PEOPLE AND STORIES THAT SHOULD NOT BE FORGOTTEN

ADVENTURES

ADVENTURES

PEOPLE AND STORIES THAT SHOULD NOT BE FORGOTTEN

Spring 2024

ISBN: (PAPERBACK) 978-1-950464-64-7
ISBN: (EBOOK) 978-1-950464-65-4

WWW.ADVENTURESBOOKZINE.COM

ADVENTURES

PEOPLE AND STORIES THAT SHOULD NOT BE FORGOTTEN

SPRING 2024　　　　　　　**ISSUE #11**

WHAT

WHERE

Editor's Note

ONE THING READERS SHOULD KNOW IS THAT WE TAKE OUR TITLE, "ADVEN-tures," quite literally. Our goal is to make every issue an adventure for the reader, by taking you on many adventures of the imagination. I think this issue does that very well, and I think you'll agree once you've perused these pages!

Let's start with the stars of the issue, the stories. Leading off, we have "Whose Body?" by Dorothy L. Sayers. This is the very first novel in which Lord Peter Wimsey appears. For those unfamiliar with Sayers' work or her famous creation, Lord Peter Wimsey was a detective who is often cited as a prototype of the "gentleman detective."

That's followed by "The Pretty Sister of Jose" by Frances Hodgson Burnett. You might recognize her as the author of "The Secret Garden." This, however, is no children's tale. It's an adult novel about murder, revenge, love and ... bullfighting! It's a fun story that we think most people aren't even aware of.

We also have original stories from Kyle Owens ("Chasing Dust in the Wind") and Suzanne Elson ("Cocktail Napkin"), a story by the legendary sci-fi writer Isaac Asimov ("Let's Get Together"), and another crime classic, this one by Wesley Long ("The Fixer").

Once you're done reading all these stories, we still have some more adventures for you. We have a fun page with cartoons and a sudoku puzzle, a review by Pretty Sinister Books, a history piece on aviator Ruth Law, and a section where we publish old opinion writings by Darryle Purcell. It's fun to look at these old opinion pieces and see how much - or how little - certain things have changed over the years.

Now, enough from me. Turn the page, and let the adventures begin!
Happy reading!

Michael Brian

Michael Brian

Letters to the editor:
Comments/Questions are
accepted. Put *Letter to Editor*
in Subject and send to:
OffBeatReads@pm.me
*Email content could
be published in future
Adventures To Go.*

WHOSE BODY?

(A LORD PETER WIMSEY NOVEL)
BY DOROTHY L. SAYERS

Dear Jim,
This book is your fault. If it had not been for your brutal insistence,Lord Peter would never have staggered through to the end of this enquiry. Pray consider that he thanks you with his accustomed suavity.

    Yours ever,
D. L. S.

CHAPTER I

"Oh, damn!" said Lord Peter Wimsey at Piccadilly Circus. "Hi, driver!"

The taxi man, irritated at receiving this appeal while negotiating the intricacies of turning into Lower Regent Street across the route of a 19 'bus, a 38-B and a bicycle, bent an unwilling ear.

"I've left the catalogue behind," said Lord Peter deprecatingly. "Uncommonly careless of me. D'you mind puttin' back to where we came from?"

"To the Savile Club, sir?"

"No—110 Piccadilly—just beyond—thank you."

"Thought you was in a hurry," said the man, overcome with a sense of injury.

"I'm afraid it's an awkward place to turn in," said Lord Peter, answering the thought rather than the words. His long, amiable face looked as if it had generated spontaneously from his top hat, as white maggots breed from Gorgonzola.

The taxi, under the severe eye of a policeman, revolved by slow jerks, with a noise like the grinding of teeth.

The block of new, perfect and expensive flats in which Lord Peter dwelt upon the second floor, stood directly opposite the Green Park, in a spot for many years occupied by the skeleton of a frustrate commercial enterprise. As Lord Peter let himself in he heard his man's voice in the library, uplifted in that throttled stridency peculiar to well-trained persons using the telephone.

"I believe that's his lordship just coming in again—if your Grace would kindly hold the line a moment."

"What is it, Bunter?"

"Her Grace has just called up from Denver, my lord. I was just saying your lordship had gone to the sale when I heard your lordship's latchkey."

"Thanks," said Lord Peter; "and you might find me my catalogue, would you? I think I must have left it in my bedroom, or on the desk."

He sat down to the telephone with an air of leisurely courtesy, as though it were an acquaintance dropped in for a chat.

"Hullo, Mother—that you?"

"Oh, there you are, dear," replied the voice of the Dowager Duchess. "I was afraid I'd just missed you."

"Well, you had, as a matter of fact. I'd just started off to Brocklebury's sale to pick up a book or two, but I had to come back for the catalogue. What's up?"

"Such a quaint thing," said the Duchess. "I thought I'd tell you. You know little Mr. Thipps?"

"Thipps?" said Lord Peter. "Thipps? Oh, yes, the little architect man who's doing the church roof. Yes. What about him?"

"Mrs. Throgmorton's just been in, in quite a state of mind."

"Sorry, Mother, I can't hear. Mrs. Who?"

"Throgmorton—Throgmorton—the vicar's wife."

"Oh, Throgmorton, yes?"

"Mr. Thipps rang them up this morning. It was his day to come down, you know."

"Yes?"

"He rang them up to say he couldn't. He was so upset, poor little man. He'd found a dead body in his bath."

"Sorry, Mother, I can't hear; found what, where?"

"A dead body, dear, in his bath."

"What?—no, no, we haven't finished. Please don't cut us off. Hullo! Hullo! Is that you, Mother? Hullo!—Mother!—Oh, yes—sorry, the girl was trying to cut us off. What sort of body?"

"A dead man, dear, with nothing on but a pair of pince-nez. Mrs. Throgmorton positively blushed when she was telling me. I'm afraid people do get a little narrow-minded in country vicarages."

"Well, it sounds a bit unusual. Was it anybody he knew?"

"No, dear, I don't think so, but, of course, he couldn't give her many details. She said he sounded quite distracted. He's such a respectable little man—and having the police in the house and so on, really worried him."

"Poor little Thipps! Uncommonly awkward for him. Let's see, he lives in Battersea, doesn't he?"

"Yes, dear; 59, Queen Caroline Mansions; opposite the Park. That big block just round the corner from the Hospital. I thought perhaps you'd like to run round and see him and ask if there's anything we can do. I always thought him a nice little man."

"Oh, quite," said Lord Peter, grinning at the telephone. The Duchess was always of the greatest assistance to his hobby of criminal investigation, though she never alluded to it, and maintained a polite fiction of its non-existence.

"What time did it happen, Mother?"

"I think he found it early this morning, but, of course, he didn't think of telling the Throgmortons just at first. She came up to me just before lunch—so tiresome, I had to ask her to stay. Fortunately, I was alone. I don't mind being bored myself, but I hate having my guests bored."

"Poor old Mother! Well, thanks awfully for tellin' me. I think I'll send Bunter to the sale and toddle round to Battersea now an' try and console the poor little beast. So-long."

"Good-bye, dear."

"Bunter!"

"Yes, my lord."

"Her Grace tells me that a respectable Battersea architect has discovered a dead man in his bath."

"Indeed, my lord? That's very gratifying."

"Very, Bunter. Your choice of words is unerring. I wish Eton and Balliol had done as much for me. Have you found the catalogue?"

"Here it is, my lord."

"Thanks. I am going to Battersea at once. I want you to attend the sale for me. Don't lose time—I don't want to miss the Folio Dante[A] nor the de Voragine—here you are—see? 'Golden Legend'—Wynkyn de Worde, 1493—got that?—and, I say, make a special effort for the Caxton folio of the 'Four Sons of Aymon'—it's the 1489 folio and unique. Look! I've marked the lots I want, and put my outside offer against each. Do your best for me. I shall be back to dinner."

"Very good, my lord."

"Take my cab and tell him to hurry. He may for you; he doesn't like me very much. Can I," said Lord Peter, looking at himself in the eighteenth-century mirror over the mantelpiece, "can I have the heart to fluster the flustered Thipps further—that's very difficult to say quickly—by appearing in a top-hat and frock-coat? I think not. Ten to one he will overlook my trousers and mistake me for the undertaker. A grey suit, I fancy, neat but not gaudy, with a hat to tone, suits my other self better. Exit the amateur of first editions; new motive introduced by solo bassoon; enter Sherlock Holmes, disguised as a walking gentleman. There goes Bunter. Invaluable fellow—never offers to do his job when you've told him to do somethin' else. Hope he doesn't miss the 'Four Sons of Aymon.' Still, there _is_ another copy of that—in the Vatican.[B] It might become available, you never know —if the Church of Rome went to pot or Switzerland invaded Italy—whereas a strange corpse doesn't turn up in a suburban bathroom more than once in a lifetime—at least, I should think not—at any rate, the number of times it's happened, _with_ a pince-nez, might be counted on the fingers of one hand, I imagine. Dear me! it's a dreadful mistake to ride two hobbies at once."

He had drifted across the passage into his bedroom, and was changing with a rapidity one might not have expected from a man of his mannerisms. He selected a dark-green tie to match his socks and tied it accurately without hesitation or the slightest compression of his lips; substituted a pair of brown shoes for his black ones, slipped a monocle into a breast pocket, and took up a beautiful Malacca walking-stick with a heavy silver knob.

"That's all, I think," he murmured to himself. "Stay—I may as well have you—you may come in useful—one never knows." He added a flat silver matchbox to his equipment, glanced at his watch, and seeing that it was already a quarter to three, ran briskly downstairs, and, hailing a taxi, was carried to Battersea Park.

MR. ALFRED THIPPS WAS A SMALL, NERVOUS MAN, WHOSE FLAXEN HAIR WAS beginning to abandon the unequal struggle with destiny. One might say that his only really marked feature was a large bruise over the left eyebrow, which gave him a faintly dissipated air incongruous with the rest of his appearance. Almost in the same breath with his first greeting, he made a self-conscious apology for it, murmuring something about having run against the dining-room door in the dark. He was touched almost to tears by Lord Peter's thoughtfulness and condescension in calling.

"I'm sure it's most kind of your lordship," he repeated for the dozenth time, rapidly blinking his weak little eyelids. "I appreciate it very deeply, very deeply, indeed, and so would Mother, only she's so deaf, I don't like to trouble you with making her understand. It's been very hard all day," he added, "with the policemen in the house and all this commotion. It's what Mother and me have never been used to, always living very retired, and it's most distressing to a man of regular habits, my lord, and reely, I'm almost thankful Mother doesn't understand, for I'm sure it would worry her terribly if she was to know about it. She was upset at first, but she's made up some idea of her own about it now, and I'm sure it's all for the best."

The old lady who sat knitting by the fire nodded grimly in response to a look from her son.

"I always said as you ought to complain about that bath, Alfred," she said suddenly, in the high, piping voice peculiar to the deaf, "and it's to be 'oped the landlord'll see about it now; not but what I think you might have managed without having the police in, but there! you always were one to make a fuss about a little thing, from chicken-pox up."

"There now," said Mr. Thipps apologetically, "you see how it is. Not but what it's just as well she's settled on that, because she understands we've locked up the bathroom and don't try to go in there. But it's been a terrible shock to me, sir—my lord, I should say, but there! my nerves are all to pieces. Such a thing has never 'appened—happened to me in all my born days. Such a state I was in this morning—I didn't know if I was on my head or my heels—I reely didn't, and my heart not being too strong,

I hardly knew how to get out of that horrid room and telephone for the police. It's affected me, sir, it's affected me, it reely has—I couldn't touch a bit of breakfast, nor lunch neither, and what with telephoning and putting off clients and interviewing people all morning, I've hardly known what to do with myself."

"I'm sure it must have been uncommonly distressin'," said Lord Peter, sympathetically, "especially comin' like that before breakfast. Hate anything tiresome happenin' before breakfast. Takes a man at such a confounded disadvantage, what?"

"That's just it, that's just it," said Mr. Thipps, eagerly. "When I saw that dreadful thing lying there in my bath, mother-naked, too, except for a pair of eyeglasses, I assure you, my lord, it regularly turned my stomach, if you'll excuse the expression. I'm not very strong, sir, and I get that sinking feeling sometimes in the morning, and what with one thing and another I 'ad—had to send the girl for a stiff brandy, or I don't know _what_ mightn't have happened. I felt so queer, though I'm anything but partial to spirits as a rule. Still, I make it a rule never to be without brandy in the house, in case of emergency, you know?"

"Very wise of you," said Lord Peter, cheerfully. "You're a very far-seein' man, Mr. Thipps. Wonderful what a little nip'll do in case of need, and the less you're used to it the more good it does you. Hope your girl is a sensible young woman, what? Nuisance to have women faintin' and shriekin' all over the place."

"Oh, Gladys is a good girl," said Mr. Thipps, "very reasonable indeed. She was shocked, of course; that's very understandable. I was shocked myself, and it wouldn't be proper in a young woman not to be shocked under the circumstances, but she is reely a helpful, energetic girl in a crisis, if you understand me. I consider myself very fortunate these days to have got a good, decent girl to do for me and Mother, even though she is a bit careless and forgetful about little things, but that's only natural. She was very sorry indeed about having left the bathroom window open, she reely was, and though I was angry at first, seeing what's come of it, it wasn't anything to speak of, not in the ordinary way, as you might say. Girls will forget things, you know, my lord, and reely she was so distressed I didn't like to say too much to her. All I said was: 'It might have been burglars,' I said, 'remember that, next time you leave a window open all night; this time it was a dead man,' I said, 'and that's unpleasant enough, but next time it might be burglars,' I said, 'and all of us murdered in our beds.' But the police-inspector—Inspector Sugg, they called him, from the Yard— he was very sharp with her, poor girl. Quite frightened her, and made her think he suspected her of something, though what good a body could be to her, poor girl, I can't imagine, and so I told the Inspector. He was quite rude to me, my lord—I may say I didn't like his manner at all. 'If you've got anything definite to accuse Gladys or me of, Inspector,' I said to him, 'bring it forward, that's what you have to do,' I said, 'but I've yet to learn that you're paid to be rude to a gentleman in his own 'ouse—house.' Reely," said Mr. Thipps, growing quite pink on the top of his head, "he regularly roused me, regularly roused me, my lord, and I'm a mild man as a rule."

"Sugg all over," said Lord Peter. "I know him. When he don't know what else to say, he's rude. Stands to reason you and the girl wouldn't go collectin' bodies. Who'd want to saddle himself with a body? Difficulty's usually to get rid of 'em. Have you got rid of this one yet, by the way?"

"It's still in the bathroom," said Mr. Thipps. "Inspector Sugg said nothing was to be touched till his men came in to move it. I'm expecting them at any time. If it would interest your lordship to have a look at it—"

"Thanks awfully," said Lord Peter. "I'd like to very much, if I'm not puttin' you out."

"Not at all," said Mr. Thipps. His manner as he led the way along the passage convinced Lord Peter of two things—first, that, gruesome as his exhibit was, he rejoiced in the importance it reflected upon himself and his flat, and secondly, that Inspector Sugg had forbidden him to exhibit it to anyone. The latter supposition was confirmed by the action of Mr. Thipps, who stopped to fetch the door-key from his bedroom, saying that the police had the other, but that he made it a rule to have two keys to every door, in case of accident.

The bathroom was in no way remarkable. It was long and narrow, the window being exactly over the head of the bath. The panes were of frosted glass; the frame wide enough to admit a man's body. Lord Peter stepped rapidly across to it, opened it and looked out.

The flat was the top one of the building and situated about the middle of the block. The bathroom window looked out upon the back-yards of the flats, which were occupied by various small outbuildings, coal-holes, garages, and the like. Beyond these were the back gardens of a parallel line of houses. On the right rose the extensive edifice of St. Luke's Hospital, Battersea, with its grounds, and, connected with it by a covered way, the residence of the famous surgeon, Sir Julian Freke, who directed the surgical side of the great new hospital, and was, in addition, known in Harley Street as a distinguished neurologist with a highly individual point of view.

This information was poured into Lord Peter's ear at considerable length by Mr. Thipps, who seemed to feel that the neighbourhood of anybody so distinguished shed a kind of halo of glory over Queen Caroline Mansions.

"We had him round here himself this morning," he said, "about this horrid business. Inspector Sugg thought one of the young medical gentlemen at the hospital might have brought the corpse round for a joke, as you might say, they always having bodies in the dissecting-room. So Inspector Sugg went round to see Sir Julian this morning to ask if there was a body missing. He was very kind, was Sir Julian, very kind indeed, though he was at work when they got there, in the dissecting-room. He looked up the books to see that all the bodies were accounted for, and then very obligingly came round here to look at this"—he indicated the bath—"and said he was afraid he couldn't help us—there was no corpse missing from the hospital, and this one didn't answer to the description of any they'd had."

"Nor to the description of any of the patients, I hope," suggested Lord Peter casually.

At this grisly hint Mr. Thipps turned pale.

"I didn't hear Inspector Sugg inquire," he said, with some agitation.

"What a very horrid thing that would be—God bless my soul, my lord, I never thought of it."

"Well, if they had missed a patient they'd probably have discovered it by now," said Lord Peter. "Let's have a look at this one."

He screwed his monocle into his eye, adding: "I see you're troubled here with the soot blowing in. Beastly nuisance, ain't it? I get it, too—spoils all my books, you know. Here, don't you trouble, if you don't care about lookin' at it."

He took from Mr. Thipps's hesitating hand the sheet which had been flung over the bath, and turned it back.

The body which lay in the bath was that of a tall, stout man of about fifty. The hair, which was thick and black and naturally curly, had been cut and parted by a master hand, and exuded a faint violet perfume, perfectly recognisable in the close air of the bathroom. The features were thick, fleshy and strongly marked, with prominent dark eyes, and a long nose curving down to a heavy chin. The clean-shaven lips were full and sensual, and the dropped jaw showed teeth stained with tobacco. On the dead face the handsome pair of gold pince-nez mocked death with grotesque elegance; the fine gold chain curved over the naked breast. The legs lay stiffly stretched out side by side; the arms reposed close to the body; the fingers were flexed naturally. Lord Peter lifted one arm, and looked at the hand with a little frown.

"Bit of a dandy, your visitor, what?" he murmured. "Parma violet and manicure." He bent again, slipping his hand beneath the head. The absurd eyeglasses slipped off, clattering into the bath, and the noise put the last touch to Mr. Thipps's growing nervousness.

"If you'll excuse me," he murmured, "it makes me feel quite faint, it reely does."

He slipped outside, and he had no sooner done so than Lord Peter, lifting the body quickly and cautiously, turned it over and inspected it with his head on one side, bringing his monocle into play with the air of the late Joseph Chamberlain approving a rare orchid. He then laid the head over his arm, and bringing out the silver matchbox from his pocket, slipped it into the open mouth. Then making the noise usually written "Tut-tut," he laid the body down, picked up the mysterious pince-nez, looked at it, put it on his nose and looked through it, made the same noise again, readjusted the pince-nez upon the nose of the corpse, so as to leave no traces of interference for the irritation of Inspector Sugg; rearranged the body; returned to the window and, leaning out, reached upwards and sideways with his walking-stick, which he had somewhat incongruously brought along with him. Nothing appearing to come of these investigations, he withdrew his head, closed the window, and rejoined Mr. Thipps in the passage.

Mr. Thipps, touched by this sympathetic interest in the younger son of a duke, took the liberty, on their return to the sitting-room, of offering him a cup of tea. Lord Peter, who had strolled over to the window and was admiring the outlook on Battersea Park, was about to accept, when an ambulance came into view at the end of Prince of Wales Road. Its appearance reminded Lord Peter of an important engagement, and with a hurried "By Jove!" he took his leave of Mr. Thipps.

"My mother sent kind regards and all that," he said, shaking hands fervently; "hopes you'll soon be down at Denver again. Good-bye, Mrs. Thipps," he bawled kindly into the ear of the old lady. "Oh, no, my dear sir, please don't trouble to come down."

He was none too soon. As he stepped out of the door and turned towards the station, the ambulance drew up from the other direction, and Inspector Sugg emerged from it with two constables. The Inspector spoke to the officer on duty at the Mansions, and turned a suspicious gaze on Lord Peter's retreating back.

"Dear old Sugg," said that nobleman, fondly, "dear, dear old bird! How he does hate me, to be sure."

CHAPTER II

"Excellent, Bunter," said Lord Peter, sinking with a sigh into a luxurious armchair. "I couldn't have done better myself. The thought of the Dante makes my mouth water—and the 'Four Sons of Aymon.' And you've saved me £60—that's glorious. What shall we spend it on, Bunter? Think of it—all ours, to do as we like with, for as Harold Skimpole so rightly observes, £60 saved is £60 gained, and I'd reckoned on spending it all. It's your saving, Bunter, and properly speaking, your £60. What do we want? Anything in your department? Would you like anything altered in the flat?"

"Well, my lord, as your lordship is so good"—the man-servant paused, about to pour an old brandy into a liqueur glass.

"Well, out with it, my Bunter, you imperturbable old hypocrite. It's no good talking as if you were announcing dinner—you're spilling the brandy. The voice is Jacob's voice, but the hands are the hands of Esau. What does that blessed darkroom of yours want now?"

"There's a Double Anastigmat with a set of supplementary lenses, my lord," said Bunter, with a note almost of religious fervour. "If it was a case of forgery now—or footprints—I could enlarge them right up on the plate. Or the wide-angled lens would be useful. It's as though the camera had eyes at the back of its head, my lord. Look—I've got it here."

He pulled a catalogue from his pocket, and submitted it, quivering, to his employer's gaze.

Lord Peter perused the description slowly, the corners of his long mouth lifted into a faint smile.

"It's Greek to me," he said, "and £50 seems a ridiculous price for a few bits of glass. I suppose, Bunter, you'd say £750 was a bit out of the way for a dirty old book in a dead language, wouldn't you?"

"It wouldn't be my place to say so, my lord."

"No, Bunter, I pay you £200 a year to keep your thoughts to yourself. Tell me, Bunter, in these democratic days, don't you think that's unfair?"

"No, my lord."

"You don't. D'you mind telling me frankly why you don't think it unfair?"

"Frankly, my lord, your lordship is paid a nobleman's income to take Lady Worthington in to dinner and refrain from exercising your lordship's undoubted powers of repartee."

Lord Peter considered this.

"That's your idea, is it, Bunter? Noblesse oblige—for a consideration. I daresay you're right. Then you're better off than I am, because I'd have to behave myself to Lady Worthington if I hadn't a penny. Bunter, if I sacked you here and now, would you tell me what you think of me?"

"No, my lord."

"You'd have a perfect right to, my Bunter, and if I sacked you on top of drinking the kind of coffee you make, I'd deserve everything you could say of me. You're a demon for coffee, Bunter—I don't want to know how you do it, because I believe it to be witchcraft, and I don't want to burn eternally. You can buy your cross-eyed lens."

"Thank you, my lord."

"Have you finished in the dining-room?"

"Not quite, my lord."

"Well, come back when you have. I have many things to tell you. Hullo! who's that?"

The doorbell had rung sharply.

"Unless it's anybody interestin' I'm not at home."

"Very good, my lord."

Lord Peter's library was one of the most delightful bachelor rooms in London. Its scheme was black and primrose; its walls were lined with rare editions, and its chairs and Chesterfield sofa suggested the embraces of the houris. In one corner stood a black baby grand, a wood fire leaped on a wide old-fashioned hearth, and the Sèvres vases on the chimneypiece were filled with ruddy and gold chrysanthemums. To the eyes of the young man who was ushered in from the raw November fog it seemed not only rare and unattainable, but friendly and familiar, like a colourful and gilded paradise in a mediaeval painting.

"Mr. Parker, my lord."

Lord Peter jumped up with genuine eagerness.

"My dear man, I'm delighted to see you. What a beastly foggy night, ain't it? Bunter, some more of that admirable coffee and another glass and the cigars. Parker, I hope you're full of crime—nothing less than arson or murder will do for us tonight. 'On such a night as this—' Bunter and I were just sitting down to carouse. I've got a Dante, and a Caxton folio that is practically unique, at Sir Ralph Brocklebury's sale. Bunter, who did the bargaining, is going to have a lens which does all kinds of wonderful things with its eyes shut, and

We both have got a body in a bath, We both have got a body in a bath— For in spite of all temptations To go in for cheap sensations We insist upon a body in a bath—

Nothing less will do for us, Parker. It's mine at present, but we're going shares in it. Property of the firm. Won't you join us? You really must put _something_ in the jack-pot. Perhaps you have a body. Oh, do have a body. Every body welcome.

Gin a body meet a body Hauled before the beak, Gin a body jolly well knows who murdered a body and that old Sugg is on the wrong tack, Need a body speak?

Not a bit of it. He tips a glassy wink to yours truly and yours truly reads the truth."

"Ah," said Parker, "I knew you'd been round to Queen Caroline Mansions. So've I, and met Sugg, and he told me he'd seen you. He was cross, too. Unwarrantable interference, he calls it."

"I knew he would," said Lord Peter. "I love taking a rise out of dear old Sugg, he's always so rude. I see by the Star that he has excelled himself by taking the girl, Gladys What's-her-name, into custody. Sugg of the evening, beautiful Sugg! But what were _you_ doing there?"

"To tell you the truth," said Parker, "I went round to see if the Semitic-looking stranger in Mr. Thipps's bath was by any extraordinary chance Sir Reuben Levy. But he isn't."

"Sir Reuben Levy? Wait a minute, I saw something about that. I know! A headline: 'Mysterious disappearance of famous financier.' What's it all about? I didn't read it carefully."

"Well, it's a bit odd, though I daresay it's nothing really—old chap may have cleared for some reason best known to himself. It only happened this morning, and nobody would have thought anything about it, only it happened to be the day on which he had arranged to attend a most important financial meeting and do some deal involving millions—I haven't got all the details. But I know he's got enemies who'd just as soon the deal didn't come off, so when I got wind of this fellow in the bath, I buzzed round to have a look at him. It didn't seem likely, of course, but unlikelier things do happen in our profession. The funny thing is, old Sugg had got bitten with the idea it is him, and is wildly telegraphing to Lady Levy to come and identify him. But as a matter of fact, the man in the bath is no more Sir Reuben Levy than Adolf Beck, poor devil, was John Smith. Oddly enough, though, he would be really extraordinarily like Sir Reuben if he had a beard, and as Lady Levy is abroad with the family, somebody may say it's him, and Sugg will build up a lovely theory, like the Tower of Babel, and destined so to perish."

"Sugg's a beautiful, braying ass," said Lord Peter. "He's like a detective in a novel. Well, I don't know anything about Levy, but I've seen the body, and I should say the idea was preposterous upon the face of it. What do you think of the brandy?"

"Unbelievable, Wimsey—sort of thing makes one believe in heaven. But I want your yarn."

"D'you mind if Bunter hears it, too? Invaluable man, Bunter—amazin' fellow with a camera. And the odd thing is, he's always on the spot when I want my bath or my boots. I don't know when he develops things—I believe he does 'em in his sleep. Bunter!"

"Yes, my lord."

"Stop fiddling about in there, and get yourself the proper things to drink and join the merry throng."

"Certainly, my lord."

"Mr. Parker has a new trick: The Vanishing Financier. Absolutely no deception. Hey, presto, pass! and where is he? Will some gentleman from the audience kindly step upon the platform and inspect the cabinet? Thank you, sir. The quickness of the 'and deceives the heye.'"

"I'm afraid mine isn't much of a story," said Parker. "It's just one of those simple things that offer no handle. Sir Reuben Levy dined last night with three friends at the Ritz. After dinner the friends went to the theatre. He refused to go with them on account of an appointment. I haven't yet been able to trace the appointment, but anyhow, he returned home to his house—9a, Park Lane—at twelve o'clock."

"Who saw him?"

"The cook, who had just gone up to bed, saw him on the doorstep, and heard him let himself in. He walked upstairs, leaving his greatcoat on the hall peg and his umbrella in the stand—you remember how it rained last night. He undressed and went to bed. Next morning he wasn't there. That's all," said Parker abruptly, with a wave of the hand.

"It isn't all, it isn't all. Daddy, go on, that's not _half_ a story," pleaded Lord Peter.

"But it _is_ all. When his man came to call him he wasn't there. The bed had been slept in. His pyjamas and all his clothes were there, the only odd thing being that they were thrown rather untidily on the ottoman at the foot of the bed, instead of being neatly folded on a chair, as is Sir Reuben's custom—looking as though he had been rather agitated or unwell. No clean clothes were missing, no suit, no boots—nothing. The boots he had worn were in his dressing-room as usual. He had washed and cleaned his teeth and done all the usual things. The housemaid was down cleaning the hall at half-past six, and can swear that nobody came in or out after that. So one is forced to suppose that a respectable middle-aged Hebrew financier either went mad between twelve and six a.m. and walked quietly out of the house in his birthday suit on a November night, or else was spirited away like the lady in the 'Ingoldsby Legends,' body and bones, leaving only a heap of crumpled clothes behind him."

"Was the front door bolted?"

"That's the sort of question you _would_ ask, straight off; it took me an hour to think of it. No; contrary to custom, there was only the Yale lock on the door. On the other hand, some of the maids had been given leave to go to the theatre, and Sir Reuben may quite conceivably have left the door open under the impression they had not come in. Such a thing has happened before."

"And that's really all?"

"Really all. Except for one very trifling circumstance."

"I love trifling circumstances," said Lord Peter, with childish delight; "so many men have been hanged by trifling circumstances. What was it?"

"Sir Reuben and Lady Levy, who are a most devoted couple, always share the same room. Lady Levy, as I said before, is in Mentonne at the moment for her health. In her absence, Sir Reuben sleeps in the double bed as usual, and invariably on his own side—the outside—of the bed. Last night he put the two pillows together and slept in the middle, or, if anything, rather closer to the wall than otherwise. The housemaid, who is a most intelligent girl, noticed this when she went up to make the bed, and, with really admirable detective instinct, refused to touch the bed or let anybody else touch it, though it wasn't till later that they actually sent for the police."

"Was nobody in the house but Sir Reuben and the servants?"

"No; Lady Levy was away with her daughter and her maid. The valet, cook, parlourmaid, housemaid and kitchenmaid were the only people in the house, and naturally wasted an hour or two squawking and gossiping. I got there about ten."

"What have you been doing since?"

"Trying to get on the track of Sir Reuben's appointment last night, since, with the exception of the cook, his 'appointer' was the last person who saw him before his disappearance. There may be some quite simple explanation, though I'm dashed if I can think of one for the moment. Hang it all, a man doesn't come in and go to bed and walk away again 'mid nodings on' in the middle of the night."

"He may have been disguised."

"I thought of that—in fact, it seems the only possible explanation. But it's deuced odd, Wimsey. An important city man, on the eve of an important transaction, without a word of warning to anybody, slips off in the middle of the night, disguised down to his skin, leaving behind his watch, purse, cheque-book, and—most mysterious and important of all—his spectacles, without which he can't see a step, as he is extremely short-sighted. He—"

"That _is_ important," interrupted Wimsey. "You are sure he didn't take a second pair?"

"His man vouches for it that he had only two pairs, one of which was found on his dressing-table, and the other in the drawer where it is always kept."

Lord Peter whistled.

"You've got me there, Parker. Even if he'd gone out to commit suicide he'd have taken those."

"So you'd think—or the suicide would have happened the first time he started to cross the road. However, I didn't overlook the possibility. I've got particulars of all today's street accidents, and I can lay my hand on my heart and say that none of them is Sir Reuben. Besides, he took his latchkey with him, which looks as though he'd meant to come back."

"Have you seen the men he dined with?"

"I found two of them at the club. They said that he seemed in the best of health and spirits, spoke of looking forward to joining Lady Levy later on—perhaps at Christmas—and referred with great satisfaction to this morning's business transaction, in which one of them—a man called Anderson of Wyndham's—was himself concerned."

"Then up till about nine o'clock, anyhow, he had no apparent intention or expectation of disappearing."

"None—unless he was a most consummate actor. Whatever happened to change his mind must have happened either at the mysterious appointment which he kept after dinner, or while he was in bed between midnight and 5.30 a.m."

"Well, Bunter," said Lord Peter, "what do you make of it?"

"Not in my department, my lord. Except that it is odd that a gentleman who was too flurried or unwell to fold his clothes as usual should remember to clean his teeth and put his boots out. Those are two things that quite frequently get overlooked, my lord."

"If you mean anything personal, Bunter," said Lord Peter, "I can only say that I think the speech an unworthy one. It's a sweet little problem,

Parker mine. Look here, I don't want to butt in, but I should dearly love to see that bedroom tomorrow. 'Tis not that I mistrust thee, dear, but I should uncommonly like to see it. Say me not nay—take another drop of brandy and a Villar Villar, but say not, say not nay!"

"Of course you can come and see it—you'll probably find lots of things I've overlooked," said the other, equably, accepting the proffered hospitality.

"Parker, acushla, you're an honour to Scotland Yard. I look at you, and Sugg appears a myth, a fable, an idiot-boy, spawned in a moonlight hour by some fantastic poet's brain. Sugg is too perfect to be possible. What does he make of the body, by the way?"

"Sugg says," replied Parker, with precision, "that the body died from a blow on the back of the neck. The doctor told him that. He says it's been dead a day or two. The doctor told him that, too. He says it's the body of a well-to-do Hebrew of about fifty. Anybody could have told him that. He says it's ridiculous to suppose it came in through the window without anybody knowing anything about it. He says it probably walked in through the front door and was murdered by the household. He's arrested the girl because she's short and frail-looking and quite unequal to downing a tall and sturdy Semite with a poker. He'd arrest Thipps, only Thipps was away in Manchester all yesterday and the day before and didn't come back till late last night—in fact, he wanted to arrest him till I reminded him that if the body had been a day or two dead, little Thipps couldn't have done him in at 10.30 last night. But he'll arrest him tomorrow as an accessory—and the old lady with the knitting, too, I shouldn't wonder."

"Well, I'm glad the little man has so much of an alibi," said Lord Peter, "though if you're only glueing your faith to cadaveric lividity, rigidity, and all the other quiddities, you must be prepared to have some sceptical beast of a prosecuting counsel walk slap-bang through the medical evidence. Remember Impey Biggs defending in that Chelsea tea-shop affair? Six bloomin' medicos contradictin' each other in the box, an' old Impey elocutin' abnormal cases from Glaister and Dixon Mann till the eyes of the jury reeled in their heads! 'Are you prepared to swear, Dr. Thingumtight, that the onset of rigor mortis indicates the hour of death without the possibility of error?' 'So far as my experience goes, in the majority of cases,' says the doctor, all stiff. 'Ah!' says Biggs, 'but this is a Court of

Justice, Doctor, not a Parliamentary election. We can't get on without a minority report. The law, Dr. Thingumtight, respects the rights of the minority, alive or dead.' Some ass laughs, and old Biggs sticks his chest out and gets impressive. 'Gentlemen, this is no laughing matter. My client—an upright and honourable gentleman—is being tried for his life—for his life, gentlemen—and it is the business of the prosecution to show his guilt—if they can—without a shadow of doubt. Now, Dr. Thingumtight, I ask you again, can you solemnly swear, without the least shadow of doubt,—probable, possible shadow of doubt—that this unhappy woman met her death neither sooner nor later than Thursday evening? A probable opinion? Gentlemen, we are not Jesuits, we are straightforward Englishmen. You cannot ask a British-born jury to convict any man on the authority of a probable opinion.' Hum of applause."

"Biggs's man was guilty all the same," said Parker.

"Of course he was. But he was acquitted all the same, an' what you've just said is libel." Wimsey walked over to the bookshelf and took down a volume of Medical Jurisprudence. "'Rigor mortis—can only be stated in a very general way—many factors determine the result.' Cautious brute. 'On the average, however, stiffening will have begun—neck and jaw—5 to 6 hours after death'—m'm—'in all likelihood have passed off in the bulk of cases by the end of 36 hours. Under certain circumstances, however, it may appear unusually early, or be retarded unusually long!' Helpful, ain't it, Parker? 'Brown-Séquard states ... 3½ minutes after death.... In certain cases not until lapse of 16 hours after death ... present as long as 21 days thereafter.' Lord! 'Modifying factors—age—muscular state—or febrile diseases—or where temperature of environment is high'—and so on and so on—any bloomin' thing. Never mind. You can run the argument for what it's worth to Sugg. _He_ won't know any better." He tossed the book away. "Come back to facts. What did _you_ make of the body?"

"Well," said the detective, "not very much—I was puzzled—frankly. I should say he had been a rich man, but self-made, and that his good fortune had come to him fairly recently."

"Ah, you noticed the calluses on the hands—I thought you wouldn't miss that."

"Both his feet were badly blistered—he had been wearing tight shoes."

"Walking a long way in them, too," said Lord Peter, "to get such blisters as that. Didn't that strike you as odd, in a person evidently well off?"

"Well, I don't know. The blisters were two or three days old. He might have got stuck in the suburbs one night, perhaps—last train gone and no taxi—and had to walk home."

"Possibly."

"There were some little red marks all over his back and one leg I couldn't quite account for."

"I saw them."

"What did you make of them?"

"I'll tell you afterwards. Go on."

"He was very long-sighted—oddly long-sighted for a man in the prime of life; the glasses were like a very old man's. By the way, they had a very beautiful and remarkable chain of flat links chased with a pattern. It struck me he might be traced through it."

"I've just put an advertisement in the _Times_ about it," said Lord Peter. "Go on."

"He had had the glasses some time—they had been mended twice."

"Beautiful, Parker, beautiful. Did you realize the importance of that?"

"Not specially, I'm afraid—why?"

"Never mind—go on."

"He was probably a sullen, ill-tempered man—his nails were filed down to the quick as though he habitually bit them, and his fingers were bitten as well. He smoked quantities of cigarettes without a holder. He was particular about his personal appearance."

"Did you examine the room at all? I didn't get a chance."

"I couldn't find much in the way of footprints. Sugg & Co. had tramped all over the place, to say nothing of little Thipps and the maid, but I noticed a very indefinite patch just behind the head of the bath, as though something damp might have stood there. You could hardly call it a print."

"It rained hard all last night, of course."

"Yes; did you notice that the soot on the window-sill was vaguely marked?"

"I did," said Wimsey, "and I examined it hard with this little fellow, but I could make nothing of it except that something or other had rested on the sill." He drew out his monocle and handed it to Parker.

"My word, that's a powerful lens."

"It is," said Wimsey, "and jolly useful when you want to take a good squint at somethin' and look like a bally fool all the time. Only it don't do to wear it permanently—if people see you full-face they say: 'Dear me! how weak the sight of that eye must be!' Still, it's useful."

"Sugg and I explored the ground at the back of the building," went on Parker, "but there wasn't a trace."

"That's interestin'. Did you try the roof?"

"No."

"We'll go over it tomorrow. The gutter's only a couple of feet off the top of the window. I measured it with my stick—the gentleman-scout's vade-mecum, I call it—it's marked off in inches. Uncommonly handy companion at times. There's a sword inside and a compass in the head. Got it made specially. Anything more?"

"Afraid not. Let's hear your version, Wimsey."

"Well, I think you've got most of the points. There are just one or two little contradictions. For instance, here's a man wears expensive gold-rimmed pince-nez and has had them long enough to be mended twice. Yet his teeth are not merely discoloured, but badly decayed and look as if he'd never cleaned them in his life. There are four molars missing on one side and three on the other and one front tooth broken right across. He's a man careful of his personal appearance, as witness his hair and his hands. What do you say to that?"

"Oh, these self-made men of low origin don't think much about teeth, and are terrified of dentists."

"True; but one of the molars has a broken edge so rough that it had made a sore place on the tongue. Nothing's more painful. D'you mean to tell me a man would put up with that if he could afford to get the tooth filed?"

"Well, people are queer. I've known servants endure agonies rather than step over a dentist's doormat. How did you see that, Wimsey?"

"Had a look inside; electric torch," said Lord Peter. "Handy little gadget. Looks like a matchbox. Well—I daresay it's all right, but I just draw your attention to it. Second point: Gentleman with hair smellin' of Parma violet and manicured hands and all the rest of it, never washes the inside of his ears. Full of wax. Nasty."

"You've got me there, Wimsey; I never noticed it. Still—old bad habits die hard."

"Right oh! Put it down at that. Third point: Gentleman with the manicure and the brilliantine and all the rest of it suffers from fleas."

"By Jove, you're right! Flea-bites. It never occurred to me."

"No doubt about it, old son. The marks were faint and old, but unmistakable."

"Of course, now you mention it. Still, that might happen to anybody. I loosed a whopper in the best hotel in Lincoln the week before last. I hope it bit the next occupier!"

"Oh, all these things _might_ happen to anybody—separately. Fourth point: Gentleman who uses Parma violet for his hair, etc., etc., washes his body in strong carbolic soap—so strong that the smell hangs about twenty-four hours later."

"Carbolic to get rid of the fleas."

"I will say for you, Parker, you've an answer for everything. Fifth point: Carefully got-up gentleman, with manicured, though masticated, finger-nails, has filthy black toe-nails which look as if they hadn't been cut for years."

"All of a piece with habits as indicated."

"Yes, I know, but such habits! Now, sixth and last point: This gentleman with the intermittently gentlemanly habits arrives in the middle of a pouring wet night, and apparently through the window, when he has already been twenty-four hours dead, and lies down quietly in Mr. Thipps's bath, unseasonably dressed in a pair of pince-nez. Not a hair on his head is ruffled—the hair has been cut so recently that there are quite a number of little short hairs stuck on his neck and the sides of the bath—and he has shaved so recently that there is a line of dried soap on his cheek—"

"Wimsey!"

"Wait a minute—and _dried soap in his mouth_."

Bunter got up and appeared suddenly at the detective's elbow, the respectful man-servant all over.

"A little more brandy, sir?" he murmured.

"Wimsey," said Parker, "you are making me feel cold all over." He emptied his glass—stared at it as though he were surprised to find it empty, set it down, got up, walked across to the bookcase, turned round, stood with his back against it and said:

"Look here, Wimsey—you've been reading detective stories; you're talking nonsense."

"No, I ain't," said Lord Peter, sleepily, "uncommon good incident for a detective story, though, what? Bunter, we'll write one, and you shall illustrate it with photographs."

"Soap in his—Rubbish!" said Parker. "It was something else—some discoloration—"

"No," said Lord Peter, "there were hairs as well. Bristly ones. He had a beard."

He took his watch from his pocket, and drew out a couple of longish, stiff hairs, which he had imprisoned between the inner and the outer case.

Parker turned them over once or twice in his fingers, looked at them close to the light, examined them with a lens, handed them to the impassible Bunter, and said:

"Do you mean to tell me, Wimsey, that any man alive would"—he laughed harshly—"shave off his beard with his mouth open, and then go and get killed with his mouth full of hairs? You're mad."

"I don't tell you so," said Wimsey. "You policemen are all alike—only one idea in your skulls. Blest if I can make out why you're ever appointed. He was shaved after he was dead. Pretty, ain't it? Uncommonly jolly little job for the barber, what? Here, sit down, man, and don't be an ass, stumpin' about the room like that. Worse things happen in war. This is only a blinkin' old shillin' shocker. But I'll tell you what, Parker, we're up against a criminal—_the_ criminal—the real artist and blighter with imagination—real, artistic, finished stuff. I'm enjoyin' this, Parker."

CHAPTER III

Lord Peter finished a Scarlatti sonata, and sat looking thoughtfully at his own hands. The fingers were long and muscular, with wide, flat joints and square tips. When he was playing, his rather hard grey eyes softened, and his long, indeterminate mouth hardened in compensation. At no other time had he any pretensions to good looks, and at all times he was spoilt by a long, narrow chin, and a long, receding forehead, accentuated by the brushed-back sleekness of his tow-coloured hair. Labour papers, softening down the chin, caricatured him as a typical aristocrat.

"That's a wonderful instrument," said Parker.

"It ain't so bad," said Lord Peter, "but Scarlatti wants a harpsichord. Piano's too modern—all thrills and overtones. No good for our job, Parker. Have you come to any conclusion?"

"The man in the bath," said Parker, methodically, "was _not_ a well-off man careful of his personal appearance. He was a labouring man, unemployed, but who had only recently lost his employment. He had been tramping about looking for a job when he met with his end. Somebody killed him and washed him and scented him and shaved him in order to disguise him, and put him into Thipps's bath without leaving a trace. Conclusion: the murderer was a powerful man, since he killed him with a single blow on the neck, a man of cool head and masterly intellect, since he did all that ghastly business without leaving a mark, a man of wealth and refinement, since he had all the apparatus of an elegant toilet handy, and a man of bizarre, and almost perverted imagination, as is shown in the two horrible touches of putting the body in the bath and of adorning it with a pair of pince-nez."

"He is a poet of crime," said Wimsey. "By the way, your difficulty about the pince-nez is cleared up. Obviously, the pince-nez never belonged to the body."

"That only makes a fresh puzzle. One can't suppose the murderer left them in that obliging manner as a clue to his own identity."

"We can hardly suppose that; I'm afraid this man possessed what most criminals lack—a sense of humour."

"Rather macabre humour."

"True. But a man who can afford to be humorous at all in such circumstances is a terrible fellow. I wonder what he did with the body between the murder and depositing it chez Thipps. Then there are more questions. How did he get it there? And why? Was it brought in at the door, as Sugg of our heart suggests? or through the window, as we think, on the not very adequate testimony of a smudge on the window-sill? Had the murderer accomplices? Is little Thipps really in it, or the girl? It don't do to put the notion out of court merely because Sugg inclines to it. Even idiots occasionally speak the truth accidentally. If not, why was Thipps selected for such an abominable practical joke? Has anybody got a grudge against Thipps? Who are the people in the other flats? We must find out that. Does Thipps play the piano at midnight over their heads or damage the reputation of the staircase by bringing home dubiously respectable ladies? Are there unsuccessful architects thirsting for his blood? Damn it all, Parker, there must be a motive somewhere. Can't have a crime without a motive, you know."

"A madman—" suggested Parker, doubtfully.

"With a deuced lot of method in his madness. He hasn't made a mistake—not one, unless leaving hairs in the corpse's mouth can be called a mistake. Well, anyhow, it's not Levy—you're right there. I say, old thing, neither your man nor mine has left much clue to go upon, has he? And there don't seem to be any motives knockin' about, either. And we seem to be two suits of clothes short in last night's work. Sir Reuben makes tracks without so much as a fig-leaf, and a mysterious individual turns up with a pince-nez, which is quite useless for purposes of decency. Dash it all! If only I had some good excuse for takin' up this body case officially—"

The telephone bell rang. The silent Bunter, whom the other two had almost forgotten, padded across to it.

"It's an elderly lady, my lord," he said. "I think she's deaf—I can't make her hear anything, but she's asking for your lordship."

Lord Peter seized the receiver, and yelled into it a "Hullo!" that might have cracked the vulcanite. He listened for some minutes with an incredulous smile, which gradually broadened into a grin of delight. At length he screamed: "All right! all right!" several times, and rang off.

"By Jove!" he announced, beaming, "sportin' old bird! It's old Mrs. Thipps. Deaf as a post. Never used the 'phone before. But determined. Perfect Napoleon. The incomparable Sugg has made a discovery and arrested little Thipps. Old lady abandoned in the flat. Thipps's last shriek to her: 'Tell Lord Peter Wimsey.' Old girl undaunted. Wrestles with telephone book. Wakes up the people at the exchange. Won't take no for an answer (not bein' able to hear it), gets through, says: 'Will I do what I can?' Says she would feel safe in the hands of a real gentleman. Oh, Parker, Parker! I could kiss her, I reely could, as Thipps says. I'll write to her instead— no, hang it, Parker, we'll go round. Bunter, get your infernal machine and the magnesium. I say, we'll all go into partnership—pool the two cases and work 'em out together. You shall see my body tonight, Parker, and I'll look for your wandering Jew tomorrow. I feel so happy, I shall explode. O Sugg, Sugg, how art thou suggified! Bunter, my shoes. I say, Parker, I suppose yours are rubber-soled. Not? Tut, tut, you mustn't go out like that. We'll lend you a pair. Gloves? Here. My stick, my torch, the lampblack, the forceps, knife, pill-boxes—all complete?"

"Certainly, my lord."

"Oh, Bunter, don't look so offended. I mean no harm. I believe in you, I trust you—what money have I got? That'll do. I knew a man once, Parker, who let a world-famous poisoner slip through his fingers because the machine on the Underground took nothing but pennies. There was a queue at the booking office and the man at the barrier stopped him, and while they were arguing about accepting a five-pound-note (which was all he had) for a twopenny ride to Baker Street, the criminal had sprung into a Circle train, and was next heard of in Constantinople, disguised as an elderly Church of England clergyman touring with his niece. Are we all ready? Go!"

They stepped out, Bunter carefully switching off the lights behind them.

As they emerged into the gloom and gleam of Piccadilly, Wimsey stopped short with a little exclamation.

"Wait a second," he said. "I've thought of something. If Sugg's there he'll make trouble. I must short-circuit him."

He ran back, and the other two men employed the few minutes of his absence in capturing a taxi.

Inspector Sugg and a subordinate Cerberus were on guard at 59, Queen Caroline Mansions, and showed no disposition to admit unofficial inquirers. Parker, indeed, they could not easily turn away, but Lord Peter found himself confronted with a surly manner and what Lord Beaconsfield described as a masterly inactivity. It was in vain that Lord Peter pleaded that he had been retained by Mrs. Thipps on behalf of her son.

"Retained!" said Inspector Sugg, with a snort. "_She'll_ be retained if she doesn't look out. Shouldn't wonder if she wasn't in it herself, only she's so deaf, she's no good for anything at all."

"Look here, Inspector," said Lord Peter, "what's the use of bein' so bally obstructive? You'd much better let me in——you know I'll get there in the end. Dash it all, it's not as if I was takin' the bread out of your children's mouths. Nobody paid me for finding Lord Attenbury's emeralds for you."

"It's my duty to keep out the public," said Inspector Sugg, morosely, "and it's going to stay out."

"I never said anything about your keeping out of the public," said Lord Peter, easily, sitting down on the staircase to thrash the matter out comfortably, "though I've no doubt pussyfoot's a good thing, on principle, if not exaggerated. The golden mean, Sugg, as Aristotle says, keeps you from bein' a golden ass. Ever been a golden ass, Sugg? I have. It would take a whole rose-garden to cure me, Sugg—

"'You are my garden of beautiful roses, My own rose, my one rose, that's you!'"

"I'm not going to stay any longer talking to you," said the harassed Sugg; "it's bad enough— Hullo, drat that telephone. Here, Cawthorn, go and see what it is, if that old catamaran will let you into the room. Shutting herself up there and screaming," said the Inspector, "it's enough to make a man give up crime and take to hedging and ditching."

The constable came back:

"It's from the Yard, sir," he said, coughing apologetically; "the Chief says every facility is to be given to Lord Peter Wimsey, sir. Um!" He stood apart noncommittally, glazing his eyes.

"Five aces," said Lord Peter, cheerfully. "The Chief's a dear friend of my mother's. No go, Sugg, it's no good buckin'; you've got a full house. I'm goin' to make it a bit fuller."

He walked in with his followers.

The body had been removed a few hours previously, and when the bathroom and the whole flat had been explored by the naked eye and the camera of the competent Bunter, it became evident that the real problem of the household was old Mrs. Thipps. Her son and servant had both been removed, and it appeared that they had no friends in town, beyond a few business acquaintances of Thipps's, whose very addresses the old lady did not know. The other flats in the building were occupied respectively by a family of seven, at present departed to winter abroad, an elderly Indian colonel of ferocious manners, who lived alone with an Indian man-servant, and a highly respectable family on the third floor, whom the disturbance over their heads had outraged to the last degree. The husband, indeed, when appealed to by Lord Peter, showed a little human weakness, but Mrs. Appledore, appearing suddenly in a warm dressing-gown, extricated him from the difficulties into which he was carelessly wandering.

"I am sorry," she said, "I'm afraid we can't interfere in any way. This is a very unpleasant business, Mr.— I'm afraid I didn't catch your name, and we have always found it better not to be mixed up with the police. Of course, _if_ the Thippses are innocent, and I am sure I hope they are, it is very unfortunate for them, but I must say that the circumstances seem to me most suspicious, and to Theophilus too, and I should not like to have it said that we had assisted murderers. We might even be supposed to be accessories. Of course you are young, Mr.—"

"This is Lord Peter Wimsey, my dear," said Theophilus mildly.

She was unimpressed.

"Ah, yes," she said, "I believe you are distantly related to my late cousin, the Bishop of Carisbrooke. Poor man! He was always being taken in by impostors; he died without ever learning any better. I imagine you take after him, Lord Peter."

"I doubt it," said Lord Peter. "So far as I know he is only a connection, though it's a wise child that knows its own father. I congratulate you, dear lady, on takin' after the other side of the family. You'll forgive my buttin' in upon you like this in the middle of the night, though, as you say, it's all in the family, and I'm sure I'm very much obliged to you, and for permittin' me to admire that awfully fetchin' thing you've got on. Now, don't you worry, Mr. Appledore. I'm thinkin' the best thing I can do is to trundle the old lady down to my mother and take her out of your way, otherwise you might be findin' your Christian feelin's gettin' the better of you some fine day, and there's nothin' like Christian feelin's for upsettin' a man's domestic comfort. Good-night, sir—good-night, dear lady—it's simply rippin' of you to let me drop in like this."

"Well!" said Mrs. Appledore, as the door closed behind him.

And—

"I thank the goodness and the grace That on my birth have smiled,"

said Lord Peter, "and taught me to be bestially impertinent when I choose. Cat!"

Two a.m. saw Lord Peter Wimsey arrive in a friend's car at the Dower House, Denver Castle, in company with a deaf and aged lady and an antique portmanteau.

"It's very nice to see you, dear," said the Dowager Duchess, placidly. She was a small, plump woman, with perfectly white hair and exquisite hands. In feature she was as unlike her second son as she was like him in character; her black eyes twinkled cheerfully, and her manners and movements were marked with a neat and rapid decision. She wore a charming wrap from Liberty's, and sat watching Lord Peter eat cold beef and cheese as though his arrival in such incongruous circumstances and company were the most ordinary event possible, which with him, indeed, it was.

"Have you got the old lady to bed?" asked Lord Peter.

"Oh, yes, dear. Such a striking old person, isn't she? And very courageous. She tells me she has never been in a motor-car before. But she thinks you a very nice lad, dear—that careful of her, you remind her of her own son. Poor little Mr. Thipps—whatever made your friend the inspector think he could have murdered anybody?"

"My friend the inspector—no, no more, thank you, Mother—is determined to prove that the intrusive person in Thipps's bath is Sir Reuben Levy, who disappeared mysteriously from his house last night. His line of reasoning is: We've lost a middle-aged gentleman without any clothes on in Park Lane; we've found a middle-aged gentleman without any clothes on in Battersea. Therefore they're one and the same person, Q.E.D., and put little Thipps in quod."

"You're very elliptical, dear," said the Duchess, mildly. "Why should Mr. Thipps be arrested even if they are the same?"

"Sugg must arrest somebody," said Lord Peter, "but there is one odd little bit of evidence come out which goes a long way to support Sugg's theory, only that I know it to be no go by the evidence of my own eyes. Last night at about 9.15 a young woman was strollin' up the Battersea Park Road for purposes best known to herself, when she saw a gentleman in a fur coat and top-hat saunterin' along under an umbrella, lookin' at the names of all the streets. He looked a bit out of place, so, not bein' a shy girl, you see, she walked up to him, and said: 'Good-evening.' 'Can you tell me, please,' says the mysterious stranger, 'whether this street leads into Prince of Wales Road?' She said it did, and further asked him in a jocular manner what he was doing with himself and all the rest of it, only she wasn't altogether so explicit about that part of the conversation, because she was unburdenin' her heart to Sugg, d'you see, and he's paid by a grateful country to have very pure, high-minded ideals, what? Anyway, the old boy said he couldn't attend to her just then as he had an appointment. 'I've got to go and see a man, my dear,' was how she said he put it, and he walked on up Alexandra Avenue towards Prince of Wales Road. She was starin' after him, still rather surprised, when she was joined by a friend of hers, who said: 'It's no good wasting your time with him—that's Levy—I knew him when I lived in the West End, and the girls used to call him Peagreen Incorruptible'—friend's name suppressed, owing to implications of story, but girl vouches for what was said. She thought no more about it till the milkman brought news this morning of the excitement at Queen Caroline Mansions; then she went round, though not likin' the police as a rule, and asked the man there whether the dead gentleman had a beard and glasses. Told he had glasses but no beard, she incautiously said: 'Oh, then, it isn't him,' and the man said: 'Isn't who?' and collared her. That's her story. Sugg's delighted, of course, and quodded Thipps on the strength of it."

"Dear me," said the Duchess, "I hope the poor girl won't get into trouble."

"Shouldn't think so," said Lord Peter. "Thipps is the one that's going to get it in the neck. Besides, he's done a silly thing. I got that out of Sugg, too, though he was sittin' tight on the information. Seems Thipps got into a confusion about the train he took back from Manchester. Said first he got home at 10.30. Then they pumped Gladys Horrocks, who let out he wasn't back till after 11.45. Then Thipps, bein' asked to explain the discrepancy, stammers and bungles and says, first, that he missed the train. Then Sugg makes inquiries at St. Pancras and discovers that he left a bag in the cloakroom there at ten. Thipps, again asked to explain, stammers worse an' says he walked about for a few hours—met a friend—can't say who—didn't meet a friend—can't say what he did with his time—can't explain why he didn't go back for his bag—can't say what time he _did_ get in—can't explain how he got a bruise on his forehead. In fact, can't explain himself at all. Gladys Horrocks interrogated again. Says, this time, Thipps came in at 10.30. Then admits she didn't hear him come in. Can't say why she didn't hear him come in. Can't say why she said first of all that she _did_ hear him. Bursts into tears. Contradicts herself. Everybody's suspicion roused. Quod 'em both."

"As you put it, dear," said the Duchess, "it all sounds very confusing, and not quite respectable. Poor little Mr. Thipps would be terribly upset by anything that wasn't respectable."

"I wonder what he did with himself," said Lord Peter thoughtfully. "I really don't think he was committing a murder. Besides, I believe the fellow has been dead a day or two, though it don't do to build too much on doctors' evidence. It's an entertainin' little problem."

"Very curious, dear. But so sad about poor Sir Reuben. I must write a few lines to Lady Levy; I used to know her quite well, you know, dear, down in Hampshire, when she was a girl. Christine Ford, she was then, and I remember so well the dreadful trouble there was about her marrying a Jew. That was before he made his money, of course, in that oil business out in America. The family wanted her to marry Julian Freke, who did so well afterwards and was connected with the family, but she fell in love with this Mr. Levy and eloped with him. He was very handsome, then, you know, dear, in a foreign-looking way, but he hadn't any means, and the Fords didn't like his religion. Of course we're all Jews nowadays, and they wouldn't have minded so much if he'd pretended to be something else, like that Mr. Simons we met at Mrs. Porchester's, who always tells everybody that he got his nose in Italy at the Renaissance, and claims to be descended somehow or other from La Bella Simonetta—so foolish, you know, dear— as if anybody believed it; and I'm sure some Jews are very good people, and personally I'd much rather they believed something, though of course it must be very inconvenient, what with not working on Saturdays and circumcising the poor little babies and everything depending on the new moon and that funny kind of meat they have with such a slang-sounding name, and never being able to have bacon for breakfast. Still, there it was, and it was much better for the girl to marry him if she was really fond of him, though I believe young Freke was really devoted to her, and they're still great friends. Not that there was ever a real engagement, only a sort of understanding with her father, but he's never married, you know, and lives all by himself in that big house next to the hospital, though he's very rich and distinguished now, and I know ever so many people have tried to get hold of him—there was Lady Mainwaring wanted him for that eldest girl of hers, though I remember saying at the time it was no use expecting a surgeon to be taken in by a figure that was all padding—they have so many opportunities of judging, you know, dear."

"Lady Levy seems to have had the knack of makin' people devoted to her," said Peter. "Look at the pea-green incorruptible Levy."

"That's quite true, dear; she was a most delightful girl, and they say her daughter is just like her. I rather lost sight of them when she married, and you know your father didn't care much about business people, but I know everybody always said they were a model couple. In fact it was a proverb that Sir Reuben was as well loved at home as he was hated abroad. I don't mean in foreign countries, you know, dear—just the proverbial way of putting things—like 'a saint abroad and a devil at home'—only the other way on, reminding one of the _Pilgrim's Progress_."

"Yes," said Peter, "I daresay the old man made one or two enemies."

"Dozens, dear—such a dreadful place, the City, isn't it? Everybody Ishmaels together—though I don't suppose Sir Reuben would like to be called that, would he? Doesn't it mean illegitimate, or not a proper Jew, anyway? I always did get confused with those Old Testament characters."

Lord Peter laughed and yawned.

"I think I'll turn in for an hour or two," he said. "I must be back in town at eight—Parker's coming to breakfast."

The Duchess looked at the clock, which marked five minutes to three.

"I'll send up your breakfast at half-past six, dear," she said. "I hope you'll find everything all right. I told them just to slip a hot-water bottle in; those linen sheets are so chilly; you can put it out if it's in your way."

CHAPTER IV

"**-S**o there it is, Parker," said Lord Peter, pushing his coffee-cup aside and lighting his after-breakfast pipe; "you may find it leads you to something, though it don't seem to get me any further with my bathroom problem. Did you do anything more at that after I left?"

"No; but I've been on the roof this morning."

"The deuce you have—what an energetic devil you are! I say, Parker, I think this co-operative scheme is an uncommonly good one. It's much easier to work on someone else's job than one's own—gives one that delightful feelin' of interferin' and bossin' about, combined with the glorious sensation that another fellow is takin' all one's own work off one's hands. You scratch my back and I'll scratch yours, what? Did you find anything?"

"Not very much. I looked for any footmarks of course, but naturally, with all this rain, there wasn't a sign. Of course, if this were a detective story, there'd have been a convenient shower exactly an hour before the crime and a beautiful set of marks which could only have come there between two and three in the morning, but this being real life in a London November, you might as well expect footprints in Niagara. I searched the roofs right along—and came to the jolly conclusion that any person in any blessed flat in the blessed row might have done it. All the staircases open on to the roof and the leads are quite flat; you can walk along as easy as along Shaftesbury Avenue. Still, I've got some evidence that the body did walk along there."

"What's that?"

Parker brought out his pocketbook and extracted a few shreds of material, which he laid before his friend.

"One was caught in the gutter just above Thipps's bathroom window, another in a crack of the stone parapet just over it, and the rest came from the chimney-stack behind, where they had caught in an iron stanchion. What do you make of them?"

Lord Peter scrutinized them very carefully through his lens.

"Interesting," he said, "damned interesting. Have you developed those plates, Bunter?" he added, as that discreet assistant came in with the post.

"Yes, my lord."

"Caught anything?"

"I don't know whether to call it anything or not, my lord," said Bunter, dubiously. "I'll bring the prints in."

"Do," said Wimsey. "Hallo! here's our advertisement about the gold chain in the _Times_—very nice it looks: 'Write,'phone or call 110, Piccadilly.' Perhaps it would have been safer to put a box number, though I always think that the franker you are with people, the more you're likely to deceive 'em; so unused is the modern world to the open hand and the guileless heart, what?"

"But you don't think the fellow who left that chain on the body is going to give himself away by coming here and inquiring about it?"

"I don't, fathead," said Lord Peter, with the easy politeness of the real aristocracy; "that's why I've tried to get hold of the jeweller who originally sold the chain. See?" He pointed to the paragraph.

"It's not an old chain—hardly worn at all. Oh, thanks, Bunter. Now, see here, Parker, these are the finger-marks you noticed yesterday on the window-sash and on the far edge of the bath. I'd overlooked them; I give you full credit for the discovery, I crawl, I grovel, my name is Watson, and you need not say what you were just going to say, because I admit it all. Now we shall—Hullo, hullo, hullo!"

The three men stared at the photographs.

"The criminal," said Lord Peter, bitterly, "climbed over the roofs in the wet and not unnaturally got soot on his fingers. He arranged the body in the bath, and wiped away all traces of himself except two, which he obligingly left to show us how to do our job. We learn from a smudge on the floor that he wore india rubber boots, and from this admirable set of finger-prints on the edge of the bath that he had the usual number of fingers and wore rubber gloves. That's the kind of man he is. Take the fool away, gentlemen."

He put the prints aside, and returned to an examination of the shreds of material in his hand. Suddenly he whistled softly.

"Do you make anything of these, Parker?"

"They seemed to me to be ravellings of some coarse cotton stuff—a sheet, perhaps, or an improvised rope."

"Yes," said Lord Peter—"yes. It may be a mistake—it may be _our_ mistake. I wonder. Tell me, d'you think these tiny threads are long enough and strong enough to hang a man?"

He was silent, his long eyes narrowing into slits behind the smoke of his pipe.

"What do you suggest doing this morning?" asked Parker.

"Well," said Lord Peter, "it seems to me it's about time I took a hand in your job. Let's go round to Park Lane and see what larks Sir Reuben Levy was up to in bed last night."

"AND NOW, MRS. PEMMING, IF YOU WOULD BE SO KIND AS TO GIVE ME A BLAN-ket," said Mr. Bunter, coming down into the kitchen, "and permit of me hanging a sheet across the lower part of this window, and drawing the screen across here, so—so as to shut off any reflections, if you understand me, we'll get to work."

Sir Reuben Levy's cook, with her eye upon Mr. Bunter's gentlemanly and well-tailored appearance, hastened to produce what was necessary. Her visitor placed on the table a basket, containing a water-bottle, a silver-backed hair-brush, a pair of boots, a small roll of linoleum, and the "Letters of a Self-made Merchant to His Son," bound in polished morocco. He drew an umbrella from beneath his arm and added it to the collection. He then advanced a ponderous photographic machine and set it up in the neighbourhood of the kitchen range; then, spreading a newspaper over the fair, scrubbed surface of the table, he began to roll up his sleeves and insinuate himself into a pair of surgical gloves. Sir Reuben Levy's valet, entering at the moment and finding him thus engaged, put aside the kitchenmaid, who was staring from a front-row position, and inspected the apparatus critically. Mr. Bunter nodded brightly to him, and uncorked a small bottle of grey powder.

"Odd sort of fish, your employer, isn't he?" said the valet, carelessly.

"Very singular, indeed," said Mr. Bunter. "Now, my dear," he added, ingratiatingly, to the kitchen-maid, "I wonder if you'd just pour a little of this grey powder over the edge of the bottle while I'm holding it— and the same with this boot—here, at the top—thank you, Miss—what is your name? Price? Oh, but you've got another name besides Price, haven't you? Mabel, eh? That's a name I'm uncommonly partial to—that's very nicely done, you've a steady hand, Miss Mabel—see that? That's the finger marks—three there, and two here, and smudged over in both places. No, don't you touch 'em, my dear, or you'll rub the bloom off. We'll stand 'em up here till they're ready to have their portraits taken. Now then, let's take the hair-brush next. Perhaps, Mrs. Pemming, you'd like to lift him up very carefully by the bristles."

"By the bristles, Mr. Bunter?"

"If you please, Mrs. Pemming—and lay him here. Now, Miss Mabel, another little exhibition of your skill, _if_ you please. No—we'll try lamp-black this time. Perfect. Couldn't have done it better myself. Ah! there's a beautiful set. No smudges this time. That'll interest his lordship. Now the little book—no, I'll pick that up myself—with these gloves, you see, and by the edges—I'm a careful criminal, Mrs. Pemming, I don't want to leave any traces. Dust the cover all over, Miss Mabel; now this side—that's the way to do it. Lots of prints and no smudges. All according to plan. Oh, please, Mr. Graves, you mustn't touch it—it's as much as my place is worth to have it touched."

"D'you have to do much of this sort of thing?" inquired Mr. Graves, from a superior standpoint.

"Any amount," replied Mr. Bunter, with a groan calculated to appeal to Mr. Graves's heart and unlock his confidence. "If you'd kindly hold one end of this bit of linoleum, Mrs. Pemming, I'll hold up this end while

Miss Mabel operates. Yes, Mr. Graves, it's a hard life, valeting by day and developing by night—morning tea at any time from 6.30 to 11, and criminal investigation at all hours. It's wonderful, the ideas these rich men with nothing to do get into their heads."

"I wonder you stand it," said Mr. Graves. "Now there's none of that here. A quiet, orderly, domestic life, Mr. Bunter, has much to be said for it. Meals at regular hours; decent, respectable families to dinner—none of your painted women—and no valeting at night, there's _much_ to be said for it. I don't hold with Hebrews as a rule, Mr. Bunter, and of course I understand that you may find it to your advantage to be in a titled family, but there's less thought of that these days, and I will say, for a self-made man, no one could call Sir Reuben vulgar, and my lady at any rate is county—Miss Ford, she was, one of the Hampshire Fords, and both of them always most considerate."

"I agree with you, Mr. Graves—his lordship and me have never held with being narrow-minded—why, yes, my dear, of course it's a footmark, this is the washstand linoleum. A good Jew can be a good man, that's what I've always said. And regular hours and considerate habits have a great deal to recommend them. Very simple in his tastes, now, Sir Reuben, isn't he? for such a rich man, I mean."

"Very simple indeed," said the cook; "the meals he and her ladyship have when they're by themselves with Miss Rachel—well, there now—if it wasn't for the dinners, which is always good when there's company, I'd be wastin' my talents and education here, if you understand me, Mr. Bunter."

Mr. Bunter added the handle of the umbrella to his collection, and began to pin a sheet across the window, aided by the housemaid.

"Admirable," said he. "Now, if I might have this blanket on the table and another on a towel-horse or something of that kind by way of a background—you're very kind, Mrs. Pemming.... Ah! I wish his lordship never wanted valeting at night. Many's the time I've sat up till three and four, and up again to call him early to go off Sherlocking at the other end of the country. And the mud he gets on his clothes and his boots!"

"I'm sure it's a shame, Mr. Bunter," said Mrs. Pemming, warmly. "Low, I calls it. In my opinion, police-work ain't no fit occupation for a gentleman, let alone a lordship."

"Everything made so difficult, too," said Mr. Bunter nobly sacrificing his employer's character and his own feelings in a good cause; "boots chucked into a corner, clothes hung up on the floor, as they say——"

"That's often the case with these men as are born with a silver spoon in their mouths," said Mr. Graves. "Now, Sir Reuben, he's never lost his good old-fashioned habits. Clothes folded up neat, boots put out in his dressing-room, so as a man could get them in the morning, everything made easy."

"He forgot them the night before last, though."

"The clothes, not the boots. Always thoughtful for others, is Sir Reuben. Ah! I hope nothing's happened to him."

"Indeed, no, poor gentleman," chimed in the cook, "and as for what they're sayin', that he'd 'ave gone out surrepshous-like to do something he didn't ought, well, I'd never believe it of him, Mr. Bunter, not if I was to take my dying oath upon it."

"Ah!" said Mr. Bunter, adjusting his arc-lamps and connecting them with the nearest electric light, "and that's more than most of us could say of them as pays us."

"FIVE FOOT TEN," SAID LORD PETER, "AND NOT AN INCH MORE." HE PEERED dubiously at the depression in the bed clothes, and measured it a second time with the gentleman-scout's vade-mecum. Parker entered this particular in a neat pocketbook.

"I suppose," he said, "a six-foot-two man _might_ leave a five-foot-ten depression if he curled himself up."

"Have you any Scotch blood in you, Parker?" inquired his colleague, bitterly.

"Not that I know of," replied Parker. "Why?"

"Because of all the cautious, ungenerous, deliberate and cold-blooded devils I know," said Lord Peter, "you are the most cautious, ungenerous, deliberate and cold-blooded. Here am I, sweating my brains out to introduce a really sensational incident into your dull and disreputable little police investigation, and you refuse to show a single spark of enthusiasm."

"Well, it's no good jumping at conclusions."

"Jump? You don't even crawl distantly within sight of a conclusion. I believe if you caught the cat with her head in the cream-jug you'd say it was conceivable that the jug was empty when she got there."

"Well, it would be conceivable, wouldn't it?"

"Curse you," said Lord Peter. He screwed his monocle into his eye, and bent over the pillow, breathing hard and tightly through his nose.

"Here, give me the tweezers," he said presently. "Good heavens, man, don't blow like that, you might be a whale." He nipped up an almost invisible object from the linen.

"What is it?" asked Parker.

"It's a hair," said Wimsey grimly, his hard eyes growing harder. "Let's go and look at Levy's hats, shall we? And you might just ring for that fellow with the churchyard name, do you mind?"

Mr. Graves, when summoned, found Lord Peter Wimsey squatting on the floor of the dressing-room before a row of hats arranged upside down before him.

"Here you are," said that nobleman cheerfully. "Now, Graves, this is a guessin' competition—a sort of three-hat trick, to mix metaphors. Here are nine hats, including three top-hats. Do you identify all these hats as belonging to Sir Reuben Levy? You do? Very good. Now I have three guesses as to which hat he wore the night he disappeared, and if I guess right, I win; if I don't, you win. See? Ready? Go. I suppose you know the answer yourself, by the way?"

"Do I understand your lordship to be asking which hat Sir Reuben wore when he went out on Monday night, your lordship?"

"No, you don't understand a bit," said Lord Peter. "I'm asking if _you_ know—don't tell me, I'm going to guess."

"I do know, your lordship," said Mr. Graves, reprovingly.

"Well," said Lord Peter, "as he was dinin' at the Ritz he wore a topper. Here are three toppers. In three guesses I'd be bound to hit the right one, wouldn't I? That don't seem very sportin'. I'll take one guess. It was this one."

He indicated the hat next the window.

"Am I right, Graves—have I got the prize?"

"That _is_ the hat in question, my lord," said Mr. Graves, without excitement.

"Thanks," said Lord Peter, "that's all I wanted to know. Ask Bunter to step up, would you?"

Mr. Bunter stepped up with an aggrieved air, and his usually smooth hair ruffled by the focussing cloth.

"Oh, there you are, Bunter," said Lord Peter; "look here——"

"Here I am, my lord," said Mr. Bunter, with respectful reproach, "but if you'll excuse me saying so, downstairs is where I ought to be, with all those young women about—they'll be fingering the evidence, my lord."

"I cry your mercy," said Lord Peter, "but I've quarrelled hopelessly with Mr. Parker and distracted the estimable Graves, and I want you to tell me what finger-prints you have found. I shan't be happy till I get it, so don't be harsh with me, Bunter."

"Well, my lord, your lordship understands I haven't photographed them yet, but I won't deny that their appearance is interesting, my lord. The little book off the night table, my lord, has only the marks of one set of fingers—there's a little scar on the right thumb which makes them easy recognised. The hair-brush, too, my lord, has only the same set of marks. The umbrella, the toothglass and the boots all have two sets: the hand with the scarred thumb, which I take to be Sir Reuben's, my lord, and a set of smudges superimposed upon them, if I may put it that way, my lord, which may or may not be the same hand in rubber gloves. I could tell you better when I've got the photographs made, to measure them, my lord. The linoleum in front of the washstand is very gratifying indeed, my lord, if you will excuse my mentioning it. Besides the marks of Sir Reuben's boots which your lordship pointed out, there's the print of a man's naked foot—a much smaller one, my lord, not much more than a ten-inch sock, I should say if you asked me."

Lord Peter's face became irradiated with almost a dim, religious light.

"A mistake," he breathed, "a mistake, a little one, but he can't afford it. When was the linoleum washed last, Bunter?"

"Monday morning, my lord. The housemaid did it and remembered to mention it. Only remark she's made yet, and it's to the point. The other domestics——"

His features expressed disdain.

"What did I say, Parker? Five-foot-ten and not an inch longer. And he didn't dare to use the hair-brush. Beautiful. But he _had_ to risk the top-hat. Gentleman can't walk home in the rain late at night without a hat, you know, Parker. Look! what do you make of it? Two sets of finger-prints on everything but the book and the brush, two sets of feet on the linoleum, and two kinds of hair in the hat!"

He lifted the top-hat to the light, and extracted the evidence with tweezers.

"Think of it, Parker—to remember the hair-brush and forget the hat—to remember his fingers all the time, and to make that one careless step on the tell-tale linoleum. Here they are, you see, black hair and tan hair—black hair in the bowler and the panama, and black and tan in last night's topper. And then, just to make certain that we're on the right track, just one little auburn hair on the pillow, on this pillow, Parker, which isn't quite in the right place. It almost brings tears to my eyes."

"Do you mean to say—" said the detective, slowly.

"I mean to say," said Lord Peter, "that it was not Sir Reuben Levy whom the cook saw last night on the doorstep. I say that it was another man, perhaps a couple of inches shorter, who came here in Levy's clothes and let himself in with Levy's latchkey. Oh, he was a bold, cunning devil, Parker. He had on Levy's boots, and every stitch of Levy's clothing down to the skin. He had rubber gloves on his hands which he never took off, and he did everything he could to make us think that Levy slept here last night. He took his chances, and won. He walked upstairs, he undressed, he even washed and cleaned his teeth, though he didn't use the hair-brush for fear of leaving red hairs in it. He had to guess what Levy did with boots and clothes; one guess was wrong and the other right, as it happened. The bed must look as if it had been slept in, so he gets in, and lies there in his victim's very pyjamas. Then, in the morning sometime, probably in the deadest hour between two and three, he gets up, dresses himself in his own clothes that he has brought with him in a bag, and creeps downstairs. If anybody wakes, he is lost, but he is a bold man, and he takes his chance. He knows that people do not wake as a rule—and they don't wake. He opens the street door which he left on the latch when he came in—he listens for the stray passer-by or the policeman on his beat. He slips out. He pulls the door quietly to with the latchkey. He walks briskly away in rubber-soled shoes—he's the kind of criminal who isn't complete without rubber-soled shoes. In a few minutes he is at Hyde Park Corner. After that—"

He paused, and added:

"He did all that, and unless he had nothing at stake, he had everything at stake. Either Sir Reuben Levy has been spirited away for some silly practical joke, or the man with the auburn hair has the guilt of murder upon his soul."

"Dear me!" ejaculated the detective, "you're very dramatic about it."

Lord Peter passed his hand rather wearily over his hair.

"My true friend," he murmured in a voice surcharged with emotion,

"you recall me to the nursery rhymes of my youth—the sacred duty of flippancy:

"There was an old man of Whitehaven Who danced a quadrille with a raven, But they said: It's absurd To encourage that bird— So they smashed that old man of Whitehaven.

That's the correct attitude, Parker. Here's a poor old buffer spirited away—such a joke—and I don't believe he'd hurt a fly himself—that makes it funnier. D'you know, Parker, I don't care frightfully about this case after all."

"Which, this or yours?"

"Both. I say, Parker, shall we go quietly home and have lunch and go to the Coliseum?"

"You can if you like," replied the detective; "but you forget I do this for my bread and butter."

"And I haven't even that excuse," said Lord Peter; "well, what's the next move? What would you do in my case?"

"I'd do some good, hard grind," said Parker. "I'd distrust every bit of work Sugg ever did, and I'd get the family history of every tenant of every flat in Queen Caroline Mansions. I'd examine all their box-rooms and rooftraps, and I would inveigle them into conversations and suddenly bring in the words 'body' and 'pince-nez,' and see if they wriggled, like those modern psyo-what's-his-names."

"You would, would you?" said Lord Peter with a grin. "Well, we've exchanged cases, you know, so just you toddle off and do it. I'm going to have a jolly time at Wyndham's."

Parker made a grimace.

"Well," he said, "I don't suppose you'd ever do it, so I'd better. You'll never become a professional till you learn to do a little work, Wimsey. How about lunch?"

"I'm invited out," said Lord Peter, magnificently. "I'll run around and change at the club. Can't feed with Freddy Arbuthnot in these bags; Bunter!"

"Yes, my lord."

"Pack up if you're ready, and come round and wash my face and hands for me at the club."

"Work here for another two hours, my lord. Can't do with less than thirty minutes' exposure. The current's none too strong."

"You see how I'm bullied by my own man, Parker? Well, I must bear it, I suppose. Ta-ta!"

He whistled his way downstairs.

The conscientious Mr. Parker, with a groan, settled down to a systematic search through Sir Reuben Levy's papers, with the assistance of a plate of ham sandwiches and a bottle of Bass.

LORD PETER AND THE HONOURABLE FREDDY ARBUTHNOT, LOOKING TOGETHER like an advertisement for gents' trouserings, strolled into the dining-room at Wyndham's.

"Haven't seen you for an age," said the Honourable Freddy. "What have you been doin' with yourself?"

"Oh, foolin' about," said Lord Peter, languidly.

"Thick or clear, sir?" inquired the waiter of the Honourable Freddy.

"Which'll you have, Wimsey?" said that gentleman, transferring the burden of selection to his guest. "They're both equally poisonous."

"Well, clear's less trouble to lick out of the spoon," said Lord Peter.

"Clear," said the Honourable Freddy.

"Consommé Polonais," agreed the waiter. "Very nice, sir."

Conversation languished until the Honourable Freddy found a bone in the filleted sole, and sent for the head waiter to explain its presence. When this matter had been adjusted Lord Peter found energy to say:

"Sorry to hear about your gov'nor, old man."

"Yes, poor old buffer," said the Honourable Freddy; "they say he can't last long now. What? Oh! the Montrachet '08. There's nothing fit to drink in this place," he added gloomily.

After this deliberate insult to a noble vintage there was a further pause, till Lord Peter said: "How's 'Change?"

"Rotten," said the Honourable Freddy.

He helped himself gloomily to salmis of game.

"Can I do anything?" asked Lord Peter.

"Oh, no, thanks—very decent of you, but it'll pan out all right in time."

"This isn't a bad salmis," said Lord Peter.

"I've eaten worse," admitted his friend.

"What about those Argentines?" inquired Lord Peter. "Here, waiter, there's a bit of cork in my glass."

"Cork?" cried the Honourable Freddy, with something approaching animation; "you'll hear about this, waiter. It's an amazing thing a fellow who's paid to do the job can't manage to take a cork out of a bottle. What you say? Argentines? Gone all to hell. Old Levy bunkin' off like that's knocked the bottom out of the market."

"You don't say so," said Lord Peter. "What d'you suppose has happened to the old man?"

"Cursed if I know," said the Honourable Freddy; "knocked on the head by the bears, I should think."

"P'r'aps he's gone off on his own," suggested Lord Peter. "Double life, you know. Giddy old blighters, some of these City men."

"Oh, no," said the Honourable Freddy, faintly roused; "no, hang it all, Wimsey, I wouldn't care to say that. He's a decent old domestic bird, and his daughter's a charmin' girl. Besides, he's straight enough—he'd _do_ you down fast enough, but he wouldn't _let_ you down. Old Anderson is badly cut up about it."

"Who's Anderson?"

"Chap with property out there. He belongs here. He was goin' to meet Levy on Tuesday. He's afraid those railway people will get in now, and then it'll be all U. P."

"Who's runnin' the railway people over here?" inquired Lord Peter.

"Yankee blighter, John P. Milligan. He's got an option, or says he has. You can't trust these brutes."

"Can't Anderson hold on?"

"Anderson isn't Levy. Hasn't got the shekels. Besides, he's only one. Levy covers the ground—he could boycott Milligan's beastly railway if he liked. That's where he's got the pull, you see."

"B'lieve I met the Milligan man somewhere," said Lord Peter, thoughtfully. "Ain't he a hulking brute with black hair and a beard?"

"You're thinkin' of somebody else," said the Honourable Freddy.

"Milligan don't stand any higher than I do, unless you call five-feet-ten hulking—and he's bald, anyway."

Lord Peter considered this over the Gorgonzola. Then he said: "Didn't know Levy had a charmin' daughter."

"Oh, yes," said the Honourable Freddy, with an elaborate detachment.

"Met her and Mamma last year abroad. That's how I got to know the old man. He's been very decent. Let me into this Argentine business on the ground floor, don't you know?"

"Well," said Lord Peter, "you might do worse. Money's money, ain't it? And Lady Levy is quite a redeemin' point. At least, my mother knew her people."

"Oh, _she's_ all right," said the Honourable Freddy, "and the old man's nothing to be ashamed of nowadays. He's self-made, of course, but he don't pretend to be anything else. No side. Toddles off to business on a 96 'bus every morning. 'Can't make up my mind to taxis, my boy,' he says. 'I had to look at every halfpenny when I was a young man, and I can't get out of the way of it now.' Though, if he's takin' his family out, nothing's too good. Rachel—that's the girl—always laughs at the old man's little economies."

"I suppose they've sent for Lady Levy," said Lord Peter.

"I suppose so," agreed the other. "I'd better pop round and express sympathy or somethin', what? Wouldn't look well not to, d'you think? But it's deuced awkward. What am I to say?"

"I don't think it matters much what you say," said Lord Peter, helpfully. "I should ask if you can do anything."

"Thanks," said the lover, "I will. Energetic young man. Count on me. Always at your service. Ring me up any time of the day or night. That's the line to take, don't you think?"

"That's the idea," said Lord Peter.

MR. JOHN P. MILLIGAN, THE LONDON REPRESENTATIVE OF THE GREAT MILLI-gan railroad and shipping company, was dictating code cables to his secretary in an office in Lombard Street, when a card was brought up to him, bearing the simple legend:

LORD PETER WIMSEY
Marlborough Club

Mr. Milligan was annoyed at the interruption, but, like many of his nation, if he had a weak point, it was the British aristocracy. He postponed for a few minutes the elimination from the map of a modest but promising farm, and directed that the visitor should be shown up.

"Good-afternoon," said that nobleman, ambling genially in, "it's most uncommonly good of you to let me come round wastin' your time like this. I'll try not to be too long about it, though I'm not awfully good at comin' to the point. My brother never would let me stand for the county, y'know— said I wandered on so nobody'd know what I was talkin' about."

"Pleased to meet you, Lord Wimsey," said Mr. Milligan. "Won't you take a seat?"

"Thanks," said Lord Peter, "but I'm not a peer, you know—that's my brother Denver. My name's Peter. It's a silly name, I always think, so old-world and full of homely virtue and that sort of thing, but my godfathers and godmothers in my baptism are responsible for that, I suppose, officially—which is rather hard on them, you know, as they didn't actually choose it. But we always have a Peter, after the third duke, who betrayed five kings somewhere about the Wars of the Roses, though come to think of it, it ain't anything to be proud of. Still, one has to make the best of it."

Mr. Milligan, thus ingeniously placed at that disadvantage which attends ignorance, manoeuvred for position, and offered his interrupter a Corona Corona.

"Thanks, awfully," said Lord Peter, "though you really mustn't tempt me to stay here burblin' all afternoon. By Jove, Mr. Milligan, if you offer people such comfortable chairs and cigars like these, I wonder they don't come an' live in your office." He added mentally: "I wish to goodness I could get those long-toed boots off you. How's a man to know the size of your feet? And a head like a potato. It's enough to make one swear."

"Say now, Lord Peter," said Mr. Milligan, "can I do anything for you?"

"Well, d'you know," said Lord Peter, "I'm wonderin' if you would. It's damned cheek to ask you, but fact is, it's my mother, you know. Wonderful woman, but don't realize what it means, demands on the time of a busy man like you. We don't understand hustle over here, you know, Mr. Milligan."

"Now don't you mention that," said Mr. Milligan; "I'd be surely charmed to do anything to oblige the Duchess."

He felt a momentary qualm as to whether a duke's mother were also a duchess, but breathed more freely as Lord Peter went on:

"Thanks—that's uncommonly good of you. Well, now, it's like this. My mother—most energetic, self-sacrificin' woman, don't you see, is thinkin' of gettin' up a sort of a charity bazaar down at Denver this winter, in aid of the church roof, y'know. Very sad case, Mr. Milligan—fine old antique— early English windows and decorated angel roof, and all that—all tumblin' to pieces, rain pourin' in and so on—vicar catchin' rheumatism at early service, owin' to the draught blowin' in over the altar—you know the sort of thing. They've got a man down startin' on it—little beggar called Thipps—lives with an aged mother in Battersea—vulgar little beast, but quite good on angel roofs and things, I'm told."

At this point, Lord Peter watched his interlocutor narrowly, but finding that this rigmarole produced in him no reaction more startling than polite interest tinged with faint bewilderment, he abandoned this line of investigation, and proceeded:

"I say, I beg your pardon, frightfully—I'm afraid I'm bein' beastly long-winded. Fact is, my mother is gettin' up this bazaar, and she thought it'd be an awfully interestin' side-show to have some lectures—sort of little talks, y'know—by eminent business men of all nations. 'How I Did It' kind of touch, y'know—'A Drop of Oil with a Kerosene King'—'Cash Conscience and Cocoa' and so on. It would interest people down there no end. You see, all my mother's friends will be there, and we've none of us any money—not what you'd call money, I mean—I expect our incomes wouldn't pay your telephone calls, would they?—but we like awfully to hear about the people who can make money. Gives us a sort of uplifted feelin', don't you know. Well, anyway, I mean, my mother'd be frightfully pleased and grateful to you, Mr. Milligan, if you'd come down and give us a few words as a representative American. It needn't take more than ten minutes or so, y'know, because the local people can't understand much beyond shootin' and huntin', and my mother's crowd can't keep their minds on anythin' more than ten minutes together, but we'd really appreciate it very much if you'd come and stay a day or two and just give us a little breezy word on the almighty dollar."

"Why, yes," said Mr. Milligan, "I'd like to, Lord Peter. It's kind of the Duchess to suggest it. It's a very sad thing when these fine old antiques begin to wear out. I'll come with great pleasure. And perhaps you'd be kind enough to accept a little donation to the Restoration Fund."

This unexpected development nearly brought Lord Peter up all standing. To pump, by means of an ingenious lie, a hospitable gentleman whom you are inclined to suspect of a peculiarly malicious murder, and to accept from him in the course of the proceedings a large cheque for a charitable object, has something about it unpalatable to any but the hardened Secret Service agent. Lord Peter temporized.

"That's awfully decent of you," he said. "I'm sure they'd be no end grateful. But you'd better not give it to me, you know. I might spend it, or lose it. I'm not very reliable, I'm afraid. The vicar's the right person—the Rev. Constantine Throgmorton, St. John-before-the-Latin-Gate Vicarage, Duke's Denver, if you like to send it there."

"I will," said Mr. Milligan. "Will you write it out now for a thousand pounds, Scoot, in case it slips my mind later?"

The secretary, a sandy-haired young man with a long chin and no eyebrows, silently did as he was requested. Lord Peter looked from the bald head of Mr. Milligan to the red head of the secretary, hardened his heart and tried again.

"Well, I'm no end grateful to you, Mr. Milligan, and so'll my mother be when I tell her. I'll let you know the date of the bazaar—it's not quite settled yet, and I've got to see some other business men, don't you know. I thought of askin' someone from one of the big newspaper combines to represent British advertisin' talent, what?—and a friend of mine promises me a leadin' German financier—very interestin' if there ain't too much feelin' against it down in the country, and I'll have to find somebody or other to do the Hebrew point of view. I thought of askin' Levy, y'know, only he's floated off in this inconvenient way."

"Yes," said Mr. Milligan, "that's a very curious thing, though I don't mind saying, Lord Peter, that it's a convenience to me. He had a cinch on my railroad combine, but I'd nothing against him personally, and if he turns up after I've brought off a little deal I've got on, I'll be happy to give him the right hand of welcome."

A vision passed through Lord Peter's mind of Sir Reuben kept somewhere in custody till a financial crisis was over. This was exceedingly possible, and far more agreeable than his earlier conjecture; it also agreed better with the impression he was forming of Mr. Milligan.

"Well, it's a rum go," said Lord Peter, "but I daresay he had his reasons. Much better not inquire into people's reasons, y'know, what? Specially as a police friend of mine who's connected with the case says the old johnnie dyed his hair before he went."

Out of the tail of his eye, Lord Peter saw the redheaded secretary add up five columns of figures simultaneously and jot down the answer.

"Dyed his hair, did he?" said Mr. Milligan.

"Dyed it red," said Lord Peter. The secretary looked up. "Odd thing is," continued Wimsey, "they can't lay hands on the bottle. Somethin' fishy there, don't you think, what?"

The secretary's interest seemed to have evaporated. He inserted a fresh sheet into his looseleaf ledger, and carried forward a row of digits from the preceding page.

"I daresay there's nothin' in it," said Lord Peter, rising to go.

"Well, it's uncommonly good of you to be bothered with me like this, Mr. Milligan—my mother'll be no end pleased. She'll write you about the date."

"I'm charmed," said Mr. Milligan. "Very pleased to have met you."

Mr. Scoot rose silently to open the door, uncoiling as he did so a portentous length of thin leg, hitherto hidden by the desk. With a mental sigh Lord Peter estimated him at six-foot-four.

"It's a pity I can't put Scoot's head on Milligan's shoulders," said Lord Peter, emerging into the swirl of the city. "And what _will_ my mother say?"

CHAPTER V

Mr. Parker was a bachelor, and occupied a Georgian but inconvenient flat at No. 12A Great Ormond Street, for which he paid a pound a week. His exertions in the cause of civilization were rewarded, not by the gift of diamond rings from empresses or munificent cheques from grateful Prime Ministers, but by a modest, though sufficient, salary, drawn from the pockets of the British taxpayer. He awoke, after a long day of arduous and inconclusive labour, to the smell of burnt porridge. Through his bedroom window, hygienically open top and bottom, a raw fog was rolling slowly in, and the sight of a pair of winter pants, flung hastily over a chair the previous night, fretted him with a sense of the sordid absurdity of the human form. The telephone bell rang, and he crawled wretchedly out of bed and into the sitting-room, where Mrs. Munns, who did for him by the day, was laying the table, sneezing as she went.

Mr. Bunter was speaking.

"His lordship says he'd be very glad, sir, if you could make it convenient to step round to breakfast."

If the odour of kidneys and bacon had been wafted along the wire, Mr. Parker could not have experienced a more vivid sense of consolation.

"Tell his lordship I'll be with him in half an hour," he said, thankfully, and plunging into the bathroom, which was also the kitchen, he informed Mrs. Munns, who was just making tea from a kettle which had gone off the boil, that he should be out to breakfast.

"You can take the porridge home for the family," he added, viciously, and flung off his dressing-gown with such determination that Mrs. Munns could only scuttle away with a snort.

A 19 'bus deposited him in Piccadilly only fifteen minutes later than his rather sanguine impulse had prompted him to suggest, and Mr. Bunter served him with glorious food, incomparable coffee, and the _Daily Mail_ before a blazing fire of wood and coal. A distant voice singing the "et iterum venturus est" from Bach's Mass in B minor proclaimed that for the owner of the flat cleanliness and godliness met at least once a day, and presently Lord Peter roamed in, moist and verbena-scented, in a bath-robe cheerfully patterned with unnaturally variegated peacocks.

"Mornin', old dear," said that gentleman. "Beast of a day, ain't it? Very good of you to trundle out in it, but I had a letter I wanted you to see, and I hadn't the energy to come round to your place. Bunter and I've been makin' a night of it."

"What's the letter?" asked Parker.

"Never talk business with your mouth full," said Lord Peter, reprovingly; "have some Oxford marmalade—and then I'll show you my Dante; they brought it round last night. What ought I to read this morning, Bunter?"

"Lord Erith's collection is going to be sold, my lord. There is a column about it in the _Morning Post_. I think your lordship should look at this review of Sir Julian Freke's new book on 'The Physiological Bases of the Conscience' in the _Times Literary Supplement_. Then there is a very singular little burglary in the _Chronicle_, my lord, and an attack on titled families in the _Herald_—rather ill-written, if I may say so, but not without unconscious humour which your lordship will appreciate."

"All right, give me that and the burglary," said his lordship.

"I have looked over the other papers," pursued Mr. Bunter, indicating a formidable pile, "and marked your lordship's after-breakfast reading."

"Oh, pray don't allude to it," said Lord Peter; "you take my appetite away."

There was silence, but for the crunching of toast and the crackling of paper.

"I see they adjourned the inquest," said Parker presently.

"Nothing else to do," said Lord Peter; "but Lady Levy arrived last night, and will have to go and fail to identify the body this morning for Sugg's benefit."

"Time, too," said Mr. Parker shortly.

Silence fell again.

"I don't think much of your burglary, Bunter," said Lord Peter.

"Competent, of course, but no imagination. I want imagination in a criminal. Where's the _Morning Post_?"

After a further silence, Lord Peter said: "You might send for the catalogue, Bunter, that Apollonios Rhodios[C] might be worth looking at. No, I'm damned if I'm going to stodge through that review, but you can stick the book on the library list if you like. His book on crime was entertainin' enough as far as it went, but the fellow's got a bee in his bonnet. Thinks God's a secretion of the liver—all right once in a way, but there's no need to keep on about it. There's nothing you can't prove if your outlook is only sufficiently limited. Look at Sugg."

"I beg your pardon," said Parker; "I wasn't attending. Argentines are steadying a little, I see."

"Milligan," said Lord Peter.

"Oil's in a bad way. Levy's made a difference there. That funny little boom in Peruvians that came on just before he disappeared has died away again. I wonder if he was concerned in it. D'you know at all?"

"I'll find out," said Lord Peter. "What was it?"

"Oh, an absolutely dud enterprise that hadn't been heard of for years. It suddenly took a little lease of life last week. I happened to notice it because my mother got let in for a couple of hundred shares a long time ago. It never paid a dividend. Now it's petered out again."

Wimsey pushed his plate aside and lit a pipe.

"Having finished, I don't mind doing some work," he said. "How did you get on yesterday?"

"I didn't," replied Parker. "I sleuthed up and down those flats in my own bodily shape and two different disguises. I was a gas-meter man and a collector for a Home for Lost Doggies, and I didn't get a thing to go on, except a servant in the top flat at the Battersea Bridge Road end of the row who said she thought she heard a bump on the roof one night. Asked which night, she couldn't rightly say. Asked if it was Monday night, she thought it very likely. Asked if it mightn't have been in that high wind on Saturday night that blew my chimney-pot off, she couldn't say but what it might have been. Asked if she was sure it was on the roof and not inside the flat, said to be sure they did find a picture tumbled down next morning. Very suggestible girl. I saw your friends, Mr. and Mrs. Appledore, who received me coldly, but could make no definite complaint about Thipps except that his mother dropped her h's, and that he once called on them uninvited, armed with a pamphlet about anti-vivisection. The Indian Colonel on the first floor was loud, but unexpectedly friendly. He gave me Indian curry for supper and some very good whisky, but he's a sort of hermit, and all _he_ could tell me was that he couldn't stand Mrs. Appledore."

"Did you get nothing at the house?"

"Only Levy's private diary. I brought it away with me. Here it is. It doesn't tell one much, though. It's full of entries like: 'Tom and Annie to dinner'; and 'My dear wife's birthday; gave her an old opal ring'; 'Mr. Arbuthnot dropped in to tea; he wants to marry Rachel, but I should like someone steadier for my treasure.' Still, I thought it would show who came to the house and so on. He evidently wrote it up at night. There's no entry for Monday."

"I expect it'll be useful," said Lord Peter, turning over the pages.

"Poor old buffer. I say, I'm not so certain now he was done away with."

He detailed to Mr. Parker his day's work.

"Arbuthnot?" said Parker. "Is that the Arbuthnot of the diary?"

"I suppose so. I hunted him up because I knew he was fond of fooling round the Stock Exchange. As for Milligan, he _looks_ all right, but I believe he's pretty ruthless in business and you never can tell. Then there's the red-haired secretary—lightnin' calculator man with a face like a fish, keeps on sayin' nuthin'—got the Tarbaby in his family tree, I should think. Milligan's got a jolly good motive for, at any rate, suspendin' Levy for a few days. Then there's the new man."

"What new man?"

"Ah, that's the letter I mentioned to you. Where did I put it? Here we are. Good parchment paper, printed address of solicitor's office in

Salisbury, and postmark to correspond. Very precisely written with a fine nib by an elderly business man of old-fashioned habits."

Parker took the letter and read:

CRIMPLESHAM AND WICKS,
Solicitors,
MILFORD HILL, SALISBURY,
17 November, 192—.

Sir,

With reference to your advertisement today in the personal column of _The Times_, I am disposed to believe that the eyeglasses and chain in question may be those I lost on the L. B. & S. C. Electric Railway while visiting London last Monday. I left Victoria by the 5.45 train, and did not notice my loss till I arrived at Balham. This indication and the optician's specification of the glasses, which I enclose, should suffice at once as an identification and a guarantee of my bona fides. If the glasses should prove to be mine, I should be greatly obliged to you if you would kindly forward them to me by registered post, as the chain was a present from my daughter, and is one of my dearest possessions.

Thanking you in advance for this kindness, and regretting the trouble to which I shall be putting you, I am,

Yours very truly,
THOS. CRIMPLESHAM

Lord Peter Wimsey,
110, Piccadilly, W.
(Encl.)

"Dear me," said Parker, "this is what you might call unexpected."

"Either it is some extraordinary misunderstanding," said Lord Peter, "or Mr. Crimplesham is a very bold and cunning villain. Or possibly, of course, they are the wrong glasses. We may as well get a ruling on that point at once. I suppose the glasses are at the Yard. I wish you'd just ring 'em up and ask 'em to send round an optician's description of them at once—and you might ask at the same time whether it's a very common prescription."

"Right you are," said Parker, and took the receiver off its hook.

"And now," said his friend, when the message was delivered, "just come into the library for a minute."

On the library table, Lord Peter had spread out a series of bromide prints, some dry, some damp, and some but half-washed.

"These little ones are the originals of the photos we've been taking," said Lord Peter, "and these big ones are enlargements all made to precisely the same scale. This one here is the footmark on the linoleum; we'll put that by itself at present. Now these finger-prints can be divided into five lots. I've numbered 'em on the prints—see?—and made a list:

"A. The finger-prints of Levy himself, off his little bedside book and his hair-brush—this and this—you can't mistake the little scar on the thumb.

"B. The smudges made by the gloved fingers of the man who slept in Levy's room on Monday night. They show clearly on the water-bottle and on the boots—superimposed on Levy's. They are very distinct on the boots—surprisingly so for gloved hands, and I deduce that the gloves were rubber ones and had recently been in water.

"Here's another interestin' point. Levy walked in the rain on Monday night, as we know, and these dark marks are mud-splashes. You see they lie _over_ Levy's finger-prints in every case. Now see: on this left boot we find the stranger's thumb-mark _over_ the mud on the leather above the heel. That's a funny place to find a thumb-mark on a boot, isn't it? That is, if Levy took off his own boots. But it's the place where you'd expect to see it if somebody forcibly removed his boots for him. Again, most of the stranger's finger-marks come _over_ the mud-marks, but here is one splash of mud which comes on top of them again. Which makes me infer that the stranger came back to Park Lane, wearing Levy's boots, in a cab, carriage or car, but that at some point or other he walked a little way—just enough to tread in a puddle and get a splash on the boots. What do you say?"

"Very pretty," said Parker. "A bit intricate, though, and the marks are not all that I could wish a finger-print to be."

"Well, I won't lay too much stress on it. But it fits in with our previous ideas. Now let's turn to:

"C. The prints obligingly left by my own particular villain on the further edge of Thipps's bath, where you spotted them, and I ought to be scourged for not having spotted them. The left hand, you notice, the base of the palm and the fingers, but not the tips, looking as though he had steadied himself on the edge of the bath while leaning down to adjust something at the bottom, the pince-nez perhaps. Gloved, you see, but showing no ridge or seam of any kind—I say rubber, you say rubber. That's that. Now see here:

"D and E come off a visiting-card of mine. There's this thing at the corner, marked F, but that you can disregard; in the original document it's a sticky mark left by the thumb of the youth who took it from me, after first removing a piece of chewing-gum from his teeth with his finger to tell me that Mr. Milligan might or might not be disengaged. D and E are the thumb-marks of Mr. Milligan and his red-haired secretary. I'm not clear which is which, but I saw the youth with the chewing-gum hand the card to the secretary, and when I got into the inner shrine I saw John P. Milligan standing with it in his hand, so it's one or the other, and for the moment it's immaterial to our purpose which is which. I boned the card from the table when I left.

"Well, now, Parker, here's what's been keeping Bunter and me up till the small hours. I've measured and measured every way backwards and forwards till my head's spinnin', and I've stared till I'm nearly blind, but I'm hanged if I can make my mind up. Question 1. Is C identical with B? Question 2. Is D or E identical with B? There's nothing to go on but the size and shape, of course, and the marks are so faint—what do you think?"

Parker shook his head doubtfully.

"I think E might almost be put out of the question," he said; "it seems such an excessively long and narrow thumb. But I think there is a decided resemblance between the span of B on the water-bottle and C on the bath. And I don't see any reason why D shouldn't be the same as B, only there's so little to judge from."

"Your untutored judgment and my measurements have brought us both to the same conclusion—if you can call it a conclusion," said Lord Peter, bitterly.

"Another thing," said Parker. "Why on earth should we try to connect B with C? The fact that you and I happen to be friends doesn't make it necessary to conclude that the two cases we happen to be interested in have any organic connection with one another. Why should they? The only person who thinks they have is Sugg, and he's nothing to go by. It would be different if there were any truth in the suggestion that the man in the bath was Levy, but we know for a certainty he wasn't. It's ridiculous to suppose that the same man was employed in committing two totally distinct crimes on the same night, one in Battersea and the other in Park Lane."

"I know," said Wimsey, "though of course we mustn't forget that Levy _was_ in Battersea at the time, and now we know he didn't return home at twelve as was supposed, we've no reason to think he ever left Battersea at all."

"True. But there are other places in Battersea besides Thipps's bathroom. And he _wasn't_ in Thipps's bathroom. In fact, come to think of it, that's the one place in the universe where we know definitely that he wasn't. So what's Thipps's bath got to do with it?"

"I don't know," said Lord Peter. "Well, perhaps we shall get something better to go on today."

He leaned back in his chair and smoked thoughtfully for some time over the papers which Bunter had marked for him.

"They've got you out in the limelight," he said. "Thank Heaven, Sugg hates me too much to give me any publicity. What a dull Agony Column! 'Darling Pipsey—Come back soon to your distracted Popsey'—and the usual young man in need of financial assistance, and the usual injunction to 'Remember thy Creator in the days of thy youth.' Hullo! there's the bell. Oh, it's our answer from Scotland Yard."

The note from Scotland Yard enclosed an optician's specification identical with that sent by Mr. Crimplesham, and added that it was an unusual one, owing to the peculiar strength of the lenses and the marked difference between the sight of the two eyes.

"That's good enough," said Parker.

"Yes," said Wimsey. "Then Possibility No. 3 is knocked on the head. There remain Possibility No. 1: Accident or Misunderstanding, and No. 2: Deliberate Villainy, of a remarkably bold and calculating kind—of a kind, in fact, characteristic of the author or authors of our two problems. Following the methods inculcated at that University of which I have the honour to be a member, we will now examine severally the various suggestions afforded by Possibility No. 2. This Possibility may be again subdivided into two or more Hypotheses. On Hypothesis 1

(strongly advocated by my distinguished colleague Professor Snupshed), the criminal, whom we may designate as X, is not identical with Crimplesham, but is using the name of Crimplesham as his shield, or aegis. This hypothesis may be further subdivided into two alternatives. Alternative A: Crimplesham is an innocent and unconscious accomplice, and X is in his employment. X writes in Crimplesham's name on Crimplesham's office-paper and obtains that the object in question, i.e., the eyeglasses, be despatched to Crimplesham's address. He is in a position to intercept the parcel before it reaches Crimplesham. The presumption is that X is Crimplesham's charwoman, office-boy, clerk, secretary or porter. This offers a wide field of investigation. The method of inquiry will be to interview Crimplesham and discover whether he sent the letter, and if not, who has access to his correspondence. Alternative B: Crimplesham is under X's influence or in his power, and has been induced to write the letter by (_a_) bribery, (_b_) misrepresentation or (_c_) threats. X may in that case be a persuasive relation or friend, or else a creditor, blackmailer or assassin; Crimplesham, on the other hand, is obviously venal or a fool. The method of inquiry in this case, I would tentatively suggest, is again to interview Crimplesham, put the facts of the case strongly before him, and assure him in the most intimidating terms that he is liable to a prolonged term of penal servitude as an accessory after the fact in the crime of murder— Ah-hem! Trusting, gentlemen, that you have followed me thus far, we will pass to the consideration of Hypothesis No. 2, to which I personally incline, and according to which X is identical with Crimplesham.

"In this case, Crimplesham, who is, in the words of an English classic, a man-of-infinite-resource-and-sagacity, correctly deduces that, of all people, the last whom we shall expect to find answering our advertisement is the criminal himself. Accordingly, he plays a bold game of bluff. He invents an occasion on which the glasses may very easily have been lost or stolen, and applies for them. If confronted, nobody will be more astonished than he to learn where they were found. He will produce witnesses to prove that he left Victoria at 5.45 and emerged from the train at Balham at the scheduled time, and sat up all Monday night playing chess with a respectable gentleman well known in Balham. In this case, the method of inquiry will be to pump the respectable gentleman in Balham, and if he should happen to be a single gentleman with a deaf housekeeper, it may be no easy matter to impugn the alibi, since, outside detective romances, few ticket-collectors and 'bus-conductors keep an exact remembrance of all the passengers passing between Balham and London on any and every evening of the week.

"Finally, gentlemen, I will frankly point out the weak point of all these hypotheses, namely: that none of them offers any explanation as to why the incriminating article was left so conspicuously on the body in the first instance."

Mr. Parker had listened with commendable patience to this academic exposition.

"Might not X," he suggested, "be an enemy of Crimplesham's, who designed to throw suspicion upon him?"

"He might. In that case he should be easy to discover, since he obviously lives in close proximity to Crimplesham and his glasses, and Crimplesham in fear of his life will then be a valuable ally for the prosecution."

"How about the first possibility of all, misunderstanding or accident?"

"Well! Well, for purposes of discussion, nothing, because it really doesn't afford any data for discussion."

"In any case," said Parker, "the obvious course appears to be to go to Salisbury."

"That seems indicated," said Lord Peter.

"Very well," said the detective, "is it to be you or me or both of us?"

"It is to be me," said Lord Peter, "and that for two reasons. First, because, if (by Possibility No. 2, Hypothesis 1, Alternative A) Crimplesham is an innocent catspaw, the person who put in the advertisement is the proper person to hand over the property. Secondly, because, if we are to adopt Hypothesis 2, we must not overlook the sinister possibility that Crimplesham-X is laying a careful trap to rid himself of the person who so unwarily advertised in the daily press his interest in the solution of the Battersea Park mystery."

"That appears to me to be an argument for our both going," objected the detective.

"Far from it," said Lord Peter. "Why play into the hands of Crimplesham-X by delivering over to him the only two men in London with the evidence, such as it is, and shall I say the wits, to connect him with the Battersea body?"

"But if we told the Yard where we were going, and we both got nobbled," said Mr. Parker, "it would afford strong presumptive evidence of Crimplesham's guilt, and anyhow, if he didn't get hanged for murdering the man in the bath he'd at least get hanged for murdering us."

"Well," said Lord Peter, "if he only murdered me you could still hang him—what's the good of wasting a sound, marriageable young male like yourself? Besides, how about old Levy? If you're incapacitated, do you think anybody else is going to find him?"

"But we could frighten Crimplesham by threatening him with the Yard."

"Well, dash it all, if it comes to that, I can frighten him by threatening him with _you_, which, seeing you hold what evidence there is, is much more to the point. And, then, suppose it's a wild-goose chase after all, you'll have wasted time when you might have been getting on with the case. There are several things that need doing."

"Well," said Parker, silenced but reluctant, "why can't I go, in that case?"

"Bosh!" said Lord Peter. "I am retained (by old Mrs. Thipps, for whom I entertain the greatest respect) to deal with this case, and it's only by courtesy I allow you to have anything to do with it."

Mr. Parker groaned.

"Will you at least take Bunter?" he said.

"In deference to your feelings," replied Lord Peter, "I will take Bunter, though he could be far more usefully employed taking photographs or overhauling my wardrobe. When is there a good train to Salisbury, Bunter?"

"There is an excellent train at 10.50, my lord."

"Kindly make arrangements to catch it," said Lord Peter, throwing off his bath-robe and trailing away with it into his bedroom. "And, Parker—if you have nothing else to do you might get hold of Levy's secretary and look into that little matter of the Peruvian oil."

LORD PETER TOOK WITH HIM, FOR LIGHT READING IN THE TRAIN, SIR REUBEN Levy's diary. It was a simple, and in the light of recent facts, rather a pathetic document. The terrible fighter of the Stock Exchange, who could with one nod set the surly bear dancing, or bring the savage bull to feed out of his hand, whose breath devastated whole districts with famine or swept financial potentates from their seats, was revealed in private life as kindly, domestic, innocently proud of himself and his belongings, confiding, generous and a little dull. His own small economies were duly chronicled side by side with extravagant presents to his wife and daughter. Small incidents of household routine appeared, such as: "Man came to mend the conservatory roof," or "The new butler (Simpson) has arrived, recommended by the Goldbergs. I think he will be satisfactory." All visitors and entertainments were duly entered, from a very magnificent lunch to Lord Dewsbury, the Minister for Foreign Affairs, and Dr. Jabez K. Wort, the American plenipotentiary, through a series of diplomatic dinners to eminent financiers, down to intimate family gatherings of persons designated by Christian names or nicknames. About May there came a mention of Lady Levy's nerves, and further reference was made to the subject in subsequent months. In September it was stated that "Freke came to see my dear wife and advised complete rest and change of scene. She thinks of going abroad with Rachel." The name of the famous nerve-specialist occurred as a diner or luncher about once a month, and it came into Lord Peter's mind that Freke would be a good person to consult about Levy himself. "People sometimes tell things to the doctor," he murmured to himself. "And, by Jove! if Levy was simply going round to see Freke on Monday night, that rather disposes of the Battersea incident, doesn't it?" He made a note to look up Sir Julian and turned on further. On September 18th, Lady Levy and her daughter had left for the south of France. Then suddenly, under the date October 5th, Lord Peter found what he was looking for: "Goldberg, Skriner and Milligan to dinner."

There was the evidence that Milligan had been in that house. There had been a formal entertainment—a meeting as of two duellists shaking hands before the fight. Skriner was a well-known picture-dealer; Lord Peter imagined an after-dinner excursion upstairs to see the two Corots in the drawing-room, and the portrait of the oldest Levy girl, who had died at the age of sixteen. It was by Augustus John, and hung in the bedroom. The name of the red-haired secretary was nowhere mentioned, unless the initial S., occurring in another entry, referred to him. Throughout September and October, Anderson (of Wyndham's) had been a frequent visitor.

Lord Peter shook his head over the diary, and turned to the consideration of the Battersea Park mystery. Whereas in the Levy affair it was easy enough to supply a motive for the crime, if crime it were, and the difficulty was to discover the method of its carrying out and the whereabouts of the victim, in the other case the chief obstacle to inquiry was the entire absence of any imaginable motive. It was odd that, although the papers had carried news of the affair from one end of the country to the other and a description of the body had been sent to every police station in the country, nobody had as yet come forward to identify the mysterious occupant of Mr. Thipps's bath. It was true that the description, which mentioned the clean-shaven chin, elegantly cut hair and the pince-nez, was rather misleading, but on the other hand, the police had managed to discover the number of molars missing, and the height, complexion and other data were correctly enough stated, as also the date at which death had presumably occurred. It seemed, however, as though the man had melted out of society without leaving a gap or so much as a ripple. Assigning a motive for the murder of a person without relations or antecedents or even clothes is like trying to visualize the fourth dimension—admirable exercise for the imagination, but arduous and inconclusive. Even if the day's interview should disclose black spots in the past or present of Mr. Crimplesham, how were they to be brought into connection with a person apparently without a past, and whose present was confined to the narrow limits of a bath and a police mortuary?

"Bunter," said Lord Peter, "I beg that in the future you will restrain me from starting two hares at once. These cases are gettin' to be a strain on my constitution. One hare has nowhere to run from, and the other has nowhere to run to. It's a kind of mental D.T., Bunter. When this is over I shall turn pussyfoot, forswear the police news, and take to an emollient diet of the works of the late Charles Garvice."

IT WAS ITS COMPARATIVE PROXIMITY TO MILFORD HILL THAT INDUCED LORD Peter to lunch at the Minster Hotel rather than at the White Hart or some other more picturesquely situated hostel. It was not a lunch calculated to cheer his mind; as in all Cathedral cities, the atmosphere of the Close pervades every nook and corner of Salisbury, and no food in that city but seems faintly flavoured with prayer-books. As he sat sadly consuming that impassive pale substance known to the English as "cheese" unqualified (for there are cheeses which go openly by their names, as Stilton, Camembert, Gruyère, Wensleydale or Gorgonzola, but "cheese" is cheese and everywhere the same), he inquired of the waiter the whereabouts of Mr. Crimplesham's office.

The waiter directed him to a house rather further up the street on the opposite side, adding: "But anybody'll tell you, sir; Mr. Crimplesham's very well known hereabouts."

"He's a good solicitor, I suppose?" said Lord Peter.

"Oh, yes, sir," said the waiter, "you couldn't do better than trust to Mr. Crimplesham, sir. There's folk say he's old-fashioned, but I'd rather have my little bits of business done by Mr. Crimplesham than by one of these fly-away young men. Not but what Mr. Crimplesham'll be retiring soon, sir, I don't doubt, for he must be close on eighty, sir, if he's a day, but then there's young Mr. Wicks to carry on the business, and he's a very nice, steady-like young gentleman."

"Is Mr. Crimplesham really as old as that?" said Lord Peter. "Dear me! He must be very active for his years. A friend of mine was doing business with him in town last week."

"Wonderful active, sir," agreed the waiter, "and with his game leg, too, you'd be surprised. But there, sir, I often think when a man's once past a certain age, the older he grows the tougher he gets, and women the same or more so."

"Very likely," said Lord Peter, calling up and dismissing the mental picture of a gentleman of eighty with a game leg carrying a dead body over the roof of a Battersea flat at midnight. "'He's tough, sir, tough, is old Joey Bagstock, tough and devilish sly,'" he added, thoughtlessly.

"Indeed, sir?" said the waiter. "I couldn't say, I'm sure."

"I beg your pardon," said Lord Peter; "I was quoting poetry. Very silly of me. I got the habit at my mother's knee and I can't break myself of it."

"No, sir," said the waiter, pocketing a liberal tip. "Thank you very much, sir. You'll find the house easy. Just afore you come to Penny-farthing Street, sir, about two turnings off, on the right-hand side opposite."

"Afraid that disposes of Crimplesham-X," said Lord Peter. "I'm rather sorry; he was a fine sinister figure as I had pictured him. Still, his may yet be the brain behind the hands—the aged spider sitting invisible in the centre of the vibrating web, you know, Bunter."

"Yes, my lord," said Bunter. They were walking up the street together.

"There is the office over the way," pursued Lord Peter. "I think, Bunter, you might step into this little shop and purchase a sporting paper, and if I do not emerge from the villain's lair—say within three-quarters of an hour, you may take such steps as your perspicuity may suggest."

Mr. Bunter turned into the shop as desired, and Lord Peter walked across and rang the lawyer's bell with decision.

"The truth, the whole truth and nothing but the truth is my long suit here, I fancy," he murmured, and when the door was opened by a clerk he delivered over his card with an unflinching air.

He was ushered immediately into a confidential-looking office, obviously furnished in the early years of Queen Victoria's reign, and never altered since. A lean, frail-looking old gentleman rose briskly from his chair as he entered and limped forward to meet him.

"My dear sir," exclaimed the lawyer, "how extremely good of you to come in person! Indeed, I am ashamed to have given you so much trouble. I trust you were passing this way, and that my glasses have not put you to any great inconvenience. Pray take a seat, Lord Peter." He peered gratefully at the young man over a pince-nez obviously the fellow of that now adorning a dossier in Scotland Yard.

Lord Peter sat down. The lawyer sat down. Lord Peter picked up a glass paper-weight from the desk and weighed it thoughtfully in his hand. Subconsciously he noted what an admirable set of finger-prints he was leaving upon it. He replaced it with precision on the exact centre of a pile of letters.

"It's quite all right," said Lord Peter. "I was here on business. Very happy to be of service to you. Very awkward to lose one's glasses, Mr. Crimplesham."

"Yes," said the lawyer, "I assure you I feel quite lost without them. I have this pair, but they do not fit my nose so well—besides, that chain has a great sentimental value for me. I was terribly distressed on arriving at Balham to find that I had lost them. I made inquiries of the railway, but to no purpose. I feared they had been stolen. There were such crowds at

Victoria, and the carriage was packed with people all the way to Balham. Did you come across them in the train?"

"Well, no," said Lord Peter, "I found them in rather an unexpected place. Do you mind telling me if you recognized any of your fellow-travellers on that occasion?"

The lawyer stared at him.

"Not a soul," he answered. "Why do you ask?"

"Well," said Lord Peter, "I thought perhaps the—the person with whom I found them might have taken them for a joke."

The lawyer looked puzzled.

"Did the person claim to be an acquaintance of mine?" he inquired. "I know practically nobody in London, except the friend with whom I was staying in Balham, Dr. Philpots, and I should be very greatly surprised at his practising a jest upon me. He knew very well how distressed I was at the loss of the glasses. My business was to attend a meeting of shareholders in Medlicott's Bank, but the other gentlemen present were all personally unknown to me, and I cannot think that any of them would take so great a liberty. In any case," he added, "as the glasses are here, I will not inquire too closely into the manner of their restoration. I am deeply obliged to you for your trouble."

Lord Peter hesitated.

"Pray forgive my seeming inquisitiveness," he said, "but I must ask you another question. It sounds rather melodramatic, I'm afraid, but it's this. Are you aware that you have any enemy—anyone, I mean, who would profit by your—er—decease or disgrace?"

Mr. Crimplesham sat frozen into stony surprise and disapproval.

"May I ask the meaning of this extraordinary question?" he inquired stiffly.

"Well," said Lord Peter, "the circumstances are a little unusual. You may recollect that my advertisement was addressed to the jeweller who sold the chain."

"That surprised me at the time," said Mr. Crimplesham, "but I begin to think your advertisement and your behaviour are all of a piece."

"They are," said Lord Peter. "As a matter of fact I did not expect the owner of the glasses to answer my advertisement. Mr. Crimplesham, you have no doubt read what the papers have to say about the Battersea Park mystery. Your glasses are the pair that was found on the body, and they are now in the possession of the police at Scotland Yard, as you may see by this." He placed the specification of the glasses and the official note before Crimplesham.

"Good God!" exclaimed the lawyer. He glanced at the paper, and then looked narrowly at Lord Peter.

"Are you yourself connected with the police?" he inquired.

"Not officially," said Lord Peter. "I am investigating the matter privately, in the interests of one of the parties."

Mr. Crimplesham rose to his feet.

"My good man," he said, "this is a very impudent attempt, but blackmail is an indictable offence, and I advise you to leave my office before you commit yourself." He rang the bell.

"I was afraid you'd take it like that," said Lord Peter. "It looks as though this ought to have been my friend Detective Parker's job, after all." He laid Parker's card on the table beside the specification, and added: "If you should wish to see me again, Mr. Crimplesham, before tomorrow morning, you will find me at the Minster Hotel."

Mr. Crimplesham disdained to reply further than to direct the clerk who entered to "show this person out."

IN THE ENTRANCE LORD PETER BRUSHED AGAINST A TALL YOUNG MAN WHO was just coming in, and who stared at him with surprised recognition. His face, however, aroused no memories in Lord Peter's mind, and that baffled nobleman, calling out Bunter from the newspaper shop, departed to his hotel to get a trunk-call through to Parker.

MEANWHILE, IN THE OFFICE, THE MEDITATIONS OF THE INDIGNANT MR. CRIMplesham were interrupted by the entrance of his junior partner.

"I say," said the latter gentleman, "has somebody done something really wicked at last? Whatever brings such a distinguished amateur of crime on our sober doorstep?"

"I have been the victim of a vulgar attempt at blackmail," said the lawyer; "an individual passing himself off as Lord Peter Wimsey—"

"But that _is_ Lord Peter Wimsey," said Mr. Wicks, "there's no mistaking him. I saw him give evidence in the Attenbury emerald case. He's a big little pot in his way, you know, and goes fishing with the head of Scotland Yard."

"Oh, dear," said Mr. Crimplesham.

FATE ARRANGED THAT THE NERVES OF MR. CRIMPLESHAM SHOULD BE TRIED that afternoon. When, escorted by Mr. Wicks, he arrived at the Minster Hotel, he was informed by the porter that Lord Peter Wimsey had strolled out, mentioning that he thought of attending Evensong. "But his man is here, sir," he added, "if you'd like to leave a message."

Mr. Wicks thought that on the whole it would be well to leave a message. Mr. Bunter, on inquiry, was found to be sitting by the telephone, waiting for a trunk-call. As Mr. Wicks addressed him the bell rang, and Mr. Bunter, politely excusing himself, took down the receiver.

"Hullo!" he said. "Is that Mr. Parker? Oh, thanks! Exchange! Exchange! Sorry, can you put me through to Scotland Yard? Excuse me, gentlemen, keeping you waiting.—Exchange! all right—Scotland Yard—Hullo! Is that Scotland Yard?—Is Detective Parker round there?—Can I speak to him?—I shall have done in a moment, gentlemen.—Hullo! is that you, Mr. Parker? Lord Peter would be much obliged if you could find it convenient to step down to Salisbury, sir. Oh, no, sir, he's in excellent health, sir—just stepped round to hear Evensong, sir—oh, no, I think tomorrow morning would do excellently, sir, thank you, sir."

CHAPTER VI

It was, in fact, inconvenient for Mr. Parker to leave London. He had had to go and see Lady Levy towards the end of the morning, and subsequently his plans for the day had been thrown out of gear and his movements delayed by the discovery that the adjourned inquest of Mr. Thipps's unknown visitor was to be held that afternoon, since nothing very definite seemed forthcoming from Inspector Sugg's inquiries. Jury and witnesses had been convened accordingly for three o'clock. Mr. Parker might altogether have missed the event, had he not run against Sugg that morning at the Yard and extracted the information from him as one would a reluctant tooth. Inspector Sugg, indeed, considered Mr. Parker rather interfering; moreover, he was hand-in-glove with Lord Peter Wimsey, and Inspector Sugg had no words for the interferingness of Lord Peter. He could not, however, when directly questioned, deny that there was to be an inquest that afternoon, nor could he prevent Mr. Parker from enjoying the inalienable right of any interested British citizen to be present. At a little before three, therefore, Mr. Parker was in his place, and amusing himself with watching the efforts of those persons who arrived after the room was packed to insinuate, bribe or bully themselves into a position of vantage. The Coroner, a medical man of precise habits and unimaginative aspect, arrived punctually, and looking peevishly round at the crowded assembly, directed all the windows to be opened, thus letting in a stream of drizzling fog upon the heads of the unfortunates on that side of the room. This caused a commotion and some expressions of disapproval, checked sternly by the Coroner, who said that with the influenza about again an unventilated room was a death-trap; that anybody who chose to object to open windows had the obvious remedy of leaving the court, and further, that if any disturbance was made he would clear the court. He then took a Formamint lozenge, and proceeded, after the usual preliminaries, to call up fourteen good and lawful persons and swear them diligently to inquire and a true presentment make of all matters touching the death of the gentleman with the pince-nez and to give a true verdict according to the evidence, so help them God. When an expostulation by a woman juror—an elderly lady in spectacles who kept a sweet-shop, and appeared to wish she was back there—had been summarily quashed by the Coroner, the jury departed to view the body. Mr. Parker gazed round again and identified the unhappy Mr. Thipps and the girl Gladys led into an adjoining room under the grim guard of the police. They were soon followed by a gaunt old lady in a bonnet and mantle. With her, in a wonderful fur coat and a motor bonnet of fascinating construction, came the Dowager Duchess of Denver, her quick, dark eyes darting hither and thither about the crowd. The next moment they had lighted on Mr. Parker, who had several times visited the Dower House, and she nodded to him, and spoke to a policeman. Before long, a way opened magically through the press, and Mr. Parker found himself accommodated with a front seat just behind the Duchess, who greeted him charmingly, and said: "What's happened to poor Peter?" Parker began to explain, and the Coroner glanced irritably in their direction. Somebody went up and whispered in his ear, at which he coughed, and took another Formamint.

"We came up by car," said the Duchess—"so tiresome—such bad roads between Denver and Gunbury St. Walters—and there were people coming to lunch—I had to put them off—I couldn't let the old lady go alone, could I? By the way, such an odd thing's happened about the Church Restoration Fund—the Vicar—oh, dear, here are these people coming back again; well, I'll tell you afterwards—do look at that woman looking shocked, and the girl in tweeds trying to look as if she sat on undraped gentlemen every day of her life—I don't mean that—corpses of course—but one finds oneself being so Elizabethan nowadays—what an awful little man the coroner is, isn't he? He's looking daggers at me—do you think he'll dare to clear me out of the court or commit me for what-you-may-call-it?"

The first part of the evidence was not of great interest to Mr. Parker. The wretched Mr. Thipps, who had caught cold in gaol, deposed in an unhappy croak to having discovered the body when he went in to take his bath at eight o'clock. He had had such a shock, he had to sit down and send the girl for brandy. He had never seen the deceased before. He had no idea how he came there.

Yes, he had been in Manchester the day before. He had arrived at St. Pancras at ten o'clock. He had cloak-roomed his bag. At this point Mr. Thipps became very red, unhappy and confused, and glanced nervously about the court.

"Now, Mr. Thipps," said the Coroner, briskly, "we must have your movements quite clear. You must appreciate the importance of the matter. You have chosen to give evidence, which you need not have done, but having done so, you will find it best to be perfectly explicit."

"Yes," said Mr. Thipps faintly.

"Have you cautioned this witness, officer?" inquired the Coroner, turning sharply to Inspector Sugg.

The Inspector replied that he had told Mr. Thipps that anything he said might be used agin' him at his trial. Mr. Thipps became ashy, and said in a bleating voice that he 'adn't—hadn't meant to do anything that wasn't right.

This remark produced a mild sensation, and the Coroner became even more acidulated in manner than before.

"Is anybody representing Mr. Thipps?" he asked, irritably. "No? Did you not explain to him that he could—that he _ought_ to be represented? You did not? Really, Inspector! Did you not know, Mr. Thipps, that you had a right to be legally represented?"

Mr. Thipps clung to a chair-back for support, and said, "No," in a voice barely audible.

"It is incredible," said the Coroner, "that so-called educated people should be so ignorant of the legal procedure of their own country. This places us in a very awkward position. I doubt, Inspector, whether I should permit the prisoner—Mr. Thipps—to give evidence at all. It is a delicate position."

The perspiration stood on Mrs. Thipps's forehead.

"Save us from our friends," whispered the Duchess to Parker. "If that cough-drop-devouring creature had openly instructed those fourteen people—and what unfinished-looking faces they have—so characteristic, I always think, of the lower middle-class, rather like sheep, or calves' head (boiled, I mean), to bring in wilful murder against the poor little man, he couldn't have made himself plainer."

"He can't let him incriminate himself, you know," said Parker.

"Stuff!" said the Duchess. "How could the man incriminate himself when he never did anything in his life? You men never think of anything but your red tape."

Meanwhile Mr. Thipps, wiping his brow with a handkerchief, had summoned up courage. He stood up with a kind of weak dignity, like a small white rabbit brought to bay.

"I would rather tell you," he said, "though it's reelly very unpleasant for a man in my position. But I reelly couldn't have it thought for a moment that I'd committed this dreadful crime. I assure you, gentlemen, I _couldn't bear_ that. No. I'd rather tell you the truth, though I'm afraid it places me in rather a—well, I'll tell you."

"You fully understand the gravity of making such a statement, Mr. Thipps," said the Coroner.

"Quite," said Mr. Thipps. "It's all right—I—might I have a drink of water?"

"Take your time," said the Coroner, at the same time robbing his remark of all conviction by an impatient glance at his watch.

"Thank you, sir," said Mr. Thipps. "Well, then, it's true I got to St. Pancras at ten. But there was a man in the carriage with me. He'd got in at Leicester. I didn't recognise him at first, but he turned out to be an old school-fellow of mine."

"What was this gentleman's name?" inquired the Coroner, his pencil poised.

Mr. Thipps shrank together visibly.

"I'm afraid I can't tell you that," he said. "You see—that is, you _will_ see—it would get him into trouble, and I couldn't do that—no, I reelly couldn't do that, not if my life depended on it. No!" he added, as the ominous pertinence of the last phrase smote upon him, "I'm sure I couldn't do that."

"Well, well," said the Coroner.

The Duchess leaned over to Parker again. "I'm beginning quite to admire the little man," she said.

Mr. Thipps resumed.

"When we got to St. Pancras I was going home, but my friend said no. We hadn't met for a long time and we ought to—to make a night of it, was his expression. I fear I was weak, and let him overpersuade me to accompany him to one of his haunts. I use the word advisedly," said Mr. Thipps, "and I assure you, sir, that if I had known beforehand where we were going I never would have set foot in the place.

"I cloak-roomed my bag, for he did not like the notion of our being encumbered with it, and we got into a taxicab and drove to the corner of Tottenham Court Road and Oxford Street. We then walked a little way, and turned into a side street (I do not recollect which) where there was an open door, with the light shining out. There was a man at a counter, and my friend bought some tickets, and I heard the man at the counter say something to him about 'Your friend,' meaning me, and my friend said, 'Oh, yes, he's been here before, haven't you, Alf?' (which was what they called me at school), though I assure you, sir"—here Mr. Thipps grew very earnest—"I never had, and nothing in the world should induce me to go to such a place again.

"Well, we went down into a room underneath, where there were drinks, and my friend had several, and made me take one or two—though I am an abstemious man as a rule—and he talked to some other men and girls who were there—a very vulgar set of people, I thought them, though I wouldn't say but what some of the young ladies were nice-looking enough. One of them sat on my friend's knee and called him a slow old thing, and told him to come on—so we went into another room, where there were a lot of people dancing all these up-to-date dances. My friend went and danced, and I sat on a sofa. One of the young ladies came up to me and said, didn't I dance, and I said 'No,' so she said wouldn't I stand her a drink then. 'You'll stand us a drink then, darling,' that was what she said, and I said, 'Wasn't it after hours?' and she said that didn't matter. So I ordered the drink—a gin and bitters it was—for I didn't like not to, the young lady seemed to expect it of me and I felt it wouldn't be gentlemanly to refuse when she asked. But it went against my conscience—such a young girl as she was—and she put her arm round my neck afterwards and kissed me just like as if she was paying for the drink—and it reelly went to my 'eart," said Mr. Thipps, a little ambiguously, but with uncommon emphasis.

Here somebody at the back said, "Cheer-oh!" and a sound was heard as of the noisy smacking of lips.

"Remove the person who made that improper noise," said the Coroner, with great indignation. "Go on, please, Mr. Thipps."

"Well," said Mr. Thipps, "about half-past twelve, as I should reckon, things began to get a bit lively, and I was looking for my friend to say good-night, not wishing to stay longer, as you will understand, when I saw him with one of the young ladies, and they seemed to be getting on altogether too well, if you follow me, my friend pulling the ribbons off her shoulder and the young lady laughing—and so on," said Mr. Thipps, hurriedly, "so I thought I'd just slip quietly out, when I heard a scuffle and a shout—and before I knew what was happening there were half-a-dozen policemen in, and the lights went out, and everybody stampeding and shouting—quite horrid, it was. I was knocked down in the rush, and hit my head a nasty knock on a chair—that was where I got that bruise they asked me about— and I was dreadfully afraid I'd never get away and it would all come out, and perhaps my photograph in the papers, when someone caught hold of me—I think it was the young lady I'd given the gin and bitters to—and she said, 'This way,' and pushed me along a passage and out at the back somewhere. So I ran through some streets, and found myself in Goodge Street, and there I got a taxi and came home. I saw the account of the raid afterwards in the papers, and saw my friend had escaped, and so, as it wasn't the sort of thing I wanted made public, and I didn't want to get him into difficulties, I just said nothing. But that's the truth."

"Well, Mr. Thipps," said the Coroner, "we shall be able to substantiate a certain amount of this story. Your friend's name—"

"No," said Mr. Thipps, stoutly, "not on any account."

"Very good," said the Coroner. "Now, can you tell us what time you did get in?"

"About half-past one, I should think. Though reelly, I was so upset—"

"Quite so. Did you go straight to bed?"

"Yes, I took my sandwich and glass of milk first. I thought it might settle my inside, so to speak," added the witness, apologetically, "not being accustomed to alcohol so late at night and on an empty stomach, as you may say."

"Quite so. Nobody sat up for you?"

"Nobody."

"How long did you take getting to bed first and last?"

Mr. Thipps thought it might have been half-an-hour.

"Did you visit the bathroom before turning in?"

"No."

"And you heard nothing in the night?"

"No. I fell fast asleep. I was rather agitated, so I took a little dose to make me sleep, and what with being so tired and the milk and the dose, I just tumbled right off and didn't wake till Gladys called me."

Further questioning elicited little from Mr. Thipps. Yes, the bathroom window had been open when he went in in the morning, he was sure of that, and he had spoken very sharply to the girl about it. He was ready to answer any questions; he would be only too 'appy—happy to have this dreadful affair sifted to the bottom.

Gladys Horrocks stated that she had been in Mr. Thipps's employment about three months. Her previous employers would speak to her character. It was her duty to make the round of the flat at night, when she had seen Mrs. Thipps to bed at ten. Yes, she remembered doing so on Monday evening. She had looked into all the rooms. Did she recollect shutting the bathroom window that night? Well, no, she couldn't swear to it, not in particular, but when Mr. Thipps called her into the bathroom in the morning it certainly _was_ open. She had not been into the bathroom before Mr. Thipps went in. Well, yes, it had happened that she had left that window open before, when anyone had been 'aving a bath in the evening and 'ad left the blind down. Mrs. Thipps 'ad 'ad a bath on Monday evening, Mondays was one of her regular bath nights. She was very much afraid she 'adn't shut the window on Monday night, though she wished her 'ead 'ad been cut off afore she'd been so forgetful.

Here the witness burst into tears and was given some water, while the Coroner refreshed himself with a third lozenge.

Recovering, witness stated that she had certainly looked into all the rooms before going to bed. No, it was quite impossible for a body to be 'idden in the flat without her seeing of it. She 'ad been in the kitchen all evening, and there wasn't 'ardly room to keep the best dinner service there, let alone a body. Old Mrs. Thipps sat in the drawing-room. Yes, she was sure she'd been into the dining-room. How? Because she put Mr. Thipps's milk and sandwiches there ready for him. There had been nothing in there—that she could swear to. Nor yet in her own bedroom, nor in the 'all. Had she searched the bedroom cupboard and the box-room? Well, no, not to say searched; she wasn't use to searchin' people's 'ouses for skelintons every night. So that a man might have concealed himself in the box-room or a wardrobe? She supposed he might.

In reply to a woman juror—well, yes, she was walking out with a young man. Williams was his name, Bill Williams,—well, yes, William Williams, if they insisted. He was a glazier by profession. Well, yes, he 'ad been in the flat sometimes. Well, she supposed you might say he was acquainted with the flat. Had she ever—no, she 'adn't, and if she'd thought such a question was going to be put to a respectable girl she wouldn't 'ave offered to give evidence. The vicar of St. Mary's would speak to her character and to Mr. Williams's. Last time Mr. Williams was at the flat was a fortnight ago.

Well, no, it wasn't exactly the last time she 'ad seen Mr. Williams. Well, yes, the last time was Monday—well, yes, Monday night. Well, if she must tell the truth, she must. Yes, the officer had cautioned her, but there wasn't any 'arm in it, and it was better to lose her place than to be 'ung, though it was a cruel shame a girl couldn't 'ave a bit of fun without a nasty corpse comin' in through the window to get 'er into difficulties. After she 'ad put Mrs. Thipps to bed, she 'ad slipped out to go to the Plumbers' and Glaziers' Ball at the

"Black Faced Ram." Mr. Williams 'ad met 'er and brought 'er back. 'E could testify to where she'd been and that there wasn't no 'arm in it. She'd left before the end of the ball. It might 'ave been two o'clock when she got back. She'd got the keys of the flat from Mrs. Thipps's drawer when Mrs. Thipps wasn't looking. She 'ad asked leave to go, but couldn't get it, along of Mr. Thipps bein' away that night. She was bitterly sorry she 'ad be'aved so, and she was sure she'd been punished for it. She had 'eard nothing suspicious when she came in. She had gone straight to bed without looking round the flat. She wished she were dead.

No, Mr. and Mrs. Thipps didn't 'ardly ever 'ave any visitors; they kep' themselves very retired. She had found the outside door bolted that morning as usual. She wouldn't never believe any 'arm of Mr. Thipps. Thank you, Miss Horrocks. Call Georgiana Thipps, and the Coroner thought we had better light the gas.

The examination of Mrs. Thipps provided more entertainment than enlightenment, affording as it did an excellent example of the game called "cross questions and crooked answers." After fifteen minutes' suffering, both in voice and temper, the Coroner abandoned the struggle, leaving the lady with the last word.

"You needn't try to bully me, young man," said that octogenarian with spirit, "settin' there spoilin' your stomach with them nasty jujubes."

At this point a young man arose in court and demanded to give evidence. Having explained that he was William Williams, glazier, he was sworn, and corroborated the evidence of Gladys Horrocks in the matter of her presence at the "Black Faced Ram" on the Monday night. They had returned to the flat rather before two, he thought, but certainly later than 1.30. He was sorry that he had persuaded Miss Horrocks to come out with him when she didn't ought. He had observed nothing of a suspicious nature in Prince of Wales Road at either visit.

Inspector Sugg gave evidence of having been called in at about half-past eight on Monday morning. He had considered the girl's manner to be suspicious and had arrested her. On later information, leading him to suspect that the deceased might have been murdered that night, he had arrested Mr. Thipps. He had found no trace of breaking into the flat. There were marks on the bathroom window-sill which pointed to somebody having got in that way. There were no ladder marks or footmarks in the yard; the yard was paved with asphalt. He had examined the roof, but found nothing on the roof. In his opinion the body had been brought into the flat previously and concealed till the evening by someone who had then gone out during the night by the bathroom window, with the connivance of the girl. In that case, why should not the girl have let the person out by the door? Well, it might have been so. Had he found traces of a body or a man or both having been hidden in the flat? He found nothing to show that they might _not_ have been so concealed. What was the evidence that led him to suppose that the death had occurred that night?

At this point Inspector Sugg appeared uneasy, and endeavoured to retire upon his professional dignity. On being pressed, however, he admitted that the evidence in question had come to nothing.

One of the jurors: Was it the case that any finger-marks had been left by the criminal?

Some marks had been found on the bath, but the criminal had worn gloves.

The Coroner: Do you draw any conclusion from this fact as to the experience of the criminal?

Inspector Sugg: Looks as if he was an old hand, sir.

The Juror: Is that very consistent with the charge against Alfred Thipps, Inspector?

The Inspector was silent.

The Coroner: In the light of the evidence which you have just heard, do you still press the charge against Alfred Thipps and Gladys Horrocks?

Inspector Sugg: I consider the whole set-out highly suspicious. Thipps's story isn't corroborated, and as for the girl Horrocks, how do we know this Williams ain't in it as well?

William Williams: Now, you drop that. I can bring a 'undred witnesses—

The Coroner: Silence, if you please. I am surprised, Inspector, that you should make this suggestion in that manner. It is highly improper. By the way, can you tell us whether a police raid was actually carried out on the Monday night on any Night Club in the neighbourhood of St. Giles's Circus?

Inspector Sugg (sulkily): I believe there was something of the sort.

The Coroner: You will, no doubt, inquire into the matter. I seem to recollect having seen some mention of it in the newspapers. Thank you, Inspector, that will do.

Several witnesses having appeared and testified to the characters of Mr. Thipps and Gladys Horrocks, the Coroner stated his intention of proceeding to the medical evidence.

"Sir Julian Freke."

There was considerable stir in the court as the great specialist walked up to give evidence. He was not only a distinguished man, but a striking figure, with his wide shoulders, upright carriage and leonine head. His manner as he kissed the Book presented to him with the usual deprecatory mumble by the Coroner's officer, was that of a St. Paul condescending to humour the timid mumbo-jumbo of superstitious Corinthians.

"So handsome, I always think," whispered the Duchess to Mr. Parker;

"just exactly like William Morris, with that bush of hair and beard and those exciting eyes looking out of it—so splendid, these dear men always devoted to something or other—not but what I think socialism is a mistake—of course it works with all those nice people, so good and happy in art linen and the weather always perfect—Morris, I mean, you know—but so difficult in real life. Science is different—I'm sure if I had nerves I should go to Sir Julian just to look at him—eyes like that give one something to think about, and that's what most of these people want, only I never had any—nerves, I mean. Don't you think so?"

"You are Sir Julian Freke," said the Coroner, "and live at St. Luke's House, Prince of Wales Road, Battersea, where you exercise a general direction over the surgical side of St. Luke's Hospital?"

Sir Julian assented briefly to this definition of his personality.

"You were the first medical man to see the deceased?"

"I was."

"And you have since conducted an examination in collaboration with Dr. Grimbold of Scotland Yard?"

"I have."

"You are in agreement as to the cause of death?"

"Generally speaking, yes."

"Will you communicate your impressions to the Jury?"

"I was engaged in research work in the dissecting room at St. Luke's Hospital at about nine o'clock on Monday morning, when I was informed that Inspector Sugg wished to see me. He told me that the dead body of a man had been discovered under mysterious circumstances at 59 Queen Caroline Mansions. He asked me whether it could be supposed to be a joke perpetrated by any of the medical students at the hospital. I was able to assure him, by an examination of the hospital's books, that there was no subject missing from the dissecting room."

"Who would be in charge of such bodies?"

"William Watts, the dissecting-room attendant."

"Is William Watts present?" inquired the Coroner of the officer.

William Watts was present, and could be called if the Coroner thought it necessary.

"I suppose no dead body would be delivered to the hospital without your knowledge, Sir Julian?"

"Certainly not."

"Thank you. Will you proceed with your statement?"

"Inspector Sugg then asked me whether I would send a medical man round to view the body. I said that I would go myself."

"Why did you do that?"

"I confess to my share of ordinary human curiosity, Mr. Coroner."

Laughter from a medical student at the back of the room.

"On arriving at the flat I found the deceased lying on his back in the bath. I examined him, and came to the conclusion that death had been caused by a blow on the back of the neck, dislocating the fourth and fifth cervical vertebrae, bruising the spinal cord and producing internal haemorrhage and partial paralysis of the brain. I judged the deceased to have been dead at least twelve hours, possibly more. I observed no other sign of violence of any kind upon the body. Deceased was a strong, well-nourished man of about fifty to fifty-five years of age."

"In your opinion, could the blow have been self-inflicted?"

"Certainly not. It had been made with a heavy, blunt instrument from behind, with great force and considerable judgment. It is quite impossible that it was self-inflicted."

"Could it have been the result of an accident?"

"That is possible, of course."

"If, for example, the deceased had been looking out of the window, and the sash had shut violently down upon him?"

"No; in that case there would have been signs of strangulation and a bruise upon the throat as well."

"But deceased might have been killed through a heavy weight accidentally falling upon him?"

"He might."

"Was death instantaneous, in your opinion?"

"It is difficult to say. Such a blow might very well cause death instantaneously, or the patient might linger in a partially paralyzed condition for some time. In the present case I should be disposed to think that deceased might have lingered for some hours. I base my decision upon the condition of the brain revealed at the autopsy. I may say, however, that Dr. Grimbold and I are not in complete agreement on the point."

"I understand that a suggestion has been made as to the identification of the deceased. _You_ are not in a position to identify him?"

"Certainly not. I never saw him before. The suggestion to which you refer is a preposterous one, and ought never to have been made. I was not aware until this morning that it had been made; had it been made to me earlier, I should have known how to deal with it, and I should like to express my strong disapproval of the unnecessary shock and distress inflicted upon a lady with whom I have the honour to be acquainted."

The Coroner: It was not my fault, Sir Julian; I had nothing to do with it; I agree with you that it was unfortunate you were not consulted.

The reporters scribbled busily, and the court asked each other what was meant, while the jury tried to look as if they knew already.

"In the matter of the eyeglasses found upon the body, Sir Julian. Do these give any indication to a medical man?"

"They are somewhat unusual lenses; an oculist would be able to speak more definitely, but I will say for myself that I should have expected them to belong to an older man than the deceased."

"Speaking as a physician, who has had many opportunities of observing the human body, did you gather anything from the appearance of the deceased as to his personal habits?"

"I should say that he was a man in easy circumstances, but who had only recently come into money. His teeth are in a bad state, and his hands shows signs of recent manual labour."

"An Australian colonist, for instance, who had made money?"

"Something of that sort; of course, I could not say positively."

"Of course not. Thank you, Sir Julian."

Dr. Grimbold, called, corroborated his distinguished colleague in every particular, except that, in his opinion, death had not occurred for several days after the blow. It was with the greatest hesitancy that he ventured to differ from Sir Julian Freke, and he might be wrong. It was difficult to tell in any case, and when he saw the body, deceased had been dead at least twenty-four hours, in his opinion.

Inspector Sugg, recalled. Would he tell the jury what steps had been taken to identify the deceased?

A description had been sent to every police station and had been inserted in all the newspapers. In view of the suggestion made by Sir Julian Freke, had inquiries been made at all the seaports? They had. And with no results? With no results at all. No one had come forward to identify the body? Plenty of people had come forward; but nobody had succeeded in identifying it. Had any effort been made to follow up the clue afforded by the eyeglasses? Inspector Sugg submitted that, having regard to the interests of justice, he would beg to be excused from answering that question. Might the jury see the eyeglasses? The eyeglasses were handed to the jury.

William Watts, called, confirmed the evidence of Sir Julian Freke with regard to dissecting-room subjects. He explained the system by which they were entered. They usually were supplied by the workhouses and free hospitals. They were under his sole charge. The young gentlemen could not possibly get the keys. Had Sir Julian Freke, or any of the house surgeons, the keys? No, not even Sir Julian Freke. The keys had remained in his possession on Monday night? They had. And, in any case, the inquiry was irrelevant, as there was no body missing, nor ever had been? That was the case.

The Coroner then addressed the jury, reminding them with some asperity that they were not there to gossip about who the deceased could or could not have been, but to give their opinion as to the cause of death. He reminded them that they should consider whether, according to the medical evidence, death could have been accidental or self-inflicted, or whether it was deliberate murder, or homicide. If they considered the evidence on this point insufficient, they could return an open verdict. In any case, their verdict could not prejudice any person; if they brought it in "murder," all the whole evidence would have to be gone through again before the magistrate. He then dismissed them, with the unspoken adjuration to be quick about it.

Sir Julian Freke, after giving his evidence, had caught the eye of the Duchess, and now came over and greeted her.

"I haven't seen you for an age," said that lady. "How are you?"

"Hard at work," said the specialist. "Just got my new book out. This kind of thing wastes time. Have you seen Lady Levy yet?"

"No, poor dear," said the Duchess. "I only came up this morning, for this. Mrs. Thipps is staying with me—one of Peter's eccentricities, you know. Poor Christine! I must run round and see her. This is Mr. Parker," she added, "who is investigating that case."

"Oh," said Sir Julian, and paused. "Do you know," he said in a low voice to Parker, "I am very glad to meet you. Have you seen Lady Levy yet?"

"I saw her this morning."

"Did she ask you to go on with the inquiry?"

"Yes," said Parker; "she thinks," he added, "that Sir Reuben may be detained in the hands of some financial rival or that perhaps some scoundrels are holding him to ransom."

"And is that _your_ opinion?" asked Sir Julian.

"I think it very likely," said Parker, frankly.

Sir Julian hesitated again.

"I wish you would walk back with me when this is over," he said.

"I should be delighted," said Parker.

At this moment the jury returned and took their places, and there was a little rustle and hush. The Coroner addressed the foreman and inquired if they were agreed upon their verdict.

"We are agreed, Mr. Coroner, that deceased died of the effects of a blow upon the spine, but how that injury was inflicted we consider that there is not sufficient evidence to show."

MR. PARKER AND SIR JULIAN FREKE WALKED UP THE ROAD TOGETHER.

"I had absolutely no idea until I saw Lady Levy this morning," said the doctor, "that there was any idea of connecting this matter with the disappearance of Sir Reuben. The suggestion was perfectly monstrous, and could only have grown up in the mind of that ridiculous police officer. If I had had any idea what was in his mind I could have disabused him and avoided all this."

"I did my best to do so," said Parker, "as soon as I was called in to the Levy case—"

"Who called you in, if I may ask?" inquired Sir Julian.

"Well, the household first of all, and then Sir Reuben's uncle, Mr. Levy of Portman Square, wrote to me to go on with the investigation."

"And now Lady Levy has confirmed those instructions?"

"Certainly," said Parker in some surprise.

Sir Julian was silent for a little time.

"I'm afraid I was the first person to put the idea into Sugg's head," said Parker, rather penitently. "When Sir Reuben disappeared, my first step, almost, was to hunt up all the street accidents and suicides and so on that had turned up during the day, and I went down to see this Battersea Park body as a matter of routine. Of course, I saw that the thing was ridiculous as soon as I got there, but Sugg froze on to the idea—and it's true there was a good deal of resemblance between the dead man and the portraits I've seen of Sir Reuben."

"A strong superficial likeness," said Sir Julian. "The upper part of the face is a not uncommon type, and as Sir Reuben wore a heavy beard and there was no opportunity of comparing the mouths and chins, I can understand the idea occurring to anybody. But only to be dismissed at once. I am sorry," he added, "as the whole matter has been painful to Lady Levy. You may know, Mr. Parker, that I am an old, though I should not call myself an intimate, friend of the Levys."

"I understood something of the sort."

"Yes. When I was a young man I—in short, Mr. Parker, I hoped once to marry Lady Levy." (Mr. Parker gave the usual sympathetic groan.) "I have never married, as you know," pursued Sir Julian. "We have remained good friends. I have always done what I could to spare her pain."

"Believe me, Sir Julian," said Parker, "that I sympathize very much with you and with Lady Levy, and that I did all I could to disabuse Inspector Sugg of this notion. Unhappily, the coincidence of Sir Reuben's being seen that evening in the Battersea Park Road—"

"Ah, yes," said Sir Julian. "Dear me, here we are at home. Perhaps you would come in for a moment, Mr. Parker, and have tea or a whisky-and-soda or something."

Parker promptly accepted this invitation, feeling that there were other things to be said.

The two men stepped into a square, finely furnished hall with a fireplace on the same side as the door, and a staircase opposite. The dining-room door stood open on their right, and as Sir Julian rang the bell a man-servant appeared at the far end of the hall.

"What will you take?" asked the doctor.

"After that dreadfully cold place," said Parker, "what I really want is gallons of hot tea, if you, as a nerve specialist, can bear the thought of it."

"Provided you allow of a judicious blend of China in it," replied Sir Julian in the same tone, "I have no objection to make. Tea in the library at once," he added to the servant, and led the way upstairs.

"I don't use the downstairs rooms much, except the dining-room," he explained as he ushered his guest into a small but cheerful library on the first floor. "This room leads out of my bedroom and is more convenient. I only live part of my time here, but it's very handy for my research work at the hospital. That's what I do there, mostly. It's a fatal thing for a theorist, Mr. Parker, to let the practical work get behindhand. Dissection is the basis of all good theory and all correct diagnosis. One must keep one's hand and eye in training. This place is far more important to me than Harley Street, and some day I shall abandon my consulting practice altogether and settle down here to cut up my subjects and write my books in peace. So many things in this life are a waste of time, Mr. Parker."

Mr. Parker assented to this.

"Very often," said Sir Julian, "the only time I get for any research work—necessitating as it does the keenest observation and the faculties at their acutest—has to be at night, after a long day's work and by artificial light, which, magnificent as the lighting of the dissecting room here is, is always more trying to the eyes than daylight. Doubtless your own work has to be carried on under even more trying conditions."

"Yes, sometimes," said Parker; "but then you see," he added, "the conditions are, so to speak, part of the work."

"Quite so, quite so," said Sir Julian; "you mean that the burglar, for example, does not demonstrate his methods in the light of day, or plant the perfect footmark in the middle of a damp patch of sand for you to analyze."

"Not as a rule," said the detective, "but I have no doubt many of your diseases work quite as insidiously as any burglar."

"They do, they do," said Sir Julian, laughing, "and it is my pride, as it is yours, to track them down for the good of society. The neuroses, you know, are particularly clever criminals—they break out into as many disguises as—"

"As Leon Kestrel, the Master-Mummer," suggested Parker, who read railway-stall detective stories on the principle of the 'busman's holiday.

"No doubt," said Sir Julian, who did not, "and they cover up their tracks wonderfully. But when you can really investigate, Mr. Parker, and break up the dead, or for preference the living body with the scalpel, you always find the footmarks—the little trail of ruin or disorder left by madness or disease or drink or any other similar pest. But the difficulty is to trace them back, merely by observing the surface symptoms—the hysteria, crime, religion, fear, shyness, conscience, or whatever it may be; just as you observe a theft or a murder and look for the footsteps of the criminal, so I observe a fit of hysterics or an outburst of piety and hunt for the little mechanical irritation which has produced it."

"You regard all these things as physical?"

"Undoubtedly. I am not ignorant of the rise of another school of thought, Mr. Parker, but its exponents are mostly charlatans or self-deceivers. '_Sie haben sich so weit darin eingeheimnisst_' that, like Sludge the Medium, they are beginning to believe their own nonsense. I should like to have the exploring of some of their brains, Mr. Parker; I would show you the little faults and landslips in the cells—the misfiring and short-circuiting of the nerves, which produce these notions and these books. At least," he added, gazing sombrely at his guest, "at least, if I could not quite show you today, I shall be able to do so tomorrow—or in a year's time—or before I die."

He sat for some minutes gazing into the fire, while the red light played upon his tawny beard and struck out answering gleams from his compelling eyes.

Parker drank tea in silence, watching him. On the whole, however, he remained but little interested in the causes of nervous phenomena and his mind strayed to Lord Peter, coping with the redoubtable Crimplesham down in Salisbury. Lord Peter had wanted him to come: that meant, either that Crimplesham was proving recalcitrant or that a clue wanted following. But Bunter had said that tomorrow would do, and it was just as well. After all, the Battersea affair was not Parker's case; he had already wasted valuable time attending an inconclusive inquest, and he really ought to get on with his legitimate work. There was still Levy's secretary to see and the little matter of the Peruvian Oil to be looked into. He looked at his watch.

"I am very much afraid—if you will excuse me—" he murmured.

Sir Julian came back with a start to the consideration of actuality.

"Your work calls you?" he said, smiling. "Well, I can understand that. I won't keep you. But I wanted to say something to you in connection with your present inquiry—only I hardly know—I hardly like—"

Parker sat down again, and banished every indication of hurry from his face and attitude.

"I shall be very grateful for any help you can give me," he said.

"I'm afraid it's more in the nature of hindrance," said Sir Julian, with a short laugh. "It's a case of destroying a clue for you, and a breach of professional confidence on my side. But since—accidentally—a certain amount has come out, perhaps the whole had better do so."

Mr. Parker made the encouraging noise which, among laymen, supplies the place of the priest's insinuating, "Yes, my son?"

"Sir Reuben Levy's visit on Monday night was to me," said Sir Julian.

"Yes?" said Mr. Parker, without expression.

"He found cause for certain grave suspicions concerning his health," said Sir Julian, slowly, as though weighing how much he could in honour disclose to a stranger. "He came to me, in preference to his own medical man, as he was particularly anxious that the matter should be kept from his wife. As I told you, he knew me fairly well, and Lady Levy had consulted me about a nervous disorder in the summer."

"Did he make an appointment with you?" asked Parker.

"I beg your pardon," said the other, absently.

"Did he make an appointment?"

"An appointment? Oh, no! He turned up suddenly in the evening after dinner when I wasn't expecting him. I took him up here and examined him, and he left me somewhere about ten o'clock, I should think."

"May I ask what was the result of your examination?"

"Why do you want to know?"

"It might illuminate—well, conjecture as to his subsequent conduct," said Parker, cautiously. This story seemed to have little coherence with the rest of the business, and he wondered whether coincidence was alone responsible for Sir Reuben's disappearance on the same night that he visited the doctor.

"I see," said Sir Julian. "Yes. Well, I will tell you in confidence that I saw grave grounds of suspicion, but as yet, no absolute certainty of mischief."

"Thank you. Sir Reuben left you at ten o'clock?"

"Then or thereabouts. I did not at first mention the matter as it was so very much Sir Reuben's wish to keep his visit to me secret, and there was no question of accident in the street or anything of that kind, since he reached home safely at midnight."

"Quite so," said Parker.

"It would have been, and is, a breach of confidence," said Sir Julian,

"and I only tell you now because Sir Reuben was accidentally seen, and because I would rather tell you in private than have you ferreting round here and questioning my servants, Mr. Parker. You will excuse my frankness."

"Certainly," said Parker. "I hold no brief for the pleasantness of my profession, Sir Julian. I am very much obliged to you for telling me this. I might otherwise have wasted valuable time following up a false trail."

"I am sure I need not ask you, in your turn, to respect this confidence," said the doctor. "To publish the matter abroad could only harm Sir Reuben and pain his wife, besides placing me in no favourable light with my patients."

"I promise to keep the thing to myself," said Parker, "except of course," he added hastily, "that I must inform my colleague."

"You have a colleague in the case?"

"I have."

"What sort of person is he?"

"He will be perfectly discreet, Sir Julian."

"Is he a police officer?"

"You need not be afraid of your confidence getting into the records at Scotland Yard."

"I see that you know how to be discreet, Mr. Parker."

"We also have our professional etiquette, Sir Julian."

On returning to Great Ormond Street, Mr. Parker found a wire awaiting him, which said: "Do not trouble to come. All well. Returning tomorrow. Wimsey."

CHAPTER VII

On returning to the flat just before lunch-time on the following morning, after a few confirmatory researches in Balham and the neighbourhood of Victoria Station, Lord Peter was greeted at the door by Mr. Bunter (who had gone straight home from Waterloo) with a telephone message and a severe and nursemaid-like eye.

"Lady Swaffham rang up, my lord, and said she hoped your lordship had not forgotten you were lunching with her."

"I have forgotten, Bunter, and I mean to forget. I trust you told her I had succumbed to lethargic encephalitis suddenly, no flowers by request."

"Lady Swaffham said, my lord, she was counting on you. She met the Duchess of Denver yesterday—"

"If my sister-in-law's there I won't go, that's flat," said Lord Peter.

"I beg your pardon, my lord, the Dowager Duchess."

"What's she doing in town?"

"I imagine she came up for the inquest, my lord."

"Oh, yes—we missed that, Bunter."

"Yes, my lord. Her Grace is lunching with Lady Swaffham."

"Bunter, I can't. I can't, really. Say I'm in bed with whooping cough, and ask my mother to come round after lunch."

"Very well, my lord. Mrs. Tommy Frayle will be at Lady Swaffham's, my lord, and Mr. Milligan—"

"Mr. who?"

"Mr. John P. Milligan, my lord, and—"

"Good God, Bunter, why didn't you say so before? Have I time to get there before he does? All right. I'm off. With a taxi I can just—"

"Not in those trousers, my lord," said Mr. Bunter, blocking the way to the door with deferential firmness.

"Oh, Bunter," pleaded his lordship, "do let me—just this once. You don't know how important it is."

"Not on any account, my lord. It would be as much as my place is worth."

"The trousers are all right, Bunter."

"Not for Lady Swaffham's, my lord. Besides, your lordship forgets the man that ran against you with a milk-can at Salisbury."

And Mr. Bunter laid an accusing finger on a slight stain of grease showing across the light cloth.

"I wish to God I'd never let you grow into a privileged family retainer, Bunter," said Lord Peter, bitterly, dashing his walking-stick into the umbrella-stand. "You've no conception of the mistakes my mother may be making."

Mr. Bunter smiled grimly and led his victim away.

When an immaculate Lord Peter was ushered, rather late for lunch, into Lady Swaffham's drawing-room, the Dowager Duchess of Denver was seated on a sofa, plunged in intimate conversation with Mr. John P. Milligan of Chicago.

"I'M VURRY PLEASED TO MEET YOU, DUCHESS," HAD BEEN THAT FINANCIER'S opening remark, "to thank you for your exceedingly kind invitation. I assure you it's a compliment I deeply appreciate."

The Duchess beamed at him, while conducting a rapid rally of all her intellectual forces.

"Do come and sit down and talk to me, Mr. Milligan," she said. "I do so love talking to you great business men—let me see, is it a railway king you are or something about puss-in-the-corner—at least, I don't mean that exactly, but that game one used to play with cards, all about wheat and oats, and there was a bull and a bear, too—or was it a horse?—no, a bear, because I remember one always had to try and get rid of it and it used to get so dreadfully crumpled and torn, poor thing, always being handed about, one got to recognise it, and then one had to buy a new pack—so foolish it must seem to you, knowing the real thing, and dreadfully noisy, but really excellent for breaking the ice with rather stiff people who didn't know each other—I'm quite sorry it's gone out."

Mr. Milligan sat down.

"Wal, now," he said, "I guess it's as interesting for us business men to meet British aristocrats as it is for Britishers to meet American railway kings, Duchess. And I guess I'll make as many mistakes talking your kind of talk as you would make if you were tryin' to run a corner in wheat in Chicago. Fancy now, I called that fine lad of yours Lord Wimsey the other day, and he thought I'd mistaken him for his brother. That made me feel rather green."

This was an unhoped-for lead. The Duchess walked warily.

"Dear boy," she said, "I am so glad you met him, Mr. Milligan. _Both_ my sons are a _great_ comfort to me, you know, though, of course, Gerald is more conventional—just the right kind of person for the House of Lords, you know, and a splendid farmer. I can't see Peter down at Denver half so well, though he is always going to all the right things in town, and very amusing sometimes, poor boy."

"I was vurry much gratified by Lord Peter's suggestion," pursued Mr. Milligan, "for which I understand you are responsible, and I'll surely be very pleased to come any day you like, though I think you're flattering me too much."

"Ah, well," said the Duchess, "I don't know if you're the best judge of that, Mr. Milligan. Not that I know anything about business myself," she added. "I'm rather old-fashioned for these days, you know, and I can't pretend to do more than know a nice _man_ when I see him; for the other things I rely on my son."

The accent of this speech was so flattering that Mr. Milligan purred almost audibly, and said:

"Wal, Duchess, I guess that's where a lady with a real, beautiful, old-fashioned soul has the advantage of these modern young blatherskites—

there aren't many men who wouldn't be nice—to her, and even then, if they aren't rock-bottom she can see through them."

"But that leaves me where I was," thought the Duchess. "I believe," she said aloud, "that I ought to be thanking you in the name of the vicar of Duke's Denver for a very munificent cheque which reached him yesterday for the Church Restoration Fund. He was so delighted and astonished, poor dear man."

"Oh, that's nothing," said Mr. Milligan, "we haven't any fine old crusted buildings like yours over on our side, so it's a privilege to be allowed to drop a little kerosene into the worm-holes when we hear of one in the old country suffering from senile decay. So when your lad told me about Duke's Denver I took the liberty to subscribe without waiting for the Bazaar."

"I'm sure it was very kind of you," said the Duchess. "You are coming to the Bazaar, then?" she continued, gazing into his face appealingly.

"Sure thing," said Mr. Milligan, with great promptness. "Lord Peter said you'd let me know for sure about the date, but we can always make time for a little bit of good work anyway. Of course I'm hoping to be able to avail myself of your kind invitation to stop, but if I'm rushed, I'll manage anyhow to pop over and speak my piece and pop back again."

"I hope so very much," said the Duchess. "I must see what can be done about the date—of course, I can't promise—"

"No, no," said Mr. Milligan heartily. "I know what these things are to fix up. And then there's not only me—there's all the real big men of European eminence your son mentioned, to be consulted."

The Duchess turned pale at the thought that any one of these illustrious persons might some time turn up in somebody's drawing-room, but by this time she had dug herself in comfortably, and was even beginning to find her range.

"I can't say how grateful we are to you," she said; "it will be such a treat. Do tell me what you think of saying."

"Wal—" began Mr. Milligan.

Suddenly everybody was standing up and a penitent voice was heard to say:

"Really, most awfully sorry, y'know—hope you'll forgive me, Lady Swaffham, what? Dear lady, could I possibly forget an invitation from you?

Fact is, I had to go an' see a man down in Salisbury—absolutely true, 'pon my word, and the fellow wouldn't let me get away. I'm simply grovellin' before you, Lady Swaffham. Shall I go an' eat my lunch in the corner?"

Lady Swaffham gracefully forgave the culprit.

"Your dear mother is here," she said.

"How do, Mother?" said Lord Peter, uneasily.

"How are you, dear?" replied the Duchess. "You really oughtn't to have turned up just yet. Mr. Milligan was just going to tell me what a thrilling speech he's preparing for the Bazaar, when you came and interrupted us."

Conversation at lunch turned, not unnaturally, on the Battersea inquest, the Duchess giving a vivid impersonation of Mrs. Thipps being interrogated by the Coroner.

"'Did you hear anything unusual in the night?' says the little man, leaning forward and screaming at her, and so crimson in the face and his ears sticking out so—just like a cherubim in that poem of Tennyson's—or is a cherub blue?—perhaps it's a seraphim I mean—anyway, you know what I mean, all eyes, with little wings on its head. And dear old Mrs. Thipps saying, 'Of course I have, any time these eighty years,' and _such_ a sensation in court till they found out she thought he'd said, 'Do you sleep without a light?' and everybody laughing, and then the Coroner said quite loudly, 'Damn the woman,' and she heard that, I can't think why, and said: 'Don't you get swearing, young man, sitting there in the presence of Providence, as you may say. I don't know what young people are coming to nowadays'—and he's sixty if he's a day, you know," said the Duchess.

BY A NATURAL TRANSITION, MRS. TOMMY FRAYLE REFERRED TO THE MAN who was hanged for murdering three brides in a bath.

"I always thought that was so ingenious," she said, gazing soulfully at Lord Peter, "and do you know, as it happened, Tommy had just made me insure my life, and I got so frightened, I gave up my morning bath and took to having it in the afternoon when he was in the House—I mean, when he was _not_ in the house—not at home, I mean."

"Dear lady," said Lord Peter, reproachfully, "I have a distinct recollection that all those brides were thoroughly unattractive. But it was an uncommonly ingenious plan—the first time of askin'—only he shouldn't have repeated himself."

"One demands a little originality in these days, even from murderers," said Lady Swaffham. "Like dramatists, you know—so much easier in Shakespeare's time, wasn't it? Always the same girl dressed up as a man, and even that borrowed from Boccaccio or Dante or somebody. I'm sure if I'd been a Shakespeare hero, the very minute I saw a slim-legged young page-boy I'd have said: 'Odsbodikins! There's that girl again!'"

"That's just what happened, as a matter of fact," said Lord Peter. "You see, Lady Swaffham, if ever you want to commit a murder, the thing you've got to do is to prevent people from associatin' their ideas. Most people don't associate anythin'—their ideas just roll about like so many dry peas on a tray, makin' a lot of noise and goin' nowhere, but once you begin lettin' 'em string their peas into a necklace, it's goin' to be strong enough to hang you, what?"

"Dear me!" said Mrs. Tommy Frayle, with a little scream, "what a blessing it is none of my friends have any ideas at all!"

"Y'see," said Lord Peter, balancing a piece of duck on his fork and frowning, "it's only in Sherlock Holmes and stories like that, that people think things out logically. Or'nar'ly, if somebody tells you somethin' out of the way, you just say, 'By Jove!' or 'How sad!' an' leave it at that, an' half the time you forget about it, 'nless somethin' turns up afterwards to drive it home. F'r instance, Lady Swaffham, I told you when I came in that I'd been down to Salisbury, 'n' that's true, only I don't suppose it impressed you much; 'n' I don't suppose it'd impress you much if you read in the paper tomorrow of a tragic discovery of a dead lawyer down in Salisbury, but if I went to Salisbury again next week 'n' there was a Salisbury doctor found dead the day after, you might begin to think I was a bird of ill omen for Salisbury residents; and if I went there again the week after, 'n' you heard next day that the see of Salisbury had fallen vacant suddenly, you might begin to wonder what took me to Salisbury, an' why I'd never mentioned before that I had friends down there, don't you see, an' you might think of goin' down to Salisbury yourself, an' askin' all kinds of people if they'd happened to see a young man in plum-coloured socks hangin' round the Bishop's Palace."

"I daresay I should," said Lady Swaffham.

"Quite. An' if you found that the lawyer and the doctor had once upon a time been in business at Poggleton-on-the-Marsh when the Bishop had been vicar there, you'd begin to remember you'd once heard of me payin' a visit to Poggleton-on-the-Marsh a long time ago, an' you'd begin to look up the parish registers there an' discover I'd been married under an assumed name by the vicar to the widow of a wealthy farmer, who'd died suddenly of peritonitis, as certified by the doctor, after the lawyer'd made a will leavin' me all her money, and _then_ you'd begin to think I might have very good reasons for gettin' rid of such promisin' blackmailers as the lawyer, the doctor an' the bishop. Only, if I hadn't started an association in your mind by gettin' rid of 'em all in the same place, you'd never have thought of goin' to Poggleton-on-the-Marsh, 'n' you wouldn't even have remembered I'd ever been there."

"Were you ever there, Lord Peter?" inquired Mrs. Tommy, anxiously.

"I don't think so," said Lord Peter; "the name threads no beads in my mind. But it might, any day, you know."

"But if you were investigating a crime," said Lady Swaffham, "you'd have to begin by the usual things, I suppose—finding out what the person had been doing, and who'd been to call, and looking for a motive, wouldn't you?"

"Oh, yes," said Lord Peter, "but most of us have such dozens of motives for murderin' all sorts of inoffensive people. There's lots of people I'd like to murder, wouldn't you?"

"Heaps," said Lady Swaffham. "There's that dreadful—perhaps I'd better not say it, though, for fear you should remember it later on."

"Well, I wouldn't if I were you," said Peter, amiably. "You never know. It'd be beastly awkward if the person died suddenly tomorrow."

"The difficulty with this Battersea case, I guess," said Mr. Milligan,

"is that nobody seems to have any associations with the gentleman in the bath."

"So hard on poor Inspector Sugg," said the Duchess. "I quite felt for the man, having to stand up there and answer a lot of questions when he had nothing at all to say."

Lord Peter applied himself to the duck, having got a little behindhand. Presently he heard somebody ask the Duchess if she had seen Lady Levy.

"She is in great distress," said the woman who had spoken, a Mrs. Freemantle, "though she clings to the hope that he will turn up. I suppose you knew him, Mr. Milligan—know him, I should say, for I hope he's still alive somewhere."

Mrs. Freemantle was the wife of an eminent railway director, and celebrated for her ignorance of the world of finance. Her _faux pas_ in this connection enlivened the tea parties of City men's wives.

"Wal, I've dined with him," said Mr. Milligan, good-naturedly. "I think he and I've done our best to ruin each other, Mrs. Freemantle. If this were the States," he added, "I'd be much inclined to suspect myself of having put Sir Reuben in a safe place. But we can't do business that way in your old country; no, ma'am."

"It must be exciting work doing business in America," said Lord Peter.

"It is," said Mr. Milligan. "I guess my brothers are having a good time there now. I'll be joining them again before long, as soon as I've fixed up a little bit of work for them on this side."

"Well, you mustn't go till after my bazaar," said the Duchess.

Lord Peter spent the afternoon in a vain hunt for Mr. Parker. He ran him down eventually after dinner in Great Ormond Street.

Parker was sitting in an elderly but affectionate armchair, with his feet on the mantelpiece, relaxing his mind with a modern commentary on the Epistle to the Galatians. He received Lord Peter with quiet pleasure, though without rapturous enthusiasm, and mixed him a whisky-and-soda. Peter took up the book his friend had laid down and glanced over the pages.

"All these men work with a bias in their minds, one way or other," he said; "they find what they are looking for."

"Oh, they do," agreed the detective; "but one learns to discount that almost automatically, you know. When I was at college, I was all on the other side—Conybeare and Robertson and Drews and those people, you know, till I found they were all so busy looking for a burglar whom nobody had ever seen, that they couldn't recognise the footprints of the household, so to speak. Then I spent two years learning to be cautious."

"Hum," said Lord Peter, "theology must be good exercise for the brain then, for you're easily the most cautious devil I know. But I say, do go on reading—it's a shame for me to come and root you up in your off-time like this."

"It's all right, old man," said Parker.

The two men sat silent for a little, and then Lord Peter said:

"D'you like your job?"

The detective considered the question, and replied:

"Yes—yes, I do. I know it to be useful, and I am fitted to it. I do it quite well—not with inspiration, perhaps, but sufficiently well to take a pride in it. It is full of variety and it forces one to keep up to the mark and not get slack. And there's a future to it. Yes, I like it. Why?"

"Oh, nothing," said Peter. "It's a hobby to me, you see. I took it up when the bottom of things was rather knocked out for me, because it was so damned exciting, and the worst of it is, I enjoy it—up to a point. If it was all on paper I'd enjoy every bit of it. I love the beginning of a job—when one doesn't know any of the people and it's just exciting and amusing. But if it comes to really running down a live person and getting him hanged, or even quodded, poor devil, there don't seem as if there was any excuse for me buttin' in, since I don't have to make my livin' by it. And I feel as if I oughtn't ever to find it amusin'. But I do."

Parker gave this speech his careful attention.

"I see what you mean," he said.

"There's old Milligan, f'r instance," said Lord Peter. "On paper, nothin' would be funnier than to catch old Milligan out. But he's rather a decent old bird to talk to. Mother likes him. He's taken a fancy to me. It's awfully entertainin' goin' and pumpin' him with stuff about a bazaar for church expenses, but when he's so jolly pleased about it and that, I feel a worm. S'pose old Milligan has cut Levy's throat and plugged him into the Thames. It ain't my business."

"It's as much yours as anybody's," said Parker; "it's no better to do it for money than to do it for nothing."

"Yes, it is," said Peter stubbornly. "Havin' to live is the only excuse there is for doin' that kind of thing."

"Well, but look here!" said Parker. "If Milligan has cut poor old Levy's throat for no reason except to make himself richer, I don't see why he should buy himself off by giving £1,000 to Duke's Denver church roof, or why he should be forgiven just because he's childishly vain, or childishly snobbish."

"That's a nasty one," said Lord Peter.

"Well, if you like, even because he has taken a fancy to you."

"No, but—"

"Look here, Wimsey—do you think he _has_ murdered Levy?"

"Well, he may have."

"But do you think he has?"

"I don't want to think so."

"Because he has taken a fancy to you?"

"Well, that biases me, of course—"

"I daresay it's quite a legitimate bias. You don't think a callous murderer would be likely to take a fancy to you?"

"Well—besides, I've taken rather a fancy to him."

"I daresay that's quite legitimate, too. You've observed him and made a subconscious deduction from your observations, and the result is, you don't think he did it. Well, why not? You're entitled to take that into account."

"But perhaps I'm wrong and he did do it."

"Then why let your vainglorious conceit in your own power of estimating character stand in the way of unmasking the singularly cold-blooded murder of an innocent and lovable man?"

"I know—but I don't feel I'm playing the game somehow."

"Look here, Peter," said the other with some earnestness, "suppose you get this playing-fields-of-Eton complex out of your system once and for all. There doesn't seem to be much doubt that something unpleasant has happened to Sir Reuben Levy. Call it murder, to strengthen the argument. If Sir Reuben has been murdered, is it a game? and is it fair to treat it as a game?"

"That's what I'm ashamed of, really," said Lord Peter. "It _is_ a game to me, to begin with, and I go on cheerfully, and then I suddenly see that somebody is going to be hurt, and I want to get out of it."

"Yes, yes, I know," said the detective, "but that's because you're thinking about your attitude. You want to be consistent, you want to look pretty, you want to swagger debonairly through a comedy of puppets or else to stalk magnificently through a tragedy of human sorrows and things. But that's childish. If you've any duty to society in the way of finding out the truth about murders, you must do it in any attitude that comes handy. You want to be elegant and detached? That's all right, if you find the truth out that way, but it hasn't any value in itself, you know. You want to look dignified and consistent—what's that got to do with it? You want to hunt down a murderer for the sport of the thing and then shake hands with him and say, 'Well played—hard luck—you shall have your revenge tomorrow!' Well, you can't do it like that. Life's not a football match. You want to be a sportsman. You can't be a sportsman. You're a responsible person."

"I don't think you ought to read so much theology," said Lord Peter.

"It has a brutalizing influence."

He got up and paced about the room, looking idly over the bookshelves. Then he sat down again, filled and lit his pipe, and said:

"Well, I'd better tell you about the ferocious and hardened Crimplesham."

He detailed his visit to Salisbury. Once assured of his bona fides, Mr. Crimplesham had given him the fullest details of his visit to town.

"And I've substantiated it all," groaned Lord Peter, "and unless he's corrupted half Balham, there's no doubt he spent the night there. And the afternoon was really spent with the bank people. And half the residents of Salisbury seem to have seen him off on Monday before lunch. And nobody but his own family or young Wicks seems to have anything to gain by his death. And even if young Wicks wanted to make away with him, it's rather far-fetched to go and murder an unknown man in Thipps's place in order to stick Crimplesham's eyeglasses on his nose."

"Where was young Wicks on Monday?" asked Parker.

"At a dance given by the Precentor," said Lord Peter, wildly.

"David—his name is David—dancing before the ark of the Lord in the face of the whole Cathedral Close."

There was a pause.

"Tell me about the inquest," said Wimsey.

Parker obliged with a summary of the evidence.

"Do you believe the body could have been concealed in the flat after all?" he asked. "I know we looked, but I suppose we might have missed something."

"We might. But Sugg looked as well."

"Sugg!"

"You do Sugg an injustice," said Lord Peter; "if there had been any signs of Thipps's complicity in the crime, Sugg would have found them."

"Why?"

"Why? Because he was looking for them. He's like your commentators on Galatians. He thinks that either Thipps, or Gladys Horrocks, or Gladys Horrocks's young man did it. Therefore he found marks on the window sill where Gladys Horrocks's young man might have come in or handed something in to Gladys Horrocks. He didn't find any signs on the roof, because he wasn't looking for them."

"But he went over the roof before me."

"Yes, but only in order to prove that there were no marks there. He reasons like this: Gladys Horrocks's young man is a glazier. Glaziers come on ladders. Glaziers have ready access to ladders. Therefore Gladys Horrocks's young man had ready access to a ladder. Therefore Gladys Horrocks's young man came on a ladder. Therefore there will be marks on the window sill and none on the roof. Therefore he finds marks on the window sill but none on the roof. He finds no marks on the ground, but he thinks he would have found them if the yard didn't happen to be paved with asphalt. Similarly, he thinks Mr. Thipps may have concealed the body in the box-room or elsewhere. Therefore you may be sure he searched the box-room and all the other places for signs of occupation. If they had been there he would have found them, because he was looking for them. Therefore, if he didn't find them it's because they weren't there."

"All right," said Parker, "stop talking. I believe you."

He went on to detail the medical evidence.

"By the way," said Lord Peter, "to skip across for a moment to the other case, has it occurred to you that perhaps Levy was going out to see Freke on Monday night?"

"He was; he did," said Parker, rather unexpectedly, and proceeded to recount his interview with the nerve-specialist.

"Humph!" said Lord Peter. "I say, Parker, these are funny cases, ain't they? Every line of inquiry seems to peter out. It's awfully exciting up to a point, you know, and then nothing comes of it. It's like rivers getting lost in the sand."

"Yes," said Parker. "And there's another one I lost this morning."

"What's that?"

"Oh, I was pumping Levy's secretary about his business. I couldn't get much that seemed important except further details about the Argentine and so on. Then I thought I'd just ask round in the City about those Peruvian

Oil shares, but Levy hadn't even heard of them so far as I could make out. I routed out the brokers, and found a lot of mystery and concealment, as one always does, you know, when somebody's been rigging the market, and at last I found one name at the back of it. But it wasn't Levy's."

"No? Whose was it?"

"Oddly enough, Freke's. It seems mysterious. He bought a lot of shares last week, in a secret kind of way, a few of them in his own name, and then quietly sold 'em out on Tuesday at a small profit—a few hundreds, not worth going to all that trouble about, you wouldn't think."

"Shouldn't have thought he ever went in for that kind of gamble."

"He doesn't as a rule. That's the funny part of it."

"Well, you never know," said Lord Peter; "people do these things just to prove to themselves or somebody else that they could make a fortune that way if they liked. I've done it myself in a small way."

He knocked out his pipe and rose to go.

"I say, old man," he said suddenly, as Parker was letting him out,

"does it occur to you that Freke's story doesn't fit in awfully well with what Anderson said about the old boy having been so jolly at dinner on Monday night? Would you be, if you thought you'd got anything of that sort?"

"No, I shouldn't," said Parker; "but," he added with his habitual caution, "some men will jest in the dentist's waiting-room. You, for one."

"Well, that's true," said Lord Peter, and went downstairs.

CHAPTER VIII

Lord Peter reached home about midnight, feeling extraordinarily wakeful and alert. Something was jigging and worrying in his brain; it felt like a hive of bees, stirred up by a stick. He felt as though he were looking at a complicated riddle, of which he had once been told the answer but had forgotten it and was always on the point of remembering.

"Somewhere," said Lord Peter to himself, "somewhere I've got the key to these two things. I know I've got it, only I can't remember what it is. Somebody said it. Perhaps I said it. I can't remember where, but I know I've got it. Go to bed, Bunter, I shall sit up a little. I'll just slip on a dressing-gown."

Before the fire he sat down with his pipe in his mouth and his jazz-coloured peacocks gathered about him. He traced out this line and that line of investigation—rivers running into the sand. They ran out from the thought of Levy, last seen at ten o'clock in Prince of Wales Road. They ran back from the picture of the grotesque dead man in Mr. Thipps's bathroom—they ran over the roof, and were lost—lost in the sand. Rivers running into the sand—rivers running underground, very far down—

Where Alph, the sacred river, ran Through caverns measureless to man Down to a sunless sea.

By leaning his head down, it seemed to Lord Peter that he could hear them, very faintly, lipping and gurgling somewhere in the darkness. But where? He felt quite sure that somebody had told him once, only he had forgotten.

He roused himself, threw a log on the fire, and picked up a book which the indefatigable Bunter, carrying on his daily fatigues amid the excitements of special duty, had brought from the Times Book Club. It happened to be Sir Julian Freke's "Physiological Bases of the Conscience," which he had seen reviewed two days before.

"This ought to send one to sleep," said Lord Peter; "if I can't leave these problems to my subconscious I'll be as limp as a rag tomorrow."

He opened the book slowly, and glanced carelessly through the preface.

"I wonder if that's true about Levy being ill," he thought, putting the book down; "it doesn't seem likely. And yet—Dash it all, I'll take my mind off it."

He read on resolutely for a little.

"I don't suppose Mother's kept up with the Levys much," was the next importunate train of thought. "Dad always hated self-made people and wouldn't have 'em at Denver. And old Gerald keeps up the tradition. I wonder if she knew Freke well in those days. She seems to get on with Milligan. I trust Mother's judgment a good deal. She was a brick about that bazaar business. I ought to have warned her. She said something once—"

He pursued an elusive memory for some minutes, till it vanished altogether with a mocking flicker of the tail. He returned to his reading.

Presently another thought crossed his mind aroused by a photograph of some experiment in surgery.

"If the evidence of Freke and that man Watts hadn't been so positive," he said to himself, "I should be inclined to look into the matter of those shreds of lint on the chimney."

He considered this, shook his head and read with determination.

Mind and matter were one thing, that was the theme of the physiologist. Matter could erupt, as it were, into ideas. You could carve passions in the brain with a knife. You could get rid of imagination with drugs and cure an outworn convention like a disease. "The knowledge of good and evil is an observed phenomenon, attendant upon a certain condition of the brain-cells, which is removable." That was one phrase; and again:

"Conscience in man may, in fact, be compared to the sting of a hive-bee, which, so far from conducing to the welfare of its possessor, cannot function, even in a single instance, without occasioning its death. The survival-value in each case is thus purely social; and if humanity ever passes from its present phase of social development into that of a higher individualism, as some of our philosophers have ventured to speculate, we may suppose that this interesting mental phenomenon may gradually cease to appear; just as the nerves and muscles which once controlled the movements of our ears and scalps have, in all save a few backward individuals, become atrophied and of interest only to the physiologist."

"By Jove!" thought Lord Peter, idly, "that's an ideal doctrine for the criminal. A man who believed that would never—"

And then it happened—the thing he had been half-unconsciously expecting. It happened suddenly, surely, as unmistakably, as sunrise. He remembered—not one thing, nor another thing, nor a logical succession of things, but everything—the whole thing, perfect, complete, in all its dimensions as it were and instantaneously; as if he stood outside the world and saw it suspended in infinitely dimensional space. He no longer needed to reason about it, or even to think about it. He knew it.

There is a game in which one is presented with a jumble of letters and is required to make a word out of them, as thus:

C O S S S S R I

The slow way of solving the problem is to try out all the permutations and combinations in turn, throwing away impossible conjunctions of letters, as:

S S S I R C

or

S C S R S O

Another way is to stare at the incoordinate elements until, by no logical process that the conscious mind can detect, or under some adventitious external stimulus, the combination:

S C I S S O R S

presents itself with calm certainty. After that, one does not even need to arrange the letters in order. The thing is done.

Even so, the scattered elements of two grotesque conundrums, flung higgledy-piggledy into Lord Peter's mind, resolved themselves, unquestioned henceforward. A bump on the roof of the end house—Levy in a welter of cold rain talking to a prostitute in the Battersea Park Road—a single ruddy hair—lint bandages—Inspector Sugg calling the great surgeon from the dissecting-room of the hospital—Lady Levy with a nervous attack—the smell of carbolic soap—the Duchess's voice—"not really an engagement, only a sort of understanding with her father"—shares in Peruvian Oil—the dark skin and curved, fleshy profile of the man in the bath—Dr. Grimbold giving evidence, "In my opinion, death did not occur for several days after the blow"—india-rubber gloves—even, faintly, the voice of Mr. Appledore, "He called on me, sir, with an anti-vivisectionist pamphlet"—all these things and many others rang together and made one sound, they swung together like bells in a steeple, with the deep tenor booming through the clamour:

"The knowledge of good and evil is a phenomenon of the brain, and is removable, removable, removable. The knowledge of good and evil is removable."

Lord Peter Wimsey was not a young man who habitually took himself very seriously, but this time he was frankly appalled. "It's impossible," said his reason, feebly; "_credo quia impossibile_," said his interior certainty with impervious self-satisfaction. "All right," said conscience, instantly allying itself with blind faith, "what are you going to do about it?"

Lord Peter got up and paced the room: "Good Lord!" he said. "Good Lord!" He took down "Who's Who" from the little shelf over the telephone and sought comfort in its pages:

FREKE, Sir Julian, Kt. _cr._ 1916; G.C.V.O. _cr._ 1919; K.C.V.O. 1917; K.C.B. 1918; M.D., F.R.C.P., F.R.C.S., Dr. en Méd. Paris; D. Sci. Cantab.; Knight of Grace of the Order of S. John of Jerusalem; Consulting Surgeon of St. Luke's Hospital, Battersea. _b._ Gryllingham, 16 March, 1872, _only son_ of Edward Curzon Freke, Esq., of Gryll Court, Gryllingham. _ Educ._ Harrow and Trinity Coll., Cambridge; Col. A.M.S.; late

Member of the Advisory Board of the Army Medical Service. _Publications_: Some Notes on the Pathological Aspects of Genius, 1892; Statistical Contributions to the Study of Infantile Paralysis in England and Wales, 1894; Functional Disturbances of the Nervous System, 1899; Cerebro-Spinal Diseases, 1904; The Borderland of Insanity, 1906; An Examination into the Treatment of Pauper Lunacy in the United Kingdom, 1906; Modern Developments in Psycho-Therapy: A Criticism, 1910; Criminal Lunacy, 1914; The Application of Psycho-Therapy to the Treatment of Shell-Shock, 1917; An Answer to Professor Freud, with a Description of Some Experiments Carried Out at the Base Hospital at Amiens, 1919; Structural Modifications Accompanying the More Important Neuroses, 1920. _Clubs_: White's; Oxford and Cambridge; Alpine, etc. _Recreations_: Chess, Mountaineering, Fishing. _Address_: 282, Harley Street and St. Luke's House, Prince of Wales Road, Battersea Park, S.W.11.

He flung the book away. "Confirmation!" he groaned. "As if I needed it!"

He sat down again and buried his face in his hands. He remembered quite suddenly how, years ago, he had stood before the breakfast table at Denver Castle—a small, peaky boy in blue knickers, with a thunderously beating heart. The family had not come down; there was a great silver urn with a spirit lamp under it, and an elaborate coffee-pot boiling in a glass dome. He had twitched the corner of the tablecloth—twitched it harder, and the urn moved ponderously forward and all the teaspoons rattled. He seized the tablecloth in a firm grip and pulled his hardest—he could feel now the delicate and awful thrill as the urn and the coffee machine and the whole of a Sèvres breakfast service had crashed down in one stupendous ruin—he remembered the horrified face of the butler, and the screams of a lady guest.

A log broke across and sank into a fluff of white ash. A belated motor-lorry rumbled past the window.

Mr. Bunter, sleeping the sleep of the true and faithful servant, was aroused in the small hours by a hoarse whisper, "Bunter!"

"Yes, my lord," said Bunter, sitting up and switching on the light.

"Put that light out, damn you!" said the voice. "Listen—over there—listen—can't you hear it?"

"It's nothing, my lord," said Mr. Bunter, hastily getting out of bed and catching hold of his master; "it's all right, you get to bed quick and I'll fetch you a drop of bromide. Why, you're all shivering—you've been sitting up too late."

"Hush! no, no—it's the water," said Lord Peter with chattering teeth; "it's up to their waists down there, poor devils. But listen! can't you hear it? Tap, tap, tap—they're mining us—but I don't know where—I can't hear—I can't. Listen, you! There it is again—we must find it—we must stop it.... Listen! Oh, my God! I can't hear—I can't hear anything for the noise of the guns. Can't they stop the guns?"

"Oh, dear!" said Mr. Bunter to himself. "No, no—it's all right, Major—don't you worry."

"But I hear it," protested Peter.

"So do I," said Mr. Bunter stoutly; "very good hearing, too, my lord. That's our own sappers at work in the communication trench. Don't you fret about that, sir."

Lord Peter grasped his wrist with a feverish hand.

"Our own sappers," he said; "sure of that?"

"Certain of it," said Mr. Bunter, cheerfully.

"They'll bring down the tower," said Lord Peter.

"To be sure they will," said Mr. Bunter, "and very nice, too. You just come and lay down a bit, sir—they've come to take over this section."

"You're sure it's safe to leave it?" said Lord Peter.

"Safe as houses, sir," said Mr. Bunter, tucking his master's arm under his and walking him off to his bedroom.

Lord Peter allowed himself to be dosed and put to bed without further resistance. Mr. Bunter, looking singularly un-Bunterlike in striped pyjamas, with his stiff black hair ruffled about his head, sat grimly watching the younger man's sharp cheekbones and the purple stains under his eyes.

"Thought we'd had the last of these attacks," he said. "Been overdoin' of himself. Asleep?" He peered at him anxiously. An affectionate note crept into his voice. "Bloody little fool!" said Sergeant Bunter.

CHAPTER IX

Mr. Parker, summoned the next morning to 110 Piccadilly, arrived to find the Dowager Duchess in possession. She greeted him charmingly.

"I am going to take this silly boy down to Denver for the week-end," she said, indicating Peter, who was writing and only acknowledged his friend's entrance with a brief nod. "He's been doing too much—running about to Salisbury and places and up till all hours of the night—you really shouldn't encourage him, Mr. Parker, it's very naughty of you—waking poor Bunter up in the middle of the night with scares about Germans, as if that wasn't all over years ago, and he hasn't had an attack for ages, but there! Nerves are such funny things, and Peter always did have nightmares when he was quite a little boy—though very often of course it was only a little pill he wanted; but he was so dreadfully bad in 1918, you know, and I suppose we can't expect to forget all about a great war in a year or two, and, really, I ought to be very thankful with both my boys safe. Still, I think a little peace and quiet at Denver won't do him any harm."

"Sorry you've been having a bad turn, old man," said Parker, vaguely sympathetic; "you're looking a bit seedy."

"Charles," said Lord Peter, in a voice entirely void of expression,

"I am going away for a couple of days because I can be no use to you in London. What has got to be done for the moment can be much better done by you than by me. I want you to take this"—he folded up his writing and placed it in an envelope—"to Scotland Yard immediately and get it sent out to all the workhouses, infirmaries, police stations, Y.M.C.A.'s and so on in London. It is a description of Thipps's corpse as he was before he was shaved and cleaned up. I want to know whether any man answering to that description has been taken in anywhere, alive or dead, during the last fortnight. You will see Sir Andrew Mackenzie personally, and get the paper sent out at once, by his authority; you will tell him that you have solved the problems of the Levy murder and the Battersea mystery"—Mr. Parker made an astonished noise to which his friend paid no attention—"and you will ask him to have men in readiness with a warrant to arrest a very dangerous and important criminal at any moment on your information. When the replies to this paper come in, you will search for any mention of St. Luke's Hospital, or of any person connected with St. Luke's Hospital, and you will send for me at once.

"Meanwhile you will scrape acquaintance—I don't care how—with one of the students at St. Luke's. Don't march in there blowing about murders and police warrants, or you may find yourself in Queer Street. I shall come up to town as soon as I hear from you, and I shall expect to find a nice ingenuous Sawbones here to meet me." He grinned faintly.

"D'you mean you've got to the bottom of this thing?" asked Parker.

"Yes. I may be wrong. I hope I am, but I know I'm not."

"You won't tell me?"

"D'you know," said Peter, "honestly I'd rather not. I say I _may_ be wrong—and I'd feel as if I'd libelled the Archbishop of Canterbury."

"Well, tell me—is it one mystery or two?"

"One."

"You talked of the Levy murder. Is Levy dead?"

"God—yes!" said Peter, with a strong shudder.

The Duchess looked up from where she was reading the _Tatler_.

"Peter," she said, "is that your ague coming on again? Whatever you two are chattering about, you'd better stop it at once if it excites you. Besides, it's about time to be off."

"All right, Mother," said Peter. He turned to Bunter, standing respectfully in the door with an overcoat and suitcase. "You understand what you have to do, don't you?" he said.

"Perfectly, thank you, my lord. The car is just arriving, your Grace."

"With Mrs. Thipps inside it," said the Duchess. "She'll be delighted to see you again, Peter. You remind her so of Mr. Thipps. Good-morning, Bunter."

"Good-morning, your Grace."

Parker accompanied them downstairs.

When they had gone he looked blankly at the paper in his hand—then, remembering that it was Saturday and there was need for haste, he hailed a taxi.

"Scotland Yard!" he cried.

TUESDAY MORNING SAW LORD PETER AND A MAN IN A VELVETEEN JACKET swishing merrily through seven acres of turnip-tops, streaked yellow with early frosts. A little way ahead, a sinuous undercurrent of excitement among the leaves proclaimed the unseen yet ever-near presence of one of the Duke of Denver's setter pups. Presently a partridge flew up with a noise like a police rattle, and Lord Peter accounted for it very creditably for a man who, a few nights before, had been listening to imaginary German sappers. The setter bounded foolishly through the turnips, and fetched back the dead bird.

"Good dog," said Lord Peter.

Encouraged by this, the dog gave a sudden ridiculous gambol and barked, its ear tossed inside out over its head.

"Heel," said the man in velveteen, violently. The animal sidled up, ashamed.

"Fool of a dog, that," said the man in velveteen; "can't keep quiet. Too nervous, my lord. One of old Black Lass's pups."

"Dear me," said Peter, "is the old dog still going?"

"No, my lord; we had to put her away in the spring."

Peter nodded. He always proclaimed that he hated the country and was thankful to have nothing to do with the family estates, but this morning he enjoyed the crisp air and the wet leaves washing darkly over his polished boots. At Denver things moved in an orderly way; no one died sudden and violent deaths except aged setters—and partridges, to be sure. He sniffed up the autumn smell with appreciation. There was a letter in his pocket which had come by the morning post, but he did not intend to read it just yet. Parker had not wired; there was no hurry.

HE READ IT IN THE SMOKING-ROOM AFTER LUNCH. HIS BROTHER WAS THERE, dozing over the _Times_—a good, clean Englishman, sturdy and conventional, rather like Henry VIII in his youth; Gerald, sixteenth Duke of Denver. The Duke considered his cadet rather degenerate, and not quite good form; he disliked his taste for police-court news.

The letter was from Mr. Bunter.

> 110, Piccadilly,
> W.1.

> My Lord:
> I write (Mr. Bunter had been carefully educated and knew that nothing is more vulgar than a careful avoidance of beginning a letter with the first person singular) as your lordship directed, to inform you of the result of my investigations.

> I experienced no difficulty in becoming acquainted with Sir Julian Freke's man-servant. He belongs to the same club as the Hon. Frederick Arbuthnot's man, who is a friend of mine, and was very willing to introduce me. He took me to the club yesterday (Sunday) evening, and we dined with the man, whose name is John Cummings, and afterwards I invited Cummings to drinks and a cigar in the flat. Your lordship will excuse me doing this, knowing that it is not my habit, but it has always been my experience that the best way to gain a man's confidence is to let him suppose that one takes advantage of one's employer.

> ("I always suspected Bunter of being a student of human nature," commented Lord Peter.)

> I gave him the best old port ("The deuce you did," said Lord Peter), having heard you and Mr. Arbuthnot talk over it. ("Hum!" said Lord Peter.)

Its effects were quite equal to my expectations as regards the principal matter in hand, but I very much regret to state that the man had so little understanding of what was offered to him that he smoked a cigar with it (one of your lordship's Villar Villars). You will understand that I made no comment on this at the time, but your lordship will sympathize with my feelings. May I take this opportunity of expressing my grateful appreciation of your lordship's excellent taste in food, drink and dress? It is, if I may say so, more than a pleasure—it is an education, to valet and buttle your lordship.

Lord Peter bowed his head gravely.

"What on earth are you doing, Peter, sittin' there noddin' an' grinnin' like a what-you-may-call-it?" demanded the Duke, coming suddenly out of a snooze. "Someone writin' pretty things to you, what?"

"Charming things," said Lord Peter.

The Duke eyed him doubtfully.

"Hope to goodness you don't go and marry a chorus beauty," he muttered inwardly, and returned to the Times.

Over dinner I had set myself to discover Cummings's tastes, and found them to run in the direction of the music-hall stage. During his first glass I drew him out in this direction, your lordship having kindly given me opportunities of seeing every performance in London, and I spoke more freely than I should consider becoming in the ordinary way in order to make myself pleasant to him. I may say that his views on women and the stage were such as I should have expected from a man who would smoke with your lordship's port.

With the second glass I introduced the subject of your lordship's inquiries. In order to save time I will write our conversation in the form of a dialogue, as nearly as possible as it actually took place.

Cummings: You seem to get many opportunities of seeing a bit of life, Mr. Bunter.

Bunter: One can always make opportunities if one knows how.

Cummings: Ah, it's very easy for you to talk, Mr. Bunter. You're not married, for one thing.

Bunter: I know better than that, Mr. Cummings.

Cummings: So do I—_now_, when it's too late. (He sighed heavily, and I filled up his glass.)

Bunter: Does Mrs. Cummings live with you at Battersea?

Cummings: Yes, her and me we do for my governor. Such a life! Not but what there's a char comes in by the day. But what's a char? I can tell you it's dull all by ourselves in that d—d Battersea suburb.

Bunter: Not very convenient for the Halls, of course.

Cummings: I believe you. It's all right for you, here in Piccadilly, right on the spot as you might say. And I daresay your governor's often out all night, eh?

Bunter: Oh, frequently, Mr. Cummings.

Cummings: And I daresay you take the opportunity to slip off yourself every so often, eh?

Bunter: Well, what do _you_ think, Mr. Cummings?

Cummings: That's it; there you are! But what's a man to do with a nagging fool of a wife and a blasted scientific doctor for a governor, as sits up all night cutting up dead bodies and experimenting with frogs?

Bunter: Surely he goes out sometimes.

Cummings: Not often. And always back before twelve. And the way he goes on if he rings the bell and you ain't there. I give you _my_ word, Mr. Bunter.

Bunter: Temper?

Cummings: No-o-o—but looking through you, nasty-like, as if you was on that operating table of his and he was going to cut you up. Nothing a man could rightly complain of, you understand, Mr. Bunter, just nasty looks. Not but what I will say he's very correct. Apologizes if he's been inconsiderate. But what's the good of that when he's been and gone and lost you your night's rest?

Bunter: How does he do that? Keeps you up late, you mean?

Cummings: Not him; far from it. House locked up and household to bed at half-past ten. That's his little rule. Not but what I'm glad enough to go as a rule, it's that dreary. Still, when I _do_ go to bed I like to go to sleep.

Bunter: What does he do? Walk about the house?

Cummings: Doesn't he? All night. And in and out of the private door to the hospital.

Bunter: You don't mean to say, Mr. Cummings, a great specialist like Sir Julian Freke does night work at the hospital?

Cummings: No, no; he does his own work—research work, as you may say. Cuts people up. They say he's very clever. Could take you or me to pieces like a clock, Mr. Bunter, and put us together again.

Bunter: Do you sleep in the basement, then, to hear him so plain?

Cummings: No; our bedroom's at the top. But, Lord! what's that? He'll bang the door so you can hear him all over the house.

Bunter: Ah, many's the time I've had to speak to Lord Peter about that. And talking all night. And baths.

Cummings: Baths? You may well say that, Mr. Bunter. Baths? Me and my wife sleep next to the cistern-room. Noise fit to wake the dead. All hours. When d'you think he chose to have a bath, no later than last Monday night, Mr. Bunter?

Bunter: I've known them to do it at two in the morning, Mr. Cummings.

Cummings: Have you, now? Well, this was at three. Three o'clock in the morning we was waked up. I give you _my_ word.

Bunter: You don't say so, Mr. Cummings.

Cummings: He cuts up diseases, you see, Mr. Bunter, and then he don't like to go to bed till he's washed the bacilluses off, if you understand me. Very natural, too, I daresay. But what I say is, the middle of the night's no time for a gentleman to be occupying his mind with diseases.

Bunter: These great men have their own way of doing things.

Cummings: Well, all I can say is, it isn't my way.

(I could believe that, your lordship. Cummings has no signs of greatness about him, and his trousers are not what I would wish to see in a man of his profession.)

Bunter: Is he habitually as late as that, Mr. Cummings?

Cummings: Well, no, Mr. Bunter, I will say, not as a general rule. He apologized, too, in the morning, and said he would have the cistern seen to—and very necessary, in my opinion, for the air gets into the pipes, and the groaning and screeching as goes on is something awful. Just like Niagara, if you follow me, Mr. Bunter, I give you _my_ word.

Bunter: Well, that's as it should be, Mr. Cummings. One can put up with a great deal from a gentleman that has the manners to apologize.

And, of course, sometimes they can't help themselves. A visitor will come in unexpectedly and keep them late, perhaps.

Cummings: That's true enough, Mr. Bunter. Now I come to think of it, there _was_ a gentleman come in on Monday evening. Not that he came late, but he stayed about an hour, and may have put Sir Julian behindhand.

Bunter: Very likely. Let me give you some more port, Mr. Cummings. Or a little of Lord Peter's old brandy.

Cummings: A little of the brandy, thank you, Mr. Bunter. I suppose you have the run of the cellar here. (He winked at me.)

"Trust me for that," I said, and I fetched him the Napoleon. I assure your lordship it went to my heart to pour it out for a man like that. However, seeing we had got on the right tack, I felt it wouldn't be wasted.

"I'm sure I wish it was always gentlemen that come here at night," I said. (Your lordship will excuse me, I am sure, making such a suggestion.)

("Good God," said Lord Peter, "I wish Bunter was less thorough in his methods.")

Cummings: Oh, he's that sort, his lordship, is he? (He chuckled and poked me. I suppress a portion of his conversation here, which could not fail to be as offensive to your lordship as it was to myself. He went on:) No, it's none of that with Sir Julian. Very few visitors at night, and always gentlemen. And going early as a rule, like the one I mentioned.

Bunter: Just as well. There's nothing I find more wearisome, Mr. Cummings, than sitting up to see visitors out.

Cummings: Oh, I didn't see this one out. Sir Julian let him out himself at ten o'clock or thereabouts. I heard the gentleman shout "Good-night" and off he goes.

Bunter: Does Sir Julian always do that?

Cummings: Well, that depends. If he sees visitors downstairs, he lets them out himself: if he sees them upstairs in the library, he rings for me.

Bunter: This was a downstairs visitor, then?

Cummings: Oh, yes. Sir Julian opened the door to him, I remember. He happened to be working in the hall. Though now I come to think of it, they went up to the library afterwards. That's funny. I know they did, because I happened to go up to the hall with coals, and I heard them upstairs. Besides, Sir Julian rang for me in the library a few minutes later.

Still, anyway, we heard him go at ten, or it may have been a bit before. He hadn't only stayed about three-quarters of an hour. However, as I was saying, there was Sir Julian banging in and out of the private door all night, and a bath at three in the morning, and up again for breakfast at eight—it beats me. If I had all his money, curse me if I'd go poking about with dead men in the middle of the night. I'd find something better to do with my time, eh, Mr. Bunter—

I need not repeat any more of his conversation, as it became unpleasant and incoherent, and I could not bring him back to the events of Monday night. I was unable to get rid of him till three. He cried on my neck, and said I was the bird, and you were the governor for him. He said that Sir Julian would be greatly annoyed with him for coming home so late, but Sunday night was his night out and if anything was said about it he would give notice. I think he will be ill-advised to do so, as I feel he is not a man I could conscientiously recommend if I were in Sir Julian Freke's place. I noticed that his boot-heels were slightly worn down.

I should wish to add, as a tribute to the great merits of your lordship's cellar, that, although I was obliged to drink a somewhat large quantity both of the Cockburn '68 and the 1800 Napoleon I feel no headache or other ill effects this morning.

Trusting that your lordship is deriving real benefit from the country air, and that the little information I have been able to obtain will prove satisfactory, I remain.

With respectful duty to all the family,

Obediently yours,
MERVYN BUNTER.

"Y'know," said Lord Peter thoughtfully to himself, "I sometimes think Mervyn Bunter's pullin' my leg. What is it, Soames?"

"A telegram, my lord."

"Parker," said Lord Peter, opening it. It said:

"Description recognised Chelsea Workhouse. Unknown vagrant injured street accident Wednesday week. Died workhouse Monday. Delivered St. Luke's same evening by order Freke. Much puzzled. Parker."

"Hurray!" said Lord Peter, suddenly sparkling. "I'm glad I've puzzled Parker. Gives me confidence in myself. Makes me feel like Sherlock Holmes.

'Perfectly simple, Watson.' Dash it all, though! this is a beastly business. Still, it's puzzled Parker."

"What's the matter?" asked the Duke, getting up and yawning.

"Marching orders," said Peter, "back to town. Many thanks for your hospitality, old bird—I'm feelin' no end better. Ready to tackle Professor Moriarty or Leon Kestrel or any of 'em."

"I do wish you'd keep out of the police courts," grumbled the Duke.

"It makes it so dashed awkward for me, havin' a brother makin' himself conspicuous."

"Sorry, Gerald," said the other; "I know I'm a beastly blot on the 'scutcheon."

"Why can't you marry and settle down and live quietly, doin' something useful?" said the Duke, unappeased.

"Because that was a wash-out as you perfectly well know," said Peter;

"besides," he added cheerfully, "I'm bein' no end useful. You may come to want me yourself, you never know. When anybody comes blackmailin' you, Gerald, or your first deserted wife turns up unexpectedly from the West Indies, you'll realize the pull of havin' a private detective in the family. 'Delicate private business arranged with tact and discretion. Investigations undertaken. Divorce evidence a specialty. Every guarantee!' Come, now."

"Ass!" said Lord Denver, throwing the newspaper violently into his armchair. "When do you want the car?"

"Almost at once. I say, Jerry, I'm taking Mother up with me."

"Why should she be mixed up in it?"

"Well, I want her help."

"I call it most unsuitable," said the Duke.

The Dowager Duchess, however, made no objection.

"I used to know her quite well," she said, "when she was Christine Ford. Why, dear?"

"Because," said Lord Peter, "there's a terrible piece of news to be broken to her about her husband."

"Is he dead, dear?"

"Yes; and she will have to come and identify him."

"Poor Christine."

"Under very revolting circumstances, Mother."

"I'll come with you, dear."

"Thank you, Mother, you're a brick. D'you mind gettin' your things on straight away and comin' up with me? I'll tell you about it in the car."

CHAPTER X

Mr. Parker, a faithful though doubting Thomas, had duly secured his medical student: a large young man like an overgrown puppy, with innocent eyes and a freckled face. He sat on the Chesterfield before Lord Peter's library fire, bewildered in equal measure by his errand, his surroundings and the drink which he was absorbing. His palate, though untutored, was naturally a good one, and he realized that even to call this liquid a drink—the term ordinarily used by him to designate cheap whisky, post-war beer or a dubious glass of claret in a Soho restaurant—was a sacrilege; this was something outside normal experience: a genie in a bottle.

The man called Parker, whom he had happened to run across the evening before in the public-house at the corner of Prince of Wales Road, seemed to be a good sort. He had insisted on bringing him round to see this friend of his, who lived splendidly in Piccadilly. Parker was quite understandable; he put him down as a government servant, or perhaps something in the City. The friend was embarrassing; he was a lord, to begin with, and his clothes were a kind of rebuke to the world at large. He talked the most fatuous nonsense, certainly, but in a disconcerting way. He didn't dig into a joke and get all the fun out of it; he made it in passing, so to speak, and skipped away to something else before your retort was ready. He had a truly terrible man-servant—the sort you read about in books—who froze the marrow in your bones with silent criticism. Parker appeared to bear up under the strain, and this made you think more highly of Parker; he must be more habituated to the surroundings of the great than you would think to look at him. You wondered what the carpet had cost on which Parker was carelessly spilling cigar ash; your father was an upholsterer—Mr. Piggott, of Piggott & Piggott, Liverpool—and you knew enough about carpets to know that you couldn't even guess at the price of this one. When you moved your head on the bulging silk cushion in the corner of the sofa, it made you wish you shaved more often and more carefully. The sofa was a monster—but even so, it hardly seemed big enough to contain you. This Lord Peter was not very tall—in fact, he was rather a small man, but he didn't look undersized. He looked right; he made you feel that to be six-foot-three was rather vulgarly assertive; you felt like Mother's new drawing-room curtains—all over great big blobs. But everybody was very decent to you, and nobody said anything you couldn't understand, or sneered at you. There were some frightfully deep-looking books on the shelves all round, and you had looked into a great folio Dante which was lying on the table, but your hosts were talking quite ordinarily and rationally about the sort of books you read yourself—clinking good love stories and detective stories. You had read a lot of those, and could give an opinion, and they listened to what you had to say, though Lord Peter had a funny way of talking about books, too, as if the author had confided in him beforehand, and told him how the story was put together, and which bit was written first. It reminded you of the way old Freke took a body to pieces.

"Thing I object to in detective stories," said Mr. Piggott, "is the way fellows remember every bloomin' thing that's happened to 'em within the last six months. They're always ready with their time of day and was it rainin' or not, and what were they doin' on such an' such a day. Reel it all off like a page of poetry. But one ain't like that in real life, d'you think so, Lord Peter?" Lord Peter smiled, and young Piggott, instantly embarrassed, appealed to his earlier acquaintance.

"You know what I mean, Parker. Come now. One day's so like another, I'm sure I couldn't remember—well, I might remember yesterday, p'r'aps, but I couldn't be certain about what I was doin' last week if I was to be shot for it."

"No," said Parker, "and evidence given in police statements sounds just as impossible. But they don't really get it like that, you know. I mean, a man doesn't just say, 'Last Friday I went out at 10 a.m. to buy a mutton chop. As I was turning into Mortimer Street I noticed a girl of about twenty-two with black hair and brown eyes, wearing a green jumper, check skirt, Panama hat and black shoes, riding a Royal Sunbeam Cycle at about ten miles an hour turning the corner by the Church of St. Simon and St. Jude on the wrong side of the road riding towards the market place!' It amounts to that, of course, but it's really wormed out of him by a series of questions."

"And in short stories," said Lord Peter, "it has to be put in statement form, because the real conversation would be so long and twaddly and tedious, and nobody would have the patience to read it. Writers have to consider their readers, if any, y'see."

"Yes," said Mr. Piggott, "but I bet you most people would find it jolly difficult to remember, even if you asked 'em things. I should—of course, I know I'm a bit of a fool, but then, most people are, ain't they? You know what I mean. Witnesses ain't detectives, they're just average idiots like you and me."

"Quite so," said Lord Peter, smiling as the force of the last phrase sank into its unhappy perpetrator; "you mean, if I were to ask you in a general way what you were doin'—say, a week ago today, you wouldn't be able to tell me a thing about it offhand?"

"No—I'm sure I shouldn't." He considered. "No. I was in at the Hospital as usual, I suppose, and, being Tuesday, there'd be a lecture on something or the other—dashed if I know what—and in the evening I went out with Tommy Pringle—no, that must have been Monday—or was it Wednesday? I tell you, I couldn't swear to anything."

"You do yourself an injustice," said Lord Peter gravely. "I'm sure, for instance, you recollect what work you were doing in the dissecting-room on that day, for example."

"Lord, no! not for certain. I mean, I daresay it might come back to me if I thought for a long time, but I wouldn't swear to it in a court of law."

"I'll bet you half-a-crown to sixpence," said Lord Peter, "that you'll remember within five minutes."

"I'm sure I can't."

"We'll see. Do you keep a notebook of the work you do when you dissect? Drawings or anything?"

"Oh, yes."

"Think of that. What's the last thing you did in it?"

"That's easy, because I only did it this morning. It was leg muscles."

"Yes. Who was the subject?"

"An old woman of sorts; died of pneumonia."

"Yes. Turn back the pages of your drawing book in your mind. What came before that?"

"Oh, some animals—still legs; I'm doing motor muscles at present. Yes. That was old Cunningham's demonstration on comparative anatomy. I did rather a good thing of a hare's legs and a frog's, and rudimentary legs on a snake."

"Yes. Which day does Mr. Cunningham lecture?"

"Friday."

"Friday; yes. Turn back again. What comes before that?"

Mr. Piggott shook his head.

"Do your drawings of legs begin on the right-hand page or the left-hand page? Can you see the first drawing?"

"Yes—yes—I can see the date written at the top. It's a section of a frog's hind leg, on the right-hand page."

"Yes. Think of the open book in your mind's eye. What is opposite to it?"

This demanded some mental concentration.

"Something round—coloured—oh, yes—it's a hand."

"Yes. You went on from the muscles of the hand and arm to leg- and foot-muscles?"

"Yes; that's right. I've got a set of drawings of arms."

"Yes. Did you make those on the Thursday?"

"No; I'm never in the dissecting-room on Thursday."

"On Wednesday, perhaps?"

"Yes; I must have made them on Wednesday. Yes; I did. I went in there after we'd seen those tetanus patients in the morning. I did them on

Wednesday afternoon. I know I went back because I wanted to finish 'em. I worked rather hard—for me. That's why I remember."

"Yes; you went back to finish them. When had you begun them, then?"

"Why, the day before."

"The day before. That was Tuesday, wasn't it?"

"I've lost count—yes, the day before Wednesday—yes, Tuesday."

"Yes. Were they a man's arms or a woman's arms?"

"Oh, a man's arms.

"Yes; last Tuesday, a week ago today, you were dissecting a man's arms in the dissecting-room. Sixpence, please."

"By Jove!"

"Wait a moment. You know a lot more about it than that. You've no idea how much you know. You know what kind of man he was."

"Oh, I never saw him complete, you know. I got there a bit late that day, I remember. I'd asked for an arm specially, because I was rather weak in arms, and Watts—that's the attendant—had promised to save me one."

"Yes. You have arrived late and found your arm waiting for you. You are dissecting it—taking your scissors and slitting up the skin and pinning it back. Was it very young, fair skin?"

"Oh, no—no. Ordinary skin, I think—with dark hairs on it—yes, that was it."

"Yes. A lean, stringy arm, perhaps, with no extra fat anywhere?"

"Oh, no—I was rather annoyed about that. I wanted a good, muscular arm, but it was rather poorly developed and the fat got in my way."

"Yes; a sedentary man who didn't do much manual work."

"That's right."

"Yes. You dissected the hand, for instance, and made a drawing of it. You would have noticed any hard calluses."

"Oh, there was nothing of that sort."

"No. But should you say it was a young man's arm? Firm young flesh and limber joints?"

"No—no."

"No. Old and stringy, perhaps."

"No. Middle-aged—with rheumatism. I mean, there was a chalky deposit in the joints, and the fingers were a bit swollen."

"Yes. A man about fifty."

"About that."

"Yes. There were other students at work on the same body."

"Oh, yes."

"Yes. And they made all the usual sort of jokes about it."

"I expect so—oh, yes!"

"You can remember some of them. Who is your local funny man, so to speak?"

"Tommy Pringle."

"What was Tommy Pringle's doing?"

"Can't remember."

"Whereabouts was Tommy Pringle working?"

"Over by the instrument cupboard—by sink C."

"Yes. Get a picture of Tommy Pringle in your mind's eye."

Piggott began to laugh.

"I remember now. Tommy Pringle said the old Sheeny—"

"Why did he call him a Sheeny?"

"I don't know. But I know he did."

"Perhaps he looked like it. Did you see his head?"

"No."

"Who had the head?"

"I don't know—oh, yes, I do, though. Old Freke bagged the head himself, and little Bouncible Binns was very cross about it, because he'd been promised a head to do with old Scrooger."

"I see. What was Sir Julian doing with the head?"

"He called us up and gave us a jaw on spinal haemorrhage and nervous lesions."

"Yes. Well, go back to Tommy Pringle."

Tommy Pringle's joke was repeated, not without some embarrassment.

"Quite so. Was that all?"

"No. The chap who was working with Tommy said that sort of thing came from over-feeding."

"I deduce that Tommy Pringle's partner was interested in the alimentary canal."

"Yes; and Tommy said, if he'd thought they'd feed you like that he'd go to the workhouse himself."

"Then the man was a pauper from the workhouse?"

"Well, he must have been, I suppose."

"Are workhouse paupers usually fat and well-fed?"

"Well, no—come to think of it, not as a rule."

"In fact, it struck Tommy Pringle and his friend that this was something a little out of the way in a workhouse subject?"

"Yes."

"And if the alimentary canal was so entertaining to these gentlemen, I imagine the subject had come by his death shortly after a full meal."

"Yes—oh, yes—he'd have had to, wouldn't he?"

"Well, I don't know," said Lord Peter. "That's in your department, you know. That would be your inference, from what they said."

"Oh, yes. Undoubtedly."

"Yes; you wouldn't, for example, expect them to make that observation if the patient had been ill for a long time and fed on slops."

"Of course not."

"Well, you see, you really know a lot about it. On Tuesday week you were dissecting the arm muscles of a rheumatic middle-aged Jew, of sedentary habits, who had died shortly after eating a heavy meal, of some injury producing spinal haemorrhage and nervous lesions, and so forth, and who was presumed to come from the workhouse?"

"Yes."

"And you could swear to those facts, if need were?"

"Well, if you put it in that way, I suppose I could."

"Of course you could."

Mr. Piggott sat for some moments in contemplation.

"I say," he said at last, "I did know all that, didn't I?"

"Oh, yes—you knew it all right—like Socrates's slave."

"Who's he?"

"A person in a book I used to read as a boy."

"Oh—does he come in 'The Last Days of Pompeii'?"

"No—another book—I daresay you escaped it. It's rather dull."

"I never read much except Henty and Fenimore Cooper at school.... But—have I got rather an extra good memory, then?"

"You have a better memory than you credit yourself with."

"Then why can't I remember all the medical stuff? It all goes out of my head like a sieve."

"Well, why can't you?" said Lord Peter, standing on the hearthrug and smiling down at his guest.

"Well," said the young man, "the chaps who examine one don't ask the same sort of questions you do."

"No?"

"No—they leave you to remember all by yourself. And it's beastly hard. Nothing to catch hold of, don't you know? But, I say—how did you know about Tommy Pringle being the funny man and—"

"I didn't, till you told me."

"No; I know. But how did you know he'd be there if you did ask? I mean to say—I say," said Mr. Piggott, who was becoming mellowed by influences themselves not unconnected with the alimentary canal—"I say, are you rather clever, or am I rather stupid?"

"No, no," said Lord Peter, "it's me. I'm always askin' such stupid questions, everybody thinks I must mean somethin' by 'em."

This was too involved for Mr. Piggott.

"Never mind," said Parker, soothingly, "he's always like that. You mustn't take any notice. He can't help it. It's premature senile decay, often observed in the families of hereditary legislators. Go away, Wimsey, and play us the 'Beggar's Opera,' or something."

"That's good enough, isn't it?" said Lord Peter, when the happy Mr. Piggott had been despatched home after a really delightful evening.

"I'm afraid so," said Parker. "But it seems almost incredible."

"There's nothing incredible in human nature," said Lord Peter; "at least, in educated human nature. Have you got that exhumation order?"

"I shall have it tomorrow. I thought of fixing up with the workhouse people for tomorrow afternoon. I shall have to go and see them first."

"Right you are; I'll let my mother know."

"I begin to feel like you, Wimsey, I don't like this job."

"I like it a deal better than I did."

"You are really certain we're not making a mistake?"

Lord Peter had strolled across to the window. The curtain was not perfectly drawn, and he stood gazing out through the gap into lighted Piccadilly. At this he turned round:

"If we are," he said, "we shall know tomorrow, and no harm will have been done. But I rather think you will receive a certain amount of confirmation on your way home. Look here, Parker, d'you know, if I were you I'd spend the night here. There's a spare bedroom; I can easily put you up."

Parker stared at him.

"Do you mean—I'm likely to be attacked?"

"I think it very likely indeed."

"Is there anybody in the street?"

"Not now; there was half-an-hour ago."

"When Piggott left?"

"Yes."

"I say—I hope the boy is in no danger."

"That's what I went down to see. I don't think so. Fact is, I don't suppose anybody would imagine we'd exactly made a confidant of Piggott. But I think you and I are in danger. You'll stay?"

"I'm damned if I will, Wimsey. Why should I run away?"

"Bosh!" said Peter. "You'd run away all right if you believed me, and why not? You don't believe me. In fact, you're still not certain I'm on the right tack. Go in peace, but don't say I didn't warn you."

"I won't; I'll dictate a message with my dying breath to say I was convinced."

"Well, don't walk—take a taxi."

"Very well, I'll do that."

"And don't let anybody else get into it."

"No."

It was a raw, unpleasant night. A taxi deposited a load of people returning from the theatre at the block of flats next door, and Parker secured it for himself. He was just giving the address to the driver, when a man came hastily running up from a side street. He was in evening dress and an overcoat. He rushed up, signalling frantically.

"Sir—sir!—dear me! why, it's Mr. Parker! How fortunate! If you would be so kind—summoned from the club—a sick friend—can't find a taxi—everybody going home from the theatre—if I might share your cab—you are returning to Bloomsbury? I want Russell Square—if I might presume—a matter of life and death."

He spoke in hurried gasps, as though he had been running violently and far. Parker promptly stepped out of the taxi.

"Delighted to be of service to you, Sir Julian," he said; "take my taxi. I am going down to Craven Street myself, but I'm in no hurry. Pray make use of the cab."

"It's extremely kind of you," said the surgeon. "I am ashamed—"

"That's all right," said Parker, cheerily. "I can wait." He assisted Freke into the taxi. "What number? 24 Russell Square, driver, and look sharp."

The taxi drove off. Parker remounted the stairs and rang Lord Peter's bell.

"Thanks, old man," he said. "I'll stop the night, after all."

"Come in," said Wimsey.

"Did you see that?" asked Parker.

"I saw something. What happened exactly?"

Parker told his story. "Frankly," he said, "I've been thinking you a bit mad, but now I'm not quite so sure of it."

Peter laughed.

"Blessed are they that have not seen and yet have believed. Bunter, Mr. Parker will stay the night."

"Look here, Wimsey, let's have another look at this business. Where's that letter?"

Lord Peter produced Bunter's essay in dialogue. Parker studied it for a short time in silence.

"You know, Wimsey, I'm as full of objections to this idea as an egg is of meat."

"So'm I, old son. That's why I want to dig up our Chelsea pauper. But trot out your objections."

"Well—"

"Well, look here, I don't pretend to be able to fill in all the blanks myself. But here we have two mysterious occurrences in one night, and a complete chain connecting the one with another through one particular person. It's beastly, but it's not unthinkable."

"Yes, I know all that. But there are one or two quite definite stumbling-blocks."

"Yes, I know. But, see here. On the one hand, Levy disappeared after being last seen looking for Prince of Wales Road at nine o'clock. At eight next morning a dead man, not unlike him in general outline, is discovered in a bath in Queen Caroline Mansions. Levy, by Freke's own admission, was going to see Freke. By information received from Chelsea workhouse a dead man, answering to the description of the Battersea corpse in its natural state, was delivered that same day to Freke. We have Levy with a past, and no future, as it were; an unknown vagrant with a future (in the cemetery) and no past, and Freke stands between their future and their past."

"That looks all right——"

"Yes. Now, further: Freke has a motive for getting rid of Levy—an old jealousy."

"Very old—and not much of a motive."

"People have been known to do that sort of thing. You're thinking that people don't keep up old jealousies for twenty years or so. Perhaps not. Not just primitive, brute jealousy. That means a word and a blow. But the thing that rankles is hurt vanity. That sticks. Humiliation. And we've all got a sore spot we don't like to have touched. I've got it. You've got it. Some blighter said hell knew no fury like a woman scorned. Stickin' it on to women, poor devils. Sex is every man's loco spot—you needn't fidget, you know it's true—he'll take a disappointment, but not a humiliation. I knew a man once who'd been turned down—not too charitably—by a girl he was engaged to. He spoke quite decently about her. I asked what had become of her. 'Oh,' he said, 'she married the other fellow.' And then burst out—couldn't help himself. 'Lord, yes!' he cried. 'To think of it—jilted for a Scotchman!' I don't know why he didn't like Scots, but that was what got him on the raw. Look at Freke. I've read his books. His attacks on his antagonists are savage. And he's a scientist. Yet he can't bear opposition, even in his work, which is where any first-class man is most sane and open-minded. Do you think he's a man to take a beating from any man on a side-issue? On a man's most sensitive side-issue? People are opinionated about side-issues, you know. I see red if anybody questions my judgment about a book. And Levy—who was nobody twenty years ago—romps in and carries off Freke's girl from under his nose. It isn't the girl Freke would bother about—it's having his aristocratic nose put out of joint by a little Jewish nobody.

"There's another thing. Freke's got another side-issue. He likes crime. In that criminology book of his he gloats over a hardened murderer. I've read it, and I've seen the admiration simply glaring out between the lines whenever he writes about a callous and successful criminal. He reserves his contempt for the victims or the penitents or the men who lose their heads and get found out. His heroes are Edmond de la Pommerais, who persuaded his mistress into becoming an accessory to her own murder, and George Joseph Smith of Brides-in-a-bath fame, who could make passionate love to his wife in the night and carry out his plot to murder her in the morning. After all, he thinks conscience is a sort of vermiform appendix. Chop it out and you'll feel all the better. Freke isn't troubled by the usual conscientious deterrent. Witness his own hand in his books. Now again. The man who went to Levy's house in his place knew the house: Freke knew the house; he was a red-haired man, smaller than Levy, but not much smaller, since he could wear his clothes without appearing ludicrous: you have seen Freke—you know his height—about five-foot-eleven, I suppose, and his auburn mane; he probably wore surgical gloves: Freke is a surgeon; he was a methodical and daring man: surgeons are obliged to be both daring and methodical. Now take the other side. The man who got hold of the Battersea corpse had to have access to dead bodies. Freke obviously had access to dead bodies. He had to be cool and quick and callous about handling a dead body. Surgeons are all that. He had to be a strong man to carry the body across the roofs and dump it in at Thipps's window. Freke is a powerful man and a member of the Alpine Club. He probably wore surgical gloves and he let the body down from the roof with a surgical bandage. This points to a surgeon again. He undoubtedly lived in the neighbourhood. Freke lives next door. The girl you interviewed heard a bump on the roof of the end house. That is the house next to Freke's. Every time we look at Freke, he leads somewhere, whereas Milligan and Thipps and Crimplesham and all the other people we've honoured with our suspicion simply led nowhere."

"Yes; but it's not quite so simple as you make out. What was Levy doing in that surreptitious way at Freke's on Monday night?"

"Well, you have Freke's explanation."

"Rot, Wimsey. You said yourself it wouldn't do."

"Excellent. It won't do. Therefore Freke was lying. Why should he lie about it, unless he had some object in hiding the truth?"

"Well, but why mention it at all?"

"Because Levy, contrary to all expectation, had been seen at the corner of the road. That was a nasty accident for Freke. He thought it best to be beforehand with an explanation—of sorts. He reckoned, of course, on nobody's ever connecting Levy with Battersea Park."

"Well, then, we come back to the first question: Why did Levy go there?"

"I don't know, but he was got there somehow. Why did Freke buy all those Peruvian Oil shares?"

"I don't know," said Parker in his turn.

"Anyway," went on Wimsey, "Freke expected him, and made arrangements to let him in himself, so that Cummings shouldn't see who the caller was."

"But the caller left again at ten."

"Oh, Charles! I did not expect this of you. This is the purest Suggery! Who saw him go? Somebody said 'Good-night' and walked away down the street. And you believe it was Levy because Freke didn't go out of his way to explain that it wasn't."

"D'you mean that Freke walked cheerfully out of the house to Park Lane, and left Levy behind—dead or alive—for Cummings to find?"

"We have Cummings's word that he did nothing of the sort. A few minutes after the steps walked away from the house, Freke rang the library bell and told Cummings to shut up for the night."

"Then—"

"Well—there's a side door to the house, I suppose—in fact, you know there is—Cummings said so—through the hospital."

"Yes—well, where was Levy?"

"Levy went up into the library and never came down. You've been in Freke's library. Where would you have put him?"

"In my bedroom next door."

"Then that's where he did put him."

"But suppose the man went in to turn down the bed?"

"Beds are turned down by the housekeeper, earlier than ten o'clock."

"Yes.... But Cummings heard Freke about the house all night."

"He heard him go in and out two or three times. He'd expect him to do that, anyway."

"Do you mean to say Freke got all that job finished before three in the morning?"

"Why not?"

"Quick work."

"Well, call it quick work. Besides, why three? Cummings never saw him again till he called him for eight o'clock breakfast."

"But he was having a bath at three."

"I don't say he didn't get back from Park Lane before three. But I don't suppose Cummings went and looked through the bathroom keyhole to see if he was in the bath."

Parker considered again.

"How about Crimplesham's pince-nez?" he asked.

"That is a bit mysterious," said Lord Peter.

"And why Thipps's bathroom?"

"Why, indeed? Pure accident, perhaps—or pure devilry."

"Do you think all this elaborate scheme could have been put together in a night, Wimsey?"

"Far from it. It was conceived as soon as that man who bore a superficial resemblance to Levy came into the workhouse. He had several days."

"I see."

"Freke gave himself away at the inquest. He and Grimbold disagreed about the length of the man's illness. If a small man (comparatively speaking) like Grimbold presumes to disagree with a man like Freke, it's because he is sure of his ground."

"Then—if your theory is sound—Freke made a mistake."

"Yes. A very slight one. He was guarding, with unnecessary caution, against starting a train of thought in the mind of anybody—say, the workhouse doctor. Up till then he'd been reckoning on the fact that people don't think a second time about anything (a body, say) that's once been accounted for."

"What made him lose his head?"

"A chain of unforeseen accidents. Levy's having been recognised—my mother's son having foolishly advertised in the _Times_ his connection with the Battersea end of the mystery—Detective Parker (whose photograph has been a little prominent in the illustrated press lately) seen sitting next door to the Duchess of Denver at the inquest. His aim in life was to prevent the two ends of the problem from linking up. And there were two of the links, literally side by side. Many criminals are wrecked by over-caution."

Parker was silent.

CHAPTER XI

"A regular pea-souper, by Jove," said Lord Peter.

Parker grunted, and struggled irritably into an overcoat.

"It affords me, if I may say so, the greatest satisfaction," continued the noble lord, "that in a collaboration like ours all the uninteresting and disagreeable routine work is done by you."

Parker grunted again.

"Do you anticipate any difficulty about the warrant?" inquired Lord Peter.

Parker grunted a third time.

"I suppose you've seen to it that all this business is kept quiet?"

"Of course."

"You've muzzled the workhouse people?"

"Of course."

"And the police?"

"Yes."

"Because, if you haven't there'll probably be nobody to arrest."

"My dear Wimsey, do you think I'm a fool?"

"I had no such hope."

Parker grunted finally and departed.

Lord Peter settled down to a perusal of his Dante. It afforded him no solace. Lord Peter was hampered in his career as a private detective by a public-school education. Despite Parker's admonitions, he was not always able to discount it. His mind had been warped in its young growth by "Raffles" and "Sherlock Holmes," or the sentiments for which they stand. He belonged to a family which had never shot a fox.

"I am an amateur," said Lord Peter.

Nevertheless, while communing with Dante, he made up his mind.

IN THE AFTERNOON HE FOUND HIMSELF IN HARLEY STREET. SIR JULIAN FREKE might be consulted about one's nerves from two till four on Tuesdays and Fridays. Lord Peter rang the bell.

"Have you an appointment, sir?" inquired the man who opened the door.

"No," said Lord Peter, "but will you give Sir Julian my card? I think it possible he may see me without one."

He sat down in the beautiful room in which Sir Julian's patients awaited his healing counsel. It was full of people. Two or three fashionably dressed women were discussing shops and servants together, and teasing a toy griffon. A big, worried-looking man by himself in a corner looked at his watch twenty times a minute. Lord Peter knew him by sight. It was Wintrington, a millionaire, who had tried to kill himself a few months ago. He controlled the finances of five countries, but he could not control his nerves. The finances of five countries were in Sir Julian Freke's capable hands. By the fireplace sat a soldierly-looking young man, of about Lord Peter's own age. His face was prematurely lined and worn; he sat bolt upright, his restless eyes darting in the direction of every slightest sound. On the sofa was an elderly woman of modest appearance, with a young girl. The girl seemed listless and wretched; the woman's look showed deep affection, and anxiety tempered with a timid hope. Close beside Lord Peter was another younger woman, with a little girl, and Lord Peter noticed in both of them the broad cheekbones and beautiful grey, slanting eyes of the Slav. The child, moving restlessly about, trod on Lord Peter's patent-leather toe, and the mother admonished her in French before turning to apologize to Lord Peter.

"Mais je vous en prie, madame," said the young man, "it is nothing."

"She is nervous, pauvre petite," said the young woman.

"You are seeking advice for her?"

"Yes. He is wonderful, the doctor. Figure to yourself, monsieur, she cannot forget, poor child, the things she has seen." She leaned nearer, so that the child might not hear. "We have escaped—from starving Russia—six months ago. I dare not tell you—she has such quick ears, and then, the cries, the tremblings, the convulsions—they all begin again. We were skeletons when we arrived—mon Dieu!—but that is better now. See, she is thin, but she is not starved. She would be fatter but for the nerves that keep her from eating. We who are older, we forget—enfin, on apprend à ne pas y penser—but these children! When one is young, monsieur, tout ça impressionne trop."

Lord Peter, escaping from the thraldom of British good form, expressed himself in that language in which sympathy is not condemned to mutism.

"But she is much better, much better," said the mother, proudly; "the great doctor, he does marvels."

"C'est un homme précieux," said Lord Peter.

"Ah, monsieur, c'est un saint qui opère des miracles! Nous prions pour lui, Natasha et moi, tous les jours. N'est-ce pas, chérie? And consider, monsieur, that he does it all, ce grand homme, cet homme illustre, for nothing at all. When we come here, we have not even the clothes upon our backs—we are ruined, famished. Et avec ça que nous sommes de bonne famille—mais hélas! monsieur, en Russie, comme vous savez, ça ne vous vaut que des insultes—des atrocités. Enfin! the great Sir Julian sees us, he says—'Madame, your little girl is very interesting to me. Say no more. I cure her for nothing—pour ses beaux yeux,' a-t-il ajouté en riant. Ah, monsieur, c'est un saint, un véritable saint! and Natasha is much, much better."

"Madame, je vous en félicite."

"And you, monsieur? You are young, well, strong—you also suffer? It is still the war, perhaps?"

"A little remains of shell-shock," said Lord Peter.

"Ah, yes. So many good, brave, young men—"

"Sir Julian can spare you a few minutes, my lord, if you will come in now," said the servant.

Lord Peter bowed to his neighbour, and walked across the waiting-room. As the door of the consulting-room closed behind him, he remembered having once gone, disguised, into the staff-room of a German officer. He experienced the same feeling—the feeling of being caught in a trap, and a mingling of bravado and shame.

HE HAD SEEN SIR JULIAN FREKE SEVERAL TIMES FROM A DISTANCE, BUT NEVER close. Now, while carefully and quite truthfully detailing the circumstances of his recent nervous attack, he considered the man before him. A man taller than himself, with immense breadth of shoulder, and wonderful hands. A face beautiful, impassioned and inhuman; fanatical, compelling eyes, bright blue amid the ruddy bush of hair and beard. They were not the cool and kindly eyes of the family doctor, they were the brooding eyes of the inspired scientist, and they searched one through.

"Well," thought Lord Peter, "I shan't have to be explicit, anyhow."

"Yes," said Sir Julian, "yes. You had been working too hard. Puzzling your mind. Yes. More than that, perhaps—troubling your mind, shall we say?"

"I found myself faced with a very alarming contingency."

"Yes. Unexpectedly, perhaps."

"Very unexpected indeed."

"Yes. Following on a period of mental and physical strain."

"Well—perhaps. Nothing out of the way."

"Yes. The unexpected contingency was—personal to yourself?"

"It demanded an immediate decision as to my own actions—yes, in that sense it was certainly personal."

"Quite so. You would have to assume some responsibility, no doubt."

"A very grave responsibility."

"Affecting others besides yourself?"

"Affecting one other person vitally, and a very great number indirectly."

"Yes. The time was night. You were sitting in the dark?"

"Not at first. I think I put the light out afterwards."

"Quite so—that action would naturally suggest itself to you. Were you warm?"

"I think the fire had died down. My man tells me that my teeth were chattering when I went in to him."

"Yes. You live in Piccadilly?"

"Yes."

"Heavy traffic sometimes goes past during the night, I expect."

"Oh, frequently."

"Just so. Now this decision you refer to—you had taken that decision."

"Yes."

"Your mind was made up?"

"Oh, yes."

"You had decided to take the action, whatever it was."

"Yes."

"Yes. It involved perhaps a period of inaction."

"Of comparative inaction—yes."

"Of suspense, shall we say?"

"Yes—of suspense, certainly."

"Possibly of some danger?"

"I don't know that that was in my mind at the time."

"No—it was a case in which you could not possibly consider yourself."

"If you like to put it that way."

"Quite so. Yes. You had these attacks frequently in 1918?"

"Yes—I was very ill for some months."

"Quite. Since then they have recurred less frequently?"

"Much less frequently."

"Yes—when did the last occur?"

"About nine months ago."

"Under what circumstances?"

"I was being worried by certain family matters. It was a question of deciding about some investments, and I was largely responsible."

"Yes. You were interested last year, I think, in some police case?"

"Yes—in the recovery of Lord Attenbury's emerald necklace."

"That involved some severe mental exercise?"

"I suppose so. But I enjoyed it very much."

"Yes. Was the exertion of solving the problem attended by any bad results physically?"

"None."

"No. You were interested, but not distressed."

"Exactly."

"Yes. You have been engaged in other investigations of the kind?"

"Yes. Little ones."

"With bad results for your health?"

"Not a bit of it. On the contrary. I took up these cases as a sort of distraction. I had a bad knock just after the war, which didn't make matters any better for me, don't you know."

"Ah! you are not married?"

"No."

"No. Will you allow me to make an examination? Just come a little nearer to the light. I want to see your eyes. Whose advice have you had till now?"

"Sir James Hodges'."

"Ah! yes—he was a sad loss to the medical profession. A really great man—a true scientist. Yes. Thank you. Now I should like to try you with this little invention."

"What's it do?"

"Well—it tells me about your nervous reactions. Will you sit here?"

The examination that followed was purely medical. When it was concluded, Sir Julian said:

"Now, Lord Peter, I'll tell you about yourself in quite untechnical language—"

"Thanks," said Peter, "that's kind of you. I'm an awful fool about long words."

"Yes. Are you fond of private theatricals, Lord Peter?"

"Not particularly," said Peter, genuinely surprised. "Awful bore as a rule. Why?"

"I thought you might be," said the specialist, drily. "Well, now. You know quite well that the strain you put on your nerves during the war has left its mark on you. It has left what I may call old wounds in your brain. Sensations received by your nerve-endings sent messages to your brain, and produced minute physical changes there—changes we are only beginning to be able to detect, even with our most delicate instruments. These changes in their turn set up sensations; or I should say, more accurately, that sensations are the names we give to these changes of tissue when we perceive them: we call them horror, fear, sense of responsibility and so on."

"Yes, I follow you."

"Very well. Now, if you stimulate those damaged places in your brain again, you run the risk of opening up the old wounds. I mean, that if you get nerve-sensations of any kind producing the reactions which we call horror, fear, and sense of responsibility, they may go on to make disturbance right along the old channel, and produce in their turn physical changes which you will call by the names you were accustomed to associate with them—dread of German mines, responsibility for the lives of your men, strained attention and the inability to distinguish small sounds through the overpowering noise of guns."

"I see."

"This effect would be increased by extraneous circumstances producing other familiar physical sensations—night, cold or the rattling of heavy traffic, for instance."

"Yes."

"Yes. The old wounds are nearly healed, but not quite. The ordinary exercise of your mental faculties has no bad effect. It is only when you excite the injured part of your brain."

"Yes, I see."

"Yes. You must avoid these occasions. You must learn to be irresponsible, Lord Peter."

"My friends say I'm only too irresponsible already."

"Very likely. A sensitive nervous temperament often appears so, owing to its mental nimbleness."

"Oh!"

"Yes. This particular responsibility you were speaking of still rests upon you?"

"Yes, it docs."

"You have not yet completed the course of action on which you have decided?"

"Not yet."

"You feel bound to carry it through?"

"Oh, yes—I can't back out of it now."

"No. You are expecting further strain?"

"A certain amount."

"Do you expect it to last much longer?"

"Very little longer now."

"Ah! Your nerves are not all they should be."

"No?"

"No. Nothing to be alarmed about, but you must exercise care while undergoing this strain, and afterwards you should take a complete rest. How about a voyage in the Mediterranean or the South Seas or somewhere?"

"Thanks. I'll think about it."

"Meanwhile, to carry you over the immediate trouble I will give you something to strengthen your nerves. It will do you no permanent good, you understand, but it will tide you over the bad time. And I will give you a prescription."

"Thank you."

Sir Julian got up and went into a small surgery leading out of the consulting-room. Lord Peter watched him moving about—boiling something and writing. Presently he returned with a paper and a hypodermic syringe.

"Here is the prescription. And now, if you will just roll up your sleeve, I will deal with the necessity of the immediate moment."

Lord Peter obediently rolled up his sleeve. Sir Julian Freke selected a portion of his forearm and anointed it with iodine.

"What's that you're goin' to stick into me. Bugs?"

The surgeon laughed.

"Not exactly," he said. He pinched up a portion of flesh between his finger and thumb. "You've had this kind of thing before, I expect."

"Oh, yes," said Lord Peter. He watched the cool fingers, fascinated, and the steady approach of the needle. "Yes—I've had it before—and, d'you know—I don't care frightfully about it."

He had brought up his right hand, and it closed over the surgeon's wrist like a vice.

The silence was like a shock. The blue eyes did not waver; they burned down steadily upon the heavy white lids below them. Then these slowly lifted; the grey eyes met the blue—coldly, steadily—and held them.

When lovers embrace, there seems no sound in the world but their own breathing. So the two men breathed face to face.

"As you like, of course, Lord Peter," said Sir Julian, courteously.

"Afraid I'm rather a silly ass," said Lord Peter, "but I never could abide these little gadgets. I had one once that went wrong and gave me a rotten bad time. They make me a bit nervous."

"In that case," replied Sir Julian, "it would certainly be better not to have the injection. It might rouse up just those sensations which we are desirous of avoiding. You will take the prescription, then, and do what you can to lessen the immediate strain as far as possible."

"Oh, yes—I'll take it easy, thanks," said Lord Peter. He rolled his sleeve down neatly. "I'm much obliged to you. If I have any further trouble I'll look in again."

"Do—do—" said Sir Julian, cheerfully. "Only make an appointment another time. I'm rather rushed these days. I hope your mother is quite well. I saw her the other day at that Battersea inquest. You should have been there. It would have interested you."

CHAPTER XII

The vile, raw fog tore your throat and ravaged your eyes. You could not see your feet. You stumbled in your walk over poor men's graves.

The feel of Parker's old trench-coat beneath your fingers was comforting. You had felt it in worse places. You clung on now for fear you should get separated. The dim people moving in front of you were like Brocken spectres.

"Take care, gentlemen," said a toneless voice out of the yellow darkness, "there's an open grave just hereabouts."

You bore away to the right, and floundered in a mass of freshly turned clay.

"Hold up, old man," said Parker.

"Where is Lady Levy?"

"In the mortuary; the Duchess of Denver is with her. Your mother is wonderful, Peter."

"Isn't she?" said Lord Peter.

A dim blue light carried by somebody ahead wavered and stood still.

"Here you are," said a voice.

Two Dantesque shapes with pitchforks loomed up.

"Have you finished?" asked somebody.

"Nearly done, sir." The demons fell to work again with the pitchforks—no, spades.

Somebody sneezed. Parker located the sneezer and introduced him.

"Mr. Levett represents the Home Secretary. Lord Peter Wimsey. We are sorry to drag you out on such a day, Mr. Levett."

"It's all in the day's work," said Mr. Levett, hoarsely. He was muffled to the eyes.

The sound of the spades for many minutes. An iron noise of tools thrown down. Demons stooping and straining.

A black-bearded spectre at your elbow. Introduced. The Master of the Workhouse.

"A very painful matter, Lord Peter. You will forgive me for hoping you and Mr. Parker may be mistaken."

"I should like to be able to hope so too."

Something heaving, straining, coming up out of the ground.

"Steady, men. This way. Can you see? Be careful of the graves—they lie pretty thick hereabouts. Are you ready?"

"Right you are, sir. You go on with the lantern. We can follow you."

Lumbering footsteps. Catch hold of Parker's trench-coat again. "That you, old man? Oh, I beg your pardon, Mr. Levett—thought you were Parker."

"Hullo, Wimsey—here you are."

More graves. A headstone shouldered crookedly aslant. A trip and jerk over the edge of the rough grass. The squeal of gravel under your feet.

"This way, gentlemen, mind the step."

The mortuary. Raw red brick and sizzling gas-jets. Two women in black, and Dr. Grimbold. The coffin laid on the table with a heavy thump.

"'Ave you got that there screw-driver, Bill? Thank 'ee. Be keerful wi' the chisel now. Not much substance to these 'ere boards, sir."

Several long creaks. A sob. The Duchess's voice, kind but peremptory.

"Hush, Christine. You mustn't cry."

A mutter of voices. The lurching departure of the Dante demons—good, decent demons in corduroy.

Dr. Grimbold's voice—cool and detached as if in the consulting room.

"Now—have you got that lamp, Mr. Wingate? Thank you. Yes, here on the table, please. Be careful not to catch your elbow in the flex, Mr.

Levett. It would be better, I think, if you came on this side. Yes—yes—thank you. That's excellent."

The sudden brilliant circle of an electric lamp over the table. Dr. Grimbold's beard and spectacles. Mr. Levett blowing his nose. Parker bending close. The Master of the Workhouse peering over him. The rest of the room in the enhanced dimness of the gas-jets and the fog.

A low murmur of voices. All heads bent over the work.

Dr. Grimbold again—beyond the circle of the lamplight.

"We don't want to distress you unnecessarily, Lady Levy. If you will just tell us what to look for—the—? Yes, yes, certainly—and—yes—stopped with gold? Yes—the lower jaw, the last but one on the right? Yes—no teeth missing—no—yes? What kind of a mole? Yes—just over the left breast? Oh, I beg your pardon, just under—yes—appendicitis? Yes—a long one—yes—in the middle? Yes, I quite understand—a scar on the arm? Yes, I don't know if we shall be able to find that—yes—any little constitutional weakness that might—? Oh, yes—arthritis—yes—thank you, Lady Levy—that's very clear. Don't come unless I ask you to. Now, Wingate."

A pause. A murmur. "Pulled out? After death, you think—well, so do I. Where is Dr. Colegrove? You attended this man in the workhouse? Yes. Do you recollect—? No? You're quite certain about that? Yes—we mustn't make a mistake, you know. Yes, but there are reasons why Sir Julian can't be present; I'm asking _you_, Dr. Colegrove. Well, you're certain—that's all I want to know. Just bring the light closer, Mr. Wingate, if you please. These miserable shells let the damp in so quickly. Ah! what do you make of this? Yes—yes—well, that's rather unmistakable, isn't it? Who did the head? Oh, Freke—of course. I was going to say they did good work at St. Luke's. Beautiful, isn't it, Dr. Colegrove? A wonderful surgeon—I saw him when he was at Guy's. Oh, no, gave it up years ago. Nothing like keeping your hand in. Ah—yes, undoubtedly that's it. Have you a towel handy, sir? Thank you. Over the head, if you please—I think we might have another here. Now, Lady Levy—I am going to ask you to look at a scar, and see if you recognise it. I'm sure you are going to help us by being very firm. Take your time—you won't see anything more than you absolutely must."

"Lucy, don't leave me."

"No, dear."

A space cleared at the table. The lamplight on the Duchess's white hair.

"Oh, yes—oh, yes! No, no—I couldn't be mistaken. There's that funny little kink in it. I've seen it hundreds of times. Oh, Lucy—Reuben!"

"Only a moment more, Lady Levy. The mole—"

"I—I think so—oh, yes, that is the very place."

"Yes. And the scar—was it three-cornered, just above the elbow?"

"Yes, oh, yes."

"Is this it?"

"Yes—yes—"

"I must ask you definitely, Lady Levy. Do you, from these three marks identify the body as that of your husband?"

"Oh! I must, mustn't I? Nobody else could have them just the same in just those places? It is my husband. It is Reuben. Oh—"

"Thank you, Lady Levy. You have been very brave and very helpful."

"But—I don't understand yet. How did he come here? Who did this dreadful thing?"

"Hush, dear," said the Duchess; "the man is going to be punished."

"Oh, but—how cruel! Poor Reuben! Who could have wanted to hurt him? Can I see his face?"

"No, dear," said the Duchess. "That isn't possible. Come away—you mustn't distress the doctors and people."

"No—no—they've all been so kind. Oh, Lucy!"

"We'll go home, dear. You don't want us any more, Dr. Grimbold?"

"No, Duchess, thank you. We are very grateful to you and to Lady Levy for coming."

There was a pause, while the two women went out, Parker, collected and helpful, escorting them to their waiting car. Then Dr. Grimbold again:

"I think Lord Peter Wimsey ought to see—the correctness of his deductions—Lord Peter—very painful—you may wish to see—yes, I was uneasy at the inquest—yes—Lady Levy—remarkably clear evidence— yes—most shocking case—ah, here's Mr. Parker—you and Lord Peter Wimsey entirely justified—do I really understand—? Really? I can hardly believe it—so distinguished a man—as you say, when a great brain turns to crime—yes—look here! Marvellous work—marvellous—somewhat obscured by this time, of course—but the most beautiful sections—here, you see, the left hemisphere—and here—through the corpus striatum— here again—the very track of the damage done by the blow—wonderful—

guessed it—saw the effect of the blow as he struck it, you know—ah, I should like to see _his_ brain, Mr. Parker—and to think that—heavens, Lord Peter, you don't know what a blow you have struck at the whole profession—the whole civilized world! Oh, my dear sir! Can you ask me? My lips are sealed of course—all our lips are sealed."

The way back through the burial ground. Fog again, and the squeal of wet gravel.

"Are your men ready, Charles?"

"They have gone. I sent them off when I saw Lady Levy to the car."

"Who is with them?"

"Sugg."

"Sugg?"

"Yes—poor devil. They've had him up on the mat at headquarters for bungling the case. All that evidence of Thipps's about the night club was corroborated, you know. That girl he gave the gin-and-bitters to was caught, and came and identified him, and they decided their case wasn't good enough, and let Thipps and the Horrocks girl go. Then they told Sugg he had overstepped his duty and ought to have been more careful. So he ought, but he can't help being a fool. I was sorry for him. It may do him some good to be in at the death. After all, Peter, you and I had special advantages."

"Yes. Well, it doesn't matter. Whoever goes won't get there in time. Sugg's as good as another."

But Sugg—an experience rare in his career—was in time.

Parker and Lord Peter were at 110 Piccadilly. Lord Peter was playing Bach and Parker was reading Origen when Sugg was announced.

"We've got our man, sir," said he.

"Good God!" said Peter. "Alive?"

"We were just in time, my lord. We rang the bell and marched straight up past his man to the library. He was sitting there doing some writing. When we came in, he made a grab for his hypodermic, but we were too quick for him, my lord. We didn't mean to let him slip through our hands, having got so far. We searched him thoroughly and marched him off."

"He is actually in gaol, then?"

"Oh, yes—safe enough—with two warders to see he doesn't make away with himself."

"You surprise me, Inspector. Have a drink."

"Thank you, my lord. I may say that I'm very grateful to you—this case was turning out a pretty bad egg for me. If I was rude to your lordship—"

"Oh, it's all right, Inspector," said Lord Peter, hastily. "I don't see how you could possibly have worked it out. I had the good luck to know something about it from other sources."

"That's what Freke says." Already the great surgeon was a common criminal in the inspector's eyes—a mere surname. "He was writing a full confession when we got hold of him, addressed to your lordship. The police will have to have it, of course, but seeing it's written for you, I brought it along for you to see first. Here it is."

He handed Lord Peter a bulky document.

"Thanks," said Peter. "Like to hear it, Charles?"

"Rather."

Accordingly Lord Peter read it aloud.

CHAPTER XIII

Dear Lord Peter—When I was a young man I used to play chess with an old friend of my father's. He was a very bad, and a very slow, player, and he could never see when a checkmate was inevitable, but insisted on playing every move out. I never had any patience with that kind of attitude, and I will freely admit now that the game is yours. I must either stay at home and be hanged or escape abroad and live in an idle and insecure obscurity. I prefer to acknowledge defeat.

If you have read my book on "Criminal Lunacy," you will remember that I wrote: "In the majority of cases, the criminal betrays himself by some abnormality attendant upon this pathological condition of the nervous tissues. His mental instability shows itself in various forms: an overweening vanity, leading him to brag of his achievement; a disproportionate sense of the importance of the offence, resulting from the hallucination of religion, and driving him to confession; egomania, producing the sense of horror or conviction of sin, and driving him to headlong flight without covering his tracks; a reckless confidence, resulting in the neglect of the most ordinary precautions, as in the case of Henry Wainwright, who left a boy in charge of the murdered woman's remains while he went to call a cab, or on the other hand, a nervous distrust of apperceptions in the past, causing him to revisit the scene of the crime to assure himself that all traces have been as safely removed as _his own judgment knows them to be_. I will not hesitate to assert that a perfectly sane man, not intimidated by religious or other delusions, could always render himself perfectly secure from detection, provided, that is, that the crime were sufficiently premeditated and that he were not pressed for time or thrown out in his calculations by purely fortuitous coincidence.

You know as well as I do, how far I have made this assertion good in practice. The two accidents which betrayed me, I could not by any possibility have foreseen. The first was the chance recognition of Levy by the girl in the Battersea Park Road, which suggested a connection between the two problems. The second was that Thipps should have arranged to go down to Denver on the Tuesday morning, thus enabling your mother to get word of the matter through to you before the body was removed by the police and to suggest a motive for the murder out of what she knew of my previous personal history. If I had been able to destroy these two accidentally forged links of circumstance, I will venture to say that you would never have so much as suspected me, still less obtained sufficient evidence to convict.

Of all human emotions, except perhaps those of hunger and fear, the sexual appetite produces the most violent, and, under some circumstances, the most persistent reactions; I think, however, I am right in saying that at the time when I wrote my book, my original sensual impulse to kill Sir Reuben Levy had already become profoundly modified by my habits of thought. To the animal lust to slay and the primitive human desire for revenge, there was added the rational intention of substantiating my own theories for the satisfaction of myself and the world. If all had turned out as I had planned, I should have deposited a sealed account of my experiment with the Bank of England, instructing my executors to publish it after my death. Now that accident has spoiled the completeness of my demonstration, I entrust the account to you, whom it cannot fail to interest, with the request that you will make it known among scientific men, in justice to my professional reputation.

The really essential factors of success in any undertaking are money and opportunity, and as a rule, the man who can make the first can make the second. During my early career, though I was fairly well-off, I had not absolute command of circumstance. Accordingly I devoted myself to my profession, and contented myself with keeping up a friendly connection with Reuben Levy and his family. This enabled me to remain in touch with his fortunes and interests, so that, when the moment for action should arrive, I might know what weapons to use.

Meanwhile, I carefully studied criminology in fiction and fact—my work on "Criminal Lunacy" was a side-product of this activity—and saw how, in every murder, the real crux of the problem was the disposal of the body. As a doctor, the means of death were always ready to my hand, and I was not likely to make any error in that connection. Nor was I likely to betray myself on account of any illusory sense of wrong-doing. The sole difficulty would be that of destroying all connection between my personality and that of the corpse. You will remember that Michael Finsbury, in Stevenson's entertaining romance, observes: "What hangs people is the unfortunate circumstance of guilt." It became clear to me that the mere leaving about of a superfluous corpse could convict nobody, provided that nobody was guilty in connection _with that particular corpse_. Thus the idea of substituting the one body for the other was early arrived at, though it was not till I obtained the practical direction of St. Luke's Hospital that I found myself perfectly unfettered in the choice and handling of dead bodies. From this period on, I kept a careful watch on all the material brought in for dissection.

My opportunity did not present itself until the week before Sir Reuben's disappearance, when the medical officer at the Chelsea workhouse sent word to me that an unknown vagrant had been injured that morning by the fall of a piece of scaffolding, and was exhibiting some very interesting nervous and cerebral reactions. I went round and saw the case, and was immediately struck by the man's strong superficial resemblance to Sir Reuben. He had been heavily struck on the back of the neck, dislocating the fourth and fifth cervical vertebrae and heavily bruising the spinal cord. It seemed highly unlikely that he could ever recover, either mentally or physically, and in any case there appeared to me to be no object in indefinitely prolonging so unprofitable an existence. He had obviously been able to support life until recently, as he was fairly well nourished, but the state of his feet and clothing showed that he was unemployed, and under present conditions he was likely to remain so. I decided that he would suit my purpose very well, and immediately put in train certain transactions in the City which I had already sketched out in my own mind. In the meantime, the reactions mentioned by the workhouse doctor were interesting, and I made careful studies of them, and arranged for the delivery of the body to the hospital when I should have completed my preparations.

On the Thursday and Friday of that week I made private arrangements with various brokers to buy the stock of certain Peruvian Oil-fields, which had gone down almost to waste-paper. This part of my experiment did not cost me very much, but I contrived to arouse considerable curiosity, and even a mild excitement. At this point I was of course careful not to let my name appear. The incidence of Saturday and Sunday gave me some anxiety lest my man should after all die before I was ready for him, but by the use of saline injections I contrived to keep him alive and, late on Sunday night, he even manifested disquieting symptoms of at any rate a partial recovery.

On Monday morning the market in Peruvians opened briskly. Rumours had evidently got about that somebody knew something, and this day I was not the only buyer in the market. I bought a couple of hundred more shares in my own name, and left the matter to take care of itself. At lunch time I made my arrangements to run into Levy accidentally at the corner of the Mansion House. He expressed (as I expected) his surprise at seeing me in that part of London. I simulated some embarrassment and suggested that we should lunch together. I dragged him to a place a bit off the usual beat, and there ordered a good wine and drank of it as much as he might suppose sufficient to induce a confidential mood. I asked him how things were going on 'Change. He said, "Oh, all right," but appeared a little doubtful, and asked me whether I did anything in that way. I said I had a little flutter occasionally, and that, as a matter of fact, I'd been put on to rather a good thing. I glanced round apprehensively at this point, and shifted my chair nearer to his.

"I suppose you don't know anything about Peruvian Oil, do you?" he said.

I started and looked round again, and leaning across to him, said, dropping my voice:

"Well, I do, as a matter of fact, but I don't want it to get about. I stand to make a good bit on it."

"But I thought the thing was hollow," he said; "it hasn't paid a dividend for umpteen years."

"No," I said, "it hasn't, but it's going to. I've got inside information." He looked a bit unconvinced, and I emptied off my glass, and edged right up to his ear.

"Look here," I said, "I'm not giving this away to everyone, but I don't mind doing you and Christine a good turn. You know, I've always kept a soft place in my heart for her, ever since the old days. You got in ahead of me that time, and now it's up to me to heap coals of fire on you both."

I was a little excited by this time, and he thought I was drunk.

"It's very kind of you, old man," he said, "but I'm a cautious bird, you know, always was. I'd like a bit of proof."

And he shrugged up his shoulders and looked like a pawnbroker.

"I'll give it to you," I said, "but it isn't safe here. Come round to my place tonight after dinner, and I'll show you the report."

"How d'you get hold of it?" said he.

"I'll tell you tonight," said I. "Come round after dinner—any time after nine, say."

"To Harley Street?" he asked, and I saw that he meant coming.

"No," I said, "to Battersea—Prince of Wales Road; I've got some work to do at the hospital. And look here," I said, "don't you let on to a soul that you're coming. I bought a couple of hundred shares today, in my own name, and people are sure to get wind of it. If we're known to be about together, someone'll twig something. In fact, it's anything but safe talking about it in this place."

"All right," he said, "I won't say a word to anybody. I'll turn up about nine o'clock. You're sure it's a sound thing?"

"It can't go wrong," I assured him. And I meant it.

We parted after that, and I went round to the workhouse. My man had died at about eleven o'clock. I had seen him just after breakfast, and was not surprised. I completed the usual formalities with the workhouse authorities, and arranged for his delivery at the hospital at about seven o'clock.

In the afternoon, as it was not one of my days to be in Harley Street, I looked up an old friend who lives close to Hyde Park, and found that he was just off to Brighton on some business or other. I had tea with him, and saw him off by the 5.35 from Victoria. On issuing from the barrier it occurred to me to purchase an evening paper, and I thoughtlessly turned my steps to the bookstall. The usual crowds were rushing to catch suburban trains home, and on moving away I found myself involved in a contrary stream of travellers coming up out of the Underground, or bolting from all sides for the 5.45 to Battersea Park and Wandsworth Common. I disengaged myself after some buffeting and went home in a taxi; and it was not till I was safely seated there that I discovered somebody's gold-rimmed pince-nez involved in the astrakhan collar of my overcoat. The time from 6.15 to seven I spent concocting something to look like a bogus report for Sir Reuben.

At seven I went through to the hospital, and found the workhouse van just delivering my subject at the side door. I had him taken straight up to the theatre, and told the attendant, William Watts, that I intended to work there that night. I told him I would prepare the body myself—the injection of a preservative would have been a most regrettable complication. I sent him about his business, and then went home and had dinner. I told my man that I should be working in the hospital that evening, and that he could go to bed at 10.30 as usual, as I could not tell whether I should be late or not. He is used to my erratic ways. I only keep two servants in the Battersea house—the man-servant and his wife, who cooks for me. The rougher domestic work is done by a charwoman, who sleeps out. The servants' bedroom is at the top of the house, overlooking Prince of Wales Road.

As soon as I had dined I established myself in the hall with some papers. My man had cleared dinner by a quarter past eight, and I told him to give me the syphon and tantalus; and sent him downstairs. Levy rang the bell at twenty minutes past nine, and I opened the door to him myself. My man appeared at the other end of the hall, but I called to him that it was all right, and he went away. Levy wore an overcoat with evening dress and carried an umbrella. "Why, how wet you are!" I said.

"How did you come?" "By 'bus," he said, "and the fool of a conductor forgot to put me down at the end of the road. It's pouring cats and dogs and pitch-dark—I couldn't see where I was." I was glad he hadn't taken a taxi, but I had rather reckoned on his not doing so. "Your little economies will be the death of you one of these days," I said. I was right there, but I hadn't reckoned on their being the death of me as well. I say again, I could not have foreseen it.

I sat him down by the fire, and gave him a whisky. He was in high spirits about some deal in Argentines he was bringing off the next day. We talked money for about a quarter of an hour and then he said:

"Well, how about this Peruvian mare's-nest of yours?"

"It's no mare's-nest," I said; "come and have a look at it."

I took him upstairs into the library, and switched on the centre light and the reading lamp on the writing table. I gave him a chair at the table with his back to the fire, and fetched the papers I had been faking, out of the safe. He took them, and began to read them, poking over them in his short-sighted way, while I mended the fire. As soon as I saw his head in a favourable position I struck him heavily with the poker, just over the fourth cervical. It was delicate work calculating the exact force necessary to kill him without breaking the skin, but my professional experience was useful to me. He gave one loud gasp, and tumbled forward on to the table quite noiselessly. I put the poker back, and examined him. His neck was broken, and he was quite dead. I carried him into my bedroom and undressed him. It was about ten minutes to ten when I had finished. I put him away under my bed, which had been turned down for the night, and cleared up the papers in the library. Then I went downstairs, took Levy's umbrella, and let myself out at the hall door, shouting "Good-night" loudly enough to be heard in the basement if the servants should be listening. I walked briskly away down the street, went in by the hospital side door, and returned to the house noiselessly by way of the private passage. It would have been awkward if anybody had seen me then, but I leaned over the back stairs and heard the cook and her husband still talking in the kitchen. I slipped back into the hall, replaced the umbrella in the stand, cleared up my papers there, went up into the library and rang the bell. When the man appeared I told him to lock up everything except the private door to the hospital. I waited in the library until he had done so, and about 10.30 I heard both servants go up to bed. I waited a quarter of an hour longer and then went through to the dissecting-room. I wheeled one of the stretcher tables through the passage to the house door, and then went to fetch Levy. It was a nuisance having to get him downstairs, but I had not liked to make away with him in any of the ground-floor rooms, in case my servant should take a fancy to poke his head in during the few minutes that I was out of the house, or while locking up. Besides, that was a flea-bite to what I should have to do later. I put Levy on the table, wheeled him across to the hospital and substituted him for my interesting pauper. I was sorry to have to abandon the idea of getting a look at the latter's brain, but I could not afford to incur suspicion. It was still rather early, so I knocked down a few minutes getting Levy ready for dissection. Then I put my pauper on the table and trundled him over to the house. It was now five past eleven, and I thought I might conclude that the servants were in bed. I carried the body into my bedroom. He was rather heavy, but less so than Levy, and my Alpine experience had taught me how to handle bodies. It is as much a matter of knack as of strength, and I am, in any case, a powerful man for my height. I put the body into the bed—not that I expected anyone to look in during my absence, but if they should they might just as well see me apparently asleep in bed. I drew the clothes a little over his head, stripped, and put on Levy's clothes, which were fortunately a little big for me everywhere, not forgetting to take his spectacles, watch and other oddments. At a little before half-past eleven I was in the road looking for a cab. People were just beginning to come home from the theatre, and I easily secured one at the corner of Prince of Wales Road. I told the man to drive me to Hyde Park Corner. There I got out, tipped him well, and asked him to pick me up again at the same place in an hour's time. He assented with an understanding grin, and I walked on up Park Lane. I had my own clothes with me in a suitcase, and carried my own overcoat and Levy's umbrella. When I got to No. 9A there were lights in some of the top windows. I was very nearly too early, owing to the old man's having sent the servants to the theatre. I waited about for a few minutes, and heard it strike the quarter past midnight. The lights were extinguished shortly after, and I let myself in with Levy's key.

It had been my original intention, when I thought over this plan of murder, to let Levy disappear from the study or the dining-room, leaving only a heap of clothes on the hearth-rug. The accident of my having been able to secure Lady Levy's absence from London, however, made possible a solution more misleading, though less pleasantly fantastic. I turned on the hall light, hung up Levy's wet overcoat and placed his umbrella in the stand. I walked up noisily and heavily to the bedroom and turned off the light by the duplicate switch on the landing. I knew the house well enough, of course. There was no chance of my running into the man-servant. Old Levy was a simple old man, who liked doing things for himself. He gave his valet little work, and never required any attendance at night. In the bedroom I took off Levy's gloves and put on a surgical pair, so as to leave no tell-tale finger-prints. As I wished to convey the impression that Levy had gone to bed in the usual way, I simply went to bed. The surest and simplest method of making a thing appear to have been done is to do it. A bed that has been rumpled about with one's hands, for instance, never looks like a bed that has been slept in. I dared not use Levy's brush, of course, as my hair is not of his colour, but I did everything else. I supposed that a thoughtful old man like Levy would put his boots handy for his valet, and I ought to have deduced that he would fold up his clothes. That was a mistake, but not an important one. Remembering that well-thought-out little work of Mr. Bentley's, I had examined Levy's mouth for false teeth, but he had none. I did not forget, however, to wet his tooth-brush.

At one o'clock I got up and dressed in my own clothes by the light of my own pocket torch. I dared not turn on the bedroom lights, as there were light blinds to the windows. I put on my own boots and an old pair of goloshes outside the door. There was a thick Turkey carpet on the stairs and hall-floor, and I was not afraid of leaving marks. I hesitated whether to chance the banging of the front door, but decided it would be safer to take the latchkey. (It is now in the Thames. I dropped it over Battersea Bridge the next day.) I slipped quietly down, and listened for a few minutes with my ear to the letter-box. I heard a constable tramp past. As soon as his steps had died away in the distance I stepped out and pulled the door gingerly to. It closed almost soundlessly, and I walked away to pick up my cab. I had an overcoat of much the same pattern as Levy's, and had taken the precaution to pack an opera hat in my suitcase. I hoped the man would not notice that I had no umbrella this time. Fortunately the rain had diminished for the moment to a sort of drizzle, and if he noticed anything he made no observation. I told him to stop at 50 Overstrand Mansions, and I paid him off there, and stood under the porch till he had driven away. Then I hurried round to my own side door and let myself in. It was about a quarter to two, and the harder part of my task still lay before me.

My first step was so to alter the appearance of my subject as to eliminate any immediate suggestion either of Levy or of the workhouse vagrant. A fairly superficial alteration was all I considered necessary, since there was not likely to be any hue-and-cry after the pauper. He was fairly accounted for, and his deputy was at hand to represent him. Nor, if Levy was after all traced to my house, would it be difficult to show that the body in evidence was, as a matter of fact, not his. A clean shave and a little hair-oiling and manicuring seemed sufficient to suggest a distinct personality for my silent accomplice. His hands had been well washed in hospital, and though calloused, were not grimy. I was not able to do the work as thoroughly as I should have liked, because time was getting on. I was not sure how long it would take me to dispose of him, and moreover, I feared the onset of _rigor mortis_, which would make my task more difficult. When I had him barbered to my satisfaction, I fetched a strong sheet and a couple of wide roller bandages, and fastened him up carefully, padding him with cotton wool wherever the bandages might chafe or leave a bruise.

Now came the really ticklish part of the business. I had already decided in my own mind that the only way of conveying him from the house was by the roof. To go through the garden at the back in this soft wet weather was to leave a ruinous trail behind us. To carry a dead man down a suburban street in the middle of the night seemed outside the range of practical politics. On the roof, on the other hand, the rain, which would have betrayed me on the ground, would stand my friend.

To reach the roof, it was necessary to carry my burden to the top of the house, past my servants' room, and hoist him out through the trap-door in the box-room roof. Had it merely been a question of going quietly up there myself, I should have had no fear of waking the servants, but to do so burdened by a heavy body was more difficult. It would be possible, provided that the man and his wife were soundly asleep, but if not, the lumbering tread on the narrow stair and the noise of opening the trap-door would be only too plainly audible. I tiptoed delicately up the stair and listened at their door. To my disgust I heard the man give a grunt and mutter something as he moved in his bed.

I looked at my watch. My preparations had taken nearly an hour, first and last, and I dared not be too late on the roof. I determined to take a bold step and, as it were, bluff out an alibi. I went without precaution against noise into the bathroom, turned on the hot and cold water taps to the full and pulled out the plug.

My household has often had occasion to complain of my habit of using the bath at irregular night hours. Not only does the rush of water into the cistern disturb any sleepers on the Prince of Wales Road side of the house, but my cistern is afflicted with peculiarly loud gurglings and thumpings, while frequently the pipes emit a loud groaning sound. To my delight, on this particular occasion, the cistern was in excellent form, honking, whistling and booming like a railway terminus. I gave the noise five minutes' start, and when I calculated that the sleepers would have finished cursing me and put their heads under the clothes to shut out the din, I reduced the flow of water to a small stream and left the bathroom, taking good care to leave the light burning and lock the door after me. Then I picked up my pauper and carried him upstairs as lightly as possible.

The box-room is a small attic on the side of the landing opposite to the servants' bedroom and the cistern-room. It has a trap-door, reached by a short, wooden ladder. I set this up, hoisted up my pauper and climbed up after him. The water was still racing into the cistern, which was making a noise as though it were trying to digest an iron chain, and with the reduced flow in the bathroom the groaning of the pipes had risen almost to a hoot. I was not afraid of anybody hearing other noises. I pulled the ladder through on to the roof after me.

Between my house and the last house in Queen Caroline Mansions there is a space of only a few feet. Indeed, when the Mansions were put up, I believe there was some trouble about ancient lights, but I suppose the parties compromised somehow. Anyhow, my seven-foot ladder reached well across. I tied the body firmly to the ladder, and pushed it over till the far end was resting on the parapet of the opposite house. Then I took a short run across the cistern-room and the box-room roof, and landed easily on the other side, the parapet being happily both low and narrow.

The rest was simple. I carried my pauper along the flat roofs, intending to leave him, like the hunchback in the story, on someone's staircase or down a chimney. I had got about half-way along when I suddenly thought, "Why, this must be about little Thipps's place," and I remembered his silly face, and his silly chatter about vivisection. It occurred to me pleasantly how delightful it would be to deposit my parcel with him and see what he made of it. I lay down and peered over the parapet at the back. It was pitch-dark and pouring with rain again by this time, and I risked using my torch. That was the only incautious thing I did, and the odds against being seen from the houses opposite were long enough. One second's flash showed me what I had hardly dared to hope—an open window just below me.

I knew those flats well enough to be sure it was either the bathroom or the kitchen. I made a noose in a third bandage that I had brought with me, and made it fast under the arms of the corpse. I twisted it into a double rope, and secured the end to the iron stanchion of a chimney-stack. Then I dangled our friend over. I went down after him myself with the aid of a drain-pipe and was soon hauling him in by Thipps's bathroom window.

By that time I had got a little conceited with myself, and spared a few minutes to lay him out prettily and make him shipshape. A sudden inspiration suggested that I should give him the pair of pince-nez which I had happened to pick up at Victoria. I came across them in my pocket while I was looking for a penknife to loosen a knot, and I saw what distinction they would lend his appearance, besides making it more misleading. I fixed them on him, effaced all traces of my presence as far as possible, and departed as I had come, going easily up between the drain-pipe and the rope.

I walked quietly back, re-crossed my crevasse and carried in my ladder and sheet. My discreet accomplice greeted me with a reassuring gurgle and thump. I didn't make a sound on the stairs. Seeing that I had now been having a bath for about three-quarters of an hour, I turned the water off, and enabled my deserving domestics to get a little sleep. I also felt it was time I had a little myself.

First, however, I had to go over to the hospital and make all safe there. I took off Levy's head, and started to open up the face. In twenty minutes his own wife could not have recognised him. I returned, leaving my wet goloshes and mackintosh by the garden door. My trousers I dried by the gas stove in my bedroom, and brushed away all traces of mud and brickdust. My pauper's beard I burned in the library.

I got a good two hours' sleep from five to seven, when my man called me as usual. I apologized for having kept the water running so long and so late, and added that I thought I would have the cistern seen to.

I was interested to note that I was rather extra hungry at breakfast, showing that my night's work had caused a certain wear-and-tear of tissue. I went over afterwards to continue my dissection. During the morning a peculiarly thick-headed police inspector came to inquire whether a body had escaped from the hospital. I had him brought to me where I was, and had the pleasure of showing him the work I was doing on Sir Reuben Levy's head. Afterwards I went round with him to Thipps's and was able to satisfy myself that my pauper looked very convincing.

As soon as the Stock Exchange opened I telephoned my various brokers, and by exercising a little care, was able to sell out the greater part of my Peruvian stock on a rising market. Towards the end of the day, however, buyers became rather unsettled as a result of Levy's death, and in the end I did not make more than a few hundreds by the transaction.

Trusting I have now made clear to you any point which you may have found obscure, and with congratulations on the good fortune and perspicacity which have enabled you to defeat me, I remain, with kind remembrances to your mother,

    Yours very truly,
    JULIAN FREKE

Post-Scriptum: My will is made, leaving my money to St. Luke's Hospital, and bequeathing my body to the same institution for dissection. I feel sure that my brain will be of interest to the scientific world. As I shall die by my own hand, I imagine that there may be a little difficulty about this. Will you do me the favour, if you can, of seeing the persons concerned in the inquest, and obtaining that the brain is not damaged by an unskilful practitioner at the post-mortem, and that the body is disposed of according to my wish?

By the way, it may be of interest to you to know that I appreciated your motive in calling this afternoon. It conveyed a warning, and I am acting upon it in spite of the disastrous consequences to myself. I was pleased to realize that you had not underestimated my nerve and intelligence, and refused the injection. Had you submitted to it, you would, of course, never have reached home alive. No trace would have been left in your body of the injection, which consisted of a harmless preparation of strychnine, mixed with an almost unknown poison, for which there is at present no recognised test, a concentrated solution of sn—

At this point the manuscript broke off.

"Well, that's all clear enough," said Parker.

"Isn't it queer?" said Lord Peter. "All that coolness, all those brains— and then he couldn't resist writing a confession to show how clever he was, even to keep his head out of the noose."

"And a very good thing for us," said Inspector Sugg, "but Lord bless you, sir, these criminals are all alike."

"Freke's epitaph," said Parker, when the Inspector had departed. "What next, Peter?"

"I shall now give a dinner party," said Lord Peter, "to Mr. John P. Milligan and his secretary and to Messrs. Crimplesham and Wicks. I feel they deserve it for not having murdered Levy."

"Well, don't forget the Thippses," said Mr. Parker.

"On no account," said Lord Peter, "would I deprive myself of the pleasure of Mrs. Thipps's company. Bunter!"

"My lord?"

"The Napoleon brandy."

END

READING BREAK!!!

SUDOKU

(MEDIUM DIFFICULTY: ANSWERS IN BACK OF BOOK)

	9		6			7	4	2
7	2			5	1			
		8						1
	6							4
1		2			8		9	7
8		5	4		6			
	5	7					2	
	1						6	
9		6						5

> "The ideal subject of totalitarian rule is not the convinced Nazi or the convinced Communist, but the people for whom... the distinction between true and false no longer exists."
> -Hannah Arendt

R. RIVETER.

AMERICAN ★ HANDMADE

BEHIND THE SCENES BATTLES FOUGHT BY THE BRAVE

PULP AVENGERS !!!

Want your short story published in *Adventures*?

Email your entire story, with "Submission" in Subject to: OffBeatReads@pm.me

When in Southern California visit Universal Studios

SEE IT THE WAY IT WAS
ORIGINALLY MADE! UNCUT!
EVERY SCENE INTACT!
THE VERSION TV DIDN'T
DARE SHOW!

ALFRED HITCHCOCK'S
PSYCHO
PSYCHO

Suggested for Mature Audiences

STARRING
ANTHONY PERKINS · VERA MILES · JOHN GAVIN · CO-STARRING MARTIN BALSAM · JOHN McINTIRE · AND JANET LEIGH AS MARION CRANE

Directed by ALFRED HITCHCOCK
Screenplay by JOSEPH STEFANO
Based on the Novel by Robert Bloch
A UNIVERSAL RE-RELEASE

No one will be admitted
except at the very
beginning of the picture!

R 88/72

THE PRETTY SISTER OF JOSÉ

BY FRANCES HODGSON BURNETT

CHAPTER ONE

It had taken him a long time, and it had cost him—José—much hard labor, to prepare for his aged grandmother and Pepita the tiny home outside Madrid, to which he at last brought them in great triumph one hot summer's day, when the very vine-leaves and orange-trees themselves were dusty. It had been a great undertaking for him in the first place, for he was a slow fellow—José; slow as he was dull and kind and faithful to Pepita and the grandmother. He had a body as big as an ox, and a heart as big as his body, but he was slow and dull in everything but one thing— that was his carpenter work. He was well enough at that, and more than well enough, for he had always had a fancy and a knack for it from the time when as a boy he had worked in his uncle's vineyards and tilled his fields and fed his beasts. His uncle had been counted a rich man among his neighbors, but when his sister and her husband died and left the two children, José and Pepita, penniless, and with no protector save himself and their grandmother, already an old woman, it was upon the grandmother that the burden fell, for he did nothing for them except to give them, grudgingly now and then, a few poor vegetables or a little fallen fruit. It is true that when José was old enough to labor in the fields he gave him work to do, but he paid him ill and treated him ill also, giving him poor food and harsh words, and often enough blows the poor lad did not deserve. So it came about that while he was at his work José fell into the way of planning to escape from all this, and make another home for himself and his pretty child-sister and the old woman. He knew there was only one way to do it: if he could carry his one gift where it would be of more use to him than it could possibly be in a poor small village; if he could carry it to a market where there were more people and where work was better paid for. Where the king and queen were, of course, there must be more money, and one could find more to do and live better. It was Padre Alejandro, the village priest, who had suggested this to him first. He was a kind, jovial old fellow, the padre, and had seen something of the world, too, long ago, which was perhaps why he was never very hard upon a simple sinner who went to confession, and could give a bit of unecclesiastical advice now and then. He had always been kind to José, and as Pepita had grown prettier and prettier every day, he had often spoken of her to old Jovita, and said she should be well taught and taken care of, and once even—when she had come into the house with a basket of grapes on her little head, rose-flushed with the hot day, her black hair curling in moist silken rings on her forehead—he had been betrayed into the worldly remark that such pretty young things ought to have something brighter to look forward to than hard work and scant fare, which made them old before their time, and left them nothing to look back upon. But he only said it to Jovita, and Jovita only stared a little, it never having occurred to her that there was anything much in the world but hard labor and poverty. And what difference did it make that one was pretty, except that it became more probable that some gay, lazy fellow would pretend to fall in love with one, and then after marriage leave one all the work to do and a houseful of hungry children to feed? She had seen that often enough. Had it not been so with Pepita's mother, who died at twenty-five almost an old woman, worn out with trouble and hard usage?

But afterward, when Padre Alejandro saw José, he spoke of Pepita to him also, though only as if incidentally among other things.

"She should marry some good fellow who could take care of her," he said.

"If you go to Madrid it will also be better for her."

And so the end of it all was that after much slow planning and many hopes and fears, and more than one disappointment, there came a day when the uncle was thrown into a violent rage by losing his best and most patient worker, and the poor cottage stood empty, and José and Pepita and Jovita found themselves in a new world.

What a new world it seemed to them all! Through the help of Padre Alejandro and an old friend of his, José had work bringing him pay which appeared absolute wealth to him. The cottage, with its good walls and roof, its neat rooms and garden, being compared with the mere hut they had left behind, seemed a palace. For the first few days, indeed, Jovita was scarce at ease; to feel no necessity for heavy labor, to have food enough, to be so comfortable, seemed unnatural, as if it might finally bring disaster. But it was not so with Pepita. All the joy of youth, all its delights and expectations filled her heart. To be so near the great, grand city, to look forward to seeing all its splendors, to walk in its streets, to share in the amusements she had heard of—this was rapture. If she had been pretty before, she became now ten times prettier; her lovely eyes grew larger with laughter and wonder and joy; her light feet almost danced; her color was like that of a damask rose. Each day brought new innocent happiness to her. When José came home from his work at night, she sat by his side and asked him a thousand questions. Had he seen the palace—had he seen the king or the queen—what were the people doing—were the public gardens beautiful?

And then she would take the guitar, which had belonged to her gay father in his gayest days, and sit out in the little garden, among the vines and lemon-trees and oleanders, and play and sing one song after another, while José smoked and rested, and wondered at and delighted in her. It was she who had inherited all her father's gayety and spirit. José had none of them, and, being slow and simple, had always found her a wonder and a strange pleasure. She had, indeed, been the one bright thing in his life, and even her wilfulness had a charm for him. He always gave way to it and was content. Had she not even once defied the uncle when no one else would have dared to do it? holding her little head up and confronting him in such a burst of pretty rage that the old curmudgeon had been quite quelled for once in his life, and had ever afterward treated her with a kind of respect, even saying to a neighbor that "the lad was a fool, but the little devil had something in her, after all."

In all his plannings it was Pepita José had thought of first. Madrid to him was only a sort of setting for Pepita; the clean, comfortable cottage a home for Pepita; the roses and lemon blossoms she would wear in her hair; under the fine grape-vines she would sit in the evening and play on her guitar. His wages would give her comfort and buy her pretty simple dresses. And then every one would see her beauty, and when she went to mass, or with himself and Jovita to the Prado or the Paseo de la Virgen del Puerto, people would look at her and tell each other how pretty she was, and all this would end in time in a good marriage perhaps. And she would be loved by some nice fellow, and have a home of her own, and be as happy as the day was long. There was only one obstacle in the way of this excellent plan; it was only a small obstacle, but—it was Pepita herself! Singularly enough, Pepita had a fixed antipathy to marriage. She had early announced her intention of remaining unmarried, and those young men who in her native village had desired to make love to her had been treated with disapproval and disdain. Knowing as little of love as a young bird unfledged, her coldness was full of innocent cruelty. She made no effort to soften any situation. She was willing to dance and laugh and sing, but when she found herself confronting lover-like tremors and emotion, she was unsparing candor itself.

"Why should I listen to you?" she had said more than once. "I do not love you. You do not please me. When you wish to marry me, I hate you. Go away, and speak to some one else."

"I will never marry any one," she said to José. "I will stay with you and be happy. Girls who marry grow ugly and are wretched. Their husbands do not love them after they are married. They must work and slave and take care of the house and the children. Look at Tessa! Her husband used to be wild about her. She could make him pale with misery if she turned away from him; he used to follow her about everywhere. Now he makes eyes at Juanita, and beats Tessa if she complains. And don't we both remember how it was with our mother? I will never love any one, and never be married. Let them love me if they are so stupid, but I will be left alone. I care nothing for any of them."

The truth is that José knew it was what she remembered of her mother's unhappiness and what Jovita had told her, which was the foundation of all this. Did he not remember it himself, and remember, with a shudder, those first miserable years of their childhood—the great, beautiful, wretched eyes of their mother, their gay, handsome father, and his careless cruelty and frequent brutality? Had not Pepita and himself clung together hidden in the loft at night, listening to their mother's sobs, and often to the sound of blows and curses rained down upon her because she was no longer a beauty, and there were beauties who had smiles to bestow on handsome fellows who were free, and even upon those who were not? It was enough to irritate any handsome fellow—this one had thought—to come home to a squalid place after enjoyment, and be forced to face poverty and children and a haggard wife with large staring eyes, red with weeping. Yes, Pepita and José remembered all this, and upon Pepita's character it had left curious traces. Young as she was, she had awakened quite grand passions in more than one heart, and on two or three occasions the suitors had been of far better fortune than herself—one of them, indeed, being the only son of a rich farmer, who might have chosen a wife of much greater importance than this pretty, scornful child, and whose family rebelled bitterly against his folly, and at last sent him away to Seville, but not before Pepita herself had coolly trodden him under her small feet.

"I like you less than any of them," she said, fixing her great, direct eyes upon him when he revealed his frenzy. "Go and marry that girl your father chose for you—if she will have you. They have no need to be afraid and speak ill of me. I don't want you. I can't bear to have you stand near me."

To José it never occurred to complain of her, but Jovita's sense of worldly advantage was outraged at this time, and she did not hesitate to express herself with much freedom and grumbling.

"God knows, I want no haste," she said; "but this is a chance for any girl. And see what a fool she is. But that is as it always happens. There will come along some worthless fellow, and she will be fooled like the rest, and be ready enough to run after him."

"I!" said Pepita, who stood in the doorway. "I!" And she opened her dark eyes in genuine anger and amazement.

"Yes, you," answered Jovita. "And you will be worse than any of them. Girls who think themselves too good to be spoken to are always easiest to coax when they find their match. Let him come, and you'll drop like a ripe grape."

"He will never come," said Pepita. "Never!" And there was not a shade of doubt in her look—nothing but cold indignation at Jovita's ill-humor.

"I am not afraid of men. They are all stupid. They think they can have anything they want, and they can have nothing. They have to ask, and it is the girls who can say 'No;' and then they are miserable, and beg and beg until one detests them. If any one said 'No' to me, I would not let them see it hurt me. They should think I did not care."

"You will not always say 'No,'" grumbled Jovita. "Wait till the day for 'Yes' comes. You'll say it fast enough. That's the way with women."

A bewitching little smile slowly curved Pepita's lips and crept into her eyes.

"I am not a woman," she said, looking out at the sun-warmed vineyards.

"He said so himself. Felipe said, 'You are not a woman; you are a witch, and no one can touch your heart or conquer you.' I will be a witch."

Secretly she had liked those words better than any of the adoring praises she had heard before. She liked the suggestion that she was invincible and safe from all danger—to be a witch—to be free from all this disastrous folly—to be unconquerable. Yes, that pleased her. It was not her fault that they would fall in love with her. What did she do to them? Nothing. She never allowed them to come near her or touch her; she never gave them tender glances or words. She laughed and was Pepita—that was all. Then it was no fault of hers.

And yet her little heart was warm enough. She loved José passionately; she loved Jo-vita; she loved little children and animals, and they loved her in return; old men and women adored her because of her simple, almost childish kindness and her readiness to help those who needed her young strength and bright spirit. It was only men who made love who were shown no mercy. She did not know that they needed mercy. She did not understand—that was all. It was as José had known it would be. When on the first holiday be took her to the public gardens with Jovita, every one who passed them gave her a second look; many turned to watch her; certainly there was not a man who did not glance over his shoulder at the bewitching girlish figure with the small round waist, at the piquant radiant face, at the well-carried little head with the red rose blooming in its cloud of soft black hair.

It was not long before two or three who were José's fellow-workmen sought him out and greeted him with great warmth. They had, it appeared, a great deal to say and many attentions to lavish upon him. Such a fine fellow, this José—such a good fellow—such a workman as was seldom seen in Madrid. And what a fine day for pleasure. And the Paseo de la Virgen del Puerto—there never were such gardens for sport. And all the time each one looked at Pepita, and lucky indeed was the man with mother and sisters to help him to make friends. And never had old Jovita met with such civilities, and encountered such deference. Pepita had the joy of a young bird in its first flight. The air of gayety enlivening everything, the people in their holiday clothes, the blue sky, the sunshine, the cheap simple pleasures of the day, were intoxicating delights to her. She made friends with the girls and their parents, and was even gracious to the young men who hung about José, and somehow seemed to find his neighborhood more attractive than any other. It was from one of these young men (his name was Manuel) she first heard of Sebastiano—the gay, the wonderful, the renowned Sebastiano. He had asked her, this Manuel, if she was going to the Plaza de Toros to see the bull-fight the following week, and when she said she did not know—that she had never seen a bull-fight— he found a great deal to say. He described the wonders of the great bull ring, where twelve thousand people could be accommodated, and where grand and beautiful ladies richly dressed and surrounded by their lovers and husbands uttered cries of joy and excitement as the fight became more dangerous, and both bulls and toreadors showed greater courage and fire; he described the costumes, the music, the picadors dashing in upon their horses; the banderilleros with their darts and ribbons; the matador with his reckless daring, his nerves and muscles of steel, and his lightning leaps. And then he described Sebastiano. Never before, it appeared from his enthusiasm, had Madrid known such a matador as Sebastiano. Never one so handsome, so dashing, so universally adored. When he appeared in the ring, what a roar of applause went up. When he made his proud bow to the president, and said, "I go to slay this bull for the honor of the people of Madrid and the most excellent president of this tourney," and threw his hat away and moved forward, waving his scarlet cloak, what excitement there was awakened. Songs were sung about him in the streets, fans were ornamented with pictures of his daring deeds, there were stories of great ladies who had wept their eyes out for love of him, and as to the women of his own class, there was not a girl in Madrid who did not dream of him.

"Why?" said Pepita, in her cold, soft voice, and with the simply cold and curious look in her great, richly lashed eyes.

"Because they are in love with him—all of them," replied Manuel, sweepingly.

"Why?" said Pepita, again.

"' Why?'" Manuel echoed, somewhat bewildered by the frank, indifferent ignoring of all natural reasons in this question—"'why?' Because he is so tall and strong and well made, because he is handsome, because he is more daring and graceful than any of the others—because he is Sebastiano."

Pepita laughed, and opened and shut her fan quickly.

"Why do you laugh?" inquired Manuel.

"I was thinking how he must despise them," she answered.

"Oh, no," said Manuel, who was not very clever; "he is always good to women. There was Sarita—a poor little thing who had always lived in the country. She saw him at her first bull-fight and was never happy afterward. She could think of nothing else, and she was too innocent to hide it. She used to slip away from home and contrive to follow him when he did not see her. She found a woman who knew some one who knew him, and she gave her all her little savings in presents to bribe her to be her friend and talk to her about him. Once or twice she met him, and because she was such a pretty little one, he spoke kindly to her and praised her eyes and her dancing. He did not know she was in love with him."

Pepita laughed again.

"Why do you do that?" Manuel asked.

"He knew," said Pepita. "He would _think_ she was, even if she cared nothing for him, and since she did care he would know before she did and would be proud of it, and make it as much worse as he could."

Manuel gazed at her a moment in silence, twirling his rather small mustacha. This beautiful, cool, mocking little person, the melting softness of whose eyes and lips should have promised such feminine tenderness and emotion, bewildered him greatly; it was plain that she was wholly unmoved by the glories of Sebastiano, and saw no glamour in his romances. What other girl would have asked "Why?"—and in that tone? It was difficult to go on with his story.

"He could not help it that she was in love with him," he said. "And she could not help it."

"Why?" inquired Pepita for the third time, and with a prettier coolness than before.

"Why," stammered Manuel, "because—because that is the way with all of them."

Pepita showed all her little gleaming teeth, and then put the stem of a rose between them and held it there like a cigarette as she looked under her eyelashes at the people. The rose was not as red as her scornful little mouth.

"He was always kind to her when he saw her," continued Manuel. "Once he gave her his _devisa_. When she died she held it in her hand and would not let it go. It was buried with her. She was a pretty child—Sarita—but she had always lived in the country and knew nothing."

"I have always lived in the country and I know nothing," said Pepita, mocking him with her great eyes; "but _I_ can help anything I choose. It should be the others who cannot help it."

She thought him dull and tiresome, and soon wished he would go away, but he could not help it, and lingered about with all sorts of stupid excuses. The more she bewildered him, the more he was fascinated. It was almost enough to stand and stare at her and hear her voice as she talked to the others. How pretty she was—that girl—how she held her head as if she was some high-born lady instead of a peasant! When some passer-by, more bold than the rest, made (loud enough to be heard) some comment upon her beauty, it did not disturb her in the least—it was as if it were nothing to her. Was it possible that there could live a girl who did not care that she was so pretty? But to imagine that she did not care was to make a great mistake—she cared very much. Ever since she had been a tiny child, her little mirror and the water of the fountain had reflected back to her this pretty face, with its soft rose of cheek and mouth, its dark liquid eyes, and soft babyish rings of hair curling on the forehead. She had always heard too that she was pretty, and as she had grown older she had found out something else, namely, that she had a power more strong and subtle than that of her beauty—a power people did not even try to resist. She did not call it by any name herself or understand it in the least. She often wondered at it, and even sometimes had a childish secret terror lest the Evil One might have something to do with it; particularly when without making any effort, when simply standing apart and looking on at the rest, with a little smile she had drawn to her side the stupid love-making for which she cared nothing. It was not so with Dolores and Maria and Isabella, who were pretty too. Somehow, handsome as they were, they must use their eyes on their lovers, they must laugh and dance and talk to be adored, while she need do nothing but be Pepita.

When, late that evening, she sat with José under the vines, the air about them heavy with jasmine and orange and lemon blossoms, she asked a great many questions about the bull-fight. It must be a grand thing to see—so many people, such gay colors, such music. José could describe it better than Manuel. He must tell her all about it.

He described it as well as he could, and in spite of his slow speech made quite an exciting picture for her; or rather she found it exciting, as she found all things just now in their novelty. Before Jovita and she had arrived, while he was making his small preparations for them, he had seen a bull-fight or so, and no point of detail had escaped his deliberate mind. He always remembered things—José.

"But you shall go," he said; "you shall go and see for yourself the very next time. It comes next week. We will go and take Jovita."

Pepita clapped her hands for joy. She sprang up and danced a few steps in her childish delight.

"That will be happiness," she said. "What happiness! Perhaps the king and queen will be there!"

"You will see Sebastiano," said José, seriously.

"I do not care for Sebastiano," cried Pepita, petulantly.

"You do not care," said José, in blank amaze, "for Sebastiano? You do not care?"

Pepita shrugged her shoulders.

"They talk too much of him," she answered, "and he is too vain. He thinks all women are in love with him, and that if a girl comes from the country she knows nothing, and will die of love if she only sees him."

"I did not know that," said José, staring. "I never heard them say so. They call him a fine fellow."

"I never heard them say so," Pepita answered scornfully; "but I know it. I am sure he is a fool," which remark caused José much bewilderment, and led him to reflect long and deeply, but did not, however, lead him to any conclusion but that Pepita was ruled by one of her caprices. He was rather afraid to admit that he himself had enjoyed the magnificent honor of seeing this great hero out of the ring; that through a quite miraculous favor he had even been allowed to speak to him and to hear him speak as he stood, the centre of a circle of admirers in a wine-shop. He had been saving this to tell Pepita, but now he thought it well to save it a little longer.

But when the day of the bull-fight arrived it was not possible to conceal it.

Ah! the wonders, the splendors of that day from the first hour! At its very dawning Pepita was up and singing. Jovita must take her rest, that she might be in her best humor to enjoy the festivities, and not spoil them by grumbling. Pepita needed no rest; her little feet danced as she moved; as she made her preparations for the morning meal she chatted incessantly to José, asking a thousand questions. Everything conspired to add to her joys. The sky was deep brilliant blue, but there was a light breeze to make the heat bearable; the birds sang until their little throats throbbed; the flowers in the garden seemed to have flung out new masses of bloom to make the small world about them brighter. In her chamber, near the roof, Pepita's gala dress lay upon her bed, her new little shoes upon the floor; she had seen them in the moonlight each time she had awakened in the night. A year ago it would not have seemed possible that such pretty finery could ever be hers, even in dreams; but now almost anything seemed possible in this new and enchanting life.

And when she was dressed how bewitching she was! how her rose of a face glowed and dimpled! how enchanting was the velvet darkness of her eyes! how airy the poise of her little black head, with its brilliant flower tucked in at the side of the knot of curly hair! Jovita stared at her and made a queer half-internal sound of exclamation. It was not her way to express approval at all freely, and she had no opinion of people who wasted time in telling girls they were pretty. But José looked at the girl as he might have looked at some rare tropical bird which had suddenly flown into the house. He looked and looked again, pulling his mustache, his not always alert face warming.

"Yes, yes," he said, "it all looks very well; that dress is pretty. None of the other girls will look better. Even Candida—"

Pepita laughed. Candida had been considered a great beauty in the village they had left, but she knew she was prettier than Candida.

José laughed also, though he scarcely knew why. Then with rather a cautious and uncertain air he produced a gay fan—a cheap one, but brilliant with color.

"This—" he began.

Pepita caught it from him, and unfurled it with a quick turn of her wrist. On one side was a picture—a dashing erect figure, in a richly hued costume.

"It is Sebastiano," said José, guiltily.

Pepita nodded her head and smiled.

"I knew it," she said; "I knew he would look like that."

"There is no other man who can slay a bull as he can," said José.

"Let him slay them," answered Pepita. And she stood and waved her fan with the prettiest inscrutable air in the world.

The journey to the Plaza de Toros was almost as delightful as the bull-fight itself to Pepita. The streaming crowds of people, all bent in one direction, and all in their gayest dress and mood, laughing, jostling each other, chatting, exchanging salutations and jokes, the grand carriages rolling by with fine ladies and gentlemen in them, the rattling old diligences, omnibuses, and _tartanes_, whose passengers seemed more hilarious than the occupants of the more splendid equipages, the ringing of mule bells, the shouts of drivers, the cracking whips, the sunshine, the color, the very dust itself, all added to the excitement of the hour. And as they made their way through the throng, it was again as it had been that first Sunday at the Paseo de la Virgen del Puerto, heads turned and exclamations were uttered when Pepita went by. And somehow it seemed that José was better known than even he himself had imagined, he received so many greetings. The truth was that already those who had seen the girl had spoken of her among themselves and to others, their readily fired Spanish natures aflame and elate. And those who had not seen, but only heard of her, were in as susceptible a condition as the more fortunate ones. She had been graphically and dramatically described again and again, so that by many a one she was recognized as "the pretty sister of José."

That was what they called her—"the pretty sister of José." She heard it half a dozen times, but never once even so much as lifted her long lashes. She was so used to admiration that it was as if they spoke of some one else, and it moved her not in the least, as she sat watching the bulls, to know that bold or languishing eyes dwelt upon her face, and that efforts were being constantly made to attract her attention.

It was a magnificent day—every one said so; there were splendid bulls and splendid dresses, and the fighters were in superb condition. The people were in good spirits too—the little breeze tempering the heat had, perhaps, something to do with it. Everything pleased them; they applauded wildly, and uttered shouts of encouragement and delight to bulls and toreadors alike. The grand people were richly attired; beautiful ladies watched with excited eyes the bulls, wearing their colors in rosettes of satin and glittering tinsel; the thousands of waving, brilliantly hued fans fluttered like a swarm of butterflies; the music filled the air. Pe-» pita sat in a dream of joy, the color coming and going on her cheeks, her rapture glowing in her eyes. She was a Spanish girl, and not so far in advance of her age that the terrible features of the pastime going on before her could obscure its brilliancy and excitement. Truth to tell, she entirely forgot Sebastiano, not even recognizing him in the pageant of the grand entry, she was so absorbed in its glitter and blaze of color. But at the killing of the bull, that was different. Just a moment before she had awakened to the fact that Manuel was near her—near enough to speak. He had been staring at her, and growing more restless every moment, until he had at last attracted the attention of José and Jovita, and his first words to her came amid shouts of applause and delight.

"Sebastiano," he said; "it is Sebastiano." Pepita turned to look. With what a proud and careless air he advanced; with what a strong, light step; how he held his head and shoulders; how his gold and silver garnishings glittered; how the people called to him with a sort of caressing ecstasy! They adored him; he was their idol. Yes, there was a thrill in it, even for her cold heart. She felt a quick pulsation. To be so proud and triumphant and daring—to be the central point of everything—to be able to awake this exultant fervor—was something after all. And he was beautiful too, though she cared nothing for that, except as she could see that it added to his triumphs and made them more complete. His athletic grace of bearing, his dark, spirited face, with its passionate Andalusian eyes, their shadows intensified by the close, long black lashes, the very arch of his foot, and superb movement of his limbs, would have set him apart from ordinary, less fortunate mortals; but to have all this and be also the demi-god of these impassioned people, it must be worth living for. If one cared for men, if one did not find them tiresome, if one was simple enough—like Sarita—to be carried away by things, there was at least something in all this to interest one a little.

"It is Sebastiano," said José.

But Sebastiano was addressing the president of the games. He extended his glittering sword, and made his announcement in a clear, rich voice. Pepita listened as he spoke. And then the most thrilling excitement of the sport began. It was no child's play Sebastiano had before him. The fierce black bull glaring at him with bent head and fiery eyes, uttering low, muttering bellowings of rage as he tore at the earth, throwing up the dust in a cloud, was a foe worthy of his mettle. He was a bull with vicious points and treacherous ones. Already goaded to fury by the play of the picadors and banderilleros, he must be watched, studied, excited, baffled; not one of his movements must be lost, or even regarded as trifling; wariness, quickness, magnificent daring, the subtlest forethought, all were needed. What play it was! what a match between brute cunning, power, and ferocity, and human courage, adroitness, and calculation! The brilliant, graceful figure was scarcely a moment in repose; it leaped and darted, the bright cloak waving, inviting, the bright sword glittering in the sun—it toyed with death and peril, evading both with an exultant grace and swiftness marvellous to behold, and rousing the on-lookers to shouts of joy and triumph. Even old Jovita wakened to a touch of fire which seemed like a renewal of her long-past youth. José and Manuel joined their cries with the rest. Pepita felt again—yes, more than once—that sudden throb and thrill.

And when at last the end was reached, with what a superb spring the last splendid blow was given! No need of a second; the bull staggered, shuddered, fell forward upon his knees, sank upon his side. Sebastiano stood erect, a brilliant, careless, triumphant figure again, the air resounding with deafening applause.

"You have seen him," cried Manuel to Pepita—"you have seen Sebastiano?"

"Yes," she answered, a little breathlessly, "I have seen him."

And even as she spoke she knew that he had seen her; she knew it even before Manuel spoke again in great excitement.

"He looks this way—he looks at us—at you."

It was quite true. Something had attracted his attention to the tier of seats in which they sat, some cry—who knows what?—perhaps some subtle magnetic influence. He turned his head with a quick movement, and his eyes fell and fastened themselves instantly upon the brilliant little face glowing like some bright flower among those humbler and less blooming.

"He looks at you, Pepita," said José.

"He looks at you and at Jovita," Pepita answered. And she laughed and turned her face away.

But not before Sebastiano had seen it well. It was Fate. Yes, he knew that. He had been loved often; he had had romantic adventures, but it had always been he who had received and the others who had given; he had always remained Sebastiano, the hero, the adored. And now he stood and looked at a little head half concealed by a fan, and forgot for a moment where he was, and that the people were still shouting their applause in deafening tumult.

CHAPTER TWO

Pepita and the others, Manuel with them, ended their gala-day with still another festivity. They dined together at a little café, and heard the bull-fight fought over again by those around them. At a table near them sat three chulos, who talked together in voices loud enough to be heard throughout their meal. And it was of Sebastiano they spoke, giving dramatic recitals of his daring deeds, telling each other of what he had done, of what he could do, and that Madrid had never seen his rival or peer. And then his conquests. It was true that noble ladies—beautiful and noble—had sent him messages and tokens. Gonsalvo, who was his intimate friend, could tell many things if he chose. Sebastiano had brilliant triumphs. Once he had even been in great danger because the woman who loved and sought him was of such rank that her relatives would have resorted to the stiletto rather than allow her infatuation to continue.

"But it is said truly that he had no love for her—that he has little for any of them," said one. "They run after him too much, these women."

"But there was one to-day—" began one of the others. "I heard it of Alfonso—he saw her at the bull-fight—Sebastiano—and tried to find out—"

He made a movement at this moment which brought Pepita directly within his view. She had been hidden from him before by the figure of

Jovita. He stopped with his wine untasted and stared at her. A moment later he bent forward and spoke in a lower tone to his companions, who turned to look also. Alfonso had pointed her out to him as she left the Plaza de Toros, and he had recognized her again.

"The little one is there," was what he said, "behind you. He asked if any of us had seen her before; if we knew her name."

Pepita did not hear him, and did not know that from that hour they would all know her, or that at least there would be few of them who did not. For Sebastiano to show an interest in a woman, to even go so far as to ask her name, was such a new thing that it must be spoken of and attract attention to her. And that she was not a fine lady, but only a pretty unknown girl with a rose in her hair, made the matter all the more exciting. When she fell asleep, tired and happy, that night, already she was on the road to fame. Sebastiano, who was the adored of his order, who in spite of his adventures sought no woman, had asked her name, had made efforts to discover it, and had learned that among those who had had the good fortune to see and speak to her she was known as "the pretty sister of José." A week from this time José came home one evening bringing Manuel with him. Manuel was often with him—in fact he had many friends; almost every day some gay or grave young fellow managed to attach himself to him, and somehow the acquaintance always shared itself soon afterward with Pepita. But Manuel appeared oftener than the rest, having a timid obstinacy, and seeming only puzzled and not discouraged by the indifference which sometimes ignored his very existence. On this particular evening he was moved from his usual calm, and so was José. They had seen Sebastiano; they had spoken to him; in the presence of a circle of his friends and admirers he had drunk wine with them. "We were passing the wine-shop and we saw him," explained Manuel, "and we went in to look on a little and hear him talk. One of the chulos who stood near spoke to him quickly when he saw us—as if he knew us—and presently the same chulo came and spoke to José, and soon Sebastiano came and spoke too. The one who approached us first was one of the three who drank at the table near us on the evening after the bull-fight. Once, in his boyhood, Sebastiano lived near the village you left; he knew Padre Alejandro and some others; he was pleased to see José and speak of them—it was as if they were friends at once."

"He has a good heart," put in José; "they all say that of him. He remembered everything—even old Juan, who lived to be a hundred and was bent double. He asked if he lived yet. It seems strange that he was once so near us, and was a little lad, ill-used and poor. He is not too proud to remember it. He would be a good friend to one in trouble—Sebastiano—though he is rich and spoken of by the whole world."

So great a celebrity José was convinced must be known to the entire universe. That night, as Pepita made ready for her bed, old Jovita, who had already retired, lay and looked at her.

The girl stood in the flood of brilliant white moonlight which bathed part of the bare room; her round dimpled arms were lifted as she unwound the soft dusky coils of her hair, to which there yet clung a few stars of jasmine. There was the shadow of a smile on her lips, and she was humming a tune.

"What does he want with José—this Sebastiano?" said Jovita, grumblingly.

"Who knows?" said Pepita.

"He wants something," Jovita went on. "They don't make friends with those beneath them for nothing, these fine ones. They all talk of you, these foolish fellows, and he has heard, and makes friends so that he can see you."

"What do they say of me?" asked

Pepita, without deigning to look up.

"Men are all fools," grumbled Jovita; "and they think girls are fools too. They say you have a pretty face; and he thinks he can make a fool of you if you are not one."

"Does he?" said Pepita, with a dimpling cruel little smile. "Let him come to-morrow—to-night. Let him begin."

"He will begin soon enough," Jovita answered. "You will see. Be sure he does not play the old game with you as he did with Sarita."

Pepita shook the small stray blossoms out of her hair and began to retwist the coil, breaking into singing in a clear voice:

"White, white is the jasmine flower; Let its stars light thee Here to my casement, Where I await thee. White, white is the jasmine flower, Sweet, sweet is the heart of the rose, Sweet my mouth's blossom—"

She stopped short and dropped her arms.

"See," she said, "let him want what he will, let him come a thousand times, and I will never speak to him."

In the gardens the next Sunday they met him. Pepita was talking to a young girl whose name was Isabella, and whose brother. Juan was following in the footsteps of Manuel and the rest. It was Isabella who first saw the matador, and uttered an exclamation.

"Your brother is coming," she cried, "with—yes, with Sebastiano."

José's simple face was on fire with delight, but Sebastiano looked less gay, and his step was less carelessly buoyant than it had been in the bull-ring. As he approached the group he looked only at Pepita. But Pepita looked only at José, her eyes laughing.

"Jovita is cross," she said; "she has been asking for you. She wishes to go home."

Sebastiano's eyes were fastened upon her face, upon her red lips, as she spoke. He had heard that she was like this; that she gave her glances to no man; that she was prettier than the rose in bloom, and as cruel as a young hawk, and his heart beat as he found himself near to her. Since the hour he had seen her he had thought only of how he might see her again, of how he might find her. He had made one bold plan after another, and had been forced to abandon each of them, and then mere chance had thrown José in his path. And now the instant he approached her she was about to elude him.

He spoke a few hurried words to José. It was too early to go away; the pleasure of the day was scarcely at its height; he wished to entertain them; they must not go.

"I will go and speak to Jovita," said José, and he went, leaving the four together.

The two simpler ones were somewhat abashed by the splendor of the dashing figure; they gazed at it with mingled curiosity and joy. To be so near it was enough, without effort at conversation. Sebastiano moved to Pepita's side. A Spanish lover loses little time.

"I saw you," he said, "at the bull-fight."

Pepita looked over his shoulder and smiled at a passing woman who had greeted her. Her face dimpled, and she showed her small white teeth. It was as if she did not see the matador at all.

"It was at the bull-fight," he persisted. "Two weeks ago. You had a red flower in your hair, as you have to-day. Ever since—"

"It was not true," Pepita said gayly, to Isabella, "what I said of Jovita. She is always cross, but she does not wish to go home. She met an old woman she knew in her young days, and is enjoying herself very much."

"Why did you say it?" asked Isabella, with simple wonder.

"Because I wished to go home myself."

"Truly!" said Isabella. "Why is that?"

"I am not entertained so much to-day," answered Pepita.

"We will make it more amusing," said Sebastiano, eagerly. "It shall be more amusing—"

"There is Jovita with her old woman now," interrupted Pepita. "I will go and speak to them."

She was gone the next instant—her movement was like the flight of a bird. Sebastiano stood and stared after her in silence until Juan addressed him respectfully.

"She is very wonderful," he said. "She changes her mind before one knows. Just before you came she said she was amused, and wished to remain."

"Perhaps," began Sebastiano, much discomforted—"perhaps it was I—"

"Ah, senor," said Juan, with great politeness, "never. It is said that she always does what she chooses, and she chooses to do a thousand things."

"That is because she is so pretty," said Isabella. "She is so much prettier than all the others, and she does not care."

"A woman who is so pretty as that," remarked Juan, sententiously, "need not care."

"She says," put in Isabella, "that if she does not care, others will; but if she should care, the others—" She stopped, meeting Sebastiano's eyes and becoming a little confused.

"What would happen then," he said, "if she should care?"

"I do not know," said Isabella; "but she never will—never."

But if she changed often toward others, Sebastiano found no change in her mood toward him. They did not leave the gardens until late in the day. Jovita was enjoying too greatly the comradeship of her old woman, and was ready to enjoy any pleasure offered to her. Sebastiano had a full purse, and perhaps understood old women of Jovita's class. He made himself very agreeable to these two, finding them the most comfortable seats and supplying them with things good to eat and drink, over which they gossiped together, leaving the young ones to amuse themselves as they pleased. They were very gay, the younger ones; even Manuel, elated by the presence and hospitalities of Sebastiano, made little jokes. But none of them were gayer than Pepita. She was the centre figure of the party; they all looked at her, listened to her, were led by her slightest caprice. They went here and there, did this or that, because she wished it. It was Sebastiano who was the host of the hour, but by instinct each knew it was Pepita who was the chief guest—who must be pleased.

"Is she pleased?" the matador asked José once in a low-toned aside.

"Does she not entertain herself?"

"Does she not say so?" answered José, with some slight secret misgiving.

"I do not know," said Sebastiano, looking down. "She does not speak to me."

José pushed his hat aside and rubbed his forehead. His respect for Pepita's whims had begun early in life and was founded on experience.

"She is young," he faltered—"she is very young. When she enjoys herself she—"

He paused with an uneasy movement of his shoulders. It was quite terrible to him that she should treat with such caprice and disdain so splendid and heroic a person; but he knew there was nothing to be done.

"She admires you," he said, with courageous mendacity. "She saw you at the bullfight."

"She will be there again? You will take her—the next time?" said Sebastiano.

"Yes," answered José. "She has asked that I will. It was the greatest pleasure of her life."

But it was true that during all the afternoon she had never once spoken to Sebas-tiano. She had been as gay as a young bird, and the spirit of the party, her laughter, her pretty mockeries and sauciness, had carried all before them. Manuel had been reduced to hopeless slavery. Isabella had looked on in secret reverential wonder. Jovita's old woman had glanced aside again and again, nodding her head, and saying, sagely:

"Yes, she will always have it her own way—the little one. You are lucky in having such a grandchild. She will never be a load." But throughout it all Pepita had managed it that not one of her words had fallen directly to Sebastiano. If he spoke to her, she gave her answer to the one nearest to him. If he did not put an actual question to her, she replied merely with a laugh or a piquant grimace or gesture, which included all the rest. It was worse than coldness. To the others it was perhaps not perceptible at all; only he who searched for her eyes, who yearned and strove to meet them, knew that they never rested upon him for an instant.

And then when he so daringly arranged that José should invite him to return home with them, to what did it all come? He was lured to old Jovita's side by the fact that at the beginning of the walk Pepita kept near her, and no sooner had the old woman involved him in tiresome talk, from which he could not escape, than the small figure flitted away and ended the journey homeward under the wing of José, and accompanied by Manuel and a certain gay little Carlos, who joked and laughed like a child.

And when after they arrived, and the moon rose, and they sat under the vines, though there was gayety and laughter, he knew, as before, that in some mysterious manner he was excluded from it, though he seemed the honored and distinguished guest. Carlos, who sat near some shrubs in bloom, made a little wreath of white flowers, and as she played and sang to her guitar, Pepita wore it on her head. Then Manuel, not to be outdone, wove a garland of pink oleander, and she threw it about her throat and sang on. Sebastiano forgot at last to speak, and could only sit and look at her. He could see and hear nothing else. It was almost the same thing with the rest, for that matter. She was somehow the centre figure round which they all seemed to have gathered, as she sat there playing, a night breeze sometimes stirring the soft ruffled hair on her forehead, which was like black floss silk; and whatsoever she sang, however passionate and tender the wild little song, however passionate and tender her voice, her young eyes had mockery in them—mocked at the words, the tenderness of her own voice, and at those who were moved by it; and most of all Sebastiano knew that she mocked at himself.

But he could not go away. Some strange thing had happened to him, it seemed; it was as if a spell had fallen upon him.

Better to be mocked than to go away. He stayed so late that Jovita fell asleep and nodded under the shadow of the grape-vines. And at last Pepita put down her guitar and rose. She stood upright in the moonlight, and extended her pretty arms and stretched them, laughing.

"Good-night," she said. "Jovita will amuse you. Already there have been too many hours in this day."

She ran into the house with no other adieu than a wave of her hand, and the next minute they could hear her singing in her room, and knew she was going to bed.

Sebastiano rose slowly.

"Good-night," he said to José.

Manuel and Carlos said good-night also, and went out together, walking side by side down the white moonlit road; but Sebas-tiano moved away from the shadowing vines with a lingering step, and José went with him a short distance. Something in his hero's air of gravity and abstraction somewhat overawed him.

"She has not been entertained," said Sebastiano at last.

"Yes, yes," said José. "She has had pleasure all the day. And she is fond of pleasure."

"She said there had been too many hours in the day."

José rubbed his head a little reflectively for a moment, and then his countenance somewhat brightened.

"She wished to lie a little for amusement," he said, affectionately.

"There is no wrong in her—Pepita—but sometimes, to be amused, she will tell a little lie without sin in it, because she knows we understand her. She does not expect us to believe. We who are used to her know her better. You will also understand in time."

"Then I may come again?" asked Sebas-tiano.

The heavy body of José almost trembled with simple pleasure.

"It is all yours, senor," he said, with a gesture including the little house and all the grape-vines and orange blossoms and oleanders. "It is poor and small, but it is yours—and we—"

Sebastiano's dark eyes rested for an instant on a little window under the eaves where a jasmine vine wreathed a thick tangle of green, starred with white flowers. And as he looked a voice broke through the fragrant barrier singing a careless, broken bit of song—

"White, white is the jasmine flower; Let its stars light thee."

"It is Pepita," said José. "She always sings when she is pleased. It is always a good sign."

If her singing was a sign of pleasure, then she must have been enjoying her life greatly in the days that came afterward, for she was singing continually. As she went about her work there was always the shadow of a smile on her lips and in her eyes, as if her thoughts amused her. And she was in such gay spirits that José was enchanted. He had only one vague source of trouble: all the rest had turned out so well! It had all occurred just as he had dreamed, but scarcely dared to hope, in those by-gone days when he had been hard-worked and ill-fed and ill-clad. He had a good place, and what seemed by comparison incredibly good wages. He had the nice little house, and Pepita had holiday garments as gay and pretty as any other girl, and looked, when dressed in them, gayer and ten times prettier than all the rest.

That was what he had looked forward to most of all, and his end was attained. And when he walked out with her, all the young fellows who were allowed to come near—and many who were not—fell in love. Yes, it was true; he saw it himself and heard it on every side. It would take the fingers of both hands to count those who were frankly enamoured, beginning with Carlos and Manuel. But it was at this point that the vague trouble came in. And it was Pepita herself who caused it, by her treatment of her adorers. To say that she dealt out scorn to them would be to say too much; she simply dealt out nothing—and less. They might come and go; they might follow and gaze and sigh—she did not even deign to seem to know they did so, unless by chance one became too pertinacious, and then she merely transfixed him with a soft, cruelly smiling eye. "She will not marry any of them," said José to Jovita in bewilderment.

"That will come soon enough," said Jovita. "She is pretty, and it makes her a little fool—all girls are like that; but one of these days you may look out—it will be all over. She is just the one to blaze up all at once."

"I do not think she is a fool like other girls," said José, with gravity. "But she does not seem to care about love; she does not seem to know. She is not even sorry for them when they are miserable." He did not consider himself when he thought of her marriage; in truth he put himself in the background, for if some other man filled her life and her heart his vocation would be gone, and there would be some dull hours for him before he could become used to it. But he had an innocent feeling that without this love, of which all men talked so much, the life he wished to be bright would not be quite complete. She was too pretty and too good never to be married—never to have a home of her own and some fine fellow to love the dust she walked on. He himself was only José, and a brother was, after all, a poor substitute for a lover who could talk and sing and make jokes, and wear such a dashing air that she would be proud of him.

"That is it," he said, sagely, to himself. "A woman must have some one to be proud of, and she could never be proud of me. If I were Sebastiano now, it would be different."

He stopped suddenly and rubbed his head, as his habit was when he was startled or confused, and his face became rather red. Perhaps this was because he remembered that among all the rest, the magnificent, the illustrious, the beautiful Sebastiano was the one to whom she showed least grace. In fact it was almost mysterious, her manner toward him. They had seen him often—he had come in many evenings to sit under the vines; when they went out for pleasure it somehow happened that they nearly always met him; but when he joined them Pepita became at once possessed of some strange wilful spirit. Upon reflection José found that he had never yet heard her speak to him: it appeared to him as he thought it over that she always by some device avoided answering directly what he said to her.

"That is a strange thing," said José, deeply mystified, as he suddenly realized this, "when one remembers how he can slay a bull. There is no one else who can slay a bull as he can. It is enough to make one weep for joy. And yet she can treat him ill."

But he did not know how ill; only Sebas-tiano knew that. Since the day he had stood in the arena and had seen all in a moment, as if a star had suddenly started into the sky, the small black head and rose of a face, he had lived in a fevered dream—a dream in which he pursued always something which seemed within his grasp and yet forever eluded him. What had he cared for all the rest of the women? Nothing. It had confused and angered him when they had thrown themselves in his way or sent him offerings, and when he had been told of this or that beauty who was in love with his proud, bearing and dashing courage. Women! What were women? He had only cared for the bulls, for the clamor of the people, and the wild excitement of the arena. All he had wished for was to learn the best stroke, the finest leap. But this girl, who had never opened her scornful little mouth to deign him a word—who had never once allowed him to look in her eyes—somehow this one drove him half mad. He could think of nothing else; he forgot even the bulls; he spent all the day and sometimes all the night in devising plans to entrap her into speaking, to force her to look at him. How obstinate she was! How she could elude him, as if by some magic!

What had he not done that he might be near her? He had followed her everywhere. José did not know that she scarcely ever went out without his following and speaking to her. He used to spring up by her side as if he had risen out of the earth, but after the first two or three times he never succeeded in making her start or show any feeling whatever.

But that first time, and even the second, she had started. The first time she had gone to the old well for water, and as she stood resting in the shade a moment he appeared With a bouquet of beautiful strange flowers in his hand.

"God be with you!" he said, and laid the flowers down a moment and drew the water for her.

She watched him draw it, smiling just a little.

"It will be a fine day for the bull-fight," he said, when her jar was filled.

She put her hand up and shaded her working eyes as she looked at the blue sky, but she said nothing.

"Do you go to-day to the Plaza de Toros?" he asked. "You shall have good places—the best. They are good bulls to-day, black Andalusians, fierce and hard to manage. There will be fine sport. You will go?"

She leaned against the side of the well and looked down into the water, where she could see her face reflected in the cool, dark depths. The next moment Sebastiano's was reflected also. He held the flowers in his hand.

"These!" he said. "It was one of the gardeners of the king who gave them to me. They are such as the queen sometimes wears. I brought them that you might wear them at the bull-fight."

She saw their beauty reflected in the water. She would not look at them directly. They were very beautiful. She had never seen such flowers. And the queen herself had worn others like them. If any one else had brought them—but it was Sebastiano. And she remembered Sarita. Perhaps he had at some time given some to Sarita, knowing that to a country girl who knew nothing they would seem very grand. Sarita would have been sure to take them.

A wicked little look came into her face. She turned as if to take up her water jar. But Sebastiano laid his hand upon it.

"You will not speak," he said passionately. "No; nor even look at the flowers I bring you. You shall tell me at least what I have done. Come, now. Am I a devil? What is it?"

She put her hands behind her back and fixed her great eyes upon him for a moment. He could not say now that she had not looked at him. He thought he could keep her, did he, when she did not choose to stay? She, Pepita! She stood there staring at him for a moment, and then turned about and walked off, leaving him with her water jar. Let him stand and watch over it all day if he would.

She went back to the house and called Jovita.

"If you want your water now," she said, "you will have to go to the well for it. It is drawn, and Senor Sebastiano is taking care of it."

"Mother of God!" said Jovita, staring, "she is mad with her Senor Sebastiano."

But not another word could she gain, and before she could reach the well she met a boy carrying the water jar toward the house, and was told that he had been paid to bring it.

They went to the bull-fight; and, as Pepita sat among the rest, out-blooming the red flower in her hair, she heard it said that Sebastiano had never before been so magnificent, had never shown such daring and dexterity.

"He looks at Pepita," said Isabella to Carlos. "When he entered, his eyes found her before he saw anything else."

Yes, he saw Pepita, and Pepita sat and watched him with as cool an interest as if the peril with which he played meant nothing. Her lovely eyes glowed under their drooping lashes, but it was only with a momentary excitement caused by the fierce sport; the man was nothing.

So it seemed at least to Sebastiano. It was a bad bull he encountered, savage and treacherous, and maddened by his rage. Once there was a moment when a shadow of a misstep would have cost him his life. There was no time to look at Pepita then, but when the danger was passed and he glanced toward her, she was softly waving her fan and smiling up at Manuel as if she had not even seen.

"She has a bad heart," he said to himself, with fierce impatience. "It is not nature that a young girl should mock at everything, and be so cruel, and have neither feeling nor even a little fear. She has a bad heart, or none at all."

He would not look at her again; he swore it to himself. And for a short time he kept his vow; but there came a moment when something, some irresistible feeling, conquered him. It was as if he must look—as if some magic forced him, drew his eyes toward her in spite of himself. And when he had looked, a sharp shock thrilled him, for she herself was looking at him; her eyes were fixed upon him with a strange steadiness, as if perhaps they had been resting upon him for some minutes and she had forgotten herself. It was a little thing perhaps, but it was enough for his hot blood and swift-veering impulsive nature. He had just given the final stroke; he was panting, glowing. The people were shouting, rising in their seats, and repeating his name with caressing, applauding epithets attached to it. Chance had brought him near the seat in which she sat, with Jovita and José and the others near her. They were applauding with the rest, all but Pepita, who only sat and smiled. And in the midst of it Sebastiano made a swift movement, so swift that it was scarcely to be understood—a mere touch of the hand to the shoulder—and something bright, like a many-hued bird, flew over the barrier and fell upon Pepita's lap. It was the knot of gay, rich ribbon which a moment before the matador had worn.

"It is the _devisa!_" exclaimed Isabella, in an awestruck tone.

"It is his _devisa_," cried José—"his _devisa_, Pepita. He has thrown it to you yourself—Sebastiano."

The next moment he was struck dumb with amazement. Pepita sat upright and broke into a little laugh. She lightly waved her fan.

"Why did he not throw it to Jovita?" she said, and with a cruel, careless little movement she swept the _devisa_ from her knee; it fell, and she set her foot upon it.

"She has trodden upon it," said old Jovita. "She has done it for pride, and to show herself above others. She is ready for the devil. Some one should beat her."

"It was the _devisa_," gasped José. "Sebastiano."

Pepita left her seat. It seemed as if something strange must have happened to her. The crimson had leaped to her cheeks, and her eyes were ablaze.

"What is it to me, his _devisa?_" she said. "I do not want it. I will not have it. Let him throw a thousand, and I will tread upon them all, one after the other. Let it lie in the dirt. Let him give it to those others, those women who want it—and him." She would go home at once; not to the pleasure-gardens, not anywhere but back to the cottage; and José followed her meekly, struck dumb. He had seen her wilful, capricious, childishly passionate, a little hard to understand, many times before, but never like this. What had occurred to her? What had Sebastiano done?

Jovita had picked up the knot of gay ribbon and brushed the dust off it, and carried it home with her, grumbling fiercely. She was never averse to grumbling a little, and here, the saints knew, was cause.

"For pride," she kept repeating; "for pride, and to show that others are beneath her! Mother of God! the king himself is not good enough for her! Let him come and pray upon his knees that she will go to the palace and wear a crown, and he will see what she will say! It is these fools of men who spoil her, as if there had never been a pretty face before. Let them treat her as she treats them, and she will be humble enough. She was always one of the devil's children with her pride!"

But Pepita, who heard it all, said nothing, though once or twice she gave her little mocking laugh.

CHAPTER THREE

By the time Pepita had reached home her mood had changed—her anger was gone, or at least the signs of it were. She sang as she prepared the supper, and chatted gayly with José. It appeared that, after all, she had enjoyed the bull-fight; it had even been better than the others; she had had great pleasure. She made delightful little jests about everything; she recounted the names of the people she had seen and known; she described to him the dresses of the girls, the airs and graces of the men. She laughed, and obliged José to laugh also, and all the time she looked so pretty, with the queer light in her eyes, the gleam of her little wicked white teeth, and the brilliant spot of color on her cheeks, that she was enough to turn one's head.

The moon was at its brightest that night. All the earth was bathed in pure, magic whiteness—the whiteness which somehow seems to bring perfume and stillness and mysterious tenderness with it. Such a night! One breathed roses and orange blossoms and jasmine. Pepita sat under the roses and sang and talked, and José smoked and was happy, but still in a state of bewilderment, though the stillness and beauty of the night soothed him and made him content to ruminate without words.

Jovita fell asleep. She always fell asleep out-of-doors on the warm summer nights, and in-doors by the fire when it was winter. Pepita ceased to talk, and sang one little song after another; then she even ceased to sing, and only touched her guitar softly now and then. After a while José, who had stretched himself upon a bench, fell asleep also.

Pepita ceased to touch her guitar. She looked out at the flowers sleeping in the moonlight, and for a few minutes was very still; then she laid the guitar down and stepped out into the brightness.

In the light of the moon one cannot see the color in a face. Perhaps this was why hers seemed to be gone. She looked quite pale, and her lovely little brows were drawn together until they made a black line across her forehead. She clasped her hands behind her head, and with her face a little thrown back, so that the light fell full upon it, wandered out among the trees and fragrant flowering things. She liked the jasmine best, and over one part of the low, rough wall there climbed one which blossomed with a myriad stars. So she went and stood by it, and looked now at it, now up and down the road, which the moon had made into a path of snow.

And as she stood there, suddenly there started up on the other side of the wall the figure she knew so well, and the next moment it had vaulted over and was close to her. Sebastiano!

She stood still, her hands still clasped behind her head, her face still upturned, and looked at him.

He folded his arms and looked at her. As for him, whether the moonlight was to blame or not, he was as pale as death.

"Yes," he said, "you are always the same. You do not change. One may come at any hour. But listen to me. You think I have come to reproach you. Why should I? I have fought bulls, but that does not teach men how to deal with women. I thought that, if a man gave you his soul and his life and the breath of his body, you would listen some day and let him think of you. You are a woman, and you are made to be loved; but there is something hard in your heart. You are proud of having mocked a man who was honest and loved you. But hear me: it is better, after all, to be less pretty and more a woman."

He stopped an instant. She had changed her position, and stood by the jasmine, stripping the blossoms from it one by one. She began to smile and sing softly, as if to herself:

"Oh, bird at my window, Sing but one song to me, My lover who is light and gay."

"And more a woman," said Sebastiano. "It is women men want."

Pepita looked up and laughed; then she sang again:

"Who stirs the blossoms in the night, Who breaks the orange flower."

Sebastiano made a swift movement and caught her wrists, his eyes flashing fire.

"That is nothing," he said. "You are woman enough. The time will come. It will not be always like this. You can be _made_ to love. Yes, you are one of those who must be _made_. Then you will suffer too, and it will be good for you. You will speak then."

He paused a moment, and held her arms a little apart, looking at her with a sudden change to mournfulness.

"How pretty you are!" he said. "How little and how pretty! If you were good and gentle, and one might touch your cheek softly or stroke your hair, how one would love and serve you! No, you cannot move. I have not fought bulls for nothing. If I let you move you will struggle and hurt yourself. Listen. I am going away. I will trouble you no more now. I will wait. If one waits long enough, pain ceases and one forgets. It is so with a wound, why not with what one feels for a woman? I said you could be _made_ to love; but let that be left for another man to do. I want no love like that. I want a woman. Some day you will not cast the _devisa_ under your feet. You will take it and hide it in your breast. It will not be mine, but some other man's who loves you less. I loved you, I was mad for you; but it shall cease. It is better to think only of the bulls than to play the fool for a woman who has no love in her heart. You are pretty, but that is not everything. You can work spells, but a man can break through them. There! Go!"

He gave her one long look, flung her hands aside, and had vaulted the wall and was gone himself one moment later.

Pepita stood still with clinched hands dropped at her side, staring with wide fierce eyes down the white moonlit road.

The next evening José came home from his work later than usual. He came down the road with a drooping head and a slow and heavy step. When he sat down to his food he ate but little, and as he bent over his soup he heard Jovita scolding.

"It is gone," she was saying. "You took it, and have thrown it away."

"Was it not mine?" said Pepita. "It was mine. I cared nothing for it, and have done what I chose with it."

José lifted his head and listened.

"What has happened?" he asked.

"She has thrown away the _devisa_, which I had saved," answered Jovita.

"I laid it away, and she has taken it. What harm did it do her that it should lie out of her sight in peace?"

"Did you do that?" José said to Pepita.

"Was it meant for her?" said Pepita. "I told you he ought to have thrown it to her and not to me."

José broke a piece of bread and crumbled it on the table mechanically.

"You need not have done that," he said. "I wish you had left it in its place. It did no hurt, and we shall not see him again. He is not coming any more. And soon he goes away; and who knows what may happen?"

Pepita walked out of the house without speaking. She did not come back for a long time, and they did not know where she had gone; but as that was her way when she was in a naughty humor, they were not anxious about her.

When she returned at last the moon was shining again, and Jovita was asleep in the shadow of the vines, and José sat on the bench outside the door, smoking.

Pepita sat down on the threshold and rested her head against the side of the door. She said nothing at all, and only looked out at the dew-laden flowers sparkling in the garden.

There was silence for several minutes, and then José turned uneasily and spoke.

"Yes," he said, "he will not come again; and soon he goes away. It is for the best. He is very strong and determined. Perhaps that comes of fighting bulls. He said he wanted you, but you did not want him, so he must forget about you. He must cease to think of you or hear of you. He asked me as a friend not to let him see me for a while, until it was over. To see me would remind him of you, and that would not do. He asked it as a friend—there was no unkind-ness—he is my friend, yes, though he is Sebastiano and I am only a poor fellow who works hard. It will all be as well as ever between us when it is all done with and we meet again. If you had wanted him we should have been brothers."

Pepita sat still. What strange thing had happened to her? She did not know. Something was the matter with her breathing. Something hurt her side—labored in it with heavy beatings like blows which suffocated her. She shut her hands and drove the nails into her palms. She could not have spoken for the world.

Before José could say more she rose with fierce suddenness, and passed him and was gone again.

The poor fellow looked after her small swift form mournfully.

"If she had wanted him," he said, "he would have made her a good husband, and we should have been brothers. But she is not easy to please, and she would not give one a chance who did not please her at first. And there is no one who slays a bull as he does!"

Pepita flew like a bird until she reached the low wall where the jasmine grew, at the spot where she had stood the night before. There she stopped, panting. The breath of the jasmine filled all the air about her. She looked up the white road.

A strange new passion filled her. She did not know whether it was anger or not, but if it was anger it was of a new kind, with more pain in it than she was used to. He would not come again—not at all again! He would not appear at her side as if he had sprung from the earth; he would not follow her or plead with her, or look at her every moment he was near her; he would not try to make her speak. Only last night he was here in this very spot, and now he would never speak like that again. He would forget her, not care for her—forget her, Pepita.

She would not believe it. She knew he could not—they never did; they always loved her best and wanted no one else. And still the labored throbbing went on in her side and she panted for breath.

"Come back," she cried, looking up the white road. "I tell you to come back. You shall. Do you hear? I tell you—I—Pepita!"

But there was no answer, no sound of any footstep, no sign of any advancing shadow. The road stretched out its white length in utter solitude, and a strange, wild look came into her beautiful little face.

"Do you not hear?" she persisted. "I will not speak to you if you do come; I will give you nothing; I will not look at you; but you shall come because I will it—because I am Pepita."

Still there was only silence and loneliness. Suddenly she flung out her hands and stamped her foot.

"I will kill you," she said. "If you do not come—I will kill you!"

Then almost immediately she put her clinched hand to her beating side and sank down upon the earth, burying her face in the dew-wet fragrant tangle of the jasmine.

But he did not come back. And yet every night she went and stood by the low wall, and looked up the white road and watched and waited. For a long time she did not know what she intended to do if he should appear. All was vague in her mind. At first it seemed only as if her whole being went out into the fierce demand that he should come, and the obstinate proud belief that it must be as she wished—that he could not resist and disobey her. Who had ever disobeyed her? Not José; not Jovita, for all her grumblings; not any of those others. And was it likely that he who had adored her more than all the rest, who had watched her with that hungry love in his eyes, could do what no other had ever done? She told herself this over and over again; but he did not come. She began to feel a feverish eagerness when she dressed herself, a passionate desire to be pretty—to be prettier than ever before. She used to stand before her scrap of looking-glass to try on one bit of simple finery after another, twisting up the soft cloud of her hair afresh a dozen times a day, and putting a fresh flower in it. She went to the well again and again and filled her jar, and emptied and filled it again, and lingered, and tried not to look round when she heard a footstep; but the right one never came, though her heart's throbbing shook her many times in false alarm. She was only a child—a passionate Spanish child, ignorant and full of fierce young natural impulses—and she knew only childish, crude methods. So she made herself beautiful, and showed herself in the places where she thought he would see her and be unable to resist her will and her beauty; but though she made José take her here and there and everywhere, she never saw Sebastiano but once. It was in the Public Garden, where they had first met. They were sitting in the shade refreshing themselves with wine, and he came toward them, not at first seeing them. Pepita clutched her fan until she broke it, and a wild exultation sprang in her breast. She had seen before she left home that she had never before been so pretty.

There had come into her face a new look—a fire that had burned deeper every charm. He would see—he would see that she was Pepita still, and that he could not keep his word if she chose—if she chose.

He drew nearer and nearer, still not seeing them. He was talking to the three companions who were with him. He was richly dressed, and looked stronger than ever, and more handsome and graceful. He came still nearer. No, she would not speak to him. No! He looked up and his eye fell upon them—upon José and Jovita and Pepita! He drew back a step and stood still; he made a low bow to them, a grand bow, such as he made when he was in the bull-ring and the people applauded. He turned away and passed on. Yes, without a word.

Jose sighed a deep and mournful sigh and rose to his feet.

"Come," he said. "We must go. It is best not to stay. He does not wish to see us, and he asked that I would keep away. It is a pity—but he asked it."

The breath was coming in sharp little puffs through Pepita's delicate nostrils. It was as if she had been struck a blow. She walked home as in a sort of delirium; she saw none of those who turned to look at her. She walked faster and faster. Jovita could not keep pace with her.

"What is the matter?" said the old woman. "You walk as if you had a devil in you. Your breath is all gone. Are you mad?"

At night, when they sat together, Pepita spoke of the next bull-fight. José must take her. She wished to go.

"It is better that we should not go there," said José. "You know why. He will not like to see you. You saw how it was to-day. He is not angry, only he is determined not to be reminded. Soon he will go away, and then you shall go with me as often as you wish; but not now. After this week he will be far away—far away."

"I will go now," said Pepita. "I will go without you if you will not take me. Isabella and Juan and Manuel will be glad enough. Let him—let him look at his bulls."

She did not know that it was desperation that had seized upon her; she thought it was defiance. Yes, yes, she told herself, breathlessly, he should see her laugh and talk with Manuel and Carlos and Juan and the rest; and then he would be punished.

She would hear nothing that José said. She would go—she would go. No other bull-fight but this would please her.

She could scarcely live until the day arrived. She had made for herself a new gala dress; she had a new fan and a necklace she had bought out of her little savings.

There was a great crowd. It was known that Sebastiano was to go away, and many had come for that reason, wishing to see him for the last time in the season.

At first Pepita was gayer than her adorers had ever seen her. She deigned to talk and smile and listen. She had the restlessness and color of some brilliant-winged bird. Isabella looked at her in wonder.

"She was never like this before," she whispered to Juan.

And then Sebastiano came, and for the time they saw only him.

When at last the bull lay an inert mass in the dust, and the people shouted and almost flung themselves from their places into the arena in their excitement, and the gay and superb actor bowed to them—bowed to them again and again—Pepita sat like a little image of stone. She was quite colorless, and her eyes were fixed. She seemed to hear and see nothing until some one spoke to her. Then she rose and looked at Manuel.

"It is too hot," she said, in a low voice not like her own. "I must go. The sun. I have a pain in my head. Come."

He had not lifted his eyes once to her. It was as if she had not lived—as if she had been Isabella or Carmenita—and he did not give her a thought. No, he had not once looked up.

The next day he was gone. She heard José say so to Jovita, who grumbled loudly. She had forgotten her old distaste for these "fine ones."

"And but for her humors he would have stayed," she said. "What more does she want than a fine well-built man like that—a man who is well-to-do, and whom every other girl would dance for joy to get? But no; nothing but a prince for her. Well, we shall see. She will work for her bread herself at last, and serve the other women who have homes and husbands."

In the middle of the night she was wakened from her slumbers by something—she knew not what. Soon she perceived it was Pepita, trembling.

"What is it now?" demanded the old woman.

"I stayed out in the dew too long," said Pepita, "and I am cold."

"That is well," said Jovita. "Get chilled through and have a fever, that we may ruin ourselves with doctors' bills; and all because you choose to remain in the night air when you should be asleep."

Pepita lay on her pillow, her eyes wide open in the darkness, her small hot hand clutching against her breast something she had hung round her neck by a bit of ribbon. It was the _devisa_ she had stolen from Jovita, and which had not been thrown away at all. In the daytime it was hidden in the bosom of her dress; at night it hung by a cord and her hand held it. By this time a sort of terror had mingled itself with her passion of anger and pain, and she lay trembling because she was saying to herself again and again:

"I am like Sarita! I am like Sarita!"

She said it to herself a thousand times in the weeks and months which followed, and which seemed to her helplessness like years. She said it in as many moods as there were hours of the day. Sometimes with wild unreasoning childish rage; sometimes with a shock of fear; sometimes in a frenzy of shame; sometimes, as she stood and looked up the road, her cheeks pale, her eyes dilated with self-pity and tears.

"I am like Sarita! Yes—Sarita!" She remembered with superstitious tremor all the things that had been said to her of the punishment that would fall upon her because of her hard-heartedness. She remembered Jovita's prophecies, and how she had mocked them; how cruel she had been to those who suffered for her; how she had laughed in their faces and turned away from their sighs.

She remembered Felipe, whom she had not spared one pang—Felipe, at whom she had only stared in scorn when he wept and wrung his hands before her. Had he felt like this when she sent him back to Seville to despair?

A cruel fever of restlessness burned her. She could find pleasure no more in the novelties of the city, in the gayeties of the gardens, in her own beauty.

Sometimes she was sure it was magic—the evil-eye. And she slipped away, poor child! and knelt in the still, cool church, and prayed to be delivered.

But once as she was doing this a sudden thought struck her.

"Not to think of him any more," she said, knitting her brows with yet another new pang. "Not to remember his face—not to remember his voice and the words he said! No, no!" And her rosary slipped from her fingers and fell upon the stone floor, and she picked it up and rose from her knees and went away.

All that day and night she thought and thought, and the next day went to pray again—but not that she might be delivered. She brought to the shrine at which she knelt substantial promises as offerings. Hers were not the prayers of a saint, but of a passionate, importunate child, self-willed and tempestuous. She would not have prayed if she could have hoped for help from any earthly means. She had never prayed for anything before. She had always taken what she wanted and gone her way; but she had had few needs. Now in this strange anguish she could do nothing for herself, and surely it was the place of the Virgin and the saints to help her. She stormed the painted wax figure in its niche with appeals which were innocently like demands.

Make him come back—make him come back to her. Mother of God, he must return! Make him come to the wall some night—yes, to-night. He must not know that she was like Sarita, but he must come; and whatsoever she did or said he must not go away again. She would sell her new necklace; the silver comb her mother had left, her—the comb her father had given her mother in the days of their courtship; she would do some work, and give to the Holy Mother some candles and flowers; but he must come back, and he must not go away again whatsoever she did.

She knelt upon the stone floor, her hands wrung together, pouring forth the same words breathlessly over and over, each reiteration more intense than the last, all her young strength going out into the appeal.

And still she had not yet reached the point of knowing what she should do and say when he came.

When she tried to rise to her feet she was obliged to make two efforts before she succeeded. She had given such a passion of strength to her siege that she was almost exhausted, and she went out into the dazzling sunlight trembling. She did this day after day, day after day, and at night she waited by the wall, but the road was always the same.

And she could hear nothing—not a word. She could not ask, even though sometimes as she sat and gazed at José with hungry eyes it seemed as if she must drop dead if he did not speak. But he did not speak because he could have told her but little, and was quite secure in his belief that the mere mention of Sebastiano's name angered her.

So the time went by—weeks and months—and at last one evening she went to the church and prayed a new prayer.

"Sacred Mother," she said, "I have sold the comb and the necklace, and I have worked and can keep my word. I have bought a little golden heart. And if he comes"—in a fainter whisper—"if he comes I will say nothing ill to him."

That night, for the first time, she heard of Sebastiano.

Little Carlos came in and was full of news.

"They say that Sebastiano has had great success, and that perhaps he will go to America."

"Where is America?" asked Jovita.

"It is at the other end of the world, and never yet have the people seen a bull-fight."

"Never?" said José, staring. "That is impossible!"

"It is true," answered Carlos. "And they are rich, and like new things; and the king has spoken of sending for Sebastiano. He will be rich enough to build a palace for his old age."

A few days later, in the dusk of the evening, there crept into the church a little figure familiar to the painted saints and the waxen Virgin. But to-day it wore a changed aspect. It moved slowly at first, reluctantly; the brilliant little face was pale; the eyes wild with torture. A moment it stood before the altar, and then flung up its arms with a fierce gesture.

"Mother of God," it cried, brokenly, "then if it must be so—tell him— tell him that I am like Sarita!" and fell upon the altar steps shuddering and sobbing like a beaten child.

CHAPTER FOUR

And yet it was again weeks and weeks before she heard another word. In those weeks there were times when she hated José because he never once spoke of what she wished to hear. She could not speak herself—she could not ask questions; she could only wait—hungry and desolate. They would not even say—these people—whether he had gone to the King of America or not; whether he was at the other end of the world, or whether he was only in some other city. The truth was that José had innocently cautioned the others against speaking of one whom Pepita disliked to hear of.

"She does not like him," he said, sorrowfully. "Girls are like that sometimes. It makes her angry when one talks of him."

But slow as he was, he could not help seeing in time that something was wrong with Pepita. Sometimes she scarcely talked at all, and she did not flame up when Jovita grumbled; it seemed as if she scarcely heard. Her eyes had grown bigger, too, and there was a burning light in them. They always appeared to be asking something; often he found himself obliged to look up, and saw them fixed upon him, as if they meant to wrest something from him. The careless bird-like look had gone, the careless bird-like laughter and mocking. He began gradually to fancy she was always thinking of something that hurt and excited her. But then there was nothing. She had all she wanted. She had as many trinkets as the other girls; she had even more. She had so little work to do that she had sought some outside her home to fill her spare moments, and she loved no one. There was not a man she knew who would not have come if she had smiled. What, then, could it be? And how pretty she was! Prettier than ever; prettier because of the burning look in her eyes, and—and something else he could not explain; a kind of restless grace of movement, as if she was always on the alert.

"Are you not pleased with Madrid any longer?" he asked her once.

"Yes," she answered.

"Do you want anything?"

"No."

"It seems to me," he said, slowly, and with much caution, "that you do not amuse yourself as you did at first."

"It is not so new," she said; "but there is still pleasure enough." And for a moment she kept her great eager eyes fixed upon him, and then she moved slowly toward him and touched him with a soft touch on his big clumsy shoulder and said: "You are a good brother! You are a good brother!"

"I have always loved you," he said, with simple pride. "When we were children, you know I always promised that you should see better days."

She had forgotten to count the weeks and days, or to take note of the changing seasons, when one hot day in the early summer he came in— José—with an innocent joy in his face.

He looked questioningly at Pepita two or three times and then coughed.

"You will not mind now," he said. "It is so long ago, and it is all over. Sebastiano has come back. He did not go to America; he is in Madrid to-day. He came to me in the street; he did not avoid me; he was rejoiced to see me. It appears that it is all well with him. Afterward Manuel told me. It appears there is a very pretty girl he met in Lisbon—she is here now. It is said he will marry her."

Pepita clinched her hands and stared at him with eyes that burned as never before.

"It is not true!" she said through her teeth. "It is not true!"

José fell back two steps.

"Not true?" he stammered. "Why not? They say so."

"A man who slays bulls as he does," she said, "does not forget a woman in a day."

José was lost in amazement.

"I thought you believed nothing but ill of him," he said. "What has happened? You are angry—angry."

"It is not true about the girl from Lisbon," she said. "It is a lie they amuse themselves with."

Never had innocent José been so thunderstruck. This was beyond his understanding. He was afraid to speak, and kept looking sidewise at her as he ate his soup; but she said no more.

"What has happened?" he said to himself over and over again. "Will she not allow him to marry another, though she does not want him herself?"

Later he went out again. It must be confessed that he went in the hope of seeing Sebastiano, or at least hearing of him. There was no difficulty in hearing of him. In the wine-shops and at the street corners he was being talked of in every group. Of what else could people speak who knew he had returned? How there would be sport—how there would be pleasure! Life began to wear a more vivacious aspect. And what had he not done since he had left Madrid? Such success—such adulation! The impression among his adorers was that the whole world had been at his feet. Here and there one could hear snatches of song of which his name was the refrain. It was only because he so loved his own people that he had refused the magnificent offers made by the King of America. He had refused them; he had chosen to remain in Spain. He had come to Madrid. Soon he would appear before them again. He had even gained in strength and dexterity; and as to his good looks—ah! what a dashing, handsome fellow!

José had the good luck to see him again, even to speak to him. What fortune—what happiness! The honest fellow felt himself overjoyed. They were to be friends again.

It was quite late when he found himself walking homeward over the white road again. He had drunk wine enough to make him feel quite gay; and as he went he sang now and then a verse of a song about the joys of the bull-fight.

When he was about half-way home he thought he heard behind him the sound of rapid feet—light feet running. He stopped and looked back. What was it he saw, or thought he saw? Was it a small dark shape which flitted instantly into the shadow of the trees? It looked like a woman who did not wish to be seen. Well, he would not look, then. What was the use of giving her trouble? He tramped on, perhaps a little more slowly. It was late for a woman to be out on the lonely road alone. It must be past midnight. Then the thought came to him that perhaps she wished to pass him. In that case he might look the other way, on the opposite side of the road. In fact, he crossed to the other side to leave the way clear, and went on good-naturedly, singing his song loudly and all out of tune. Yes, he had been right. Soon the footsteps drew nearer; the shadow within the shadow slipped past—ran swiftly. But by that time they were nearing his home, and there was a stretch of road unshaded by anything. The shadow hesitated, darted across the white space, and José, seeing it in the full light, uttered a cry, and started in pursuit. In but a few moments he had reached it and held it by the arm, feeling all the slender body breathless and panting.

"Pepita!" he cried. "It is you?"

She let the mantilla drop from her face and stood and looked at him.

"Yes," she answered, "it is Pepita; and you need not ask—I will not tell you. I have been to—to look at something—and I will tell you nothing."

He put his hand up and rubbed his forehead violently. Then he let it drop.

"I shall not ask," he said. "You would do no wrong. You are a good girl; but—"

"You think I have gone mad," she said, with a sudden change of voice and a piteous little shiver. "Who knows? Perhaps some one has cast the evil-eye upon me. But I have done no harm, and I shall do none."

"No," he said, rather stupidly. "You would do no harm. Let us go in, then."

And without another word they went into the house, Pepita to her bed to be awake and gaze at the darkness, José to sit with his head in his hands and thinking a thousand wild thoughts until he fell asleep.

He could not know that where he had been she had been also; that when the snatches of song had been sung she had heard them; that when the people had talked of Sebastiano she had listened; that when Sebastiano had stood in the bright light she had stood in the shadow and watched. She had not thought of danger or of being discovered. She had only thought of one thing and listened for one thing—and once she had heard this thing discussed by some chattering young chulos.

"She is a pretty young girl," they said. "Not as pretty as that other, but handsome enough. She was a little devil, that other. But it is a mistake for a man like him to marry. How can a man feel free to risk his life gayly when he has a woman hung about his neck?"

"He will not," she whispered, growing hot all over. "No, he has not forgotten. I have given the little heart and the flowers and candles. And he could not forget while I—He will come back."

She struggled with the passionate persistence of a child. Since she would not give him up, he was hers.

But she did not know what to do. There was nothing but to wait in this fever of strange misery and unrest, which grew more cruel every day; and at the bull-fight if he would only look—perhaps—yes, if he saw her face, he would understand and come.

In the days before the great entertainment took place she was like some little savage creature at bay. She could scarcely bear to hear the voices of those who spoke to her. Once she went into the church and threw herself upon her knees as usual, but when she looked up her eyes were fierce.

"If he does not come," she cried to the waxen Virgin, "I will pray to you no more—no more."

She knew that it was blasphemy, but she did not care; and before she went home she bought a sharp little knife and hid it in her breast.

"This," she whispered, "this—if it is true about the girl from Lisbon; but it is not true."

For many years afterward the day of the great bull-fight was remembered. No one who saw it forgot it as long as he lived. Affairs used to date from it in the minds of many.

A year had passed since that first brilliant day when Pepita had gone forth in her first festal dress. She remembered it all as she dressed herself on this other morning. The same day seemed to have come again; the same sunshine and deep blue sky. There were the same flowers nodding their heads; Jovita was grumbling a little in her haste, just as she had done then; and in the looking-glass there was the same little figure in the bright attire—the soft black hair, the red rose, the red mouth. As she looked, a sudden triumph made her radiant.

"I have not grown ugly," she said.

No, she had not grown ugly. She was too young and strong for that, and excitement had flushed her into new brilliance.

When she found herself seated among the fluttering fans of rainbow colors, that moment's glow of exultation left her. Strangely enough, she could not help thinking of the empty church and the waxen figure before which she had knelt, and then of the nights when she had stood watching by the wall, and then of the sharp little knife in her breast. And then came the clamor of the music and the grand entry of the moving stream of color and glitter dazzling her eyes. No; just at first she had not the power to look. Could it be she—Pepita—who felt dizzy and could not see? who could distinguish nothing in the splendid panorama of the triumphal march? And what clamor, what excitement there was on every side! "What bulls! What men!" they were saying about her.

Only she seemed, in the midst of all the loud-voiced eagerness and delight, to sit alone, a cold little figure vaguely tormented by the gayety and the voices and the color of fluttering fans and ribbons and costumes. The deep rose had fled from her face; she sat with her hands wrung on her knee and waited for one moment to come.

The great bull ran bellowing around the arena; little beribboned darts were flung at him and stuck in his shaggy shoulders; brilliant cloaks were flaunted in his face; taunting cries mocked him. He charged hither and thither in blind fury, scattering men and horses, who only returned again to the attack.

"It takes too long," communed Pepita, "It takes too long."

And then the voices began to call for Sebas-tiano. "Sebastiano! Sebastiano!" on every side—even the grand ladies and their cavaliers clapping their hands and calling also. The beauties in the high places were always ready to see him come, and to give him a welcome when he risked his life to amuse them.

He stepped forth in his rich dress and with his gallant bearing, a more beautiful and gay figure than ever, it seemed the excited people thought. He had grown finer, without doubt, they said. His face was a little pale, but that only made more beautiful his long dark eyes, under their dense, straight, black lashes. It was the women who said this, and who saw the richness of his dress, the colors of his _devisa_, the close curl of his crisp hair, the grace of his movement. The men saw his superb limbs, his firm step, his quick glance, his bright sword.

"Come, little slayer of bulls," they shouted, "and show us what you would have taught the people of America."

And it appeared they were not to be disappointed in their expectation of sport. They saw that when he stood before the bull and made a little mocking bow of salute, he looked into its small, furious eyes with a smile, as it drew near—a bellowing black mass, snorting and throwing up the dust. It was as ready to begin as he. It rushed upon him, and he was gone. He played with it, led it on, defied it, eluded it. The flashing sword seemed to become a score of glittering blades; the people shouted—rose in their seats—leaned forward—laughed—mocked the bull—cried out praises of sword and man and beast—of each leap—each touch of the steel's point.

"He plays with it as if it were a little lamb," they cried. "Sebastiano! Sebastiano!"

Of what use to tell what must be seen in all its danger to be understood? The joy and exultation rose to fierce fever-heat, the cries swelled higher, faces flushed and eyes sparkled and flamed, while the brilliant figure darted, leaped, attacked, played with death as it had done scores of times before.

Only Pepita sat without color or applause—only Pepita's fan was motionless amidst all the fluttering—though her breast moved up and down, and the throbbing in her side was like the beating of a hammer. She was speaking to herself, though her lips were closed; she was speaking to Sebastiano.

"He will look soon," she was saying. "He will look as he did that first day. My eyes will make him look. They will force him to it. Listen! it is Pepita whose eyes are on you. You must feel them. You have not forgotten. No. And it is Pepita—Pepita!"

All the strength of her body and soul she threw into her gaze—all the fire of her young wildly beating heart and throbbing pulses.

"You must hear," she said. "Pepita! Pepita!"

And unconsciously she leaned forward so that her white face and great eyes, and the little black head with the rose burning in its hair, stood out among the faces of those about her.

And he looked up and saw her, and their eyes met; and without knowing she started to her feet.

No one knew, no one but herself saw, how it happened: even she did not understand until all was past. Their eyes met, as they had done on the day a year before. No, not as they had done then, but with a strange new look. Sebastiano started; the arena swam before him; there was a second—a fatal second in which he saw only a small face without color and the red rose which was the color of blood. Then there was a roar near him—a roar among the people—a wild shriek from the women. The bull was upon him; he made a misstep, and was caught, amid the shrieks and bellows, and flung inert far out upon the hoof-trodden dust with the blood pouring from his side.

"But," they said in the wine-shops at night, "when they took him up, though they thought him gasping in death, he had not lost himself; and as they carried him out they came upon a girl—the one who is called 'the pretty sister of José'—her brother was taking her away. She looked like one dead three days; and Sebastiano—there is a man for you!—tore the _devisa_ from his shoulder and dropped it at her feet; and she snatched it up—all wet with his blood—and thrust it in her breast, and dropped like a stone. It is said that he loved her, and she had a devil of a temper and treated him badly. He is a good fellow—her brother José—and wept like a child for Sebastiano, and has begged to be allowed to nurse him, and Sebastiano will have it so."

"I am strong as an ox," José had said, weeping. "I can watch like a dog. I want neither sleep nor food, if it comes to that; and once when one of my comrades fell from a scaffold I was the only one who could nurse him without killing him with the pain. He will tell you that I nursed him well, and was never tired."

"Let him stay," said Sebastiano.

In his struggle with death, which lasted so long, it was always the large form and simple, anxious face of José he saw when he knew what passed around him, and even when the fever brought him delirious visions he was often vaguely conscious of his presence. For himself, he did not know whether he was to live or die; but one night he found out.

It was a beautiful night which came after a long day in which those about his bed had looked at him with pitying eyes, and at last a priest had come and absolved him of his sins, and left him with a solemn, kindly blessing, with a soul clear of stain and ready for paradise.

He had fallen asleep afterward, and had dreamed not of heaven but of earth, of a red rose in soft black hair, and of a passionate little face whose large eyes glowed upon him.

And suddenly he was wide awake, and found his dream a living truth.

José was no longer in the room. The moonlight made everything clear, and upon the floor beside him knelt Pepita, her eyes fixed upon his.

"Dios! Dios!" he murmured.

"Hush!" she said. "Do not speak. It is Pepita. Look at me. They said that perhaps to-night you would die. I have prayed until I can pray no more, and when I came to José the tears were falling from his eyes, and he said perhaps you would not see the day. Then I showed him the little knife hidden in my breast, and told him if he did not let me come to you alone I would not live. I said I could force you to remain on earth. I love you—I love you. It has all happened, that which you said would happen; and when the _devisa_ fell at my feet I hid it in my breast with the other which was there before. And because I love you so, you cannot die. I will do anything you say I must do. I am Pepita, and I give myself to you. I would give my blood and my life and my soul for you. Every night I have waited by the wall in the hope that you would come. I have watched you when you did not see me. If you had not come I should have killed myself; if you die, I will drive the knife to its hilt in my heart. I can love more than those women who love so easily and so often. I knew nothing about it when I was so proud and mocked you. I know now. Mother of God! it is like a thousand deaths when one cannot see the face one wants. What hunger night and day!—one is driven mad by it!"

She bent more closely over him, crushing his un wounded hand against her heart—searching his soul with her look.

"They said there was a girl in Lisbon whom you loved," she said. "I knew it was a lie."

"Yes," he whispered, "it was a lie. Kiss me on the mouth."

His arm curved itself around her neck, and the red lips which had mocked melted upon his own.

"Did you suffer?" he murmured.

She began to sob like a child, as she had sobbed at the feet of the Virgin.

"I told you that you would suffer! It was the same thing with me. Saints of Heaven! human beings cannot bear that long. I shall not die, and I will make you forget the pain. Stay with me, and let me see your eyes and touch your lips every hour, that I may know you are Pepita, and that you have given yourself to me."

"I will stay through all the day and night," she answered. "They cannot make me go away if I do not wish it. They always give me my way. I have always had it—the Virgin herself has given it to me."

It seemed this was true. In a few months from then the people who strolled in the Public Garden on Sunday looked at a beautiful young couple who walked together.

"There are two who are mad with love for each other," it was said.

"Sebastiano and his wife. She is the one he threw his _devisa_ to when he thought himself a dead man. They used to call her 'the pretty sister of Jose.'"

END

LET X BE THE MURDERER by Clifford Witting. Originally published in
1947. New edition Galileo Publishers, 2023

ALL THESE YEARS I WAS UNDER THE IMPRESSION THAT HAD SOMETHING TO DO
with mathematics. Anyone would think so based on the title. Then when
you open the book and see that the books is divided into four sections —
Theorem, Hypothesis, Construction, Proof — once again most readers
would be expecting an academic mystery perhaps about a murdered cal-
culus or geometry professor. However, Inspector Charlton does not meet
anyone involved in mathematics or geometry or even physics. Instead it's
almost as if he travels back to the 19th century because this detective novel
turns out to be very much a homage to the Victorian sensation novel. As
a bonus, adding to the anachronistic atmosphere, Witting throws in eerie
occult dabbling and explorations into the world of spiritualism and para-
normal events.

Inspector Henry Charlton, Witting's usual protagonist detective, is paired up with the flippant Cockney copper, Det-Sgt Martin this time and they make an amusing pair. Yet another surprise — Peter Bradfield (who appears in several other Witting detective novels as a constable and in as one of the lead characters) pops up in the last couple of chapters to help Charlton gather crucial evidence in an entirely surreptitious slightly unethical manner. Bradfield eventually makes it to the rank of Chief Inspector, I think, and he becomes the lead detective in Witting›s novels that were written and published in the 1950s and 1960s.

In essence this book can be interpreted as Wilkie Collins redux. The machinations of Mrs. Gulliver, a scheming housekeeper, and the Harlers, a devilish husband and wife, reminded me of the diabolical trio of Count Fosco, Lady Fosco and Percival Glyde in . Mr & Mrs Harler in are intent on sending a poor old man to the madhouse just as those other three set their sinister designs on Laura Fairlie. Similarly, the bulk of the novel involves a highly convoluted history of philandering, adultery and questionable parentage. The often dizzying explanations of who was jumping into whose beds and who fathered what child got to be rather head spinning. The climax of the book involves...well, I can't really mention it without spoiling a genuine surprise. But I must tell you that plot device is something that occurred in two other books I recently read and made me not only raise my eyebrows in surprise but burst out laughing. Not so much because it's both absurd and so utterly unexpected but because who could believe that I would read three different books from three different decades over a period of three months that all featured the same bizarre revelation? It was beyond surreal!

It's not just the slew of dastardly villains all of whom get what they deserve in the end that make this such an engaging page-turner. Cast in the role of the apparent victim of the Harler's "Gaslighting" plot is elderly Sir Victor Warringham, head of the household at the dilapidated estate known as Elmsdale. Sir Victor had recently lost his wife and daughter in a wartime bombing and he's been devastated by their deaths. He turns to spiritualism for solace and has been acting increasingly eccentric. Someone caught him playing at witchcraft spells and black magic in the kitchen, he's written a book on haunted houses, and is currently involved in researching folklore and legends. When Charlton interviews Sir Vincent he reveals what all his experiments have been about. It was a clever bit of misdirection very early in a novel teeming with reversals, upsets and topsy-turvy perceptions.

Perhaps the only drawback to this mystery novel is Witting's tendency to have his characters indulge in long monologues to fill in backstory or to explain themselves. It's another aspect of the book that recalls a Victorian sensibility; an insistence that characters speak at length about their motivations or to dissemble and mislead. Clement Harler, in particular, talks voluminously and pompously. He also calls the lead detective Clayton for much of the book and it's only when Charlton has finally got Harler to come clean and stop lying that he humiliates Harler by sternly correcting him.

Clifford Witting (1907-68) was educated at Eltham College London and served in the Royal Artillery and the Ordinance Corps during WW2. He married Ellen Marjorie Steward in 1934 and worked as a clerk in Lloyds bank from 1924 to 1942. Sadly he is also an undeservedly forgotten writer well worth the attention of any devotee of crime fiction. After languishing in the limbo of Out-of-Printdom for decades Witting's devilishly clever, often hilarious, detective and mystery novels have been reprinted by Galileo Publishing. They are available at the usual online bookselling sites and if you live in the UK perhaps even in real bookstores. In addition to the delightfully bizarre story of   I would highly recommend the following from Clifford Witting's varied output: , and . All of which are available in reprint editions form Galileo.

JF Norris is a part time writer and bookseller. In 1999 he started an internet bookselling business from which his blog gets its name. The blog is solely devoted to of out-of-print & vintage crime, supernatural, adventure and other genre fiction. JF has also written critical essays and reviews on detective & supernatural fiction for fanzines, internet sites, and small press publishers.
The Blog: prettysinister.blogspot.com

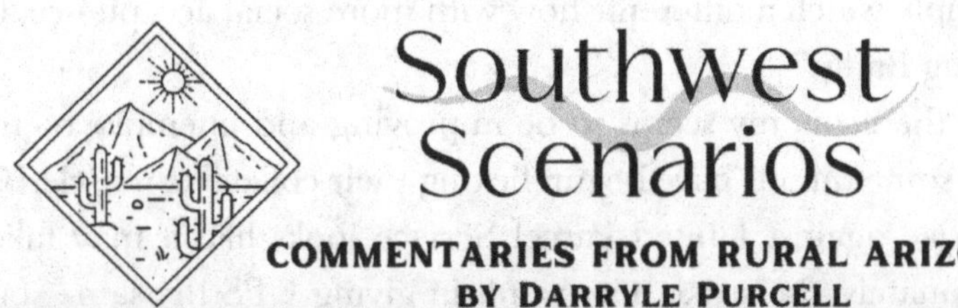

(Protesting has changed immensely in the last few decades. Complaining about PETA putting people in pig suits to protest Weinermobiles seems very naïve by today's standards, in that putting ANTIFA thugs in pig suits would definitely be an improvement.)

Make sausage, not war

Aug, 14, 1997

ONE WOULD THINK THE FINE ART OF PROTESTING IS IN MONUMENTAL DECLINE. THE ANGRY CROWDS THAT USED TO FILL THE STREETS TO HEAR HANOI JANE denounce American imperialism are now sweating to the oldies with her workout tapes. The outraged college students who staged campus sit-ins to protest ROTC programs, conservative newspaper opinions, Ronald Reagan or the lack of black- Hispanic- women- and gay-studies classes presently sip the right kind of wine as they watch HBO Barbra Streisand specials in their time-share vacation condos.

Times they are a-changin'. And protesters have become a thing of the past ... until just recently.

It seems American whining has increased, again, to the level reminiscent of the 1960s.

It began with a religious group announcing a boycott of Disney. On the surface, that action could be equated with Bill Clinton being shocked by the But, as Southern Baptists pointed out, Disney isn't just Pooh-bears and friendly dwarfs anymore. The corporation is now involved in a lot of entertainment offerings, some of which contain sex and violence and not-so-G-rated humor.

The Disney-produced "Ellen" TV sitcom, which features a comic lesbian portraying a comic lesbian, sent the Baptists into their protest. One would think that if they were shocked by the content of the program they could simply watch a different show with more social acceptance, like "Men Behaving Badly."

Now that the economy seems to be improving and unemployment is at a low level, some unions have begun flexing their collective muscle. The Teamsters' strike against United Parcel Service looks like it may take a while. Unfortunately, the strike may result in giving UPS the same status as Railroad Express.

But the big Kahoona of protesters for the '90s is People For the Ethical Treatment of Animals (PETA). These animal rightists are known for their Missing-In-Action style raids on laboratories where they rescue mistreated rats and such.

PETA is presently deployed in an anti-Weinermobile operation. Everywhere the Oscar Meyer Weinermobile shows up, PETA people also show up dressed as pigs with meat protest signs. They attempt to hog the spotlight to preach their tasteless baloney against the eating of meat.

Once again, it would seem that free people have a choice not only in what they want to read and view on TV and at the theater, but in whether they eat meat and/or vegetables. And maniacal vegetarians certainly have the American right to carry signs demanding everyone else stop eating meat. But PETA people in pig suits are hard to take seriously. (I would hope they don't wear their costumes when they protest in the town near where "Deliverance" was filmed.)

I've always wondered what PETA people feed their pets. Do they give their dogs a daily diet of PETA bread? Can a cat live on grits? Do they avoid vitamins derived from shark livers? Would one squeeze melon balls into the shape of a rat to feed to a pet boa constrictor?

Now that I think about it, today's protesters haven't quite reached the level of the whiners of the 1960s. The hippie costumes were rather silly looking, but they outclass pig suits.

Southwest Scenarios

The commentaries that follow here and in future issues were originally published by *The Mohave Valley Daily News* between 1993 & 2013--and in many ways they apply to today. We are grateful to republish these commentaries written by Darryle Purcell in full and unedited. His own brand of humor and style can deliver insight, provoke thought, and even boil blood.

HISTORICAL EMPORIUM
Est. 2003

Hollywood-fawcz Lanon-Creme Shampoo
Never Dries—
it Beautifies!

In ten cent tins
SHORTBREAD
Little cakes of rich shortbread.
Serve with tea, coffee and cocoa.
NATIONAL BISCUIT COMPANY

COCKTAIL NAPKIN

A NEW ORIGINAL BY SUZANNE ELSON

This dirty stained napkin has my future wrapped in it, Jackson thought. How eloquent. He stuffed it in his pocket and watched the beautiful girl exit.

Jackson was a fourth-year student out with his roommates, with no intention of meeting anyone. But the moment he noticed her he was completely mesmerized. She had white-blonde hair and light hazel eyes that were so large and round, he was lost in them. She sat on the barstool to his right. Her friends dumped their coats with her and maneuvered through the crowd to the vacant pool table. "Is the band any good?" she asked, fishing in her purse for change for her drink. He took a long swig of his beer and pivoted his stool to face her. Small talk about the headliner band turned into deep conversations. They chatted about their classes, families, pasts, and dreams. They never left their seats or took their eyes off each other. By the end of the night, Jackson was clearly infatuated with the girl called Linda, if not head over heels in love. He watched her leave with her friends, the napkin folded in his palm. He didn't realize how tightly he was squeezing it until the bartender announced last call and he stared at his hand.

Back at his apartment, Jackson closed the door to his tiny room. The soft, warm glow of the rising sun pierced through the blinds. An old easel leaned against the walls in the corner. He ripped off the top sheet of paper and painted Linda's face, so she would stay in his mind. He was shocked at how quickly she came to life. Linda's angelic eyes smiled at him, and her long hair shone under the lamp. He pulled the napkin out of his pocket. He could only make out three of the ten numbers. That sucks, he thought. But… how hard can it be to find the most beautiful girl in the world? I'll sit on her barstool every night and comb every French class on campus until I find her, thought Jackson.

For three months, Jackson frequented the bar as much as he could. He sat between loud, drunk students night after night, sipping rum and cokes and rereading 1984. He strolled the red-bricked campus walk daily in the hopes of seeing her. He was excited, impatient, and nervous, all twisted together. Jackson finished his last year and waited for acceptance into Teacher's College, but never forgot Linda or removed her picture from his easel. Living in a bachelor's apartment, surviving on macaroni and cheese, he dreamt of the day she would round the corner, and he could finally tell her how he felt, so they could start their life together.

JACKSON'S HAIR HAD GRAYED OVER THE YEARS. HE STILL KEPT HIS MUSTACHE closely trimmed. Lines creased at the corners of his eyes, but he still had the same zest for life and art he had when he was young.

Linda stuffed her long, dark hair under her ball cap. She was tall and willowy, like her dad, but with her mom's deep, dark eyes. She watched her brother Mackenzie grunt and curse as he hauled overstuffed suitcases up the stairs.

"Dad, remember when you were talking about da Vinci last week?" Linda asked, snapping her headphones around her neck.

"Yes…"

"Tell me more."

Jackson smiled and spun around on his stool. "Where were we… Leonardo was born in 1452. Like I said, a time when your social status was very important and vital to your success. And although his father was a wealthy bourgeois, Leonardo was unschooled and apprenticed like any working-class child, since he was illegitimate. Do you remember me telling you about Salai? Well, he came to him as a boy."

Linda nodded as her father continued. "Leonardo was stigmatized for his illegitimacy and bigotry, which made it much harder for him to be appreciated and recognized. But he was. When he met Melzi, he was a newly appointed painter and engineer to Louis XII."

Jackson turned back to his painting. "And why the sudden interest? Have you changed your mind about your future?"

Linda laughed, knowing where this was heading. "No. I just wanted to know why they gave him such a hard time about stuff that doesn't make much difference nowadays, if you think about it."

Jackson's wife, Sharon, entered through the side door and hung up her jacket. She waved to their kids and kissed her husband on the cheek.

"How was work, hon?" Jackson asked as she continued down the hallway.

Sharon came back wrapped in a robe. "Work was okay. More of a sales job and less of a banking position every single day," she said, heading out to the hot tub.

Jackson loved his wife. It was a safe, satisfying love. Nothing extraordinary like what stories are made of, or like the love for another girl hiding in his heart. He never saw Linda again after that night at the bar. But she was never far from his mind, surfacing whenever he was lonely or insecure. He stared at the portrait of his daughter he had just finished. same name, totally different features, he thought.

Jackson and Sharon's 19-year-old son Mackenzie was leaving to spend the summer backpacking through Europe before his final year of college. When his friends came to pick him up, Jackson answered the door. He stared at the young lady in front of him. For a moment he thought his dreams were answered. She had long, white-blonde hair, large hazel eyes, and the fairest complexion he had seen in years. He smiled, assuming the girl would recognize him, but when he saw her discomfort, he immediately realized this girl was at least 20 years younger than him, and it was nothing more than a coincidence.

"Marlowe, is it?" he stumbled.

She nodded.

"Please come in. Sorry, you just look so familiar, I didn't mean to stare," he said. "And you must be Calvin." The young man nodded and shook

Jackson's hand. As Jackson followed Marlowe down the hall, he instantly found himself back at the bar, listening to her silky voice fill his ears.

Mackenzie came up from the den carrying more bags. "I'll call as soon as we get settled, Dad. And don't worry, we'll stay out of trouble." He grinned at his friends. Jackson watched the weighted-down car drive away, wanting so badly to run out and ask Marlowe who her mother was. It was uncanny how much she looked like the girl from the bar.

"What are you doing, dear?" Sharon asked, seeing Jackson's face pressed against the screen door. "Nothing, darling," he said, turning around as she ran her fingers through his hair. "Just thinking about how I'm going to miss our boy."

"30 YEARS OF MARRIAGE. IT WASN'T THAT BAD, WAS IT?" SHARON ASKED, FINishing off her glass of wine.

Jackson smiled at her and squeezed her hand. His hair was completely white now, with deep wrinkles across his forehead. "Not at all hon. There have been difficult times, but we made it through. Here we are now, on the honeymoon we never got to have."

"That's because I was seven months pregnant," she laughed.

"You were radiant when you were pregnant. Well, when you weren't vomiting," he laughed back.

They had two days left on their trip before flying out of Manchester. The elegant little restaurant they were dining at in Calais was directly opposite the large hypermarket where they had spent their entire morning. The elderly waiter brought the bill. "Merci, Madame et Monsieur."

Three hours remained before they needed to catch the shuttle back to Folkestone in Kent. They spent the remaining time strolling through the crowded, cobbled roads. Jackson held Sharon's hand as they passed the locals chatting outside their shops. A young lady bumped into him as she hurried out of one of the boutiques. She spun around to apologize and stopped, realizing she recognized him, but couldn't place his face. Jackson stared back. Those eyes. He knew her. The beautiful lady shook her head, apologized, and continued walking. As she turned the corner, he remembered who she was.

"Back in a second," he said, letting go of Sharon's hand. He caught up with the woman as she was climbing into a taxi. "Excuse me, miss," he breathed as she closed the door.

She grinned and lowered the window. "Now I recognize you, you're Mr. Huxley, Mackenzie's dad, aren't you? My God, it's been a long time. Fancy meeting you in Europe."

"Marlowe, I've been meaning to ask you something for years, if you can just hang on a sec."

"Okay," she said, mumbling something to the driver.

Jackson recomposed himself. "May I be so blunt as to ask your mother's name?"

Marlowe frowned. "Why?"

"I wonder if she might have been an old friend of mine."

She looked at him, confused. "Linda," she said as the taxi pulled away. Jackson stood there, stuck to the ground, as the taxi disappeared down the street. His hands clasped his chest as he struggled to take a breath. He realized Sharon was now beside him, but he couldn't bring himself to look at her. He turned and ran back to the shop Marlowe had exited from earlier.

Jackson asked the portly man behind the counter what he knew about Marlowe. "Oh yes, monsieur. Mademoiselle Marlowe lives on the country road near the big cotton mill. Rue 6," he offered.

"Thank you for your help," Jackson said, dropping money on the counter for a handful of hastily chosen magnets.

Sharon stood behind him, arms crossed, eyes fighting away tears. "What the hell is going on here, Jackson?" she shouted. "What's your connection with that woman? Who is she?"

"There's something I really need to do," he said, kissing her on her forehead before hurrying out of the shop. "Go back to the room, hon. I'll meet you there shortly. Promise," he shouted as he left.

THE CURTAINS WERE DRAWN. NOT A HINT OF BREEZE MOVED THEM. SOUNDS OF children playing on the pavement drifted up into the darkness as Marlowe led him in. A single white candle burned by the side of the bed. An older lady lay on her side, her cropped, damp hair pressed against her head. Her fair skin was taut, pulled over fine cheekbones. Her eyes rarely opened, but when they did, the most beautiful light hazel color filled them. Jackson cradled her clasped hands. He managed to gather from her sparse words that she left for Italy shortly after meeting him - with the intent of returning - but was in a horrible automobile accident and spent the next several years recovering, eventually staying in France. Although she got pregnant with Marlowe, she never married. She kept his memory close to her heart.

For several nights, Jackson sat, holding her hands and talking quietly to her. He knew she didn't have much time left. As the early morning sun shouldered the neighboring houses, Linda opened her watery eyes. His beautiful girl was still beautiful, so radiant, even in her last minutes. He squeezed her hands as she gasped for air, her weak chest rising and falling less. Jackson softly cried as Marlowe closed her eyes, remembering the first time he saw her. I searched a lifetime for you, he thought, and now I have to say goodbye.

BACK AT HOME, JACKSON ENTERED THROUGH THE SIDE DOOR AND SET DOWN his luggage. Sharon was in the den, reading. "Please forgive me, sweetheart," he started, "I had to say goodbye to an old friend."

Sharon's shoulders were shaking. He was sure she was crying. But instead, when she looked up, there was only anger in her eyes. "You didn't even call or respond to my texts, Jackson. How could you do that to me? Did you think I would just sit here and patiently wait for you after you left me completely alone with two days remaining on our vacation? I will never, forgive you for that."

Sharon stared at him with total contempt. He frantically tried to think of something to say. "And before you come up with any more excuses, all your clothes are in the spare room. I want you gone by morning. You have hurt me beyond words, and I don't know where we stand now. I need time, Jackson."

Jackson was at a loss for words. Looking at his belongings neatly piled on the bed made his life seem so small. On top of the pile was his old easel. Clipped onto it was a yellowed sheet of paper he instantly recognized as the old drawing of Linda. The cocktail napkin was stapled to it.

"What did you take me for?" Sharon asked, standing at the door. "You even named our girl after her." Jackson watched the tears roll down her face. "Please, let me…"

Sharon shook her head. She walked out of the room without saying another word.

ALONE, AFTER ART CLASS, JACKSON PAINTED. HIS EYES SWELLED AS THE COLors danced and chased across the paper. He let the brush do the work as he thought about the stupid way he had led his life and the terrible pain he had caused Sharon. The brush smoothly swept across the sheet, filling in the white, completing the painting before he really had a chance to look. He laid down his brush and studied the result. He had captured the raw beauty of a fine lady, a lady that was meant to be Linda, but instead, Sharon's sad face looked back at him. A face he had never really appreciated until now. Dark wavy hair fell loosely down her forehead. Faint freckles sprinkled across the bridge of her nose, and the slightest curve of a smile lit up her deep, dark eyes. Tears ran down his cheeks as he realized what a fool he was to have chased a 30-year dream. He wept for this beauty who was always there, always loving, always supportive. Jackson grabbed his keys and briefcase. He was determined to chase after the woman, starting now, even if it took him the rest of his life.

LINDA UNFOLDED THE DAMP FACE CLOTH, PRESSING THE COOL SIDE AGAINST her father's skin. A new baby slept soundly on her lap. Jackson's sparse white hair was slicked back and his face was now heavily wrinkled with prominent laugh lines. His breaths were coming less and less often. He hadn't opened his eyes for days. Mackenzie sat on the other side of the bed, reading his favorite book, , to him, for the second time.

Suddenly, the side door opened. Light footsteps squeaked on the old hardwood floor. A chair screeched over to the bed. Jackson felt warmth in his hand. He felt a familiar squeeze. Jackson took a long, deep breath, and slowly released it. With everything he had, he fluttered open his eyes.

"You came back," he whispered.

Sharon held his hand tighter. "I did. I wanted to see you one last time, Jackson. I love you."

Jackson nodded. Tears rolled down his face. "I prayed every day that you would." His words were forced, separated. Sharon gently brushed his tears away and ran her fingers through his hair.

He sighed, and slowly closed his eyes for the last time. As Sharon glanced up at their children, she noticed a large painting on the wall beside the window. It was beautifully done, the most elegant piece of artwork she had ever seen. It was definitely Jackson's best work.

And it was her.

END

RUTH LAW

One of the reasons *ADVENTURES* BookZine gives such weight to people and stories from long ago is that they are so fascinating. Today's culture takes much for granted and assumes so much. In our social media age we are teaching ourselves to do things based on how it appears to others, because that is what gains attention.

What we esteem from long ago are those things which were authentic. It was a classier time when people valued life. People did things in a celebration of life and exploration. Recognition and publicity was a result, not the sole aim.

Case in point: Ruth Law Oliver. Born in Lynn, Massachusetts in 1887. As a child, instead of seeing herself as a victim, Ruth worked to physically keep up with her stuntman brother Rodman.

RUTH LAW.

Later, as history has it, Orville Wright refused to give Ruth flying lessons because he believed women were not inclined to understand the mechanics involved. Ruth became more determined yet. "The surest way to make me do a thing is to tell me I can't do it," she is quoted as saying.

Regardless of circumstances that may have threatened her chosen path, Ruth became a pilot, and a mechanic. She went on to break an air-speed record and set other records after World War 1. Other details are worth mentioning, but we encourage you to take a moment to look her up. Because Ruth was eventually hindered from flying, she suffered a nervous breakdown. Imagine what a loss it would have been if she hadn't been determined at all. If she hadn't been willing to fight, not for attention, but for what she loved.

1916; Ruth after landing in New York (from Chicago).

CHASING DUST IN THE WIND

A NEW ORIGINAL BY KYLE OWENS

"Will that be all?"

"Yeah, that'll do it. I also got some gas."

"Okay. I made some coffee if you want a cup?

"No, I'm fine. Thank you."

As George rung up the man's items on the cash register the man noticed a joke book off to the side and asked, "You like joke books?"

"Yeah, when people come in and yell at you constantly about the gas prices you have to try and find some humor in life somehow."

"I guess that's true."

"So, I just hit 'em with this."

The man laughed, "That should work."

"That's $42.73."

The man handed him the money. George gave him his change and said, "Have a good one."

"You too."

The man left and George sat back down and began reading his joke book when Nancy Francis walked in a bit frazzled. "Sorry I'm late, George."

"No problem."

"I fell asleep on the couch and the next thing I noticed it was after three."

"It's after six now."

"Well, I would have been here sooner, but I didn't really want to come," she said as she walked behind the counter.

"At least you're honest."

"Been busy today?"

"I was changing the gas prices and the wind blew the six away. Or was it the nine? Did anything exciting happen to you?" asked George as he placed his joke book on the counter.

"Just the nap," Nancy said as she put on her blue vest with her name tag pinned to it and then noticed George's joke book. "Are you reading another joke book?"

"Yeah," George said as he took his store vest off and hung it on a nail in the closet.

"Who is it this time?"

"Milton Berle. Of course, when you read Milton Berle's jokes, you're probably reading several comedians' jokes."

"Tell me one. I need me some funny."

"Let's see here-" George mumbled as picked up his joke book and thumbed through it quickly. "Here's one. A man buys thermometers in the winter because they're lower then."

"That's a Milton Berle joke?" asked Nancy with an expression on her face like she has just smelled something gross.

"Yeah."

"That's terrible."

"Well, he is dead."

"Your stuff is better than that."

"I just write jokes for fun- hey is that a pun?"

"Jokes are worthless without an audience. You need to perform your act somewhere."

"There's no place in Yellow Knife, South Dakota to perform comedy."

"I didn't say in Yellow Knife," said Nancy. "You could go to Hollywood or New York or something."

"I don't know how I would do in front of an audience," George said.

"Look around you George. Yellow Knife's a dying town. Maybe comedy is your way out of here. You just graduated High School- the world is ahead of you so you should use this time to pursue your dream. I tell you if I had your talent and I didn't have any kids- oh boy, if I didn't have kids-"

"Maybe you're right."

"I know I'm right. And what's more is that you know I'm right."

"I better head on out. Oh, I need a carton of cigarettes."

"I thought your mom quit smoking."

"She'll never quit. She's smoked so much they should at least name a cancer after her."

Nancy reached up to the top shelf behind the counter and got a carton of down, handed them to George and he gave her the money for them.

"I think you should do it."

George smiled a wicked smile at her and with a come-hither voice said, "Why Nancy, you beast."

"I mean go to Hollywood to try to make it as a comedian."

"I appreciate your confidence, but I'd probably stink at it."

"You're funny. Funnier than Milton Berle."

"See you tomorrow."

"Think about it."

"Okay."

George walked out of the store carrying his mother's carton of cigarettes in one hand and his joke book in the other. He slowly made his way down the deserted road that ran through the town of mostly abandoned storefronts until he got to his house on the corner of Avenue West.

George walked in and as usual found his mother lying on the couch watching "The Wheel of Fortune" with the volume up as loud as she could get it.

"That you, George?" his mother screamed without looking, which was chased with a cough.

"It's me."

"You're late."

"Nancy over napped."

"You got my cigarettes?"

"Yeah, I got 'em."

George handed the carton over to her, she opened them up, took out a pack, tore off the top, slid out a cigarette, lit it and took a big puff on it, closed her eyes and said, "Ah- cancer, take me away."

"You really should quit that you know."

"Why?"

"Why? You're the only person left on earth that asks that."

"I like smoking. I'm retired, not hurting anyone but me. What's the big deal?"

"What about all of this second-hand smoke that gets on me."

"I'll smoke harder."

"At least you try."

George then gave his mother a kiss on the head then went into the kitchen where he poured himself a bowl of cereal. He walked over to the kitchen sink and ran water over the cereal for his supper before he headed to his bedroom to eat.

GEORGE WAS SITTING ON HIS BED LISTENING TO A WOODY ALLEN COMEDY CD through his headphones. On his wall were posters and pictures of come-dians, everyone from Bill Cosby, Richard Pryor, Jerry Seinfeld and Johnny Carson. On a shelf were several rows of comedy CDs from all his favorite stand ups. On another shelf were an unimaginable number of joke books from various publishers.

Suddenly his best friend Mandel appeared at his window wearing a red T-Shirt with the words "It doesn't say anything" written across the front of it.

"You home?" asked Mandel.

George jumped at the sound of his voice and said, "Scare me to death."

"I usually just have that effect on women."

"No, it's universal."

George turned off his CD player and pulled down his headphones until they collared around his neck.

"Look what I found," said Mandel as he held his cell phone up and showed George a webpage.

"When did you get a cell phone?"

"It belongs to my sister's boyfriend."

"Willie Jack?"

"No this is Rodney's phone. Willie Jack went to Alabama to start a worm farm. He said there were a lot of upfront costs, but then it would pay for itself."

"Upfront costs? I guess you do have to build a fence to keep the fish out. Why are you showing me the Hollywood Reporter website?"

"Just read it," commanded Mandel.

"Comedian Star Search, top Hollywood agent looking for new comedians to sign. The top ten finalists will be cast for a reality show."

"I thought of you when I saw that," said Mandel.

"Reality show- that sounds terrible."

"It's a way in, man. Don't knock it."

George handed the phone back to Mandel and said, "I don't have any money to get to Hollywood."

"It won't cost that much. I wrote the address down for you," Mandel said as he pulled a piece of paper put of his right pant pocket and handed it to George.

George took the paper, glanced it over then whispered out, "I'm not interested."

"I thought you wanted to be a comedian?"

"You're the second person that has brought that up to me today."

"Don't you see what this means?"

"I have nosey friends."

"We're just looking out for you is all."

"Well, you can stop now."

"It's fate. You have to do this. In school you always told me how you wanted to be a comedian."

"Yes, but it was a foolish kid dream- like playing shortstop for the Yankees."

"But that dream came true for somebody. And I'm pretty sure they were playing baseball when the call came."

George just looked away as he stroked the piece of paper with his fingers.

"You have to be in the game, George. You can't become a star in Yellow Knife."

"It's where I live."

"Do you know what they call comedians in Yellow Knife?"

"I think they're still called comedians."

"Convenience store clerks."

"Oh. What do they call cake in Yellow Knife?"

"What?"

"I was just curious."

"Listen, you have to do this for us."

"Us?"

"I got nothing. No talent, no money, no nothing. All I got is you."

"That's both sweet and disturbing."

"Maybe I should have gone with Willie Jack and helped him with that worm farm. I'm pretty handy at building fences."

"Listen, I need to get to sleep because I've got to do the morning shift tomorrow."

"Okay, but at least think about it."

"I'll think."

"Peace out," Mandel said as he left.

"Uh- Shake well before using. Man, I really need to cool up my goodbyes."

George looked at the address on the piece of paper before placing it on the nightstand. He thought about what Mandel said then turned out the light.

THE NEXT MORNING, AT 4:15 AM, GEORGE WAS SITTING AT THE STORE counter with no one else around thumbing through his joke book.

"My nephew put too many stamps on a letter and he kept worrying that it would go too far. That's kind of funny."

A car pulled up.

"Word must be getting out that I'm lonely."

In walked the store's manager, Holston Fritters, and hollered, "Jason-"

"George."

"Yeah, I need you to go in the back for a second."

"Why?"

"Just do as I say."

George stared at him before reluctantly going to the small back office. Once in the office he noticed the manager getting money out of the cash register.

"Hold on now!" George shouted as he hurried over to him.

"I told you to go in the back."

"You can't steal money from the cash register."

"I'm not stealing it. I'm just borrowing it is all."

"I'll be held responsible for this."

"No, you won't because it didn't happen," said the manager as he put the money into his pocket. "Besides, everybody does it."

"I don't."

"Which is why you're broke. Face the facts Jason, we're nothing. Our lives are worthless. Take it where you can get it and screw the consequences."

"The people's lives in this town aren't worthless."

"Name someone that has accomplished something that has come from Yellow Knife, South Dakota."

George had no answer.

"This is where the losers live. And they aren't allowed to leave," said the manager.

"I don't believe that."

"You will."

"No, I won't. There are good people that live here. We're not all thieves and losers."

"Do you know what we sell the most in here? Huh? Alcohol and cigarettes. Does that sound like a community with high hopes about itself. There are more alcoholics in this town than dreamers, boy."

"It's not going to happen to me."

"It already has."

"What are you talking about?"

"Your father died an alcoholic."

"You leave my father out of this!"

"I knew your father, Jason-"

"My name is George!"

The manager looked at George confused and muttered, "Who the heck is Jason then?"

"I don't know. But just because my father fell down in life doesn't mean I will. Failure isn't genetic," said George.

"We're all doomed to a life of nothing here. This is what this little town does to people. There's no industry, no college, we don't even have a stop light or a movie theater here. This town is just nothing. And if you stay here, you'll be nothing too."

George didn't think. He just acted.

"No! I'm out of here! I quit!"

George then headed for the door.

"You can't quit. Someone has to be here. Hey! Come back here!"

George walked out of the store into the early morning darkness. His mind began tracing his life's past and possible future. He got to his house, walked inside, made his way over to his mother's bedroom, opened the door then turned on the light that sat on the nightstand.

"Oh- turn the light off," his mother said as she squinted her eyes."

"I have to talk to you."

"Can't you wait until I'm conscious?"

"No."

"What's wrong?"

"Do you think I'll become a failure like Dad?"

"What?"

"Do you?"

"No. You woke me up for this?"

"I've got to get out of here."

"Then turn the light off."

"I mean out of this town."

"Out of town? You mean you're leaving me?"

"There's nothing here for me, Mom."

"You got that job down at the store."

"I quit."

"What'd you steal?"

"I didn't steal anything. That's what got me into trouble."

"Baby, if you want me to help you steal something I'll do it."

"No, mom.

"Because you're my boy."

"I'm not trying to steal something. I want to do something I like doing for once."

His mother started laughing, "You want to do something you like? We are talking about life now, aren't we?"

"Yes, mom."

"You never get to do what you want."

"People all over the world are doing jobs that they enjoy."

"Yeah, but they ain't an Indian living in Yellow Knife."

George looked away from her fearing that she might be right and said, "I want to try it though. Try and achieve my dream."

"What dream?

"Comedy."

"Comedy? You mean telling jokes?"

"Yeah."

"For a living?"

"Yeah."

She started laughing again and said, "That's crazy talk."

"Mandel told me about a comedy contest in Hollywood. He gave me the address," George said as he pulled the paper with the address on it out of his pocket and handed it to her. She tried to read it, but couldn't and handed it back to him.

"I can't read this unless it's on a bottle label."

"A Hollywood Agency is looking for new comedians to sign."

"Why?"

"The old ones died I guess."

"Be a joke teller here."

"There's no place around here to tell jokes for a living."

"You can tell 'em to me."

"Mom, how's that going to help me?"

"I promise to laugh."

"You don't understand," George said as he stood up then began to pace the room in frustration.

"Of course, I understand. I'm not drunk all of the time you know. You have a dream that you'd like to give a shot before you lose your chance."

"Listen, I'm going to do this. I want to know if I have your support?"

"Where do you have to go?"

"Hollywood."

"Hollywood? But if you go to Hollywood who'll get my cigarettes?"

"I'll get Mandel to get your cigarettes."

"Mandel?"

"He'll help check on you."

"I'm not a child you know."

"You do tend to put things in your mouth that shouldn't go there," George said.

"I've been meaning to ask you- what kind of name is Mandel anyway?"

"I don't know," George said as he rubbed his face with his opened hand.

"I don't want to be here without you."

"I know. I'm going to miss you too, but I've got to try and better myself instead

of-"

"Repeating your parents mistakes."

Her statement hit George like a freight train. "Don't say that. You're a good mother."

"No, I'm not. I've known that for some time now. Maybe if I support you in this, I can start changing things around here for me too."

"Thank you."

George bent down and kissed his mother on the top of her head.

"Now, you get on out of here before I start crying."

"Okay," George said with a smile.

He then walked to the door, opened it then started to walk out, but stopped and turned to his mother.

"I love you, Mom," he said then closed the door.

His mother laid in the bed with tears in her eyes and whispered, "Don't turn out like me. God, please don't let him turn out like me."

The next morning George had the car hood up as he checked the engine on an old yellow, 1950 Chevy, trying to get it in shape to go to Hollywood.

"Hey George," said Mandel as he walked into the yard.

"I'm doing it."

Mandel quickly turned his back, slightly embarrassed and said, "Oh, I'm sorry- tell me when you're done."

"No. I'm going to Hollywood."

"You're kidding?"

"Nope. I'm going to do it."

"I inspired you?"

"In your own way I guess you did."

"I'll take my ten percent off the top."

George jokingly showed him his fist. "You'll take your ten percent from this five percent."

"That seems fair," Mandel said with a laugh as he helped George look over his car. "Does this thing even run?"

"It'll get you to where you need to go as long as you don't have to be there at a certain time."

"Why don't you fly?"

"I ain't flying."

"Are you afraid of it crashing?"

"Yes."

"More people die in a bathroom than on a plane."

"How big is that bathroom?"

"You know what I mean," said Mandel.

George poured a bottle of motor oil into a funnel perched atop the engine.

"Have you been working on any routines?" asked Mandel as he looked over the car engine.

"I've been looking through my notebooks and piecing some stuff together. I think I've got a pretty good idea what I'm going to do. I'll just rehearse it on the road while I'm going there."

"Where did you get this car anyway?"

"My Dad lost it in a poker game," said George as he removed the empty oil bottle, placed it into a plastic bag and wiped his hands with a rag. "The only thing that is worrying me is that I don't really have a hook. You know- something to stand out."

"What do you mean you don't have a hook? You're an Indian in Hollywood. That should stand out all by itself."

"I guess that's true. Just tell jokes about my life, my town, friends-"

"Exactly. Take me for instance. I'm half Indian and half white. I'm at war with myself."

"Yeah. Every time you go camping you burn your tent down."

They both laughed as George got into the car and turned the key. It made a struggling noise like a drowning victim before it finally started up.

"Just call me Johnny Nascar," said George over the revs of the engine.

"Do you think it'll get you to Hollywood?"

They both stared at the thick black plume of smoke that exited the exhaust pipe.

"I don't even think it'll get me out of the yard," said George.

THAT NIGHT, IN HIS BEDROOM, GEORGE PACKED HIS SUITCASE THEN WENT over to his bed and took out his notebooks of jokes where he began reading through them. He then stopped then looked at the posters of comedians he had on his walls.

"Were you all this scared when you started?"

He placed his notebook down as his eyes locked onto his small alarm clock.

"My world changes tomorrow. But I don't know which way."

THE NEXT MORNING GEORGE CAME INTO HIS MOTHER'S BEDROOM TO TELL her goodbye. However, she was drunk and passed out to the world. He looked at an empty bottle of liquor on the nightstand crisscrossed with shadows from the mini blinds. He picked it up as a sigh whispered out of his mouth. "You could have told me goodbye first."

He then placed the bottle back down onto the table and kissed his mother on the forehead then left.

George came out of the house carrying his suitcase, walked to the car, put the suitcase in the trunk then looked about the yard and said aloud, "I'm leaving this town now and I'm not coming back until I'm somebody."

He got into the car, placed the key in the ignition then turned it, but it wouldn't start.

"I guess I'm back."

AN HOUR LATER MANDEL CAME OVER IN HIS TRUCK WITH A PAIR OF BOOSTER cables, hooked them up to the battery and shouted, "Try her now!" from beneath the car hood.

George turned the key chased with a quick prayer as the engine roared to life.

"Hey!" George shouted in celebration as he got out of the car and joined Mandel at the front of it. "Thanks for getting up early to help me out."

"Glad to help. Which way are you going to get to Hollywood?"

"I'm going through Rapid City on I-90 and then I get on I-25 and hook up on I-80 and get on I-15 in Salt Lake City and from there I go straight to L.A."

"Are you going through Vegas?"

"Yeah."

"Are you going to gamble?"

"That's what the car's for."

Mandel then reached into his pocket, pulled out some change and said, "Here's a quarter. You have to play a slot for me."

"But I'm not going into a casino. I'm just going through Vegas."

"This is the closest I'll ever come to Vegas. You have to play it for me."

"Mandel-"

"All you have to do is go into a casino, put this quarter in the slot, pull the handle then leave. What's so hard about that?"

"Okay- okay," George said as he took Mandel's quarter and put it into his front pocket. "Which casino do you want me to go to?"

"Doesn't matter. If I win just call me."

"If you win, you'll never hear from me again."

They both laughed.

"I guess I better head on out," said George.

"Yeah. Don't worry about your mom, I'll get her cigarettes and check on her for you."

"I appreciate that."

They both just sort of stood there not really knowing what to say or do.

"See ya," Mandel said as he reached his hand out to shake George's hand goodbye.

"That ain't going to work," said George as he gave Mandel a hug.

"I'm very uncomfortable right now," said Mandel.

"So am I," George said as he let go. "Next time you see me I'll be a star."

"I'll watch every night to check if you're on it."

"You do that," George said as he got into the car then stuck his head out of the open driver's side window and yelled, "Hollywood look out! There's a crazy Indian heading your way in a car called Cough Drop!"

George then drove off and Mandel watched him disappear into the morning dark and shouted, "Win it for all of us, George!"

THE NEXT DAY GEORGE WAS DRIVING ALONG WHEN HE CAME UPON A SIGN THAT read Las Vegas one mile.

"Welcome to Las Vegas. Las Vegas, that's Latin for 'Where'd my money go?'"

He drove through the famous city's downtown where he was mesmerized by not only what he was seeing, but by its haunted past of gangsters and Hollywood stars that came in and out of its midst.

George parked the car then hurried into the first casino he saw, walked over to a slot machine, pulled out a quarter and whispered, "The is for you Mandel." He then put the quarter in the slot, pulled the handle and promptly didn't win.

"I told him there was no reason for me to come into one of these casinos."

As George turned to leave, he saw a sign that read, 'Amateur Talent Show' with an arrow pointed toward a door.

"Well, I be a cigar Indian-" he said to himself as he headed toward the door.

George walked in and saw a juggling act on stage in front of a small audience. He wondered how he could get on stage when he saw a man in the front at a table along with a few other people. He walked over to them.

"Excuse me. I was wondering if it was too late to go on?"

"We can put you on. What's your name?"

"George Running Bear."

"Uh- have you been drinking?"

"No. That's my name. I'm an American Indian. You know- Native American. Go Redskins."

"Oh. We can put you on next. What do you do?"

"Comedy."

"That's great. Just go in the back and wait your turn. Dan will take you back there."

"Okay.

A man stood up, who was obviously Dan said, "Just follow me."

He led George to the back of the stage where they stood just behind the curtain.

"Are you excited?" Dan asked.

"I guess I am. Not a lot of people here, huh?"

"Mostly tourists. They get tired of gambling or they don't have anything left to gamble so they come in here thinking they might find their big break, sort of their last gasp at success before heading back home to their ordinary lives."

"Do any of them find success here?"

"No. How long is your act?"

"Seven minutes."

"Can you make it longer?"

"What do you mean? Seven minutes is all I've got. It's what I've been rehearsing on the road."

"Where are you from?"

"Yellow Knife, South Dakota."

"Sounds like a small town."

"It actually sounds like a town for cowardly serial killers."

"We need you to do forty minutes."

"Forty minutes?"

"Our next three acts passed out. You're on."

George was stunned by the time request and walked to the edge of the curtains and just stood there frozen.

Dan went over to him where he whispered, "Unless you're doing a puppet act, the audience needs to see you."

"Yeah- I guess that's right. Here goes nothing."

"I'm sure it is," said Dan under his breath as George walked to the center of the stage where the microphone was located.

George stood in front of the microphone with his hands by his side. The audience had no idea who he was or what his act would be. He simply stood there in the bright lights and said nothing.

After about twenty seconds George hurried off the stage. He passed by Dan who said, "That's the first mime stand-up comedy routine I've ever seen, kid."

George walked by people laughing at him.

George walked out of the casino and went to his car. He opened the door and got in.

Then George began crying.

As the day melted away, George finally made it out of his car and sat on the hood watching cars go by along with his life.

"You've done it now George. You're all alone and scared to death. No one can help me, but me. Now I've got to decide, do I go back to my home of nothing or do I go on to Hollywood and possibly embarrass myself?"

He looked one way and said to himself, "That way leads home." He then looked the other way and said, "That way leads to Hollywood. I know what home is like. I have no idea what waits for me in Hollywood. Could be failure or perhaps something big could happen. I have no chance at home of anything happening big."

He thought about it.

"Look out Hollywood, George Running Bear is on his way."

George got in his car, started it up and headed out of the parking lot toward Hollywood, but before he got out of the parking lot the car sputtered and stopped.

"I can't believe I'm out of gas."

After George got some gas, he headed out toward Hollywood and finally seen his destination in the form of a sign stating it was just ahead on the right.

"I made it, Hollywood, California, where the high school mascots are minks."

He then looked at the address Mandel had given him.

"Doheny Road- Doheny Road- where are you? There it is."

He turned down the street and went about looking for the correct address.

"That's it. Now to find a parking place, I thought nobody owned cars out here because they were all environmentalists."

George parked his car, headed into the large building and followed the signs that led inside a door where he saw a secretary at her desk.

"Excuse me-"

"Yes."

"I'm here about the comedian search that was on The Hollywood Reporter website."

"Yes. Just fill out this form," she said as she handed him the paperwork.

"Thank you?"

"Just have a seat over there and fill it out and then give it back to me," she said with a nod.

"Sure."

George went over to the couch, down and began filling out the form as an African-American man in his middle forties walked in then headed over to the secretary.

"Hi- I'm here about the comedian search."

She handed him a form. "Okay. Just fill this out then give it back to me."

"Sure," he said as he took the form then went over and sat down beside George.

"Hello," said the man.

"Hey. I'm George."

"I'm Leroy."

George stared at him and couldn't help but say, "I've seen you before."

"I've been on TV a few times."

"I thought this was just an amateur contest?"

"Nah, they let anyone sign up."

"Oh, I didn't know that," George muttered with a great deal of concern in his voice.

"I don't recall the last name-"

"Running Bear."

"Running Bear?"

"It's Irish."

Leroy laughed, "That's good. You been on TV before?"

"No."

"Where have you performed at?"

"I guess you could say that I performed in Vegas."

"Could say?"

"I had technical problems. Nothing came out of my mouth."

"Oh- was it your first time?"

"Yeah. I got up there and I was ready- but as soon as I seen everybody staring back at me, I froze. I couldn't think of my routine at all."

"How many people were in the room?"

"About thirty or so I guess."

"You do know that this show is going to be on network TV?"

"You mean the reality show part?"

"Yeah, but the ten finalists have to do a live routine on The Tonight Show."

George's concern began growing.

"I'm going to die on network TV. Of course, I won't be the first Indian to die on TV thanks to Bonanza."

"You won't die. Everyone struggles the first time."

"Did you?"

"I got a standing ovation."

"I feel better now."

"Where are you staying?" asked Leroy.

"The Cough Drop. That's the name of my car."

"You been sleeping in your car?"

"It's all I can afford."

"You can bunk with me."

"Where are you staying?"

"The Delilah."

"What in the world is The Delilah?"

EXACTLY THIRTY-FIVE MINUTES LATER GEORGE AND LEROY WERE STANDING IN front of a rundown motel with a flashing sign in the front that had the word Delilah splashed across it, though the letter 'h' was lying on the side-walk propped up against the bottom of the building.

"That's The Delilah," said Leroy.

"Looks like its seen better days."

"Interesting comment coming from the owner of that car," Leroy said as he pointed at George's car.

"I guess that's true. How much will this cost me?"

"We'll split the bill."

"How much will that be?"

"It's fifty a night."

All the strength went out of George's legs. "I appreciate your help and all, but I can't afford it."

"You can't afford $25.00 a night?"

"All my money is kind of hiding from me right now."

"I know that feeling. So how much will you charge me to stay in your car?"

George was shocked by his question. "You mean you can't afford this either?"

"Not really."

"But you've been on The Tonight Show".

"I was on it one time."

"But I thought that's all it took. People would see you and book you and bam- you're bigger than a reality show prison reunion special."

"I was big for a while, but even at that I was just scraping by. Money would come in and I'd spend it on bills and it was gone. Then everyone stopped calling."

"I guess I never thought of it like that."

"Comedy can be cruel."

"Then why do you keep doing it?"

"It's what I'm supposed to do. I just haven't quite convinced anybody else of that yet."

"Hence the contest?"

"Exactly. I'm afraid it's my last stand."

"Well, let me show you to your room," said George as they walked over to his car. "Would you like a room with a view?"

"Yes, I would and a waterbed if possible."

"I'll bring the water hose up to your room myself."

As the day drifted into night George and Leroy sat on the hood of the car and watched traffic go by from the motel parking lot. George began writing in his notebook under the street light as his quiet intensity forced a smile of admiration from Leroy.

"You working on your routine?" asked Leroy.

"Yeah. I'm scared to death too."

"No reason to be. The worst thing they can do to you is kill you."

"I guess that's true. Do you have your routine down yet?"

"Sure. Ever since I heard about the contest, I've been trying out new material every night at the clubs."

"That's a huge advantage."

"Yeah. I know what works and what doesn't. It's the only way to tell."

"I guess it is."

"Lay some lines on me."

"Nah- I'll just keep 'em to myself."

"You don't think I'll steal your stuff, do you?"

"Oh no- I didn't mean it like that. I'm just afraid it's not any good."

"You'll never know until you do it."

George thought it over. "I guess that's right."

"Go stand over there in the spotlight and see if you can impress me."

"Okay."

George got up off the car then went and stood under the parking lot lights. He took a deep breath then began his routine.

"I'm George Running Bear- and no my father's name isn't Smokey. I'm a Cherokee Indian from Yellow Knife, South Dakota, the home of- well, nothing. There's not a whole lot to do in Yellow Knife. We don't have any stop lights. No movie theaters. No big chain stores. However, we do have a hospital- because we have no stop lights. It's a very poor town. I remember growing up the first time I heard the phrase 'The Government's War on Poverty'- it scared me to death. I thought they were going to kill us. My Mom and Dad are good people- in their own way. Dad was a good provider. He always brought home half of his unemployment check. My parents had a hate-hate relationship. I know statistics show that married men live longer than single men, but single men don't usually die from poisoning. I've been reading the news here lately and illegal immigration comes up a lot. If it's one thing Indian's know about its illegal immigration. You all better build that wall."

Then George's demeanor changed. He became soft spoken and appeared to be looking inside himself.

"You know I almost didn't come here tonight. I didn't think I had the courage to stand up here in front of everyone. My first attempt at standup was a disaster. I couldn't even think of anything to say. I just didn't want to put myself through that again. Then the other night when I couldn't sleep worrying about this contest, I turned on the TV and happened upon one of the cable news channels and they were doing a story about this guy that wanted to accomplish his dream. He wanted to climb a mountain. You see, he was blind. And he was the nicest man you could ever meet. He didn't blame anyone for his being born blind. He was happy and joking around- he's what we're supposed to be like as human beings. And I got to thinking if he can climb that mountain while blind then surely, I could get up in front of you all and tell a few jokes. It was truly an inspirational story- well, until he fell off. He walked right off the side. I'm George Running Bear, goodnight, everybody!"

Leroy applauded, "That's great, man."

"Really?" George asked as he rejoined him on the hood of the car.

"Absolutely. I think you have a great chance of making the cut."

"Is that what they're going to do tomorrow?"

"Yeah, they'll take the top ten and then they put 'em on TV in a reality type show of some kind. I don't really know what happens then. They probably don't either."

"Will we be on TV tomorrow?"

"Maybe. They'll highlight the better ones and the worst ones."

"Oh, if they're highlighting the worst ones then I'm guaranteed to be on then."

"You have to think positive."

"I keep thinking of Vegas."

"We all have that one show that haunts us. You've already got it out of the way."

"I guess it's best to do it when you're not on TV than when you are."

"Exactly."

"What time is it?"

Leroy looked at his watch and said, "A little after eleven."

"Man, I'm so nervous, but you don't look nervous at all."

"That's because I'm cool. Say, if you win the grand prize what are you going to do with it?" asked Leroy.

"Get my mom out of debt."

"Ah- the good son."

"I'd like to buy a better used car too."

"That I would have to agree with."

"I have a tendency to lose it in the parking lot because when I go looking for it, I can't find it because I keep looking through the thing because of all the rust."Leroy laughed as he suggested, "Let's try and get us some sleep."

"Yeah. You know, I'm starting to get a little hungry."

"Why didn't you say so."

Leroy reached into his pocket and pulled out a candy bar and said, "A black man always carries a candy bar and an alibi in case of an emergency."

Leroy broke off half of the candy bar and gave it to George.

"To fame and fortune," toasted Leroy.

"To fame and fortune."

They clanked their bars together and ate them.

"Do you think fame will change you?" asked George.

"I sure hope so because I'm about to go to bed with an Indian on the hood of his car."

They both laughed and slowly drifted off to sleep.

THE NEXT MORNING GEORGE AND LEROY WALKED INTO A LARGE AUDITORIUM filled with comedians whom had dreams of stardom. In the front was a stage with hand drawn pictures hanging on the back wall as if it had been made for a children's play or a really under budgeted sitcom. In front of the stage was a table with three people sitting at it and a long line of people standing at it.

"Hey, that's John Fox," George pointed out as he whispered.

"Sure, looks like it."

"He had his own sitcom in the nineties."

"He probably got a private invite to be on the show by the producers."

"I thought everyone here was supposed to be an amateur. I can't compete with known talent."

"He's just like me," assured Leroy. "No one is here because we're known talent anymore. Now relax."

"My hand is shaking."

"Well, stop it. An Indian shaking might cause it to rain or something. Let's go see when we're up."

"Okay."

They walked over to the table in the front and waited in line.

"I should probably call home," said George.

"I'll let you use my cell phone after you get your card."

"What's the card for?"

"It tells when you go on."

"Leroy, what if I freeze up there?"

"I'll go all John Wayne on you."

"Thanks. You should have been a psychiatrist."

Leroy turned to the man behind him and asked, "Is this the line for the lottery?"

"For somebody," he said.

Leroy shouted out, "All you other people need to go on back home. I've got this thing won. It's all fixed. This is a rerun today. Me and my buddy saw it at the Playboy mansion last night and I won it. So, you all just head on back."

Nobody reacted to Leroy's taunts as George said, "I don't think they believed you."

"I noticed that. They're all acting like my parole officer."

"Name?" asked the woman at the table.

"Just put Leroy on it."

"Okay, Leroy. Here's your card. You go on thirty-fifth."

"Thirty-five. That's my lucky number," said Leroy. "I'm number thirty-five everybody. So be sure you see me before I become famous because I will change."

"Next," said the woman.

George walked up and said, "Hello."

"Name," the woman replied not interested in any small talk.

"George Running Bear."

"George Running Bear? Interesting name. Are you a Native American?"

"Sure am. I can trace my family tree all the way back to, who's those white guys?"

The woman laughed, "You're thirty-sixth."

"Thank you."

George took the card and went over to where Leroy stood and observed, "Looks like we have a wait."

"Yeah. Now here's my phone so you can call home," said Leroy as he took the phone from his pocket and handed it to George.

"I really appreciate this. I'll be right back."

"Okay. I'm going to get a seat."

"Yeah, I'll catch up to you."

George went out into the lobby, stood in front of a large window and dialed home.

"Hello?" said a familiar voice.

"Mandel?"

"Hey, George. How's it going in ole Hollywood?"

"We have our tryouts today."

"You'll do great. I just know it."

"Thanks. Uh- why are you at my house? Shouldn't you be at work now?"

There was a pause.

"Mandel- what's wrong?"

"It's your mom-"

"Is she okay?"

"I don't like giving you bad news-"

"Come on man, you're scaring me."

"She had a mild heart attack."

"A mild heart attack? There's no such thing as a mild heart attack. Mild is only for weather and cheese."

"That's what the doctor called it."

"Where's she at now?"

"She's in the hospital."

"Is she going to be okay?"

"The doctors think she'll be strong enough to go home in a few days."

"Why are you at the house?"

"She wanted me to come and get her cigarettes."

"Don't you dare take her any cigarettes."

"But I said I'd get 'em."

"Are you crazy?"

"I'll plead the fifth on that one."

"Do not do it."

"But I'm scared of your mother."

"She's in the hospital after having a heart attack, Mandel. If a fight breaks out, I think you can take her."

"Maybe if you called her."

"I'll call her, what's the number?"

"555-9363."

"I got it. Thanks for looking out for her for me."

"Anytime. Say I looked in the refrigerator and saw some Cokes. Can I have one?"

"Yes, Mandel- you can have a Coke."

"Can I have two?"

"I'm hanging up now."

George hung up the phone and started dialing as he kept repeating the phone number aloud. A voice answered, "Yellow Knife Regional."

"Yes, I'd like to talk with Mrs. Rachel Running Bear. She's a patient."

"Do you know the room number?"

"No. She'll be the one demanding cigarettes."

"Sounds like room seventeen. I'll connect you."

"I bet she becomes the first patient paroled from a hospital," George whispered to himself.

After a few seconds his mother answered the phone, "Mandel, where's my cigarettes?"

"It's not Mandel, its George."

"When did you get home?"

"I'm not home, I'm still in Hollywood."

"How did you know I was here?"

"I called home and Mandel told me."

"Did he say anything about my cigarettes?"

"You're not getting any cigarettes."

"You sound like those blasted doctors."

"You can't smoke in a hospital."

"Did they get rid of the Bill of Rights or something since I've been in here?"

"It has nothing to do with- listen, you can't smoke. It's dangerous for your health, plus there's other people in there with breathing problems, not to mention oxygen tanks that could explode if you smoked near them."

"It's my body."

"That's probably very tired of you right now. Are you okay?"

"Son, I've never been okay."

"I'll come on home."

"No, no no."

"Mom, you just had a heart attack. My place is to be with you."

"I'm not worth throwing your dream away."

"I'm not throwing my dream away. I didn't have a chance to start with. I'm just chasing dust in the wind."

"You're there. You have to see it through."

"But what about you?"

"The doctors and Mandel will take care of me. So, stop thinking of me and start thinking of you for once."

"I feel guilty that I'm not there."

"Do you want to be like your father?"

"What do you mean?"

"Your father threw his dream away and he never recovered."

"What dream?"

"He wanted to be an actor. He was too scared to try though and regretted it for the rest of his life. The way he dealt with it was booze."

"I never knew that," whispered George.

"If you never try to achieve your dream you will never forgive yourself. So, you have to try. Promise me."

"I promise."

"Also, I think I'm falling in love with Mandel."

"What?"

"I think we have an eye thing going."

"I don't want Mandel as a Step Dad. He's terrible at playing catch."

"I never said I was going to marry him. We'd just live together."

"But he's scared to death of you."

"That's how I like my men."

"Goodbye, Mom."

"Bye son. I love you."

"I love you too."

George hung up the phone, walked back inside the auditorium, sat down beside Leroy and gave him his phone back.

"How's everything back home?" asked Leroy.

"Well, my mother had a mild heart attack and wants to move in with my best friend."

"At least she's keeping active. Is she okay?"

"I don't know. It's hard to believe anything she says. Those stupid cigarettes she smokes is killing her and she still won't stop. I don't know how I'm going to do this with my mom on my mind."

"You have to try and push through it."

"I'm scared enough as it is without being worried about her. Look at my hands," George said while he held his hands out that were shaking.

"They're shaking like a black man walking on the right side of tracks."

"What number are they up to?"

"Thirty."

"Thirty? Already?"

"They don't listen to the whole act. They just listen for thirty seconds or so then tell them to go sit down."

"I feel like I'm about to throw up."

A voice called out, "Thirty-five."

"That's me," said Leroy.

"Knock 'em dead."

Leroy headed to the front, walked up on the stage and over to the microphone.

"I'm Leroy and I'm from Warsaw Mississippi. The home of- well nothing. It's a small town. It has no stop lights. No movie theaters- it does have a hospital- because it has no stop lights."

George became stunned as he listened to the people laugh.

"My parents don't get along that well. I told my father that statistics show that married men live longer than single men. He said, yeah, but single men don't usually die from poisoning."

The laughter got George upset as he watched his act being performed in front of his face.

"Okay, that's good," interrupted one of the judges. "Very good act."

"Thank you," replied Leroy.

"Just wait outside."

"Okay."

Leroy walked back toward the exit where George intercepted him by grabbing him by the arm and asked, "What was that?"

"Survival."

"Number thirty-six," called the man in the front.

"You stole my jokes. I've got enough to worry about with my mother having a heart attack and you pull this."

"Number thirty-six."

"I'm sorry about your mother-"

"I thought we were friends."

"Listen, this could be my last chance and I'll do whatever it takes to make it."

"Number thirty-six. This is your last call."

"They're calling you," said Leroy.

"What am I going to do without an act?"

"I don't care."

Leroy left and George turned toward the stage.

"I'm thirty-six! I'm thirty-six!" George shouted as he ran toward the stage.

"We were about to pass you up."

"Yeah- sorry about that."

George walked upon the stage and took the microphone in his hand.

"Uh- I'm George Running Bear. No, my father isn't named Smokey. I work- I work at a convenience store in Yellow Knife South Dakota. It's a small- I was working there one day and this woman came in with seven kids. Seven kids? Can you imagine that. I didn't see her husband anywhere so I just assumed she had killed him by now. Uh- I bet they have a time at the supper—at the supper table. After they eat, the mother probably has to count the kids to make sure they're all still there."

George's mind was racing between his mother's health and the stealing of his routine. He tried to calm himself and think of all the jokes he had written in all of his notebooks, but they were gone from his mind. He was lost and he couldn't think of anything to say as the judges at the table just stared at him which brought forth his surrender.

"Uh- I- well, that's all I got."

"Thank you, just wait outside," said the man at the table.

George walked down from the stage and headed out into the lobby area and just kept walking to the exit, went outside and over to a bench where he sat down. He put his head in his hands and tried to keep from crying.

Later, inside the auditorium the comics were seated as the agent sponsoring the contest walked upon the stage.

"I want to first say that I was really impressed with everyone here today. It's hard to narrow it down to just ten. But I have the finalists here and when I call your number please come upon the stage. Sixteen, eight, twenty-two, fifty, seventy, ten, forty-four, sixty-one, eighty, and thirty-five. Again, I want to thank everyone for coming. And just because you weren't chosen doesn't mean you should give up on your dream. Thank you."

In the Yellow Knife hospital lobby, Mandel was sitting in a chair with his eyes closed when a familiar voice brought his eyes opened.

"Hey, buddy."

"George!" Mandel screamed out as he stood up and hugged his dear friend. "How are you?"

"Okay, I guess. How's Mom?"

"They said she can go home in a couple of days, but she has to take it easy. They said no smoking under any circumstances."

"I'll make sure of that. Listen I want to thank you for being here for her."

"No problem."

"I owe you one."

"Nah."

"I do."

"How was Hollywood?"

"I didn't do too good."

"They didn't pick you?"

"No. I was too nervous and messed up."

"You can always try again."

"Nah, I don't think I'm made for Hollywood."

"You can't give up on your dream."

"Sometimes people have the wrong dream."

"Not you. Remember the first day we met in first grade? You made me laugh so hard that milk came out of my nose and I was drinking soda at the time. Now that's funny."

George laughed, "Maybe you should have gone to Hollywood instead of me."

"Well, you just relax, work on some new material and you can have at 'em again."

"We'll talk about it later. Let's go see Mom."

"Okay."

In the hospital room George's mother laid in bed reading a magazine when Mandel walked in.

"Hello, Mrs. Running Bear," said Mandel.

"I thought I sent you home to get me some cigarettes?"

George walked in and said, "They'll be no more cigarettes for you."

"When did you get back?" asked a surprised Rachel as a large smile formed across her mouth.

"Just now."

"Are you going to yell at me or are you going to give me a hug?"

"I can do both," George said as hugged his mother.

"I'll leave you two alone," said Mandel.

"Thanks, Mandel. I really mean that."

"You bet," Mandel said as he left.

"He's a good boy," said his mother.

"Yes, he is."

"I could see myself married to him."

"Don't you think there's a slight age difference?"

"Yeah. Maybe if he was a few years younger it would work out better."

George sat down in the chair beside the bed.

"How did the contest go?" she asked.

"Not too good."

"What place did you come in?"

"They only chose the top ten, so I guess I came in somewhere between eleven and last."

"You can try again soon."

"You just get better."

"I'll try. I'm getting a little sleepy."

"You go on and rest. I'll be outside."

"Okay."

"I love you, Mom," George said as he got up and kissed her on the head.

"George, promise me you'll try again."

"Just rest."

George walked out of the room and walked over to where Mandel stood.

"You know, for having a heart attack she doesn't look half bad," said George.

"I have to say I'm impressed with her too."

"I guess it's my turn to be the parent."

"What are you going to do now?" asked Mandel.

"I guess I've got to find a job."

"Hey, I heard the other day that the manager of that store you used to work at was arrested for embezzlement."

"Hmmm," George mused to himself.

A FEW DAYS LATER GEORGE UNLOCKED THE DOOR AND WALKED INSIDE THE convenience store. He went over to the cash register, put his blue vest on with his name tag pinned to it and got things ready for the day.

He sat down and began looking through his joke book when a car pulled up and a man got out and came inside.

"Hello," said the man as he walked to the soft drink cooler.

"I thought I was the only person that got up this early."

I wish you were," said the man as he walked to the counter and placed a ' down on it.

George picked up the joke book and said, "Let me get this out of your way." He then tossed the joke book into the trash can.

"I'm about to brew up some coffee if you want some."

"Nah, I've got to head on out. Thanks though," the customer said as he picked up a candy bar and placed it down on the counter beside the soft drink.

George rang up the total, the customer paid it in cash then left.

George sat down then looked over at the trash can. He got up, reached down into the trash can where he retrieved his joke book and stared at the picture of Milton Berle on the cover.

"Okay, Uncle Miltie, if you can make me laugh, I won't give up on my dream."

George randomly parted the pages with his thumb where his eyes fell upon the joke at the top left of page 159.

"How does the ocean say hello? It waves."

A hearty laugh filled the store.

THE END

From 1935, Fred MacMurray and Carol Lombard in a publicity still for the film

Let's Get Together
by Isaac Asimov

Originally published in <u>Infinity Science Fiction</u>
Magazine, 1957

A kind of peace had endured for a century and people had forgotten what anything else was like. They would scarcely have known how to react had they discovered that a kind of war had finally come.

Certainly, Elias Lynn, Chief of the Bureau of Robotics, wasn't sure how he ought to react when finally found out. The Bureau of Robotics was headquartered in Cheyenne, in line with the century-old trend toward decentralization, and Lynn stared dubiously at the young Security officer from Washington who had brought the news.

Elias Lynn was a large man, almost charmingly homely, with pale blue eyes that bulged a bit. Men weren't usually comfortable under the stare of those eyes, but the Security officer remained calm.

Lynn decided that his first reaction ought to be incredulity. Hell, it incredulity! He just didn›t believe it!

He eased himself back in his chair and said, "How certain is the information?"

The Security officer, who had introduced himself as Ralph G. Breckenridge and had presented credentials to match, had the softness of youth about him; full lips, plump cheeks that flushed easily, and guileless eyes. His clothing was out of line with Cheyenne but it suited a universally air-conditioned Washington, where Security, despite everything, was still centered.

Breckenridge flushed and said, "There's no doubt about it."

"You people know all about Them, I suppose," said Lynn and was unable to keep a trace of sarcasm out of his tone. He was not particularly aware of his use of a slightly-stressed pronoun in his reference to the enemy, the equivalent of capitalization in print. It was a cultural habit of this generation and the one preceding. No one said the "East," or the "Reds" or the "Soviets" or the "Russians" any more. That would have been too confusing, since some of Them weren't of the East, weren't Reds, Soviets, and especially not Russians. It was much simpler to say We and They, and much more precise.

Travelers had frequently reported that They did the same in reverse. Over there, They were "We" (in the appropriate language) and We were "They."

Scarcely anyone gave thought to such things any more. It was all quite comfortable and casual. There was no hatred, even. At the beginning, it had been called a Cold War. Now it was only a game, almost a good-natured game, with unspoken rules and a kind of decency about it.

Lynn said, abruptly, "Why should They want to disturb the situation?"

He rose and stood staring at a wall-map of the world, split into two regions with faint edgings of color. An irregular portion on the left of the map was edged in a mild green. A smaller, but just as irregular, portion on the right of the map was bordered in a washed-out pink. We and They.

The map hadn't changed much in a century. The loss of Formosa and the gain of East Germany some eighty years before had been the last territorial switch of importance.

There had been another change, though, that was significant enough and that was in the colors. Two generations before, Their territory had been a brooding, bloody red, Ours a pure and undefiled white. Now there was a neutrality about the colors. Lynn had seen Their maps and it was the same on Their side.

"They wouldn't do it," he said.

"They are doing it," said Breckenridge, "and you had better accustom yourself to the fact. Of course, sir, I realize that it isn't pleasant to think that they may be that far ahead of us in robotics."

His eyes remained as guileless as ever, but the hidden knife-edges of the words plunged deep, and Lynn quivered at the impact.

Of course, that would account for why the Chief of Robotics learned of this so late and through a Security officer at that. He had lost caste in the eyes of the Government; if Robotics had really failed in the struggle, Lynn could expect no political mercy.

Lynn said wearily, "Even if what you say is true, they're not far ahead of us. We could build humanoid robots."

"Have we, sir?"

"Yes. As a matter of fact, we have built a few models for experimental purposes."

"They were doing so ten years ago. They've made ten years' progress since."

Lynn was disturbed. He wondered if his incredulity concerning the whole business were really the result of wounded pride and fear for his job and reputation. He was embarrassed by the possibility that this might be so, and yet he was forced into defense.

He said, "Look, young man, the stalemate between Them and Us was never perfect in every detail, you know. They have always been ahead in one facet or another and We in some other facet or another. If They're ahead of us right now in robotics, it's because They've placed a greater proportion of Their effort into robotics than We have. And that means that some other branch of endeavor has received a greater share of Our efforts than it has of Theirs. It would mean We're ahead in force-field research or in hyper-atomics, perhaps."

Lynn felt distressed at his own statement that the stalemate wasn't perfect. It was true enough, but that was the one great danger threatening the world. The world depended on the stalemate being as perfect as possible. If the small unevennesses that always existed over-balanced too far in one direction or the other—

Almost at the beginning of what had been the Cold War, both sides had developed thermonuclear weapons, and war became unthinkable. Competition switched from the military to the economic and psychological and had stayed there ever since.

But always there was the driving effort on each side to break the stalemate, to develop a parry for every possible thrust, to develop a thrust that could not be parried in time—something that would make war possible again. And that was not because either side wanted war so desperately, but because both were afraid that the other side would make the crucial discovery first.

For a hundred years each side had kept the struggle even. And in the process, peace had been maintained for a hundred years while, as byproducts of the continuously intensive research, force-fields had been produced and solar energy and insect control and robots. Each side was making a beginning in the understanding of mentalics, which was the name given to the biochemistry and biophysics of thought. Each side had its outposts on the Moon and on Mars. Mankind was advancing in giant strides under forced draft.

It was even necessary for both sides to be as decent and humane as possible among themselves, lest through cruelty and tyranny, friends be made for the other side.

It couldn't be that the stalemate would now be broken and that there would be war.

Lynn said, "I want to consult one of my men. I want his opinion."

"Is he trustworthy?"

Lynn looked disgusted. "Good Lord, what man in Robotics has not been investigated and cleared to death by your people? Yes, I vouch for him. If you can't trust a man like Humphrey Carl Laszlo, then we're in no position to face the kind of attack you say They are launching, no matter what else we do."

"I've heard of Laszlo," said Breckenridge.

"Good. Does he pass?"

"Yes."

"Then, I'll have him in and we'll find out what he thinks about the possibility that robots could invade the U. S. A."

"Not exactly," said Breckenridge, softly. "You still don't accept the full truth. Find out what he thinks about the fact that robots have invaded the U. S. A.»

Laszlo was the grandson of a Hungarian who had broken through what had then been called the Iron Curtain, and he had a comfortable above-suspicion feeling about himself because of it. He was thick-set and balding with a pugnacious look graven forever on his snub face, but his accent was clear Harvard and he was almost excessively soft-spoken.

To Lynn, who was conscious that after years of administration he was no longer expert in the various phases of modern robotics, Laszlo was a comforting receptacle for complete knowledge. Lynn felt better because of the man's mere presence.

Lynn said, "What do you think?"

A scowl twisted Laszlo's face ferociously. "That They're that far ahead of us. Completely incredible. It would mean They've produced humanoids that could not be told from humans at close quarters. It would mean a considerable advance in robo-mentalics."

"You're personally involved," said Breckenridge, coldly. "Leaving professional pride out of account, exactly why is it impossible that They be ahead of Us?"

Laszlo shrugged. "I assure you that I'm well acquainted with Their literature on robotics. I know approximately where They are."

"You know approximately where They want you to They are, is what you really mean,» corrected Breckenridge. «Have you ever visited the other side?»

"I haven't," said Laszlo, shortly.

"Nor you, Dr. Lynn?"

Lynn said, "No, I haven't, either."

Breckenridge said, "Has any robotics man visited the other side in twenty-five years?" He asked the question with a kind of confidence that indicated he knew the answer.

For a matter of seconds, the atmosphere was heavy with thought. Discomfort crossed Laszlo's broad face. He said, "As a matter of fact, They haven't held any conferences on robotics in a long time."

"In twenty-five years," said Breckenridge. "Isn't that significant?"

"Maybe," said Laszlo, reluctantly. "Something else bothers me, though. None of Them have ever come to Our conferences on robotics. None that I can remember."

"Were They invited?" asked Breckenridge.

Lynn, staring and worried, interposed quickly, "Of course."

Breckenridge said, "Do They refuse attendance to any other types of scientific conferences We hold?"

"I don't know," said Laszlo. He was pacing the floor now. "I haven't heard of any cases. Have you, Chief?"

"No," said Lynn.

Breckenridge said, "Wouldn't you say it was as though They didn't want to be put in the position of having to return any such invitation? Or as though They were afraid one of Their men might talk too much?"

That was exactly how it seemed, and Lynn felt a helpless conviction that Security's story was true after all steal over him.

Why else had there been no contact between sides on robotics? There had been a cross-fertilizing trickle of researchers moving in both directions on a strictly one-for-one basis for years, dating back to the days of Eisenhower and Khrushchev. There were a great many good motives for that: an honest appreciation of the supra-national character of science; impulses of friendliness that are hard to wipe out completely in the individual human being; the desire to be exposed to a fresh and interesting outlook and to have your own slightly-stale notions greeted by others as fresh and interesting.

The governments themselves were anxious that this continue. There was always the obvious thought that by learning all you could and telling as little as you could, your own side would gain by the exchange.

But not in the case of robotics. Not there.

Such a little thing to carry conviction. And a thing, moreover, they had known all along. Lynn thought, darkly: We've taken the complacent way out.

Because the other side had done nothing publicly on robotics, it had been tempting to sit back smugly and be comfortable in the assurance of superiority. Why hadn't it seemed possible, even likely, that They were hiding superior cards, a trump hand, for the proper time?

Laszlo said, shakenly, "What do we do?" It was obvious that the same line of thought had carried the same conviction to him.

"Do?" parroted Lynn. It was hard to think right now of anything but of the complete horror that came with conviction. There were ten humanoid robots somewhere in the United States, each one carrying a fragment of a TC bomb.

TC! The race for sheer horror in bomb-ery had ended there. TC! Total Conversion! The sun was no longer a synonym one could use. Total conversion made the sun a penny candle.

Ten humanoids, each completely harmless in separation, could, by the simple act of coming together, exceed critical mass and—

Lynn rose to his feet heavily, the dark pouches under his eyes, which ordinarily lent his ugly face a look of savage foreboding, more prominent than ever. "It's going to be up to us to figure out ways and means of telling a humanoid from a human and then finding the humanoids."

"How quickly?" muttered Laszlo.

"Not later than five minutes before they get together," barked Lynn, "and I don't know when that will be."

Breckenridge nodded. "I'm glad you're with us now, sir. I'm to bring you back to Washington for conference, you know."

Lynn raised his eyebrows. "All right."

He wondered if, had he delayed longer in being convinced, he might not have been replaced forthwith—if some other Chief of the Bureau of Robotics might not be conferring in Washington. He suddenly wished earnestly that exactly that had come to pass.

The First Presidential Assistant was there, the Secretary of Science, the Secretary of Security, Lynn himself, and Breckenridge. Five of them sitting about a table in the dungeons of an underground fortress near Washington.

Presidential Assistant Jeffreys was an impressive man, handsome in a white-haired and just-a-trifle-jowly fashion, solid, thoughtful and as unobtrusive, politically, as a Presidential Assistant ought to be.

He spoke incisively. "There are three questions that face us as I see it. First, when are the humanoids going to get together? Second, where are they going to get together? Third, how do we stop them before they get together?"

Secretary of Science Amberley nodded convulsively at that. He had been Dean of Northwestern Engineering before his appointment. He was thin, sharp-featured and noticeably edgy. His forefinger traced slow circles on the table.

"As far as   they›ll get together,» he said. «I suppose it›s definite that it won›t be for some time.»

"Why do you say that?" asked Lynn, sharply.

"They've been in the U. S. at least a month already. So Security says."

Lynn turned automatically to look at Breckenridge, and Secretary of Security Macalaster intercepted the glance. Macalaster said, "The information is reliable. Don't let Breckenridge's apparent youth fool you, Dr. Lynn. That's part of his value to us. Actually, he's 34 and has been with the department for ten years. He has been in Moscow for nearly a year and without him, none of this terrible danger would be known to us. As it is, we have most of the details."

"Not the crucial ones," said Lynn.

Macalaster of Security smiled frostily. His heavy chin and close-set eyes were well-known to the public but almost nothing else about him was. He said, "We are all finitely human, Dr. Lynn. Agent Breckenridge has done a great deal."

Presidential Assistant Jeffreys cut in. "Let us say we have a certain amount of time. If action at the instant were necessary, it would have happened before this. It seems likely that they are waiting for a specific time. If we knew the place, perhaps the time would become self-evident.

"If they are going to TC a target, they will want to cripple us as much as possible, so it would seem that a major city would have to be it. In any case, a major metropolis is the only target worth a TC bomb. I think there are four possibilities: Washington, as the administrative center; New York, as the financial center; and Detroit and Pittsburgh as the two chief industrial centers."

Macalaster of Security said, "I vote for New York. Administration and industry have both been decentralized to the point where the destruction of any one particular city won't prevent instant retaliation."

"Then why New York?" asked Amberly of Science, perhaps more sharply than he intended. "Finance has been decentralized as well."

"A question of morale. It may be they intend to destroy our will to resist, to induce surrender by the sheer horror of the first blow. The greatest destruction of human life would be in the New York Metropolitan area—"

"Pretty cold-blooded," muttered Lynn.

"I know," said Macalaster of Security, "but they're capable of it, if they thought it would mean final victory at a stroke. Wouldn't we—"

Presidential Assistant Jeffreys brushed back his white hair. "Let's assume the worst. Let's assume that New York will be destroyed some time during the winter, preferably immediately after a serious blizzard when communications are at their worst and the disruption of utilities and food supplies in fringe areas will be most serious in their effect. Now, how do we stop them?"

Amberley of Science could only say, "Finding ten men in two hundred and twenty million is an awfully small needle in an awfully large haystack."

Jeffreys shook his head. "You have it wrong. Ten humanoids among two hundred twenty million humans."

"No difference," said Amberley of Science. "We don't know that a humanoid can be differentiated from a human at sight. Probably not." He looked at Lynn. They all did.

Lynn said heavily, "We in Cheyenne couldn't make one that would pass as human in the daylight."

"But They can," said Macalaster of Security, "and not only physically. We're sure of that. They've advanced mentalic procedures to the point where they can reel off the micro-electronic pattern of the brain and focus it on the positronic pathways of the robot."

Lynn stared. "Are you implying that they can create the replica of a human being complete with personality and memory?"

"I do."

"Of specific human beings?"

"That's right."

"Is this also based on Agent Breckenridge's findings?"

"Yes. The evidence can't be disputed."

Lynn bent his head in thought for a moment. Then he said, "Then ten men in the United States are not men but humanoids. But the originals would have had to be available to them. They couldn't be Orientals, who would be too easy to spot, so they would have to be East Europeans. How would they be introduced into this country, then? With the radar network over the entire world border as tight as a drum, how could They introduce any individual, human or humanoid, without our knowing it?"

Macalaster of Security said, "It can be done. There are certain legitimate seepages across the border. Businessmen, pilots, even tourists. They're watched, of course, on both sides. Still ten of them might have been kidnapped and used as models for humanoids. The humanoids would then be sent back in their place. Since we wouldn't expect such a substitution, it would pass us by. If they were Americans to begin with, there would be no difficulty in their getting into this country. It's as simple as that."

"And even their friends and family could not tell the difference?"

"We must assume so. Believe me, we've been waiting for any report that might imply sudden attacks of amnesia or troublesome changes in personality. We've checked on thousands."

Amberley of Science stared at his finger-tips. "I think ordinary measures won't work. The attack must come from the Bureau of Robotics and I depend on the chief of that bureau."

Again eyes turned sharply, expectantly, on Lynn.

Lynn felt bitterness rise. It seemed to him that this was what the conference came to and was intended for. Nothing that had been said had not been said before. He was sure of that. There was no solution to the problem, no pregnant suggestion. It was a device for the record, a device on the part of men who gravely feared defeat and who wished the responsibility for it placed clearly and unequivocally on someone else.

And yet there was justice in it. It was in robotics that We had fallen short. And Lynn was not Lynn merely. He was Lynn of Robotics and the responsibility had to be his.

He said, "I will do what I can."

He spent a wakeful night and there was a haggardness about both body and soul when he sought and attained another interview with Presidential Assistant Jeffreys the next morning. Breckenridge was there, and though Lynn would have preferred a private conference, he could see the justice in the situation. It was obvious that Breckenridge had attained enormous influence with the government as a result of his successful Intelligence work. Well, why not?

Lynn said, "Sir, I am considering the possibility that we are hopping uselessly to enemy piping."

"In what way?"

"I'm sure that however impatient the public may grow at times, and however legislators sometimes find it expedient to talk, the government at least recognizes the world stalemate to be beneficial. They must recognize it also. Ten humanoids with one TC bomb is a trivial way of breaking the stalemate."

"The destruction of fifteen million human beings is scarcely trivial."

"It is from the world power standpoint. It would not so demoralize us as to make us surrender or so cripple us as to convince us we could not win. There would just be the same old planetary death-war that both sides have avoided so long and so successfully. And all They would have accomplished is to force us to fight minus one city. It's not enough."

"What do you suggest?" said Jeffreys, coldly. "That They do not have ten humanoids in our country? That there is not a TC bomb waiting to get together?"

"I'll agree that those things are here, but perhaps for some reason greater than just mid-winter bomb-madness."

"Such as?"

"It may be that the physical destruction resulting from the humanoids getting together is not the worst thing that can happen to us. What about the moral and intellectual destruction that comes of their being here at all?

With all due respect to Agent Breckenridge, what if They for us to find out about the humanoids; what if the humanoids are never supposed to get together, but merely to remain separate in order to give us something to worry about.»

"Why?"

"Tell me this. What measures have already been taken against the humanoids? I suppose that Security is going through the files of all citizens who have ever been across the border or close enough to it to make kidnapping possible: I know, since Macalaster mentioned it yesterday, that they are following up suspicious psychiatric cases. What else?"

Jeffreys said, "Small X-ray devices are being installed in key places in the large cities. In the mass arenas, for instance—"

"Where ten humanoids might slip in among a hundred thousand spectators of a football game or an air-polo match?"

"Exactly."

"And concert halls and churches?"

"We must start somewhere. We can't do it all at once."

"Particularly when panic must be avoided?" said Lynn. "Isn't that so? It wouldn't do to have the public realize that at any unpredictable moment, some unpredictable city and its human contents would suddenly cease to exist."

"I suppose that's obvious. What are you driving at?"

Lynn said strenuously, "That a growing fraction of our national effort will be diverted entirely into the nasty problem of what Amberley called finding a very small needle in a very large haystack. We'll be chasing our tails madly, while They increase their research lead to the point where we find we can no longer catch up; when we must surrender without the chance even of snapping our fingers in retaliation.

"Consider further that this news will leak out as more and more people become involved in our counter-measures and more and more people begin to guess what we're doing. Then what? The panic might do us more harm than any one TC bomb."

The Presidential Assistant said, irritably, "In Heaven's name, man, what do you suggest we do, then?"

"Nothing," said Lynn. "Call their bluff. Live as we have lived and gamble that They won't dare break the stalemate for the sake of a one-bomb headstart."

"Impossible!" said Jeffreys. "Completely impossible. The welfare of all of Us is very largely in my hands, and doing nothing is the one thing I cannot do. I agree with you, perhaps, that X-ray machines at sports arenas are a kind of skin-deep measure that won't be effective, but it has to be done so that people, in the aftermath, do not come to the bitter conclusion that we tossed our country away for the sake of a subtle line of reasoning that encouraged do-nothingism. In fact, our counter-gambit will be active indeed."

"In what way?"

Presidential Assistant Jeffreys looked at Breckenridge. The young Security officer, hitherto calmly silent, said, "It's no use talking about a possible future break in the stalemate when the stalemate is broken now. It doesn't matter whether these humanoids explode or do not. Maybe they only a bait to divert us, as you say. But the fact remains that we are a quarter of a century behind in robotics, and that may be fatal. What other advances in robotics will there be to surprise us if war does start? The only answer is to divert our entire force immediately, , into a crash program of robotics research, and the first problem is to find the humanoids. Call it an exercise in robotics, if you will, or call it the prevention of the death of fifteen million men, women and children."

Lynn shook his head, helplessly, "You . You'd be playing into their hands. They want us lured into the one blind alley while they're free to advance in all other directions."

Jeffreys said, impatiently, "That's your guess. Breckenridge has made his suggestion through channels and the government has approved, and we will begin with an all-Science conference."

"All-Science?"

Breckenridge said, "We have listed every important scientist of every branch of natural science. They'll all be at Cheyenne. There will be only one point on the agenda: How to advance robotics. The major specific sub-heading under that will be: How to develop a receiving device for the electromagnetic fields of the cerebral cortex that will be sufficiently delicate to distinguish between a protoplasmic human brain and a positronic humanoid brain."

Jeffreys said, "We had hoped you would be willing to be in charge of the conference."

"I was not consulted in this."

"Obviously time was short, sir. Do you agree to be in charge?"

Lynn smiled briefly. It was a matter of responsibility again. The responsibility must be clearly that of Lynn of Robotics. He had the feeling it would be Breckenridge who would really be in charge. But what could he do?

He said, "I agree."

Breckenridge and Lynn returned together to Cheyenne, where that evening Laszlo listened with a sullen mistrust to Lynn's description of coming events.

Laszlo said, "While you were gone, Chief, I've started putting five experimental models of humanoid structure through the testing procedures. Our men are on a twelve-hour day, with three shifts overlapping. If we've got to arrange a conference, we're going to be crowded and red-taped out of everything. Work will come to a halt."

Breckenridge said, "That will be only temporary. You will gain more than you lose."

Laszlo scowled. "A bunch of astrophysicists and geochemists around won't help a damn toward robotics."

"Views from specialists of other fields may be helpful."

"Are you sure? How do we know that there   any way of detecting brain waves or that, even if we can, there is a way of differentiating human and humanoid by wave pattern. Who set up the project, anyway?»

"I did," said Breckenridge.

" did? Are you a robotics man?»

The young Security agent said, calmly, "I have studied robotics."

"That's not the same thing."

"I've had access to text-material dealing with Russian robotics—in Russian. Top-secret material well in advance of anything you have here."

Lynn said, ruefully, "He has us there, Laszlo."

"It was on the basis of that material," Breckenridge went on, "that I suggested this particular line of investigation. It is reasonably certain that in copying off the electromagnetic pattern of a specific human mind into a specific positronic brain, a perfectly exact duplicate cannot be made. For one thing, the most complicated positronic brain small enough to fit into a human-sized skull is hundreds of times less complex than the human brain. It can't pick up all the overtones, therefore, and there must be some way to take advantage of that fact."

Laszlo looked impressed despite himself and Lynn smiled grimly. It was easy to resent Breckenridge and the coming intrusion of several hundred scientists of non-robotics specialties, but the problem itself was an intriguing one. There was that consolation, at least.

It came to him quietly.

Lynn found he had nothing to do but sit in his office alone, with an executive position that had grown merely titular. Perhaps that helped. It gave him time to think, to picture the creative scientists of half the world converging on Cheyenne.

It was Breckenridge who, with cool efficiency, was handling the details of preparation. There had been a kind of confidence in the way he said, "Let's get together and we'll lick Them."

Let's get together.

It came to Lynn so quietly that anyone watching Lynn at that moment might have seen his eyes blink slowly twice—but surely nothing more.

He did what he had to do with a whirling detachment that kept him calm when he felt that, by all rights, he ought to be going mad.

He sought out Breckenridge in the other's improvised quarters.

Breckenridge was alone and frowning. "Is anything wrong, sir?"

Lynn said, wearily, "Everything's right, I think. I've invoked martial law."

"What!"

"As chief of a division I can do so if I am of the opinion the situation warrants it. Over my division, I can then be dictator. Chalk up one for the beauties of decentralization."

"You will rescind that order immediately." Breckenridge took a step forward. "When Washington hears this, you will be ruined."

"I'm ruined anyway. Do you think I don't realize that I've been set up for the role of the greatest villain in American history: the man who let Them break the stalemate. I have nothing to lose—and perhaps a great deal to gain."

He laughed a little wildly, "What a target the Division of Robotics will be, eh, Breckenridge? Only a few thousand men to be killed by a TC bomb capable of wiping out three hundred square miles in one micro-second. But five hundred of those men would be our greatest scientists. We would be in the peculiar position of having to fight a war with our brains shot out, or surrendering. I think we'd surrender."

"But this is impossible. Lynn, do you hear me? Do you understand? How could the humanoids pass our security provisions? How could they get together?"

"But they getting together! We›re helping them to do so. We›re ordering them to do so. Our scientists visit the other side, Breckenridge. They visit Them regularly. You made a point of how strange it was that no one in robotics did. Well, ten of those scientists are still there and in their place, ten humanoids are converging on Cheyenne.»

"That's a ridiculous guess."

"I think it's a good one, Breckenridge. But it wouldn't work unless we knew humanoids were in America so that we would call the conference in the first place. Quite a coincidence that you brought the news of the humanoids suggested the conference suggested the agenda are running the show and know exactly which scientists were invited. Did you make sure the right ten were included?»

"Dr. Lynn!" cried Breckenridge in outrage. He poised to rush forward.

Lynn said, "Don't move. I've got a blaster here. We'll just wait for the scientists to get here one by one. One by one we'll X-ray them. One by one, we'll monitor them for radioactivity. No two will get together without being checked, and if all five hundred are clear, I'll give you my blaster and surrender to you. Only I think we'll find the ten humanoids. Sit down, Breckenridge."

They both sat.

Lynn said, "We wait. When I'm tired, Laszlo will spell me. We wait."

Professor Manuelo Jiminez of the Institute of Higher Studies of Buenos Aires exploded while the stratospheric jet on which he traveled was three miles above the Amazon Valley. It was a simple chemical explosion but it was enough to destroy the plane.

Dr. Herman Liebowitz of M. I. T. exploded in a monorail, killing twenty people and injuring a hundred others.

In similar manner, Dr. Auguste Marin of L'Institut Nucléonique of Montreal and seven others died at various stages of their journey to Cheyenne.

Laszlo hurtled in, pale-faced and stammering, with the first news of it. It had only been two hours that Lynn had sat there, facing Breckenridge, blaster in hand.

Laszlo said, "I thought you were nuts, Chief, but you were right. They humanoids. They to be.» He turned to stare with hate-filled eyes at Breckenridge. «Only they were warned. warned them, and now there won›t be one left intact. Not one to study.»

"God!" cried Lynn and in a frenzy of haste thrust his blaster out toward Breckenridge and fired. The Security man's neck vanished; the torso fell; the head dropped, thudded against the floor and rolled crookedly.

Lynn moaned, "I didn't understand, I thought he was a traitor. Nothing more."

And Laszlo stood immobile, mouth open, for the moment incapable of speech.

Lynn said, wildly. "Sure, he warned them. But how could he do so while sitting in that chair unless he were equipped with built-in radio transmission? Don't you see it? Breckenridge had been in Moscow. The real Breckenridge is still there. Oh my God, there were of them.»

Laszlo managed a hoarse squeak. "Why didn't explode?»

"He was hanging on, I suppose, to make sure the others had received his message and were safely destroyed. Lord, Lord, when you brought the news and I realized the truth, I couldn't shoot fast enough. God knows by how few seconds I may have beaten him to it."

Laszlo said, shakily, "At least, we'll have one to study." He bent and put his fingers on the sticky fluid trickling out of the mangled remains at the neck end of the headless body.

Not blood, but high-grade machine oil.

The End

From October 1921 Photoplay Magazine; Marie Prevost was a Canadian-born actress who made 121 silent & sound films during her 20 year career.

THE FIXER

BY WESLEY LONG

(From Astounding Science-Fiction, May 1945)

The Telfan tailors didn't understand Solarian tailoring; Sandra was forced to admit that they were good—for Telfans. But for Solarians, they didn't come up to the accepted standards.

They had tried, she gave them credit for that. But the Telfan figure did not match the Solarian, especially the four-breasted female Telfan woman did not match Sandra's thin-waisted, high breasted figure. Her total lack of the Telfan skin; part feathers, part hair, but actually classifiable as neither, caused a different "hang" to the clothing. Telfans wore practically nothing because of the pelt and though Sandra's figure was one of those that should have been adorned in practically nothing, Telfu was not sufficiently warm to go running around in a sunsuit.

And making over Telfan clothing to fit her was out of the question. She stood half a head above their tallest women, and the only clothing that would have fit was clothing made in outsizes for extremely huge Telfan women. Needless to say this size of garment was shapeless.

Sandra finished her mending, tried on the garment and made a wry face. "I used to curse the lack of humans here," she told her image in the mirror, "but now I'm glad I'm the only one. I'd sure hate to have any of my old friends see me looking like this."

The image that repeated silently was not too far a cry from the Sandra Drake that had called the in for a landing on Telfu some months ago. But they hadn't waited, and she now knew why. Well, she was forced to admit that her try at either trapping them here or getting off with them had failed, and therefore she had been outguessed.

That made her burn. Being outguessed by a man was something that Sandra didn't care to have happen. She could live through it; but it was the aftermath that really hurt. The Telfans came to understand her too well after that incident. They no longer looked upon her as a leading figure in her system. They knew that her knowledge of Solarian science was sketchy and incomplete. Therefore she had lost her hold upon Telfu, and was now forced to do her own mending.

On the other hand, Sandra Drake was an intelligent woman. Her contempt for the Telfan language was gone. It went on that memorable day when she discovered that everyone who understood any Terran had gone to greet the landing and had left her unable to convey her desires. From that time on, Sandra plied herself and was quite capable of conversing in Telfan, and fluently.

So Sandra Drake had been living with the Telfans for several months. She had been forced to live with her wits and her mind and she found it interesting. Telfans were quite cold to her charms, which made her angry at times; on Terra she was used to admiration from anything masculine from fourteen to ninety-eight. Below fourteen they didn't know any better and over ninety-eight they didn't care, but the years between were aware of Sandra Drake. On Telfu, posturing, posing, and offering had no effect. They looked upon her as an encyclopedia; an animate phonograph, which, upon proper stimulation, could be made to sound interesting.

They had their machinery of action, too. Either Sandra assisted them—or she did not find things easy. It was adjustable, too, and the better assistance she gave, the better she found things.

Well, thought Sandra, it has been interesting—

She was startled by a knock upon her door. She admitted two Telfan men and a Telfan woman. The woman she knew.

"Yes, Thuni?" she asked the woman.

"Sandrake," announced the woman, putting the Telfan pronunciation on the Terran name, "These are Orfall and Theodi, both of whom are among the leading medico-physicists of Telfu. They desire your help."

Sandra reflected quickly. After all, this ability to be of assistance did give her a sop to her vanity. The fact that as little as she really knew of Terran science she could assist, and at times direct, gave her first feeling of real self-assurance.

"I shall, if I can," she told them.

"You, in spite of your untrained mind, have been extremely valuable," Orfall said simply. "While you do not know the details, you at least have some knowledge of the channels of Terran science, and you may, and have, explained down which channel lies truth, and along which line of endeavor lies but a blank wall. That in itself is valuable."

"Another item of interest," said Theodi, "is the fact that the books left us by the   are ponderous and often obscure; they assume that we have a basic knowledge which we have not. You have been able to direct us to the proper place in them to find the proper answer to many of our questions.»

"I see," said Sandra. All too seldom had anyone told her she was valuable and interesting. It had been more likely a statement of her headstrong nature, her utter uselessness, and her nuisance value.

"As you know, we of Telfu are slightly ahead of you in chemistry. Yet there are things in chemistry that can not be solved without an advanced knowledge in the gravitic spectrum that Terra has exploited. Perhaps it was the lack of a channel in the gravitic that drove us into higher chemical development; but we are planet-locked until your people return to remove the block."

"Go on," said Sandra impatiently. "I gather that you are in trouble of some sort?"

"We are, indeed. A plague of ... ah, there is no word for it in Terran"—he switched to Telfan, "Andryorelitis," and back again to Terran—"which is an air-borne disease of the virus type. No inoculation has been discovered, and no immunity zone can be established. Telfu is in danger of halving the population."

"Bad, huh?"

"It is terrible. It strikes unknown. Its incubation period is several days, and then the victim gets the first symptoms. Nine days later, the victim is dead. Unfortunately, the victim is a carrier of andryorelitis during the incubation period, and therefore isolation is impossible."

"Sounds like real trouble to me," said Sandra. "Will examination reveal it?"

"Of course," answered Orfall. "But what planet can examine the population daily?"

"I see the impossibilities. Then what do you hope? We have nothing that will combat it; knowing nothing of it in Sol would preclude any possibility. What can we do?"

"To return to chemistry," said Theodi, "I will explain. Our chemico-physicists have predicted the combination of a molecule which will combat the virus selectively. It is a complex protein molecule of unstable nature—so unstable, unfortunately, that it will not permit us to compound it. We have used every catalyst in the book, and nothing works. Follow?"

"I think so," said Sandra. "What keeps it from forming?"

"As I said, it is very unstable. The atomic lattice appears to be structurally unsound. That happens in a lot of cases, you know. At any rate, we can make this molecule—and have made it successfully. But its yield is less than four ten-thousandths of one percent, and the residue precipitates out in an insoluble compound that can not be reprocessed."

"Otherwise you would keep the process going until completion?"

"Precisely. If reprocessing would work, we could leave the batch to cook until all of it went into combination. Or we could add fresh 'mix' to the processing batch and make the process continuous. But the stuff is not re-processable. We must complete each batch, and then go on a long process of fractionation to distill the proper compound out of the useless residue."

"I can see that a process of that inefficiency would be bothersome," said Sandra.

"Not bothersome, Sandrake. Impossible. Imagine going into a project giving about .000,37% yield for two hundred-fifty billion Telfans. The required dose of the antibody is forty-seven milligrams. Call it fifty, for round numbers, Sandrake, and you get a total figure of one trillion, two hundred-fifty billion milligrams, or one million two hundred fifty thousand kilograms. At four ten-thousandths of one percent yield, we'd have to process something like three hundred billion kilograms of raw material and then rectify it through that long and laborious process of fractional crystallization, partial electrolysis, and fractional distillation—with a final partial crystallization. Processing that much raw material would be a lifetime job at best. Doing it under pressure, with the planning and procurement problems intensified by the certainty of the few short weeks we have ... ah, Sandrake, it is impossible."

"What is this trouble specifically?"

"The final addition of silicon. It will not enter the compound, but forces something less active from the combination."

"Making it useless?"

"Right."

"You've tried it?"

"And it works," nodded Orfall.

"And knowing that you of Terra have some wonders in science, we would like to know—"

"You see," interrupted Orfall, "they've figured that the catalyst would be less than sixty-one percent efficient, if we could combine the silicon with it and let it replace into the other compound. That would work. But again we are stuck. The catalyst is stable as it is. What has Terra done to assist in forcing combination in unstable compounds?"

"Must be something," said Sandra, thoughtfully. "May I have a moment to think?"

"Certainly."

"And one thing more. Haven't you anything that even resembles tobacco on this sterile planet?"

"I'm afraid not," said Theodi. "Believe me, we have sought it."

"Thanks," said Sandra. "I know it was for me. But, fellows, I think better with a cigarette."

"We have analyzed the one you gave us, and haven't found a similar weed—"

"O.K., I'll do my thinking in a higher plane," smiled Sandra.

A thought, fleeting as the touch of a moth's wing, crossed Sandra's mind. She fought to reclaim it. It had some association with an experience—some experience in which she had failed, somewhere.

Recently? It might have been.

Long ago?

Sandra didn't think so.

She sat there silent, and the Telfans left with a short statement to the effect that she might be able to think better alone. They would return later.

It had to do with something highly scientific; something of a nature that staggered her imagination. It was coupled with something vast, something deep, something complex.

Her eyes fastened on a spot of brilliant light, reflected from a polished and silvered glass vase at her bedside, and as she sat there with her eyes unseeing, deep in concentrated thought, her mind focused upon the one thing of vastness that she had been involved in.

Sandra's mind was good, in spite of her inferiority complex. It was sharp, retentive, and above all, imaginative. It is a point for speculation whether the imaginative qualities might not have been responsible for her antics; certainly her escapades were the result of some imaginative desire to excel. At any rate, she fastened her eyes on the spot of light, and concentrated herself into a partial self-hypnosis. The train of thought went on before her unseeing eyes with the vividness of a color moving picture, and she was not living the scene, but seeing herself live through a train of events that seemed to jump the unimportant parts like a well-planned motion picture.

Her semihypnotized mind seemed to know the right track, though Sandra's wide-awake mind either ignored the key to the problem or was not certain of the right path to follow.

She was in a room of steel. Steel and machinery and gleaming silver bars. There was some chaos there, too. The silver busbars had lost their die-straightness, and in one place, a single lamination of the main bus hung down askew. It was about a foot wide and one inch thick, and the nine-foot section that hung from the ceiling was slightly lower than the top of her head.

There was blood on the sharp corner, and Sandra looked down to see the red splotch on the floor. She shuddered.

Cables ran in wriggly tangles across the floor. Some were still smoking from some overload, and others, still new from their reels, were obviously part of a jury-rigged circuit. Boxes of equipment were broken open and their contents missing, though the spare parts in the boxes were intact. The whole scene spelled—

Trouble!

The floor was not level; a slight tilt made standing difficult, until a man from some other room shouted:

"The mechanograv is working—hold on!"

And the floor rotated until it was the usual, level platform. The huge busbar swung gently on its loose mooring like a ponderous, irresistible mass.

And there was a man who came striding in. His contempt for her still hurt, and Sandra winced. Even in that motion-picture dreaming, wherein the girl in the picture seemed apart from Sandra Drake, the ire vented upon the red-headed image made Sandra writhe in sympathy.

And then she heard the words come from the man's lips. They were clear and concise, and seemed to come from the man himself instead of from within her own memory:

"The electronic charge is great enough to force an inert element— xenon—to accept an additional electron in its ring-system. This permits combination with active elements such as bromine. When xenon-bromide forms, we know that our intrinsic charge is highly electro-negative. See?"

The scene within Sandra's mind dissolved, and she shook her head. It cleared, but the words remained.

"Orfall," she called. "Theodi! Thuni—bring them here!"

They returned. "McBride," she said. "He can do it!"

"How?" asked Theodi skeptically.

"You've read their books," said Sandra Drake. "You know the principle of the Plutonian Lens—and also that the alternating stations require terrible electronic charges to maintain the lens that focuses Sol on Pluto. They check that with the formation of xenon-bromide for negative, and decomposition of tetrachloro dibromo-methane for the positive charge. They can do it."

"Can't they do it on a planet?" asked Orfall sadly.

"Not unless they can raise the whole planet to a high negative charge," snapped Sandra. "What do you think?"

"I don't know—none of us do. Can they?"

"No."

"Then—?"

"We'll call them, tell McBride what's the matter and what we need. He'll fix it."

"It sounds like a fool's gesture to me," said Theodi.

"Utterly impossible. How are we going to get in touch with them in the first place?"

"Look," said Theodi. "We can call them. See what McBride says and put the problem to them. If there's a way out, fine. If not, we've lost nothing."

"But how are we going to call them over nine light-years of space?"

"Ah—yes," said Theodi. "We can't."

"Maybe I can," said Sandra. "That'll be my contribution. I think I can call them."

"Nine light-years—" objected Theodi.

"Remember that the gravitic spectrum propagates at the speed of light raised to the 2.71828 ... th power. That'll make talking to Terra like calling across the room. May I try?"

"You think they'll be listening for you?"

"Can't miss," said Sandra with a positive gesture. "My ship, the   , is equipped with the standard communications set. It puts out right in the middle of the main communications band of the electrogravitic. If I can get enough power to beam towards Sol, it'll hit them right in the middle."

"You intend to use the set in the   ?"

"Overloaded to the utmost. They tell me that they'll take one hundred percent overloads for an hour. Make that one thousand percent, and it may last ten minutes. Ten minutes is all I need to give them our trouble—they have recorders if McBride isn't there to hear it in person."

"Where are you going to get that power?" asked Theodi.

"From you."

"Impossible, Sandrake. You know that there is not sufficient power available to make such a program possible."

"Ridiculous. The resources of a planet are unmeasurable."

"Perhaps so," said Theodi. "But remember that our power, like Terra's power, is spread out all over the face. The transmission of power such as you will require would be impossible because the line losses will be greater than the power input. It might be possible to connect the networks together and draw the entire power output of Telfu into one district, but line losses would prohibit its operation."

"I only need ten minutes maximum," said Sandra.

"You're asking us to sacrifice—? You mean—overload every plant within efficiency-distance of your ship until it breaks down?"

"What have you to lose?"

"Can we do it?" asked Orfall.

"Of course," said Sandra. "You run your machinery at low load until it is running at ten times the velocity, and then I cram on the power. Momentum will carry me through."

"And if one machine goes, under that load, the entire district will go completely dead."

"Oh no," said Sandra. "The closer and most powerful one will not be used. That one will be used to talk to the boys when they arrive. They'll only have a distress signal, and the details must be held until they come investigating. They can't land, and so we'll have to tell 'em the story while they're in space. We'll need that power."

"Small consolation. Then Indilee will be an oasis of power in a radius of powerless country."

Sandra looked Theodi in the eye and said in a cold voice:

"Then go on out and die with the rest of your kind. What good will your machinery do you if you're all dead?"

"This is a democracy, Sandrake. We cannot just take the machinery and the equipment of others—even to save ourselves."

"How's your red tape factory?" she asked with a smile.

"Meaning?"

"Either you get those power plants or die. I don't care if you steal them, buy them, or borrow them. But get them—and quick."

"But there is a chance to save Telfu," suggested Orfall.

"Sensible fellow," smiled Sandra. In her mind she cursed the whole planet. This was a place for Sandra to undulate a bit; to turn on those two-million kilovolt-ampere eyes; to stretch one rounded arm out straight, putting the other hand below the ear and raising the elbow to a level just above those eyes and shielding the victim from the warmth in them. This showed off Sandra's svelte figure to perfection, and few men in Sol could have refused Sandra anything after that perfect performance.

But they were very few.

The Telfan ideal of beauty did not include Sandra Drake's perfection. She could have postured from now until galaxy's end, and they wouldn't have known her intent. Against their women, Sandra was alien—not sickeningly ugly or deformed, but alien and acceptable—and totally undesirable.

Sandra sighed, told the subconscious mind not to bother with the spotlights and provocative sultriness, and tried to think her way to the mastery of these Telfans.

"Couldn't we divert the electrical supply plants across Telfu?" objected Theodi. "Seems to me—"

"Not a chance," said Sandra. "You have no idea of the power required. I must shoot the works all at once. The set, the generators, and the supply lines will all go out at once. That'll give me ten minutes, I hope."

"But the dissipation of such power—Where can we collect it?"

"There's only one place on Telfu. That's in the power room of the . That is still intact?"

"Yes. Handled, inspected, photographed, and manipulated without driving power, of course, but it is still intact."

"Should be," commented Sandra wryly. "After all, my trouble was not being able to make the drive work. Couldn't get any push. Used up my entire stock of cupralum. So, do we?"

"I hate to say 'yes,'" said Theodi.

"Look," said Sandra, realizing something for the first time. "We have lots of gravitic machinery. Give me your useless power plants and I'll see that you get gravitic machinery to replace them."

"Um-m-m."

"Look, Theodi, you're used to thinking in Telfan terms—which means no gravitics. Think in Terran terms. You are no longer alone in the universe. You are in contact with a race that has gravitic power."

"Well—"

Sandra smiled. "Take it or leave it—and die," she told him. "Think of it. Andryorelitis comes like a thief in the night, giving no warning. Like the black wings of a gigantic, clutching bat, silent and ominous and unseen it comes and spreads its horde of hell on the city. Men go on in their way, meeting other men and inoculating them, passing the germ of death to whomever the black visitor may have missed on his visit. Men take it to their families and spread it from hand to hand, from lip to lip, from mother to babe to grandparent and beyond. The unborn is as cursed as the almost-dead, for it is within their bodies. The days pass in which every soul is given the opportunity of catching and spreading the dread disease.

"Then in this peaceful, unawareness of the terror, nine days pass and one sees a red spot on his arm. He shies away from his friends not knowing that they, too, have red blotches. The city is made of slinking men, ashamed women, and scared children. The newspaper headlines scream of the plague, but none will buy, for they fear inoculation on the part of the newsboy. They fight and fear one another, and the plague has its way, spreading across the city like the falling of night and missing none.

"The Grim Reaper swings his sharp scythe, and the populace falls like shorn wheat.

"And the stricken city becomes a place of horror. The smell of rotting bodies taints the air and makes life impossible for those unlucky few who have not been given the peace of death. None are interested in the cries of the dying, and no one sees the sunken cheeks, the withered bodies, the redding flesh. Do you like that picture, Theodi?"

"You speak harshly, Sandrake."

"You paint a prettier one," said Sandra, scorning him. "Go home and dream. Let your imagination roam—or haven't you Telfans got imagination?"

"We have, but—"

"You utter fool! To stand there like a stick of wood between Telfu and some lumps of worthless metal! Like the drowning man that clutched his gold—which pulled him under. Fool's gold. Theodi."

"There is much in what she says, Theodi," added Orfall.

"It is hard to think, sometimes," said Theodi slowly.

"Men!" sneered Sandra. "The whole sex is the same, here or on any inhabited planet. You know so much! Your vaunted power of reasoning is so brilliant. You pride yourselves on your inflexible wills or your willingness to accept new ideas, depending upon which your utter self-esteem thinks is best to exhibit at the instant. Thuni, what do you think?"

"The metal is of little importance to dead men," said Thuni promptly. "And you claim that Terra and Pluto have machines in abundance. The answer is obvious."

"You see?" said Sandra triumphantly.

"I've forgotten," admitted Theodi. "I'd been taught from childhood that high power was hard to get. It is hard to think that another star has it a-plenty and is willing, and able, to give us enough for our needs. It is a revolutionary thought and seems unreal. A story, perhaps. Yes, Sandrake, you shall have your power."

"Good," said Sandra, taking a deep breath. "And thanks. I'll also need your best students for the job."

"Our best are poor enough. Gravitics were known in theory only. A detectable phenomenon, utterly useless. We could not pass the initial doorway—the power generating bands—because of our satellite's absorption of the primary effects. To study the higher and more complex effects was impossible save in theory. But you shall have them."

"I have some practical working knowledge of the stuff," said Sandra. "One can't live and work with McBride and Hammond and the rest without getting a bit of it. Oh, I was only with them for a few weeks at best, but they are ardent teachers. I'll get along with the help of your students."

"You're certain?"

"Not certain—but fairly sure. At best, you have nothing to lose and everything to gain."

"I think we have misjudged you," said Theodi. "You're fundamentally fine—"

"Thank you," said Sandra, simply. "Convincing you was the hardest job I've ever done, believe me."

"Convincing the Terrans—?"

"Will be the second hardest job. Darn it, we can't use television."

McBride shook his head at Steve Hammond. "Don't believe it," he said.

"You don't."

"No, I don't. Drake has something up her sleeve."

"It's a pretty big sleeve, then," grinned Hammond. "Rigging anything to call from Telfu to Sol is no small potatoes."

"She overloaded everything in sight. That'd about make it right," said McBride. "It went blooey right in the middle of the third sentence—'McBride or Hammond: Telfu in grip of serious epidemic. Need highly charged laboratory to prepare mis-valenced compound for synthetic serum. Danger is imminent, so implore your help for the lives of—' and that's all. Either she's as dramatic as Shakespeare, or this is the real juice."

"And you think it is joy-juice."

"Her past record—and yet we can't afford to pass this up. She should know, though, that if this is the malarkey, she'll be scorned out of the system. Both systems."

"She wrecked the lens—and she's still here," reminded Hammond.

"'Here' is right," said the pilot cheerfully. "In case you birds are wondering about our position, Telfu is right below us by ten million miles."

"Suppose she's got anything left of that set?" asked McBride.

"Imagine so. The thing couldn't have gone to pieces like the Wonderful One Horse Shay. Give a call and see. If Sandra's not kidding, she'll be listening."

"Kidding or not," laughed McBride, "Sandra will be listening."

Hammond turned on the communications set and coughed into the microphone, watching the meters swing. Then, satisfied, he said: "This is the answering S. D. I. from Telfu. Calling Sandra Drake. If you are listening, break in. This is Hammond of the   listening for a repeat of previous S. D. I.» Hammond broke into Telfan and repeated the message.

Then the answer-light winked on the panel and he heard:

"This is Sandra Drake. Is it really you?"

"No," said Hammond. "Just a reasonable facsimile. What's the matter?"

"Oh!" said Sandra. There was a world of feeling in the word. "This has been the longest seven days in my life. It worked, then."

"What worked then?"

"The communications set."

"Obviously. What did you do to it?"

"Not much, personally. I sort of managed it, though. They lent me their best gravitic students and we went to work on the thing. We remade everything in the set—everything that could stand it, that is—about four times their size. That's where I came in. Some things couldn't be increased in size without ruining the tuning, and I knew which ones. Is my output all right?"

"Shaky, but strong enough for service."

"I'm running without an output stage. We used the output stage to drive a super-power stage made of the beefed-up parts and when the works went blooey, it took the Telfan output and my output with it. I'm running off to my own driver stage."

"You've been a busy little girl," said Hammond. "What did you use for power?"

"I talked them into giving me every power plant in the district so that I could call you. It all went in eight minutes flat. The is a mess—again.»

"Are you brave or foolish?" asked Hammond.

"Both," answered Sandra. "After all, this is no tea party. There isn't a good generator on the ; I ruined them all trying to call you. Can you understand how urgent this is?"

"I think so," said Hammond. "How did you wreck the whole shooting-match?"

"I used the gravitic generators to generate local fields and used 'em as communications-band reflectors. Part of it was theory on the part of the Telfans and part of it was ideas given me by your experiments with the super-drive. Anyhow, I'll bet that Soaky is fifty degrees hotter, now, with all the soup we put into the transmitter. That'll make your problem easier—hey?"

"Yup," smiled Hammond. "Just like the guy whose only reason for sending telegrams was that he hated to see the mail-carrier work so hard."

"Well, fifty degrees is one percent of the way, anyway."

"That's right," grinned Hammond. "But look, we're killing valuable time if this is as important as it sounds. What's needed?"'

Sandra explained.

"And you say the silicon won't combine? Shucks, we can do that all right," said John McBride.

"Fine."

"Our problem is delivering the goods."

"Why?"

"Name me a container that will carry the electronic charge."

"Oh? I was thinking—"

"Don't bother," said McBride. "There isn't anything better than ten million miles of pure and absolute space. She'll corona, and then arc, and then she'll assume the normal charge and the stuff will come unstuck again. And you couldn't possibly send every Telfan out into space for a treatment. There aren't enough years in a century to do that."

"First, we'll have to do away with Soaky," said Hammond.

"We can do that," said McBride. "The converted spacecraft are about ready. We can get 'em off in twenty-four hours. But landing this compound is the tricky job. How are we going to do it?"

"Let's assume that we can think of something and get the rest of this yarn. How do you feel, Sandra?"

"Tired, sort of. I've been busy."

"I gather."

"But this slight relaxation is doing me a lot of good. Is the Lady Thani with you? Her sister, Thuni, asked me to ask."

"She and her husband are on Terra. We didn't pass that way. But you may tell Thuni that they are well, happy, and being treated with Terra's best. Our main trouble is shooing away vaudeville agents, flesh merchants, and screwball politicians who either want to tie their wagon on behind or run their wagon up against."

"You'll never get rid of them," said Sandra. "Are they pointing with pride or viewing with alarm?"

"The pointers-with-pride hold a very slight majority."

"That's a fair sign."

"You're right. It is. Luckily, most of the newspapers follow the pointers-with-pride and the general feeling is that way. Most of the malcontents fear that Telfu will have a finger in the division of the universe and they are not going to get as much because of it. They think we should step in and run Telfu, or Telfu may step in and run us."

"We're far enough apart to save 'em the trouble," said Sandra. "But look, fellows, you're running back to Terra—or Sol, anyway. Can you bring me something the next time you come? Please?"

"If possible," said Hammond.

"I need cigarettes, and clothing. I look seedy. I'm frantic for a smoke; I know where you can buy a corpus delectable, dressed in old clothing, for a pack of smokes."

"Willing to sell your body for a mess of potash?"

"Just about. But remember the old one— "

"Knowing you—I'll remember," laughed Hammond. "How have you enjoyed your visit?"

"So-so. It's been an experience. A lonely experience, believe me. I've had my troubles, and I've had my triumph. Aside from the complete lack of human companionship, it's been interesting enough."

"You mean male adoration?"

"Might as well admit it," said Sandra. "These birds look upon me as they might view one of those platter-lipped Ubangis. I'm not interesting nor disgustingly repulsive. Here I am, and I'd have been washing floors for a living if it hadn't been for the fact that I do have some experience and knowledge in gravitics. At least, I know where to find the answer."

"Well, take it easy, Sandra, and we'll be back. Look, I'm dropping a message-carrier with a radio spotter in it. It'll carry all of our spare cigarettes. Can't do much about clothing. None of us wear lace undies."

"I'll bear up," answered Sandra with a laugh. "Thanks."

"O.K., then, see you later."

"Right," said Sandra. "So long!" the set died, but before it went completely off, they heard her say to someone in the background: "You can turn the lights on again."

"What did she mean by that?" asked Hammond.

"I'll bet a cooky that they had the entire output of some city diverted into her communications set. After all, what with Soaky's absorption plus the normal power-gravitic communication, they'd do a lot of running on a waterfall plant, or a coal burning plant to make up for what we accomplish with a single machine in Sol. Our power took a beating, as far as we are from it, and we know what kind of power it takes to do anything with the gravitics on Telfu. Well, let's get going. This seems to be the beginning of Our Busy Week."

At Hellsport, on Pluto, twenty-four huge ships were grouped. They looked like the Devil's spawn; their upright ovoid shapes set in the glimmering background of the light that danced from the open-hearth furnaces of Mephisto. In the sky, the reflection glowed, and it was known for hundreds of miles as The Eternal Fire.

But the men that were arriving were too busy to notice the picture it presented. They were too close to that scene, although they had seen the photographs in the   and , where almost identical pictures filled a whole page in the roto-gravure sections.

They kept arriving, these men who were going to Sirius to set up another Lens. They came from resorts on the Sulphur Sea near Hell and they all asked the reason. They came from Sharon, which lies across the River Styx from Hell, and they asked the same question. The hurried call sought men from their play-spots in the Devil's Mountains and from the vacation wonderlands of the Nergal Canyon. The Great Cave of Loki in the Æsir Plains lost a dozen or so, and Fafnir's Abyss no longer rang to the click of camera shutters as the group left for Hellsport. Vulcan, the frustrated volcano, felt the downward-moving footsteps of the seven who were studying the embryonic crater that was beginning to show signs of life under the heat of Pluto's synthetic sun; the men left eagerly to be on their way to Sirius, but they all prayed that the cold of Pluto's interior would remain cold until they returned.

The Hall of the Mountain King rang to their laughter as they returned to their hotel accommodations near Hellsport, and then again was silent as they went to Hellsport and made the last finishing touches on their equipment.

Just before take-off time, the old familiar cry of "Where's Carlson?" went the rounds until Carlson himself took up the general communicator microphone and called "Here, dammit!" and was informed that it was good because they couldn't start the lens without him. That cooled Carlson off, because it was true and all of them knew it.

Then the two dozen mighty ships lifted in the air above Pluto and headed for Sirius. They joined the on her way from the Plutonian Lens, and after a few minutes of discussion—all done while accelerating at one hundred and fifty feet per second per second—they fell silent and started on the run to Sirius, nine light-years away.

The trip was made without mishap.

"Now," said McBride, through the general communicator, "in order that we understand, I'm going to repeat the general plan again.

"This is a problem different from the central heating system. We are not going to make a planet livable— ! Honestly, it is but a satellite, but the problem is only made more difficult since it is harder to hit with a stellar beam. But enough of that, we've got the calculations necessary.

"We intend to burn Soaky. Our trick, then, is to set up the maximum possible heat-energy field around or on Soaky. Therefore a lens-system such as the Plutonian Lens is out of the question. Far better is a duplex system. We shall, therefore, send twelve of our ships to a point in space less than thirty million miles from Sirius. This will give us a solid-angle of considerable magnitude—a power intake, if you will—that will extract about all that we can handle.

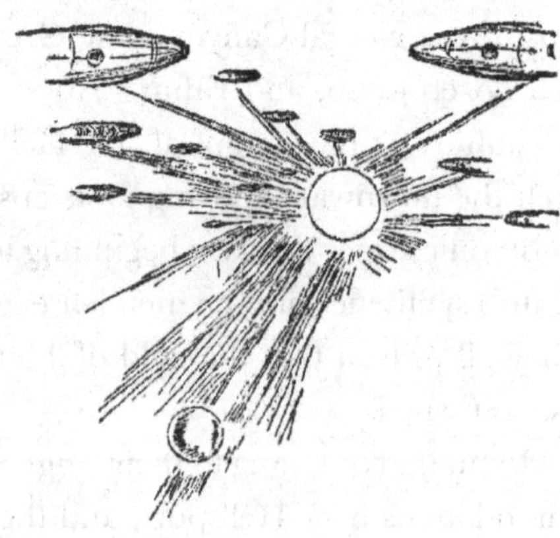

"The front lens-element will cause the divergent rays from Sirius to become parallel or nearly so. We can't help but lose some.

"Now these parallel rays will hit the second element, which will be set up less than ten million miles from Telfu. That's about as close as we can get without losing our control due to Soaky's field-absorption. And it will focus the entire possible bundle of energy on Soaky. Unless Soaky is utterly impossible, we'll cook his goose. Right?"

The answer came with a laugh. Then someone asked about Soaky.

"Soaky," continued McBride, "is a satellite of Telfu. It is approximately one quarter million miles from the planet, and is invisible from Telfu, being less than a hundred miles in diameter. The Telfans, by means of crude gravitic detectors, have discovered Soaky plotted his orbit pretty well, and so we really have little to do."

Steve Hammond went to the microphone and laughed. "McBride is a master at the art of understatement," he said. "But my contribution to the art of eliminating planets is an anachronism. We have, on the , one of the most useless things in the universe. I shudder to mention it, fellows, but there must be some good place for everything, no matter how useless it may seem. We—and hold your hats—have a rocket ship."

A series of groans and catcalls returned over the communicator, and there was the shrill whistle of someone outrageously murdering " ."

"Yep," continued Hammond, "Skyways, who boast that they can furnish transportation anywhere within reason or realm of operating practice, have furnished the , which, named, appropriately, may operate on or near Soaky. It is a useless bit of machinery for anything else, and once the has landed on Soaky and planted spotter generators for us to get a precise ‹fix› on, the will be relegated to some museum—if she doesn›t get scuttled on the way in.»

At this point McBride returned and finished by saying: "We shall set up our lens, and exceeding Archimedes, 'Having a place to stand, we shall burn up a satellite.' So now go on and make the thing cook, fellows. You all have your orders. The will be a roving factor, feel free to call us for any trouble. We›ve got our own job cut out for us.»

The twenty-four great ships of space, already spread out across the space between Sirius I and Telfu, began to jockey for their selected positions in space. McBride listened to the quick-running patter of the lens-technicians and the astrogators as they juggled their ships into the first semblance of order. Then he turned and nodded to Larry Timkins. Larry shook his head and left, going aloft to the rocket ship.

The loft opened and the diverged from the opening. Hannigan, the regular pilot, snapped the switches briefly and the darted away from the free-running for several miles. Then the first burst of flame came searing out in a mushroom, which lengthened to a long rapier of white fire. The moved off ponderously, and the sky was cut into two parts by the river of flame that burned in the rocket›s jets. The rapier of flame curved slightly and pointed toward Telfu.

"No worrying about him," said McBride. "We'll know where he is."

"So will the rest of the system. O.K., Jawn, you've got the boys running—now for our problem. How do we make Silicon-acetyldiethyl-sulfanomid?"

"Yeah. How?"

"Well, according to La Drake, their trouble is the lack of stability. We can probably make it under high electronic charge—in fact, that's what she was suggesting."

"What'll it do when we remove the intrinsic charge? Remember the xenon-bromide. It falls apart when we leave the high negative."

"It's more than likely that the stuff will collapse when we neutralize."

"Do you suppose we could get it there before it falls apart?"

"You mean like the guy who used to put the light switch off and get into bed before it got dark?" laughed McBride. "What would happen to our xenon-bromide if we were to get it to zero charge all at once?"

"I don't know, but file that one away for future reference," said Hammond, thoughtfully. "Make up a batch of xenon krypto-neide, or any of that ilk which might be crystalline, and then heave it in an electrostatically charged shell at the enemy. Upon neutralization, what with the hellish electronic charge plus the reversion to gas—probably white-hot from electrical discharges—we'd have an explosive that would really be good."

"Good!" exploded McBride. "Look, my little munitions expert, the neutralizing charge—happening instantaneously—would paralyze everything electronic in nature for seventy miles even in space, and the electronic charge, reaching zero in nothing flat, would cause instantaneous decomposition of the compound. Since it is held together electrically, the decomposition, or   rate, would propagate at the speed of light, or approaching that velocity.   Blooey for everything in sight!»

"Funny how the human animal can always dream up a scheme for something lethal out of every invention."

"Yeah—even while they're trying to figure out something to save a planetful of people, they'll invent something deadly. That's one of the things that makes us . But what do we do with the Telfans?"

"Theodi says it is stable once made—do you suppose it would be stable even if made in the forced process?"

"Let's try. Got the stuff?"

"Barrels of it," said McBride. He went to the shelves of bottles and removed the ingredients for Telfu's antibody. He weighed the chemicals, and placed them in a combustion boat. This he placed under a cover-glass and then called for Hannigan to run the intrinsic-charge generator.

As the collectors began to load the ship with electrons, and the various chemical indicators began to change color at various levels of charge, McBride and Hammond set up long-focus microscopes to watch the compound.

The final tube on the indicator panel changed from the mixture of xenon and bromine to a gray-green gas, and then McBride called: "Enough, Hannigan."

"Right, boss," said Hannigan.

"Any action?"

"Not yet. First the atmosphere of pure nothing so the stuff won't try to combine with the aforementioned atmosphere. Then twelve hundred degrees Kelvin, and finally the slow-cooling to form large crystals." McBride opened a valve and the trapped air under the sealed glass whipped out into space. "This stuff is stubborn," he added, turning on the heater. The mixture grayed a bit, and then started to turn cherry red all over at once. Hammond manipulated the color-temperature meter and when the color was right, he motioned and McBride cut the heater, riding the control all the way to room temperature.

"Anything?"

"Won't form."

"Huh?" asked Hammond. "I thought we could form anything."

"We can. But we might not live to tell about it. Some items of unstable planetary systems are easily converted from their normal valence-ratings to others of wide and ridiculous values. We picked xenon for our final indicator because it fits in nice with the negative value we need. But this stuff has valence-inertia beyond that value. According to this stuff here, I'd say that its instability was less than that of the carbon-chains that go into the human body."

Hammond whistled.

"And that means, little brother, that by the time we hit the right negative charge to make this stuff combine, we'll end up with being completely and irreplaceably dead."

"Ugh!" grunted Hammond. "Did we get anything?"

"Can't tell," said McBride. "Darned stuff sets like cement when it cools. Warm up the tensile strength machine and we'll crush it and paw through the wreckage."

He inspected the crushed mass a few minutes later and managed to separate two minute crystalline specks under the microscope. "I don't know whether these are the stuff, Steve," he said, "or whether it is just wishful thinking. Is it better than that four ten-thousands of one percent yield?"

"Not if you can weigh it. We started off with a hundred grams. One percent is one gram; four ten-thousandths of one gram is four hundred micrograms. The balance will swing over on less than ten micrograms. This isn't even that much. No good, Mac."

"Call Theodi and ask about that catalyst-conversion stunt."

"Huh?"

"He intimated that if they could combine the silicon with the catalyst, they'd be able to cause metathesis at better than sixty-one percent efficient. Trick is getting silicon to combine with an already-filled compound."

"They are better at chemistry than we," admitted Hammond. "I'll call."

Apparently the receiver in the was attended constantly, for the sleepy voice of a Telfan answered. He answered that he would get Theodi, and as he was about to shut off the transmitter, another voice came over. It was Thuni.

"Hello, Thuni," said Hammond cheerfully. "How goes it?"

"Bad," said the woman. "But I must go."

"I wouldn't," advised Steve. "Your sister Thani and her husband would like to talk to you."

"Oh," said Thuni in a strained voice. "I'd like to speak, too. But this expenditure of power ... I fear—"

"Nonsense. Thani has been nine light-years away for almost a year. Think, Thuni, the light that started from our star is only one ninth of the distance on the way, and Thani has been there and back."

"I know, but this power—"

"What's power?" laughed Hammond. "We've plenty of power."

"But we have not. Realize that the entire city of Indilee is in darkness because of my desire to speak."

"So what?" asked Hammond. "You have the chance, have you not?"

"But I am not Sandrake, who would think nothing of expending the entire power-availability of a whole city just to talk."

"Sandra is pretty much a human being in spite of her faults," said Hammond. "I'm certain that any of us would have done it, just in the same manner. In fact, I'm not too certain that Drake is inclined to be a little inefficient, not knowing too much about the finer points of operation. probably divert the power output of the whole planet just to be sure I was heard.»

"Does nothing stop Terrans?"

"Not for long," laughed Hammond. "And here's Thani. And the operator won't be asking for another thirty thousand dollars after the first three minutes, because there's no operator."

"I fear," started Thuni, and then ceased her worry. She finished: "I'll hold this open until Theodi comes, at least."

"Good. That's learning to use the gifts of the universe to your own comfort and pleasure. See you later, Thuni." To Thani, standing at his side, he said: "Here's your sister. She needs cheering up."

Thani flashed him a smile that might have been enticing in a Terran woman, and then turned to talk to her sister.

"Meanwhile," said McBride, "I've a thought. Not a good one, but a couple of dark ones. We know that silicon is a tough character. It doesn't take to planetary changes with the ease of xenon, for instance. It is way high up on the electronic-stability table."

"That's correct," said Hammond. "But we've been thinking in terms of not trying to add the silicon, but to combine the sulphur to the rest of the compound containing the silicon already."

"Frankly, not too much is known about the electro-combining processes with the more complex organic compounds. But what I'm thinking is this: A chain is as strong as its weakest link, and the attempt to add silicon to the compound only fails. When the more active sulphur is added, it automatically forces the silicon out of the compound, and will continue to do so until the right electro-negative charge is reached. Electro-combining silicon at a level less than its electro-stability level is impossible."

"That means trouble, Mac," said Hammond slowly. "Want to try the decomposition of silicon-fluoride?"

"Might, to kill some time." McBride reacted fluorine with silicon in a combustion chamber and then called for Hannigan to run the charge down again. They watched, and as they expected, nothing happened.

"That's it," said McBride. "We're stumped."

"I wonder—" mused Hammond.

"Have you any doubt? Are you thinking of automatically operated space-chambers set up for the formation of Silicon-acetyldiethyl-sulfanomid?"

"That might work if we had time to build 'em. But look, Mac. Suppose we generate a terrific electrogravitic field, monopolar as according to the first orders of gravitic fields. Generate this field in a volume of less than a foot in diameter, and accordingly intense. Then we'll negatize the ship, and at the same time bombard the electrogravitic sphere with electrons from a standard electron-gun. It'll take gobs of power, John, to drive 'em in, but the field will help, and also keep 'em there. What do you think?"

"Sort of localizing our collection of electrons, hey? Hm-m-m. We'll have to do that in vacuo—but that'll keep the atmosphere from combining, too, and is better as she goes. We have plenty of electrons when the ship runs negative, and that'll tend to collect them in the place where they're needed the most. Might work, Steve. Break out the E-grav and we'll try."

Hammond called Pete Thurman and James Wilson and told them what he wanted. They all set to work, but an interruption came for Hammond and Hannigan as the returned in a blaze of fire.

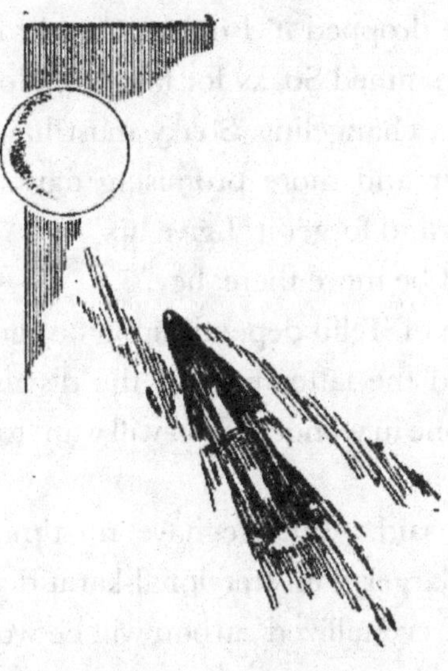

The rocket went off, and the pilot did some fancy work until the inert rocket ship entered the space lock above. Larry Timkins emerged, holding his head between his hands. «It›s murder,» he said. «Downright murder!»

"What's murder?"

"Manipulating that fire-breathing gargoyle. Y'know how the regular drive takes hold all at once? Well, this thing sort of hangs fire. There's a bit of a lag—ever so little—since the jets are sheer mechanical and the time-function requires that the mechanical linkages from lever-turn to fuel-release, ignition, and ultimate movement—well, they act in considerably less time than the electrogravitic drive."

"Do you have to use it again?"

"Nope. I planted the spotter-generators and—picked up a souvenir of Soaky. Look," and he pulled a piece of crystal from his spacesuit pouch and dropped it on the table.

"Dirty looking hunk of glass," said Hammond. "Going to use it for a paperweight?"

"It'd go better on the gal friend's finger, but I'm going to sell it and lay away the profits for my edification and amusement. It'll assay four karats if it's worth a dime, and that ain't quartz."

"Diamond?" asked Hammond in surprise.

"It has an index of refraction higher than 2.4, and is harder than Sandra Drake's heart."

"Sounds like. How did it get there?"

"Ask the bird that dropped it. I only picked it up. If I'd found it in a blue-clay flue, I'd have mined Soaky for fair, but a loose diamond lying on the surface is strictly a changeling. Soaky must have known high-falutin' friends in his younger and more promising days. Call it one of those inexplicable mysteries and forget it. I give up."

"Hm-m-m. Might be more there, hey?"

"Yeah, but the life of Telfu depends upon our getting rid of Soaky."

Thani, who heard the latter part of the discussion, came over and looked at the uncut stone in wonder. "You will want to inspect our satellite?" she asked Hammond.

"I'd like to," he said. "But we have no time. While we've never synthesized anything larger than fractional-karat diamonds, and this four to five karats worth of crystallized carbon will be worth a small fortune to

Timkins, here, the idea of forestalling help to Telfu whilst we chase a will-of-the-wisp is strictly a phony. Besides, it looks to us as though this one was a sport—an impossible find. Chances are that Larry was extremely lucky."

Thani shook her head. The chances of a huge fortune in precious stones going up the chimney because of danger to an alien race gave her food for thought.

McBride's shout cut all future conversation along this line. Hammond called for Larry to follow, and they went to the room in which the electrogravitic generator was being worked on.

McBride met them. "We're about ready," he said. "There's peepholes for all."

"Peepholes?"

"Unless you want to be in an airless room along with umpty-gewhillion electron volts. Better take a peephole."

McBride's hole was equipped with telescope and controls for the equipment. They set their eyes to the windows and watched. McBride explained: "First off, I open the space cock and let the vacuum of space in. Said vacuum drives the air out, leaving the place filled with hard nothing. That eliminates the possibility of corona with the voltages we are going to use."

Then he depressed the generator-on control button, and the pilot lights winked. He read the meters through the telescope, and adjusted the variable controls until a faintly outlined sphere formed between the radiator gravitodes of the generator. This sphere was invisible in that it reflected no light and was transparent, but the light from the wall beyond was refracted slightly, and the sphere was constantly changing in index of refraction, so that the sphere shimmered like heat waves over a meadow.

"We set the spherical warp, so. Now on the boom we insert the combustion tube containing the mix. The insertion of the boom is easy due to the heavy gravitic field, which attracts proportional to the square of the distance. I think it increases the inertia-constant—"

" , Mac. Inertia is a of matter, not a phenomenon.»

"You can stir up a good argument later, here or at the annual meeting of the Gravitic Society. Right now I'm about to turn on the heat." McBride withdrew the boom, leaving the combustion tube in the warp, where it was fixed against the infinitesimal point of zero-attraction, with all sides of the boat in contracting-urge. He snapped the button and watched through the color-temperature meter. Then, as the color was reached, he threw over a series of controls, and the spherical field became a riot of color.

It fluoresced, as the bombardment of electrons hit it, coming from all sides. The sphere grew, and McBride tightened the warp by applying more power. Still it grew as the repulsion of the electrons tried to nullify the gravitic attraction, and McBride continued to step up the power of the electrogravitic generator to keep the sphere from expanding.

"Hannigan," he called. "Give me just a bit more?"

"We can stand about six more electrons," laughed Hannigan. "No more."

"Give 'em to me," returned McBride cheerfully.

And then the sphere refused to be confined. It grew, and McBride made comic motions with the hand that held the control, as if to turn the knob from its shaft in a supreme effort to increase the power by a single alphon.

The sphere grew to huge proportions, and McBride cranked the control to zero just as the surface of the sphere grew instable and threatened to expand without limit.

His other hand turned the heat control slowly down, and the color of the combustion tube died. A hiss of air entered, and they ran inside to see the result.

The combustion boat was ablaze with scintillating crystals. Beautiful blue-green crystals that were half-hidden in the gray-yellow powder of the catalyst. Their surfaces caught the lights, and sent little darting spots of blue fire dancing over the approaching people.

McBride lifted the combustion tube with a pair of tongs. "This is the pure stuff," he said quietly. "Looks like a good crop this year, too. What's it insoluble in, Steve?"

"Sulphur dioxide, according to Theodi."

"Good. We'll remove the catalyst with that and weigh the residue which will be the entire output of our hundred grams of stuff. The percentage will be higher than .004%, I'd say. Come on—"

The communicator barked: "McBride! McBride! This is Peters on Number One, Telfan element."

McBride answered: "What's the matter?"

"Nothing. We're in! We had a bit of trouble getting the warp going at this end. The image-size of Sirius when projected by a lens as close as the fore element is larger in diameter than Sirius is according to the distances involved, you know, and getting the warp started across the face of the Telfan Lens was some going. But we're about to thicken the center and shorten the focal length of the aft element right now."

"O.K. No trouble, hey?"

"Excepting it is hot in the hind-end stations. The interstices that give the spill-overs from Lens One do a swell job of heating up the stations when it hits."

"Sirius is hot stuff."

"Look, Mac, how much energy will it take to ruin Soaky?"

"Well," grinned McBride, "Lothar's 'Handbook of Useless Facts' says that a globe of ice the size of Terra, if dropped into Sol, would melt and boil so quick it wouldn't go ' .' Is Carlson handy?"

"Here, Mac. On the hind surface in the flitter and it is hotter than the hinges of Hell."

"The one on Pluto?"

"No, the one in the real Nether Regions."

"O.K., Carl. You're the balance wheel in this outfit. If you must aberrate, lean outward a bit, will you? I'd hate to singe the pants off of a couple of billion Telfans whilst trying to save their lives."

"I'll keep an eye on it," promised Carlson.

" " grunted Peters. "He means . Or has Carlson got his semicircular canals in his eyes?"

Hammond interrupted with a gloating shout. "Mac! We're in! Ninety-one percent. Pure, crystalline Silicon-acetyldiethyl-sulfanomid. And the charge is almost equal to the galactic mean; meaning that the stuff is stable."

McBride nodded and said into the communicator: "Our half is did, boys. All that stands between we-all and Telfu is a stinking, one-hundred mile satellite. Frankly, I'm agin it!"

Peters did not answer McBride. He shouted, his voice strained with excitement: "Here comes Soaky now, around the edge of Telfu. This is it, gang. Bore him deep and give him Hell!"

Sandra Drake sat down on the edge of a hard bench and took a deep breath. With her free hand, she rubbed her eyes and pushed the stray hair out of them. Her eyes were red-rimmed and puffed with lack of sleep. She stretched and took a longing look at the surface of the hard bench; one of those looks that was calculating not the hardness of the bench but wondering if she could catch forty winks without having trouble call her away again. She decided not. She knew herself, and she knew that as long as she kept going she could stay awake, but if she slowed down for a moment, she'd drop off and nothing would awaken her. And forty winks would actually make her feel worse than no sleep at all.

Outside of the window, dawn was just breaking. It was a strange dawn, an alien sunrise, but one that was nothing new to Sandra Drake. Sirius II was just above the horizon, but almost lost in the mists because of its low radiation. Sirius I was not above the horizon yet, but his strong radiation was coloring the sky blue-gray.

Sandra looked out of the window at the graying sky above. Carefully and hopefully she scanned it but she was not surprised that nothing was there for her to see. The idea of doing away with a hundred-mile satellite was too much, even for McBride, Hammond, and the rest of their gang. A hundred miles of celestial body was not large as celestial bodies go, but against man's futile efforts it was simply vast.

In all of the man-made works on Terra, Pluto, Venus, Mars, and Luna, considerably less than the volume of a hundred-mile sphere had been moved. Affected, perhaps, but not man-moved; the pile-up of rivers behind a dam could not be counted.

So man pitting himself against a celestial object seemed almost like sacrilege, though Sandra Drake knew that these men would take a job of analyzing the course-constants of the Star of Bethlehem if they thought they knew where it was now.

And as small as Soaky was against the giants of the galaxy, it was none the less a celestial object.

So she searched the sky hopefully and was not surprised that nothing was there. Her search was more "Will it happen" instead of "When will it happen?"

And then a Telfan stuck his head in the room and called: "Sandrake! Can you come?"

Sandra shook her head, rubbed her eyes again, and went.

"Now what?" she asked wearily. "We don't have to evacuate another district?"

"No," smiled Theodi, "not that bad this time. But we are going out to Loana—a small town not too far from here—and try out some of this latest stuff."

"Have any hope for it?"

"I must have hope," said Theodi.

"That's selling yourself a bill of goods," said Sandra.

"I know. But unless I play self-deception to the limit, I'll quit from sheer futility. No, Sandrake, I must hope with all my soul and I must force myself to believe that this may work."

"I won't even mention my friends," she said.

"You are beginning to give up?"

"I hate to think of it," said Sandra honestly. "It'll be the first time that they failed to do what they said they could do. I know they planned it, perhaps it takes longer than they think. Or perhaps they came unprepared; their equipment not complete. After all," and Sandra managed a reminiscent smile in spite of her feelings, "I've seen them running some of the haywirest equipment in the world and making it perform. Maybe this time the law of averages caught up with them."

"You think perhaps they are finding that our satellite is too much for them?"

"I hate to think of it. I'd hate to admit that they could fail."

"You have changed, Sandrake."

"Have I? I wonder if it is my hope that they will take me home. No, Theodi, in spite of what I may say about them, they know their potatoes. They're the typical genius-type. Whether they rate as genius I wouldn't know, but they're that kind of people. Give them a situation, and from somewhere in their memory they can bring forth the darnedest things which fit in like jigsaw pieces to complete the whole picture."

"I hope they continue," said Theodi. "Feel up to coming along?"

"Sure."

"Good. We need you."

"Who, me?" asked Sandra.

"Yes."

"Why?"

"Because you are alien. You are impartially alien. Though you have friends on Telfu, they are few, and in your secret mind you class us all as 'Telfan' and forget about sub-classifications. This experimentation is just that, to you, and we are the subjects. Therefore when you select one hundred victims out of a district, we get a perfect, impartial selection; a true cross-section of the district."

"Any of you could do that."

"No. We'd be biased by our knowledge of who is important, who is the sicker, who is young and who is old. And, though it may seem strange to you, you have absolutely no idea of beauty. Therefore you are impartial among the ugly and the beautiful."

"So what?"

"In experimentation on humans, we are inclined to pick those of less value to the community. We pick the lame and the halt and the ugly. We are inclined to pick those who are likely not to live anyway, and this biases our selection. Come, let's get going."

"O.K. Lead on."

Three hours later, and still without sleep, Sandra strode up the line of Telfans and pointed out one after the other. Those selected followed silently to the auditorium in the center of the village and seated themselves. They looked neither happy nor regretful, but rather a resignation was upon them.

Sandra said: "Is this the best place you could pick?"

"Sorry," smiled Theodi. "I didn't know it made any difference."

"I suppose it is good from a functional standpoint," said Sandra. "Being on the stage permits them to pass before us from one side to the other. It is the only clear place in the auditorium in which to work, and as far as I could see, there isn't any other suitable place in town. But being on the stage sort of makes me ... oh, come on. I'm just tired, I guess. Where's the pills?"

"No pills on this deal," said Theodi, opening a case and removing a set of large hypodermics. "This goes into the vein. Right in the main line. You'll have to help."

"Me? Look, Theodi, I don't feel well enough to go shoving needles into people."

Theodi looked up sharply. Her brash-sounding statement was made in a hard voice in spite of its humanitarian and pleading sound. Sandrake, to Theodi's opinion, was really feeling ill.

"It must be done," he said simply. "You fill and hand them to me."

Sandra took the first hypo, inserted it into the disinfectant, and then filled it from an ampule. She handed it to Theodi and watched him with fascination as he took the first Telfan in line and thrust the needle into his arm. It went in and in, and Theodi felt around with the needle-point until he found the vein, and then he emptied the cylinder. "Next!" he called, and so on until the hundred had been inoculated.

"Now," said Theodi, "we'll proceed to Dorana and do likewise."

Sandra was silent all the way to the next village, and as she started down the line of people, picking them out one by one, her face began to whiten.

Halfway through, Sandra stopped.

"Go on," urged Theodi.

" " screamed Sandra. "Go on? No!"

"But—"

"Go on and on and on and on and on?" shrieked Sandra in a crescendo that ended in a toneless, inarticulate screech. She stopped the sentence only because her voice had no more range and she had no more breath. "Theodi, I feel like a murderess! I go on selecting people as I would select specimens to be speared with a mounting pin and stuck on a cardboard. I point them out. They follow dumbly with a look of resignation. They come and you try something new on them—every time it is something new, and you don't know whether it'll kill 'em or not! I can't stand it."

"But who can we have to do this?"

"Get one of your own to do your own dirty work! You need me! Bah! Suppose—?"

"Suppose we have the right combination?"

"Suppose you have? You haven't—and you know it."

"I wouldn't say that."

"I would. You're just experimenting." Sandra's lip curled over her perfect teeth in a perfect sneer. "Experimenting on your own kind. And I'm no better. You should hate me—and I'm beginning to hate you and every one of you."

"This must go on—"

"It'll go on without me."

"Come on, Sandrake. Buck up. Here, I'll give you a sedative and you sleep for an hour. You're over-tired. Then—"

"Then nothing. I can't go on murdering your people any more."

"It's not murder. It's—"

"It's worse than murder. You go on filling them with colored water and telling them that you think that this is the works—and you know it is just another blind try! Go away!" Sandra whirled and ran blindly. Across the field she ran, out and away from the village. On and on she ran, until she fell breathless beside a small brook.

Thankfully, she dabbled in the brook with her tired feet, and laved the cool water on her wrists and forehead. She drank sparingly, and then stretched on her back to relieve the strained muscles that seemed to make her back arch almost to the breaking point.

Unknowing, Sandra relaxed as the ground supported her back, and with the suddenness of falling night, Sandra slept.

Her dreams were less restful than the sleep. They were filled with a whirling panorama of lights, disembodied faces, grinning, leering faces who watched long, brutal needles find the vitals of mute sufferers whose only visible admission of unbearable pain was the tortured look on their mobile faces. And through the dream, McBride and Hammond fought against a huge metal barrier against which their mightiest efforts were futile.

THE DAY WORE ON AS SANDRA SLEPT, AND NIGHT CAME, AND IN ALL THAT TIME Sandra had hardly moved. As the darkness fell, she aroused enough to drink from the brook and settle herself in a more comfortable position. Afterward she did not recall awakening at all but she did select a thick thatch of soft moss the second time and she wondered about it later. And it was about midnight when Sandra awoke.

She was slept out, rested. But the self-hatred was still vivid. The dream had kept it there, and though her body was rested, her mind was still tired from the furious mental action that went on even as she slept.

She stretched, rolled over on her back, and considered her actions of before with distaste. That had been a spectacle, and she hated spectacles except when they made her appear in a better light. She searched the sky wearily, picking out Garna, which was Telfu's sister planet, and Ordana, the behemoth of the Sirian system, both of which were shining close to the bright Geggenschein of Sirius. Above her, she spotted the place where all Telfans watched—the spot where Soaky should be according to their calculations. It was not a spot, but an area, and Sandra scanned it in a futile manner.

Nothing yet.

A minute change in the sky along the horizon made her turn quickly, hopefully. She scanned the sky carefully, and yet she knew that looking at the starry curtain was futile unless the scene became so evident that it could not be missed. She could see nothing, and besides, Soaky was supposed to be above, not on the horizon.

She looked above again, but there was nothing to see. Puzzled at that—that that had caught her attention along the horizon. She shrugged, and in trying to rationalize she admitted that it might have been a meteorite; and she knew that she was overanxious.

It was the same, she knew.

But was it? Was it?

No, but what in the name of—?

Garna and Ordana and Geggenschein were gone from the Telfan sky. What was this? Why should planets disappear?

Planets were about as permanent as—but they must still remain, it was their light that was gone! Sandra shouted. McBride! The lens. In her mind she saw the scaled layout; Sirius, Telfu, the other planets, and Soaky, the satellite that was oh, so close to Telfu. Place two biconvex lenses, one near Sirius and one near Telfu—and any light from Sirius that could normally reach Telfu—and the planets in line from Sirius—would be cut off by the lens, refracted into the energy beam that would ultimately be focused on Soaky.

They'd started at last! Sandra looked upward into the area containing Soaky.

And as she looked, a mite of colored pinpoint appeared in the sky above. It did not rise into the incandescence, it leaped. It passed upward through the red, the orange, the yellow, and the blue with lightning-flash speed, and then settled down in color to an intolerable white. It seared the eyes, that microscopic speck, and its brightness made it appear huge.

Sandra shook her head and looked down. The darkness was fading, and sharp shadows of the low bushes and herself marked the ground. The stars beside Soaky began to fade to the eye, and as the brightness took on solar brilliance, it was like the sudden return of daylight.

A flicker of the light caused Sandra to look into that intolerable light again. No, Soaky was still going strong. But it was scintillating, now, and there were streamers of incandescent vapor leaving the coruscating nucleus that was Soaky.

Full against Soaky the Sirian beam drove, and the surface vaporized. The streamers were the high-temperature vapors of incandescent metal, being driven away from the tortured satellite by the radiation pressure of that intolerable brilliance. The vapors condensed in finely divided droplets of metal, but still floated away in lines and whorls.

The landscape around Sandra was in full light, now, and the shadows were no longer sharp. The boiling, blue-white vapors were rushing from the satellite at high velocity, and they spoiled the point-source of light. They danced and flickered in the sky, and as Sandra watched, a slight twinge of terror crossed her, and she caught her breath.

This was not right. This was—was defying God Himself. And Sandra, never awed by the men themselves, fell in fear before the visible evidence of their ability. It was not right, this utter destruction of a celestial body by man. Men were supposed to be motes—bacterium on the skin of an apple—not mighty motes capable of almost literally eating the apple that—not eating but destroying ruthlessly—the apple that was spoiling their barrel.

And Sandra, not even awed by the God of her people, prayed to Him in fear. Fear, because people of her race dared to tamper with the universe.

But then the light passed away, and no omnipotent lightning flashed across the universe to destroy it. The night fell again, and darkness, unspoiled, crowded the landscape leaving Sandra light-blind. She fumbled aimlessly in the darkness that was by contrast the utter blackness of no-light.

Sandra Drake was not alone in that. Half of the people on the planet of Telfu were blinking in the darkness; silently groping their way into their houses. Their tongues were stilled by the awesome sight.

Sandra brushed her tattered skirt and smiled. She was a long way from Indilee and she wanted to be there as soon as she could. She was beginning to feel the pinch of the months of loneliness; before, it was futility to lie awake at night and think of the touch of a human hand and the sound of a human voice. Yes, she even admitted to the desire for a bit of admiration, after all, it had been her meat and drink.

But now it was a dream about to come true. There would be people of her own kind. People who could laugh at the hardy jokes of her race, and appreciate the casual acceptance of doing absolutely nothing for periods of time. The verbal sparring and blocking would be there, too; the nice trick of forcing someone into a trap of his own making and springing it with—not double talk—but triple talk. The sound of people who could discuss both downright earthy things and high theory with the same words but with slightly different inflections in their voices, and be understood by others who knew both lines of talk.

She gave a short laugh. They would never know whether she did it from sheer altruism or because she was scared to death at the idea of being exposed to andryorelitis.

She blinked. The sky flared briefly ahead of her in a brilliant and colorful display of some auroral discharge. It illuminated one full quarter of the celestial hemisphere in flowing color. Sandra thought and remembered a man saying: "The charge on Station One is so great that at twenty thousand feet it would arc a million miles or more." The words and the distances were forgotten, and probably wrong due to her faulty memory for those details, but she did remember something of that nature.

Obviously, one of the Stations had landed with a load of Silicon-acetyldiethyl-sulfanomid. The not-quite-perfectly neutralized electronic charge must have ionized the upper air in a sprinkling corona.

From another corner of the sky, a similar flare of color flashed, and it was followed by flashes from near and far, each one creating a streaking display of celestial fireworks.

At the sight of that auroral display, Sandra's head went up, her shoulders went back, and there returned to her step a bit of that lilting walk. She smiled crookedly and then broke into that saucy grin. She set her foot on the road to Dorana, from where she could get a ride back to Indilee.

There were Terrans here, all right. Her Terrans that nothing ever stopped. They came—and brought the goods with them.

But—who brought them?

Sandra Drake.

Throughout the night, the flashing of the celestial fireworks told the whole planet that Terrans were bringing the needed drug to Telfu. And with each flash, as with each mile, a bit of the old Sandra Drake returned.

There were a lot of miles back to the *Haywire Queen*.

END.

SODUKO ANSWERS

5	9	1	6	8	3	7	4	2
7	2	4	5	1	9	3	8	6
6	3	8	7	4	2	5	1	9
3	6	9	1	2	7	8	5	4
1	4	2	3	5	8	6	9	7
8	7	5	4	9	6	2	3	1
4	5	7	8	6	1	9	2	3
2	1	3	9	7	5	4	6	8
9	8	6	2	3	4	1	7	5

We hope you enjoyed reading!

Don't forget to visit AdventuresBookZine.com for more and subscribe so you never miss an issue.